THE ORPHANAGE GIRLS COME HOME

London, 1910. When Amy is chosen to be a part of a programme to resettle displaced children in Canada, her life changes overnight. Her great sadness is having to say goodbye to Ruth and Ellen, the friends who became family to her during the dark days at the orphanage. As she steps on board the ship, the promise of a new life lies ahead. But during the long crossing, Amy discovers a terrifying secret.

Canada, 1919. As the decades pass, Amy's Canadian experience is far from the life she imagined. She always keeps Ruth's address to hand, longing to return to London and reunite with her dear friends. With the world at war, it seems an impossible dream. Separated from her loved ones by the ocean, will Amy the orphanage girl ever come home?

SPECIAL MESSAGE TO READERS

THE ULVERSCROFT FOUNDATION
(registered UK charity number 264873)
was established in 1972 to provide funds for
research, diagnosis and treatment of eye diseases.
Examples of major projects funded by the
Ulverscroft Foundation are:

- he Children's Eye Unit at Moorfields Eye ospital, London
- The Ulverscroft Children's Eye Unit at Great Ormond Street Hospital for Sick Children
- Funding research into eye diseases and treatment the Department of Ophthalmology, University f Leicester
- The Ulverscroft Vision Research Group, Institute of Child Health
- Twin operating theatres at the Western Ophthalmic Hospital, London
- The Chair of Ophthalmology at the Royal Australian College of Ophthalmologists

You can help further the work of the Foundation
by making a donation or leaving a legacy. Every
contribution is gratefully received. If you would like
to help support the Foundation or require further
information, please contact:

THE ULVERSCROFT FOUNDATION
The Green, Bradgate Road, Anstey
Leicester LE7 7FU, England
Tel: (0116) 236 4325

website: www.ulverscroft-foundation.org.uk

MARY WOOD

◆

THE ORPHANAGE GIRLS COME HOME

Complete and Unabridged

MAGNA
Leicester

First published in Great Britain in 2023 by
Pan Books
an imprint of Pan Macmillan
London

First Ulverscroft Edition
published 2024
by arrangement with
Pan Macmillan
London

*A catalogue record for this book is available
from the British Library.*

ISBN 978–0–7505–5084–0

Published by
Ulverscroft Limited
Anstey, Leicestershire

Printed and bound in Great Britain by
TJ Books Ltd., Padstow, Cornwall

This book is printed on acid-free paper

For my darling Roy as we celebrate
sixty years of happy marriage. Thank you.

1

Amy

SEPTEMBER 1910

Twelve-year-old Amy clutched her small case, her tummy tickling with excitement as she waited in the queue to board the huge ship. She couldn't believe she'd been chosen to begin a new life in Canada.

Her days in the Carlton Orphanage in Bethnal Green were behind her. No more of the stinking Mr Belton pawing her and hurting her.

The queue wormed from the gangplank and along the dock where most of the men of the East End of London tried to get a day's work. She'd seen them standing together, blowing plumes of smoke from their rolled-up fags, just waiting — hoping. All looked downtrodden, though they had a cheery word for the kids, calling out to them to have a good life and make the most of this chance they were being given.

Amy decided that she was going to do that, though she couldn't deny the feeling in her chest of having swallowed something that had stuck there. It had started when Ruth had run away from the orphanage weeks ago and had worsened when Ellen's father had turned up there soon after and taken Ellen away with him. Being parted from them both hurt so much.

Ruth had been her saviour, taking care of her from the first night she'd entered the orphanage where she'd been taken from the workhouse she'd been housed in since her time with the nuns — a time she could only just remember. The nuns had always told her that her mum had abandoned her as a baby, but then one day they told all the kids they had in their care that they could no longer stay there, and were to go to other places.

When she arrived at the workhouse the nun handing her over spoke in a low voice to the warden. Amy remembered hearing the words, 'She should be made to care for her,' but never knew what they meant.

She only knew that she'd been happy from that day as, though conditions were bad, the women inmates looked after the kids, and one in particular, Ethel, had loved her and she'd loved Ethel.

But then, a day came when the warden told Ethel, 'That child should be in the orphanage by rights. Seeing as no one has claimed her, you will be the one to take her there.'

Amy could remember feeling she'd lost something precious when Ethel left her inside the orphanage gate. Memories of what happened that same night and how it set the pattern of her life in the orphanage shuddered through her and gave her nightmares that left her screaming in terror.

But though she hated the place, it did bring Ruth into her life.

She'd loved Ruth. Ruth had tended to her when Belton had brought her back to the dormitory, bleeding and in pain.

Always, she'd wanted to look like Ruth — beautiful with dark hair and huge dark eyes — and she hated her own mousy-coloured hair and how her face was covered in freckles. She thought this was why she hadn't ever been loved enough by anyone for them to keep looking after her — until she met Ruth. Although Ruth couldn't be with her now, Amy remembered her words when she'd told her she would always love her. And Ellen would too. Lovely, quiet Ellen, who looked a lot like Ruth, only her dark hair was curly.

Ellen had always seemed full of sadness, but it had been lovely to see her face light up when her dad had come for her — that was the picture Amy wanted to always stay with her.

The sigh that she released was gasped back in with joy as a voice called out her name.

'I'm here, Ruth! Oh, Ruth, Ruth!'

Within moments she was enclosed in Ruth's arms. Their tears wet each other's hair and cheeks. 'Oh, Amy, luv. I can't believe you're going so far away.'

'I know. I'm excited, but scared too.'

'You don't mind going?'

'No, they said it's a wonderful opportunity for us to travel to Canada. To see a new world. I've got all new clothes.'

'And they've cut yer lovely hair!'

'I know, they said it will be better. I don't know why. I'm going to miss yer, Ruth.'

They were crying again. But Amy felt cheered when Ruth said, 'I've written me address down. You can write and send letters from Canada.'

'Ta, mate. I will write, and I'll let yer know where you can write back to . . . Will I ever see yer again, Ruth?'

Through her sobs she heard Ruth say, 'I'll never forget yer, Amy. When we're older, maybe things'll be different and then we can travel to see each other. Look, I'll definitely come to see you, so hang on to

3

that. I'm going to make me fortune making hats. And when I do, I'll buy a ticket to travel on this ship to Canada, and that's a promise.'

They clung to each other again.

A stern voice forced them apart. 'You, there, what are you doing? Amy, who is this?'

'It's me friend, miss. She's come to say goodbye.'

'All right then, but hurry, we'll be moving forward shortly.'

The queue began to move. Ruth walked alongside her until they reached a barrier that stopped her.

Amy didn't take her eyes off her as they were hoarded up the gangplank. She couldn't. She could see Ruth's lovely smile, and the tears running down her face, as she frantically waved. And then just as it was her turn to step inside the ship, she heard Ruth shout, 'I love you, Amy. Don't forget me.'

Taking a deep breath, she shouted as loud as she could, 'And I love you, Ruth. I won't, I promise.'

And then all she could see was the inside of a corridor.

Her lungs filled with the musty smell of damp carpet. A stuffiness threatened to choke her. She could hardly breathe as bodies behind pushed her forward, but those in front weren't moving fast enough.

Still, the loud booming voice urged them on. 'Move, you little tykes, move! Yer'll hold the bleedin' ship up!'

Amy couldn't see who it was who was shouting, but she heard crying and wails of, 'I'm going to be sick!'

Not able to get enough air, Amy felt her head begin to swim, then her legs go like jelly and a darkness take everything around her.

* * *

4

When she came to, she was lying on a bed. The bed was moving from side to side. A mask was over her face and glaring down at her was an ugly woman in a nurse's outfit. Her voice snarled, 'What have you been up to? You shouldn't have been allowed on this trip in your state, you dirty tyke! A prostitute, are you? Oh yes, I've heard of them as young as you. Depraved, I call it. Born evil!'

Amy knew what a prostitute was. Ethel was one and there had been many more of them in the workhouse. Kind women they were, sharing what they'd managed to earn when they'd sneaked out, and sometimes she'd heard them say they'd been lying with the night warden. Always they were there for her, and she loved them, but she didn't understand how this nurse could think that she was one of them.

As she took the mask off Amy's face, the nurse said, 'Oxygen's wasted on you. A girl of your age getting yourself with child! So, now you're a problem for us. The doctor will explain what we're going to do.'

As her face disappeared from above Amy, the doctor leaned forward. 'You're a very sick girl, Amy. You're losing blood. When did you first see your period?'

Amy felt confused. Was she really awake?

'Amy! Answer the doctor. He is here to help you!'

The nurse's voice frightened Amy into stammering, 'I were ten. The women at the workhouse helped me. I had none after I went to the orphanage, but —'

'That's all we need to know. No excuses . . . Well, Doctor, you see what we're dealing with. It will be a good thing to get all these scum off the ship. I fear it's going to be a long trip this time. I've already got two of them with chicken pox, so that'll be rife and we're hardly out of the dock!'

5

'Sister, what has happened may not be this child's fault.'

'Of course it is. Why do you think she was picked to go? They get rid of all the troublesome ones.'

Amy's confusion deepened. Were they being 'got rid of' and not going to a new life?

'Well, she won't keep the child. It's obviously coming away.'

As he said this, a pain creased Amy's back. It shot around to the front causing her to draw up her knees.

The nurse didn't help her but made a noise as if triumphant. 'Huh, she's wanting to push already. Well, what she's in for will be her punishment and might deter her from her tricks in the future.'

Amy heard her own scream drown the nurse out. So piercing was it, it seemed as if it split the room in two and brought down more terrible pain on her. 'Help — help me. Please, help me!'

'There is no help, child. You should have thought of this before you cajoled some poor bloke to lie with you. You'll have to push the poor little mite out of you . . . How far gone is this pregnancy, Doctor?'

Horror gripped Amy. They were talking about her having a baby! She couldn't take it in.

'I'd say approximately four to five months, but that's only an estimate. Without dates, it's difficult to tell. But in any case, we're looking at her delivering a fully developed baby, but not one that can live.'

'Oh my God. They must have known back at the orphanage. How dare they send her to Canada in this state!'

'Look, let's be thankful for her sake, and for the baby's, that this will all be behind her after tonight. This has no need to be recorded anywhere. Perhaps

6

the child will have a better, new start, and this will change her ways — that is, if it was her own fault. Wasn't there talk of two wardens having been beaten near to death — thought to be a revenge attack by a former orphan of the home for acts done to them?'

'This lot will say anything to discredit those who are put in charge of them and who try to give them a good start.'

'Sister, sometimes I wonder if you are right for this job. Whatever made you so bitter towards children I will never know.'

With this the sister humphed and left them.

'Now, Amy. I am sorry, but you may have a lot of pain. I have nothing that I can give you for it, but it will go once your dead child comes away from you. Do you understand?'

'No! No, I don't want to have a baby. I didn't do anything . . . Belton —'

'Shush, now. Allegations won't do you any good. I'll send someone along to you as soon as I can, but everyone is tied up right now as the other children are dropping like flies from various ailments. You'll be all right, you're strong, and when this is over you can live your life in a good way having learned a very painful lesson.'

As he left, the doctor put out the light and closed the door. Amy had seen that the room she was in wasn't very big and had no window. A terror entered her as she hated the dark, but this was an impenetrable blackness that gave her a silver haze in front of her eyes. Her scream bounced back at her and seemed to trigger a pain far worse than the one she'd just experienced. 'Help me . . . help me-eee!'

No one came.

An urge to push as if she wanted to go to the lavatory came over her. She felt for the bedstead and clung on to it. Her face contorted with the effort and her neck felt as though it had swelled. She thought her head would explode, but that was nothing compared to the indescribable pain that gripped her back.

As it subsided, huge sobs wracked her. She put her hand between her legs, felt a river of sticky liquid coming from her. Her terror deepened. Would her baby come out of where she peed from? But how? A baby is too big to do that . . . *A baby . . . a baby . . . My baby . . .* 'I — I don't want it to die! Don't let it die, please. Ruth! Ruth!'

Her cry hit the blackness and went no further. Her sobs rasped her throat, but once more went into a holler of pain as she grasped the bedstead again. This time she felt a split down below that was far greater than the one Belton had caused. The sting of it made her catch her breath. Then it was as if she was releasing a huge object from herself, and the pain subsided.

She lay back exhausted. But a small whimper roused her. She sat up. Felt around. Her hands touched a tiny wet form. She was about to search further when the jelly-like form moved. She ran her hands over it, touched limbs so tiny they would have fitted into a matchbox. *My baby, my baby.* Lifting the form in one hand and bringing it to her breast, she so wished she could see it. 'This is your mummy, baby. I'll call you Ruth Ellen.'

The baby didn't move.

'Ruth Ellen? Come on, my baby. I'll take care of you.'

The form lay so still Amy knew, but didn't want to know . . . She went to cuddle her child to her, but it almost slipped off her hand. Keeping her hand very still, she lay back.

The motion of the ship rocked the bed and reminded her of one of the women in the workhouse singing to her baby. In her mind she repeated the words while she stroked her child's head.

Rock-a-bye baby, on the treetop,
When the wind blows, the cradle will rock,
When the bough breaks, the cradle will fall,
And down will come baby, cradle and all.

2

Amy didn't know how long it was before someone came as she'd slept a restless dream-filled sleep since her baby had arrived. It was someone taking her child from her hand that woke her. 'No . . . no!'

'It's dead. It's nothing. It didn't live, so it has no soul.'

'It did. There was a murmur.'

'That'd be a natural expelling from the body of any fluid. It hasn't lived, so will go into the incinerator. You just forget it.'

The horror of this sent a pain through Amy. 'Ruth, Ruth!'

'Who's Ruth? Don't tell me you're going out of your mind now? We've enough trouble . . . Look, you did wrong, and you've paid the price. Now for reasons unbeknown to man you're being given a second chance. Pull yourself together and take it. I'll get a porter to come and wheel you to the bathroom. Wash yourself off. I'll put your case down there for you. Find some clean clothes and then look at the list on the wall to find which cabin you're allocated to and the rules. Go there and don't cause any more trouble — I take it you can read?'

'Yes, I can.'

'Right, don't let me come across you again!'

When she left, she switched off the light, as the doctor had done. Amy called after her. Her unanswered calls became screams till her throat and ears hurt. But the nurse didn't reappear. Exhausted and distraught over the fate of her baby, who she'd decided was a girl, even though she didn't know, she lay back. In her mind she went over some of the prayers she remembered from the convent's Catholic chapel. When a prayer called 'Hail Mary' came to her, she remembered the words. They were to the lady Ruth called Holy Mary: *Hail Mary, full of grace. The Lord is with thee. Blessed art thou amongst women, and blessed is the fruit of thy womb* . . . With this she felt some comfort as she thought, *Mary had a baby, just like me!*

It came to her then how they had once had a lesson about babies who die and what happens to their souls. The nun said they went to a place called limbo as they weren't pure, because every baby was born with a sin on their soul. But if the child was baptized, it would go to heaven. In her mind she baptized her child, begging God to forgive the original sin she was stained with and take her to heaven to be with Him.

When she next woke, though all was darkness, she saw a light. A tiny one floating up and then disappearing through the ceiling. A warm feeling washed over her. *My little Ruth Ellen is going to heaven. Thank you, God.*

But then the little light turned into a flash of reds and blues and yellows and even though she frantically blinked her eyes, she couldn't control them. They frightened her. She rolled off the bed, thinking to hide under it, but it was a lot higher than she thought and she fell heavily onto the floor. As she landed, she heard a crack just before a pain zinged through her ribs. Gasping increased the pain and yet didn't give her the air she wanted. She tried again. The air seemed to stick in her throat, suffocating her.

11

Mustering as much breath as she could, she tried to call out, but only a whimper came from her. 'Help me . . . help me!'

The door opened and light swathed the room.

A man's voice said, 'What the bloomin' 'eck are yer doing down there? And look at the state of yer . . . Christ! Yer bleedin' to death!'

There was a pause. No one came over to her, then she heard the same voice frantically calling, 'Help! I need help 'ere! This one's copping it!'

Amy didn't know what happened after that as she went back into the blackness, a place where she couldn't see or hear anything.

The blackness parted sometimes and an urge to leave it came to her as a lovely bright light shone, but the darkness kept pulling her back into its depth, until the light brightened and she floated towards it without resistance. It was a voice that stopped her. She opened her eyes and saw the doctor looking down at her. 'Amy, fight! You want to live, don't you? Don't give in. You cracked your ribs, but they will heal. You were haemorrhaging — losing a lot of blood — but we stopped that happening. Now you need to get stronger. You need to eat a little soup every day and remain conscious so you can fight for your life. We can only do so much.'

She couldn't answer him. If she could, she would've said that she didn't want to live. She wanted to go to her baby.

A salty tear trickled into her mouth.

'That's good, Amy, you are crying. That means you're feeling something again. Let it happen.'

'Where . . . where am I?'

'You're on board a ship bound for Canada. You

12

remember? You have left the orphanage and are going to a new life. Grasp it with both hands, Amy.'

For the first time, Amy saw him properly. Saw that he looked young for a doctor and that under his white coat he wore a sailor's uniform.

'Are you in the navy?'

'I am. I'm in the medical corps. I'm the ship's doctor . . . Look, I'm sorry I left you like that. And in the dark. I meant to come back but there are so many falling ill, I'm run off my feet. I thought the darkness would be restful for you as you seemed to have a long way to go with your labour. I've never known one come so quick.'

Amy managed a small smile. She liked him. He seemed to really care for her and about her. That didn't happen often.

'But you're all right now. Whatever happened to you back there is behind you. You can only live a full life if you leave it there in the past. Will you try?'

She nodded, suddenly feeling shy to talk about it all. Shy and lonely. She had no one in the world now. Though Ruth and Ellen would always love her, they weren't here and never would be.

'Don't cry any more, Amy . . . Look, I must go. You will be well enough to go to your cabin soon, and then in no time you'll find that you'll make friends, and things won't seem so bad.'

When he left her, her loneliness deepened. She thought of Ruth and Ellen again and how she longed to be with them. To sit once more on the steps of the orphanage with them, giggling. Always they were by each other's side sharing their pain but making happy moments too. Now it was just her.

She tried to think what Ruth would say to her and

knew she'd want her to get better as one day, she was going to come and find her. *I'll think of that happening every day till you come to me, Ruth.*

★ ★ ★

The days all went into each other after that. The cabin she shared with four others was a small, hot, window-less room. It had two sets of bunk beds and there was a bathroom along the corridor that served all the chil-dren, so when she wanted to pee, she had to wait in a queue. It had been here that she'd met Lucy, a small girl who didn't tower over Amy as most of her age did.

Lucy told her she'd been in an orphanage in Lon-don, but she didn't know where exactly, or how she got there, nor, like Amy, did she know her true birth date but had been given the date when she'd arrived at the home as her birthday and so, she thought her-self to be eleven.

They sat together in the corridor, as they were now, whenever they could and when it was time for them to walk on the deck, they would hold hands. Amy loved Lucy. She could talk to her about any-thing and thought her pretty with a mass of blonde curls and blue eyes. And she found it fascinating how Lucy loved all things, noticing beauty in everything and never seeing any object just as it was, but finding more to it. It was as if she had special powers.

Cutting into these thoughts, Lucy was doing it again — the seeing of things that weren't there. 'Look, Amy, there's a donkey!'

'A what? Yer bonkers, Lucy.'

'I'm not. Look there, in the lino.'

Amy peered at the spot where Lucy was looking.

14

There was a stain, and yes, the more she looked, the more it did look like a donkey. She laughed out loud. A laugh she'd thought she would never give again.

'How do yer see all these things? I don't see them till yer point them out.'

'I don't know. I can draw things out of me head too. I wish I had a crayon and paper with me. I used to pinch some from the classroom.'

'The doctor's a kind man. I'll pretend I don't feel well and go and ask him for some, eh?'

'Would yer?'

'Can yer really draw things?'

'Anything. I'm not lying. I drew a picture for a girl at the orphanage. They brought her in after her mum and dad died. She told me that she saw a vision of her mum sat in a wooden armchair, holding her on her knee. I used to get her to tell me about it over and over as I hadn't ever known a mum and I liked to imagine it. Then one day it came alive to me, and it were me sitting on the woman's knee. I drew the picture of it for her. She said it was just as she remembered it . . . It made me cry to give it to her, Amy, but happy that it made her happy.'

Amy dug her hand through Lucy's arm. 'That were kind of yer. But why don't yer draw one for yerself, eh? Make it how yer think your mum might have looked. I reckon she'd have hair like you and them blue eyes too.'

Lucy giggled and snuggled into Amy. 'I never thought of that. I do have a picture in me head of what me mum looked like . . . Would you like one? Would the doctor give yer two sheets?'

'I don't know if he'll give me one yet, but I think he will.'

A sudden shout and clapping of hands caught their attention. They stood up.

'All get your coats. Time for your daily walk, children.'

'Miss White's all right, ain't she?'

'She is. I'll tell her I ain't well and see if I can go to the doctor while yer all on deck.'

Getting permission was easy. Amy ran as fast as she could to the hospital ward, even though her chest still hurt to take deep breaths. It was as if she had to hurry as she felt that anything she gained could be taken from her and that gave an urgency to everything. She didn't want to lose the chance of having a picture.

She felt herself glowing inside when she found Lucy again. 'I have it! He gave me three sheets and two pencils!'

'Oh, Amy, ta.'

Just to see Lucy's smile thanked Amy. She wanted to hug her. The same thought must have come to Lucy as she flung her arms around her. It felt good. She clung on to Lucy and hoped with all her heart that they stayed together.

★ ★ ★

A few days later, Amy sat alone in a quiet corner staring at the drawing Lucy had done from the descriptions she'd given her. It was so real. Herself, Ruth and Ellen, at the orphanage. They were sitting on the landing at the top of the stairs leading from the building to the playground, their legs dangling and their expressions happy as they were all giggling. Ruth and Ellen's portrait was a very near likeness to them, with herself just as she was.

16

But as she stared at it, her heart began to thump and the tears that had run silently down her cheeks plopped onto the paper as the image had awoken her to this no longer being a trip to a better life, but a trip to take her away from everything she'd known. It didn't matter that what she had known had been horrific as all she could think of was that she'd had Ruth and Ellen. And she so wanted them now . . . but might never see them again. Just like her own little Ruth Ellen. Though she'd never seen her, she often tried to imagine her. In her mind she'd become like the doll she'd seen on the journey from the workhouse to the orphanage. She and Ethel had walked down a street lined with shops and Ethel had said, ''Ere, I reckon we can slow our pace a little, luv, and look in the windows. And we might just get ourselves a cup of tea.'

One shop window had been very dark. They'd had to put their faces on the pane and cup their hands around their eyes to block out the sun so that they could see inside.

A mishmash of objects, from a kettle to a baby's pram, were displayed as second-hand. Sitting in the pram was what Amy at first thought was a real-life baby. She'd stared at it, then realized it was a doll. A beautiful doll with black hair curled around the brim of a white bonnet. She was dressed all in white and had very rosy cheeks and huge brown eyes that seemed to follow you wherever you went. Amy had longed to hold her.

Now, she felt she did in her imagination as she pretended to hold her own little Ruth Ellen to her. But in her darkest hours when she woke from a nightmare, she remembered Belton, the man who must have put little Ruth Ellen inside her.

17

She didn't want these thoughts and fought against them, as nothing must taint the memory of her child. She just so longed for her.

18

3

When the ship finally reached its destination Amy found she was bustled down the gangplank with what seemed like hundreds of other kids pushing and shoving. She and Lucy clung to each other's hands.

The heat was unbearable, the crush making it hard to breathe. Amy forced her other hand into her pocket. It reassured her to feel the carefully folded picture and to know that safe in its folds was the scrap of paper with Ruth's address written on it.

Two days later they arrived at Marchmont Home and were told they were in Belleville, Ontario, which to Amy meant nothing except that it wasn't London.

The house looked lovely. White, large and with what looked like a lace balcony wrapped around it, it stood in its own grounds.

She looked at Lucy, whose hand she'd held for much of the last two days since they had left the ship. This new land had held wonderment for them with its many lakes shimmering with reflections of snow-capped mountains — the backdrop to every part of this country that they had travelled through.

Once they alighted from the rickety old coach, they were assembled in a large room where they listened in awe to the lady in charge of the home. She seemed kindly and had a nice smile. Amy filled with hope.

'Now then, children, my name is Mrs Peterson. You won't be here long, as our aim is to get you living with families who will take care of you and give you a much better life than you've had till now. But while you are here you will be expected to be on good behaviour, and to apply yourselves to your studies, and other things you will be taught.'

She went on about rules and housekeeping, which seemed to be the main occupation of the girls, whereas the boys would be learning farming skills. This was to prepare them as they were to take up these roles when they went to a family.

Mrs Peterson told them that Canada was a great farming country and that they would enjoy life here very much.

Amy began to feel that everything was going to be all right. That all the bad was behind her, and she told herself that she'd work hard and make Mrs Peterson proud of her.

* * *

She didn't have long to do that as two days later all of the girls stood once more in the hall, this time to be 'picked', or not, by the visiting families looking for help.

Amy didn't feel ready to go. She liked it in the home and had begun to settle into the routine. She knew Lucy felt the same as she sidled up to her and found her hand. 'Let's keep our heads down, Amy. They might not pick us then.'

But this didn't work.

'You!'

Amy cringed. She'd seen the boots sticking out of the long skirt stop in front of her.

'Look up, girl.'

Amy looked up. The woman had an expression on

her face that struck fear into her heart. Pinched is what she'd call the face of the woman. Tight-lipped. Hair pulled severely back into a bun. Beady eyes that peered. 'You look strong.'

Amy couldn't imagine why she thought this. She was small for her age, and didn't feel strong, hadn't since . . . but she wouldn't think of that.

'Ma, she's puny!'

'Shut up, Martha. I think she has a good day's work in her. Little ones can be strong and get through a lot of work and don't need as much food . . . How old are you, girl?'

'Twelve, miss.'

'Mrs Miller, not miss! Have you begun your monthlies?'

'Yes, Mrs Miller.'

'Hmph. Well, do you know how to behave yourself? I don't want you getting into trouble. If you do, you'll be in a convent and forgotten about.'

Amy trembled. She felt Lucy's hand tighten on hers and knew that she was afraid for her. Amy prayed the lady would move on. She sniffed away the tears that threatened.

'Right. I'll take you. I just need to find a strong boy now . . . Mrs Peterson, Mrs Peterson!'

At Mrs Peterson's, 'Yes, may I help you?' Mrs Miller, in a voice unrecognizable to Amy, said, 'I'll take this one, dear. She's an appealing little thing, and I think I could give her a good home and a good start in life. As God is my witness, it is what I came here today to do, dear lady.'

'That's wonderful. Amy has only been with us for a couple of days and to have found a placement already is very good . . . I don't suppose you could consider

21

taking both girls, could you? Amy and Lucy are insep-
arable. We were told that was so on the journey here,
only we find the children settle easier if they have a
companion.'

Mrs Miller turned and looked at Lucy.

Lucy, normally shy, looked up and smiled. Amy
kept the fingers of her free hand crossed.

'Mmm, well, it could be useful to have two girls. As
they aren't very old, and small for their age, they can
share the very few duties I have for them to do and
accompany each other to school . . . Yes, I'll take them
both, but I still need a helping hand on the farm. Have
you a good strong lad needing a home?'

'They are over in the fields, dear. Let me take you
to see them . . . Amy, Lucy, go to your dormitory and
fold all your things into your cases. Don't dawdle now
as you don't want to hold Mrs Miller up.'

Martha hadn't moved but stood staring at them.
Amy thought she was about thirteen as she was taller
by a foot than they were, and overweight. She looked
silly with her golden hair tied in bunches each side of
her face, in a child's way.

'What are you staring at?'

Amy cast her eyes down. Martha put out her foot
and stamped on Amy's. Amy bent double but didn't
cry out. There was something menacing about Martha's smirk. It seemed to say, 'Don't even dare to tell.'

In the dormitory, Lucy plonked on her bed. Tears
filled her eyes.

Going to her, Amy told her, 'It'll be all right, mate.
At least we'll be together.'

Lucy stood. The hug they went into took some of
the loneliness from Amy's heart. 'Ta for getting Mrs
Miller to like yer, Lucy. I wouldn't have blamed yer if

yer'd have wanted to put yourself in a bad light so as not to be chosen.'

'I just want us to be together. I never want us to be apart.'

'Nor me. Come on, let's get sorted. We'll look out for one another, and if we work hard, maybe it won't be so bad.'

When they set off, sitting in the back of a long, flat cart, they were joined by a shy lad who looked as old as Martha. He told them his name was Ivan.

Mrs Miller, Martha and a man driving the horses, who they knew to be Mrs Miller's husband and Martha's father from the conversations they were having, sat on a comfy-looking bench at the front of the cart.

They hadn't gone far when they pulled up at a ramshackle wooden building that had a sign saying *General Store*.

Mr Miller got down. 'You three, come with me.'

When they walked inside the store, they found it to be more like a pub. Men sat or stood around a bar drinking.

'Load that lot on the cart!'

Amy looked at the huge, bulky sacks knowing she couldn't move even one of them an inch, let alone lift them onto the cart.

Ivan gallantly tackled the nearest one. 'Give me a hand, girls.'

Both got the bottom corners but couldn't lift it much. Ivan tugged for all he was worth, his face red with the effort, till gradually they slid it along.

'Ha! Looks like you got yerself some good workers there, Ralph!' All the men in the bar roared with laughter. Mr Miller scowled as he looked around at them. His fists clenched. A hush descended. Some

23

of the men shuffled their feet and looked like they wanted to run. Amy felt afraid.

The man behind the bar calmed things. 'Come and have your beer, Ralph, and you, Phil, and you, Randy, give them kids a hand. There'll be a drink in it for you.'

With Phil and Randy's help the goods were soon loaded. Ivan surprised them all by copying the men and mastering the technique of throwing sacks onto his back.

'You girls sit on the sacks. Go on, you're useless at anything else.' Randy gave them a cheeky smile. They giggled and clambered up, snuggling on one of the sacks together. Mrs Miller didn't turn around or acknowledge anyone. Nor did she complain when what seemed like hours passed and Ralph hadn't come out of the pub.

Martha did. 'Ma, when is Pa going to come and take us home? I'm getting cold.'

'Hush, girl. Don't complain. Pa works hard, he's entitled to have his drink and enjoy the company of the men.'

'I know, but I want to pee.'

Hearing Martha say this, Amy suddenly had the urge to go too, and beside her, Lucy began to wriggle on her bottom. Not for herself, but for Lucy, Amy piped up, 'Please may we go to the lavatory, Mrs Miller?'

Mrs Miller let out a deep sigh. 'Oh, for goodness' sake! Martha, you go and take them with you.'

'They can go on their own when I come back.'

'Take them!'

Martha jumped down, her bulk causing dust to rise from the ground. She didn't wait for them but

24

hurried around to the back of the building. Amy and Lucy found it easy to keep up with her, but couldn't help giggling at how she waddled when she tried to get ahead.

When they came to a lean-to Martha spoke for the first time. 'I'll go first, you keep watch in case one of the men come around.'

When she opened the door, the smell knocked Amy for six and she saw it did Lucy. They both retched.

'I ain't going in there, Lucy. Keep watch.' With this, Amy went around the side of the lean-to, lifted her lifted her skirt and squatted.

She'd just finished relieving herself when Martha came out. 'What do you think you're doing? You dirty thing . . . Ma . . . Ma!'

Mrs Miller came running around the corner. 'What? What's happening? Are you all right?'

Amy didn't have enough time to pull her skirt straight. Mrs Miller looked down at the tell-tale wet patch in the dust.

'You dirty tyke!' Her vicious slap sent Amy reeling backwards. She landed in her own urine. Lucy cried out in protest. Mrs Miller reeled around. 'And don't you dare give backchat! Go into the lavatory and behave like a civilized human being! Go on.'

With this she turned. Amy, feeling dizzy from the slap, tried to get up, but then she saw Martha's look and saw her take a sly look at her ma's back before lifting her foot.

Pain shot through Amy's leg.

Lucy helped her up. Leaning against the wall, her face smarted and her leg burned, but she was determined that Lucy wouldn't have to go into the stinking lav. 'I'll keep a look out, Lucy, luv. They won't come back, but I'll call if I hear one of the men coming. Squat just around the corner of the lean-to.'

Misery filled Amy as the horses trundled along for what seemed like miles and miles over rough terrain, but she tried not to show it as she comforted Lucy. Ivan sat on the edge of the cart, his head bent, not uttering a word.

The waft of alcohol came over them as Mr Miller swayed in his seat, his head flopping forward from time to time, until Mrs Miller nudged him when it seemed the horses would take them into the ditch.

On the third time of her doing this, he lifted his hand and swiped Mrs Miller across her head.

'Pa! Don't hit Ma like that!'

'Yer'll get one in a minute, Little Miss Fatso!'

Martha burst into tears, her sobs loud and overdone.

'Shurrup, can't yer. Or I'll do as I say and put yer across my knee. Yer ma indulges yer too much. If it were up to me, I'd lock yer in yer room and leave yer there for a week. It wouldn't do yer any harm, girl.'

Amy never thought she would, but she felt pity for Martha. Mr Miller was a pig of a man. But then she felt envy as Mrs Miller gathered Martha to her and rocked her backwards and forwards while she gently stroked her back.

How Amy had longed to have a mum do that to her. As she stared at the scene, she felt a weight on her shoulder. Turning, she saw that Lucy had fallen asleep. Gently manoeuvring her, Amy managed to get Lucy's head into her lap. Mimicking Mrs Miller, she stroked Lucy's back. The action felt good and comforted her.

It was dark when they finally pulled up. Lucy woke and stretched herself. Amy tried to, but her limbs were stiff and tired. They waited. Mr Miller, sober now, went up the steps of the wooden house and lit a lamp that hung above the door.

The light showed the building, its many windows reflecting the glow of the lamp.

To Amy, it looked lovely with its net curtains and tied-back drapes and a porch along the front of the house. On this stood a type of swing seat, the like of which she'd never seen before.

'This way. Bring your stuff.'

Mr Miller's gruff voice barked this as an order as he came back down the stairs carrying the lamp.

They turned away from the house and followed him down what felt like a muddy path as Amy's boots squelched under her. She lifted her frock to stop it sweeping the ground but had a job to hold it with needing both hands to keep swapping her case between.

Ahead of them she could see a barn. Once inside Mr Miller said, 'That's where you sleep.' He pointed to an open hatch, accessed by a wooden ladder. They could see that the barn was full of hay bales.

As Mr Miller lit another lamp, he said, 'Up there. Yer'll find a blanket each and a bowl. There's a tap outside to wash yerselves. Mrs Miller is a stickler for cleanliness, so don't forget to do behind yer ears.'

He laughed, but Amy didn't see anything funny.

'I'll bring a jar of coffee down. Get yerselves sorted, I want yer up sharp in the morning! So, it'll be lights out when I give you yer hot drink.'

'I'm hungry, sir.'

Amy felt Lucy quiver as she said this.

Mr Miller hesitated then said, 'I'll bring yer a crust each,' before turning and almost marching away from them.

'It's cold, Amy.'

'It might not be up top, luv. We'll huddle together and keep each other warm, eh?'

Amy didn't feel as brave as she sounded. The thought of the darkness above and the unfamiliar calling of birds and creaks of the barn door had spooked her.

'Come on, you two. Let's go up, eh? We'll sort it. But I'm glad yer asked for food, Lucy. I could eat a scabby cat.'

Feeling a bit braver as Ivan said this in a jovial voice, Amy asked, 'Where're you from, Ivan?'

'Me 'ome's in Bethnal Green. Me mum told the authorities that she couldn't cope. She has fifteen kids in a one-down, two-up cottage, yer see. She thought they'd help her out, but they took me and two of me brothers into care. The next day I were boarding the ship. Me mum don't know I'm 'ere, and I don't know where me brothers are.'

Amy felt his agony in the pit of her stomach. She wanted to put her arms around Ivan. 'You can write to yer mum, Ivan. Put her mind at rest.'

'I can't write.'

As they climbed the ladder, she said, 'I'll write for yer then.'

'And where are yer going to get paper, pen and ink and a stamp from?'

Amy's heart sank as the impossibility of doing so sank in. *How am I going to write to Ruth?*

Brushing this thought away as it threatened to

undo her, she climbed the last few steps of the ladder and surveyed the loft. In the little light that glowed through the hatch, she saw it had nothing in it other than what Mr Miller had told them: straw, two blankets and an enamel bowl.

'You should go downstairs while me and Lucy get undressed, Ivan.'

'I'm going to find somewhere to pee, so don't worry.'

'Watch he don't catch yer,' Lucy told him. 'They don't like us doing it except in a lav.'

'Well, there ain't one, is there, eh?'

This sounded a bit gruff to Amy. 'She's only telling yer. I'll ask Mr Miller when he comes back.'

'I can't wait that long.'

Amy hoped it was tiredness making Ivan grumpy. She felt sorry for him and determined she'd help him all she could.

When Mr Miller came back, he brought three huge chunks of bread, and a hot can of coffee as promised. The bread was spread with dripping and smelled delicious. He told them there was a bucket around the back they were to use as a lav and were to tip it into the cesspit. 'Yer nose'll lead you to that. It's down the bottom of the field. Just make sure you clean the bucket thoroughly using the tap and the wire brush that hangs next to it.'

With this he left them.

Amy's spirits fell as he turned the lamp off, and she heard a sob from Lucy.

'Don't worry, girls, it's a full moon. When our eyes get used to it, we'll be able to see . . . 'Ave a drink out of that can each, then pass it to me,' Ivan told them, making Amy feel glad that he'd returned to his former self.

29

It was as he said, the moon did light the loft.

They soon cheered as they drank the bitter liquid that they tolerated to warm them and to quench their thirst, even though it made them grimace.

When they'd finished eating the delicious chunks of bread and dripping, Ivan set about making two beds from the hay, telling them to go to the lav. 'Don't worry about using the bucket, squat down outside.'

They did this, both shivering in their nightgowns.

It was when they were huddled up together that Amy felt Lucy's body shuddering. She could only hold her close as her own fear and sadness trembled through her. But then she heard a muffled sob from Ivan, and felt herself sink into the depths of despair.

4

The days and nights seemed the same — drudgery, sparse food, a few swipes around the ear from Mrs Miller and spitefulness from Martha, then little rest as they tried to ease their aching bodies on their beds of hay.

And now a year had passed and here it was, October 1911.

As she worked, cleaning out the back room, which the family called the dining room but was nothing more than a dumping ground for anything they couldn't be bothered to put away, Amy thought about how she, Lucy and Ivan had somehow managed to get through the year.

Their friendship had sustained them, and it had made her happy to see Ivan and Lucy become close. They chatted for hours, and Ivan had made Lucy pieces of charcoal to draw with. He'd learned how when he'd worked for a blacksmith who'd made it to sell to the schools. He sat for hours after they had settled down, paring the bark off the bits of wood he'd collected during the day. He would put these into a blackened tin, made that way by the many times he'd placed it, full of wood, into the kiln that was lit to boil the pig swill. Magically, when the tin cooled, there were the finished pieces of charcoal inside it.

Lucy was overjoyed with the supply, even though she only had the floorboards to use as a canvas, which they had to hide with hay in case Martha ever saw them and caused trouble. It was something that Amy hated doing as some of the drawings she thought were masterpieces. Especially the portraits of Ivan.

But, for the most part, the year had brought acceptance that life wasn't what they had dreamed it would be and that they had to make the most of it, doing what they could to avoid the beatings and tending to whichever one was hurt with love and offering comfort.

'Haven't you finished in here yet, you lazy English slut?'

Amy's stomach muscles tightened. She stared at Mrs Miller.

'Well?'

As she took a quick glance at the clock on the mantelshelf, Amy's fear deepened. She was shocked to realize that the task had taken her longer than usual. Her heart sank. No matter what she said, she knew it wouldn't make any difference.

'Speak to me, girl, or you'll end up like your idle mate.'

'Lucy? What have you done to Lucy? Where is she?'

'She deserved all she got, making eyes at my husband. Letting him paw her.'

'No! Lucy would never do that. What's happened?' Pushing past Mrs Miller, Amy ran towards the barn. 'Lucy! Lucy!'

Ivan appeared at the barn door. His look of devastation made Amy realize before he spoke that this was worse than usual, but she couldn't prepare herself for what he told her. 'She's hurt bad, Amy. That woman took a stick to her. Said she'd been going with Mr Miller, but she ain't, Amy. Lucy would never do that.'

Clambering up the ladder to the sound of moans

of pain, Amy gasped when she saw the bloodied state of Lucy's back. Torn almost to ribbons, some of the gashes gaped open, showing her raw flesh.

Falling onto to her knees, she held Lucy's arm. 'When did this happen? Why didn't I hear anything?'

'Mis-mister Miller . . . he told me to go . . . to the bottom barn . . . Oh, Amy, he tried . . . he kissed me . . . and touched me . . . and I screamed and kicked him . . . Martha came. Her . . . her dad was on his knees as I'd caught him in his privates. She went screaming across the yard. And then . . . Mrs Miller . . . Oh, Amy, she beat me. She . . . she used a thin stick!'

'No! Oh, Lucy, I didn't hear anything. I was in the back of the house. I'll go and get a jug of water, luv. We'll clean you up and make you feel better, eh?'

Amy's heart thudded in her chest as she went towards the water pump. How could this happen to such a delicate soul? Because that's what Lucy was. Yes, she'd developed rapidly since they'd been here. Her breasts had grown, and her shape had changed, making her appear to be a young woman rather than a young girl. Her clothes stretched over her curves which were accentuated by her tiny waist. And yet, she hadn't lost her slender gracefulness. To Amy, she was how she imagined a fairy would be — beautiful and almost as if she wasn't of this world.

To think of Lucy's fragility being spoiled by the rotten Mr Miller and her hurting was too much to bear. Men were pigs and she never wanted to be touched by one again.

These thoughts left her when she returned with the water as shock zinged through her at the sight of Lucy trembling violently. Froth foamed around her mouth.

'LUCY!'

The sound of footsteps on the ladder steadied Amy, until she saw Mr Miller's head appear. 'Is she all right?'

Amy's temper boiled over. 'Yer a pig . . . A pig!' Without thinking, she kicked out at him but then was horror struck to see him reel backwards and disappear. The crash of him and the ladder landing made her sick with fear but when she looked down and saw him get up and shake his fist at her, she filled with defiance and stuck her tongue out at him.

'No . . . Amy, no . . . Don't . . . he'll beat you . . . Oh, help me . . . please, help me.'

'It's all right, Lucy. I'll help yer, luv.' Glad to see the froth had dripped onto the floor and there was no more of it, though Lucy's body still shook, Amy felt torn between warming her up and making her even colder by bathing her back. She decided she must clean the jagged wounds, so gritted her teeth, gently bathed the cuts and picked out little splinters of wood.

Awash with tears, as Lucy sobbed and begged her to stop, she ripped the sheet that they were now allowed and covered the wounds, afraid as she did that she might not have cleaned them enough, but knowing she could not put Lucy through any more.

Lying down beside her, she gently stroked Lucy's hair. Her curls, now damp with sweat, sprang back into coils with each touch.

'Did . . . I mean, did he do that thing to yer, luv?'

'No . . . Oh, Amy, it was awful. The taste of him when he kissed me . . . he made me retch. And his hands . . . he — he kept saying that soon it wouldn't just be his hands touching me and that I would like it, but I didn't, Amy, I hated it and wanted him to stop.

34

It was when . . . he . . . he put his hand up me skirt that I kicked out. I — I couldn't stop, Amy. He was on the floor crying, but I couldn't stop kicking him. Then Martha appeared . . . She screamed at him . . . she said . . . I — I heard her say . . . that she was his girl. That . . . that he shouldn't do those things to anyone but her!'

'What? Yer mean, he's been interfering with Martha . . . his own daughter?'

'Yes . . . She was hysterical. She said he'd told her that there was no one else. That she was better than her ma!'

Amy felt shocked to her core. For a moment, she pitied Martha, but then hated her even more for allowing what she and Lucy had fought against and had had forced on them. Then, seeing the sweat on Lucy's brow, she put that out of her mind. 'Don't think about it all now, luv. You'll be ill. We have to be stronger than them. If we give in, we'll be lost.'

'I want to leave here, Amy. We could run away during the night.'

'Where would we go? How would we live?'

'Just go till we come to another farm. We know how all of the farms are crying out for workers.'

'What about Ivan?'

'He'll come. We . . . we've talked about it — planned it even.'

This shocked Amy and made her feel left out and, yes, alone. Would they have gone and left her?

The sound of screams took these thoughts away and replaced them with fear. This deepened when Ivan appeared, his face ghastly white, his voice shaking . . . 'He's killed her!'

Amy stared at him.

'He's killed Martha. She were going mad at him . . . he hit out at her . . . she fell . . . her 'ead cracked open . . . her eyes just stared. Mrs Miller's fainted and . . . and he's gone!'

Lucy's sobs brought Amy out of the stupor that hearing all this had put her in and made her face the reality of it as Lucy cried, 'I want to go . . . Ivan, take me away from here.'

Ivan hurried over and kneeled beside Lucy. His voice gentle, his hand touching her hair, he told her, 'We'll go as soon as yer better, luv . . . Yer'll come an' all, won't yer, Amy?'

Amy nodded. She went to ask when, but sobs of, 'Help me! Help me,' drew her to the hatch. There on the ground, on her knees, was a different Mrs Miller — broken, begging of them to do something.

Ivan took charge. 'I'm coming.' As he went down the ladder he said, 'Yer'll 'ave to send for the doctor, Mrs Miller . . . Amy, come and 'elp me, we need to get Martha inside.'

Amy obeyed but didn't want to. Her mind screamed against seeing the dead Martha, or helping the hateful Mrs Miller, but for all that, it was the decent thing to do, so she went without protest. 'I'll be back soon, Lucy, luv. Try to sleep, eh? Everything'll be all right. I promise.'

Martha's body lay across the entrance to the kitchen. There was a scraper for boots just outside the door and Amy could see that Martha had fallen onto this. Her face looked ugly and distorted and as if made of wax. Amy had the urge to scream at her that she'd got her just deserts, but instead lifted her legs as Ivan instructed. The weight of them bent her double. 'I can't, Ivan. She's too heavy for me.'

'We can't leave her out 'ere.' He turned to the sobbing Mrs Miller. 'Yer'll have to 'elp us, missus. We'll need to drag her.'

Amy didn't like the sound of this. 'But that'll scrape all her skin off, Ivan. Why don't we cover her up and get the doctor and some help, eh?'

Seeming to calm a little, Mrs Miller told him, 'Take the pony and trap and head for town. Get the police! Tell them he did it. Tell them he's gone, and to go after him as he'll head south. They need to catch him before he gets to the border.'

Ivan didn't argue. He ran across the yard and within minutes reappeared with the horse and trap. Amy stared after him, wanting to call him back, feeling afraid now she was left with Mrs Miller, but he disappeared into a cloud of dust.

'You've caused this! You and that other one! You drove my Ralph mad, you lured him away from me with flaunting yourselves . . . Oh, my baby, my Martha. She couldn't bear it. She loved her da.'

Wanting to scream at her that it was Martha who'd taken her husband and lain with her own da, and that none of it was their doing, Amy stopped herself as she could see the deep grief and shock this woman was in. 'I'll make yer a hot coffee, eh? It might help yer.'

Turning and going into the kitchen, Amy heard Mrs Miller's wails turn to a kind of chanting of Martha's name. She prayed that, concentrating on her daughter, Mrs Miller would forget her anger.

As she lifted the jug of hot coffee off the stove, the smell of it made her want to retch. She'd never taken to it and longed for a decent cup of tea, but Mrs Miller said it was too expensive and only kept for visitors.

Sighing, Amy turned to pour the coffee into the

37

mugs that always stood on the sideboard next to the stove. A shadow caught her eye. A kind of growl made her jump. She dropped the jug. Hot coffee splashed on her legs; scolding pains seared her. Mrs Miller looked like the devil as she lunged at her with the copper stick they used to agitate the washing and lift it from the tub. Amy stepped to the side, but the blow caught her shoulder, sending an excruciating pain shooting down her arm. Dodging around the table and out of the door, she ran for all she was worth to the barn and climbed the ladder faster than she ever had done. With the screams of the mad woman ringing in her ears, she closed the trapdoor and sat on it.

Lucy's large eyes stared out at her.

'She can't get to us, Lucy, don't worry, luv.' But the sound of the iron bar that kept the hatch closed during the day being shoved into place struck a terror into her. She and Lucy were trapped!

They huddled together as best they could with the pain that Lucy was in. Amy prayed that Ivan wouldn't be long, but knew it took over an hour to do the trip to the shanty town that stood on the side of the lake.

It was then that she smelled burning. Panic rose in her. Terror gripped her as if a vice had been clamped around her chest. She couldn't breathe.

Lucy stirred, then coughed.

They both stared at the tendrils of smoke seeping through the edges of the hatch. It was then that cackling laughter sounded and they heard a strange chant. 'Burn, you witches, burn!'

'Put the blanket over the hatch, Amy. Stop the smoke getting to us.'

'But ... Oh God, Lucy, all the dry hay ... the wooden barn ...'

38

'Don't. Amy, luv, we must stay calm. Think . . . Wait a minute, the knife Ivan uses to shave the bark off the sticks is under his blanket. Get it, Amy! See if there's anything you can do with it to get us out . . . The walls are wood — see if you can prise a panel open.'

Following Lucy's instructions, Amy threw the blanket over the hatch, then remembered the remaining water in the jug. She doused the blanket with it, hoping that might help.

With the knife in her hand now, she frantically looked around, not sure what to do. Her eyes fell on the place where Ivan had nailed a piece of wood over a hole in the wall to stop the draughts. Desperately she hacked away at it till she could put her hand through and then tugged the panel with all her might. A creak gave her hope, but it didn't budge enough for them to get through.

The floor beneath her felt hot. Fear sent her running to the other side of the barn. Here some old skins hung. She pulled at them. One came down. Relief flooded her as she saw a handle. Grabbing it, she couldn't move it . . . 'It's a door, Lucy, but it's locked!'

Lucy whimpered. The sound triggered Amy's anger. She kicked out again and again at the door. Behind her the loft began to fill with smoke. Her throat burned. Panic spurred her on. One almighty shove with her least painful shoulder and it gave way but with such suddenness she almost fell through it.

Relief was soon replaced with horror as the rush of air ignited the heat into flames.

Roaring, creeping flames.

Agonized cries of, 'Lucy, Lucy!' felt futile as she watched in horror the ball of flames engulf her beloved friend, then seem to thunder towards her, searing her with unbearable heat. She turned and jumped.

The ground gave no mercy. Pain shot through her already bruised shoulder. A crack hailed a desperate pain in her arm. But the heat spurred her on as the sparks that spat at her stung her body and forced her to roll away and keep rolling till she was out of range. Then it happened. The roof of the barn collapsed, and Amy knew that she would never see the beautiful, kind, talented Lucy again. It was all too much to bear. She allowed the blackness that threatened to enclose her take her into its peace.

* * *

When she came to, she was lying on a soft bed. Above her the ornate ceiling with its swirls and lovely chandelier made her think of Lucy. 'Lucy?'

'Hush, Amy, yer in Mrs Miller's room. We can't find Lucy . . . What happened? She ain't . . . ?'

The scene came back to her. She opened her mouth to scream, but nothing came out.

'Oh, Amy, what happened? How did the barn catch fire?'

'Mrs . . . Mrs Miller.'

'She's dead. Hung herself. Tell me where Lucy is.'

Amy turned her head. Ivan's face was full of pain. 'She . . . The fire . . . It . . . it wrapped around her . . . Oh, Ivan, help me!'

'No . . . no, Amy . . . no!'

'I — I found a door . . . She'd locked us in . . . behind the skins . . .'

'Amy, you ain't making sense. What door? Who locked you in?'

'Mrs Miller. She went mad. I ran . . .'

40

Amy couldn't stop the torrent of words pouring from her as she related every detail. When she came to the end of the telling, she lay back exhausted.

'Let me examine her, son.'

The kindly voice gave her hope. Another voice said, 'Well, it sounds like it happened as we said. Ralph was always saying his wife had mad bouts. He feared her when she did as she seemed to turn into the devil.' Then a cough, followed by, 'Are yer sure it was Ralph — Mr Miller — who hit his daughter? He was very fond of her, and it seems more likely it was Mrs Miller did it, given what has been said.'

Ivan didn't answer. Amy wanted to shout that it was Mr Miller. That the love he had for his daughter wasn't natural, but a pain in her arm made her scream.

'You've broken your arm, my dear, and probably a few ribs too. It will hurt while I set it in place, then it will feel more comfortable. Bite on this.'

Something that tasted like dirty leather was shoved into Amy's mouth. She spluttered, tried to remove it, but then a pain much worse than any she'd had made her bite down on it. Her scream rasped her tonsils.

Unable to take any more, she went back into the blackness only to be dogged for hours by nightmarish dreams.

★   ★   ★

This time when she woke she felt a hand holding hers. She turned her head. Ivan's tear-stained face looked haggard. He sniffed and wiped his sleeve over his cheeks. 'Yer awake then?'

For some reason this made Amy smile.

41

'It's just us, Amy. Me and you. We're 'ere on our own. The police are looking for Ralph and they say we can stay till they find him, but in the meantime, they will contact Mrs Peterson of Marchmont Home to get us some new places.'

'I don't want to go to another, I just want to go home, or to stay with Mrs Peterson.'

'Yer can't, Amy, luv. I asked the policeman to tell her we wanted to stay together . . . You do want to stay with me, don't yer?'

Amy nodded.

'Lucy . . . Lucy's body — what remained of it — were found.'

Amy heard a noise. She knew it had come from herself but couldn't stop it. Her sore throat burned as she hollered out her pain.

Ivan's hand tightened on hers, but he didn't try to stop her cries. His own tears flowed down his face. She clung to his hand as if he would be the saviour of her, but she doubted anyone could be that.

When he released her hand, the bed sagged as he climbed onto it. Lying beside her, he gently put his arm over her. Amy grasped it as if it was a lifeline. Together, they broke their hearts for their loss of the lovely, delicate Lucy.

5

When they reached Marchmont Home three weeks later, Mrs Peterson welcomed them with open arms. To be held by her, even though it hurt her splinted arm and cracked ribs, warmed a small patch of Amy's cold, sad heart.

'I am so sorry, my dear. We try. We really try hard to keep an eye on our children when they leave us, but the volume coming into our country is overwhelming. We did have a visit scheduled to the Millers' farm for early next year. That you should go through all you have is unforgiveable.'

Amy found she couldn't answer, but Ivan did. 'It's not your fault, Mrs Peterson. We only want one thing and that's to be placed together.'

'I will try but don't hold out your hopes. Anyway, that's weeks away. Amy must heal physically and mentally first, and you, too, need a respite, Ivan, to heal from the horror of it all.'

'I want to go home to London, Mrs Peterson. I've friends there who'll look after me.'

'Oh, Amy, I can understand that, dear, but it isn't possible. We don't have any way of returning you to your homeland.' Mrs Peterson gave a pitying smile. 'I'm really sorry, Amy. We have failed you, and most of all we have failed dear Lucy. I can only promise we will do our best for you from now on.'

Amy thought of all she'd had, and had lost: her little baby, lovely Lucy and the drawing she'd done for her, the paper with Ruth's address — not that she didn't know it, it was ingrained in her memory, but she'd loved touching Ruth's handwriting. Somehow, she would get back to London and begin again. Be with Ruth and Ellen, for if Ruth hadn't found Ellen, they would do so together.

As she followed Mrs Peterson to the dormitory, she caught sight of her reflection in a mirror hung on the corridor wall. She was shocked to see how haggard she looked. How greasy her hair was, how much more freckled her face was from being in the fields in the blazing sun and how her eyes had somehow died.

She looked around and noticed for the first time that Ivan was no longer with her, but then, he'd probably been sent to the boys' quarters. At this moment she was so tired that she felt glad. Coping with his grief as well as her own had weighed her down.

* * *

The days seemed to flow along, but gradually Amy recovered and Ivan looked more like his old self. They often met in the gardens and chatted and, yes, sometimes had a laugh together. Ivan had become like the brother she'd never had.

Life had become bearable again, with just a few nightmares to mar it. Her waking hours were when she would think of Lucy in heaven with Ruth's Holy Mary and her little Ruth Ellen and she began to feel better. It helped, too, when Mrs Peterson told them that she now had a report into Lucy's death. 'I thought you should both know, my dears, that our dear Lucy died instantly and wouldn't have felt any pain. They say the fireball that engulfed her would have killed

44

her, she wouldn't have suffered any feeling of burning first as its heat was so intense . . . I know, it is still horrible to think about and a horrendous memory for you both, especially you, Amy, who witnessed it, but I wanted you to know as I am sure you have tried to imagine how it had felt for her. May she rest in peace.'

Amy had a picture of how it happened, how the flames seared up from nowhere when she opened the door to the barn. What Mrs Peterson said was the truth. She'd not heard a sound from Lucy — not a scream or a moan.

In the garden a couple of days later, wrapped up warm against the November chill, and talking to Ivan, Amy told him, 'I've been thinking. We never had a service for Lucy. Something that'd put her soul to rest — like a funeral, although that can't happen.'

'A memorial service, yer mean?'

'Yes. We should, Ivan. There's only us who can do that. She had no one else.'

'What yer thinking of, going to church or what?'

'I don't know. We could do that. Would yer come if I can arrange it?'

'I would. I ain't that keen on all that stuff and I'm glad Mrs Peterson don't enforce it, but you go now and then, so is it what yer want?'

Amy wasn't sure. Lucy had never talked about God much, so she didn't know if she was a believer or not. If she wasn't, would she be sitting with Ruth's Holy Mary?

Brushing this thought away, she told Ivan, 'I'll ask Mrs Peterson. She might have an idea.'

When she found Mrs Peterson, Amy was surprised to learn that she had been looking for her. 'Ah, Amy. I have news. I have a family who want a girl of your age!'

45

Amy's heart sank. All she could think to say was, 'Oh? Will they take Ivan as well?'

'I don't know yet. I've made contact and told them about you. They're coming to meet you. They should be here any day, but weren't sure when they could set out . . . Now, what were you looking for me for?'

Amy told her with an even heavier heart than she'd already had. It had come as a shock that she would soon be leaving.

'I think that's a lovely idea, though I would have reservations because I don't want to frighten the children who are looking forward to placements. So, that would mean not revealing how our dear Lucy died.'

'I don't mind no one knowing, I just want her to be remembered, to have a service that puts her to rest.'

'Well, that is what we will do. How about we make it a picnic, say prayers for Lucy, but make it fun too?'

'Lucy would like that, ta, Mrs Peterson.'

'And, Amy, I will make sure that this time you're all right and treated well, dear. This family are known for their kindness.'

Amy knew her fear to wobble the nerves in her stomach as she couldn't believe this to be true. But what mattered most was that she didn't want to be parted from Ivan.

★ ★ ★

Two days later, the planning was done, and the picnic was to take place. Amy had some words she wanted to say, and Ivan had surprised her by forming them into a poem. The smaller children were all excited, but those around her own age and younger were unsure. Amy knew how they felt. Even treats were something to be sceptical of as all their lives they hadn't had many.

It was a beautiful day, what Mrs Peterson called 'the fall' but what they called autumn. The trees in the garden and for as far as the eye could see were a kaleidoscope of golds, reds and browns. Amy knew that if Lucy were here, she would have painted the landscape and it would have been a beautiful likeness. Her heart ached for her lovely friend.

It was lovely to see the excited faces of the younger ones, and even the older kids, who hadn't been sure of all this, looked happy and relaxed. All munched on their jam sandwiches and eyed the jam tart that sat on their plates as if to protect it from predators.

When they'd eaten, Mrs Peterson told them the reason for the picnic and called everyone to say a prayer, which she led. Then it was time for Amy to stand and read out hers and Ivan's poem.

Mrs Peterson's words surprised Amy as she introduced her. 'Children, you can all be inspired by Amy. She, like you, came to Canada to begin a new life. She has suffered the loss of her friend, who was chosen by God to live in heaven, but Amy is carrying on in true British spirit. Not only is she paying this tribute to her friend, but she is prepared to go out very soon and begin her journey in the land that welcomes you all . . . Now, Amy, you won't be forgotten here, nor will Lucy. I have asked the gardener to make a rose garden in the corner over there and it will be called the 'Lucy and Amy Garden'. It is a tribute and for future children who come here to know and remember the pioneers of our venture to bring a new life to the underprivileged.'

With tears stinging her eyes, Amy took a deep breath. She didn't want to falter. These words were for Lucy, and she wanted them to be heard clearly by her:

> 'Lucy was our mate
> She didn't know how to hate
> Only to love and to draw
> Flowers, birds and more
> Ivan and I loved her so
> We didn't want her to go
> But we want her soul to rest
> For she was one of the best.'

As she read this last line, Mrs Peterson began to clap and then all the children joined in. For Amy, it was a good moment. She looked over at Ivan and he was grinning. She grinned back. She and he had given Lucy a good send-off and that's all they'd wanted to do.

★ ★ ★

The next day, the family arrived. Amy didn't feel at all ready. She just wanted to stay where she was if she couldn't get home to London.

'Now, Amy, dear, to give you a chance, we haven't said anything about what has happened to you in the past year. I wouldn't advise it, as though these farmers live miles apart from each other, they hear all that goes on. Most will have made their mind up that the home child, as they call you children, would be more to blame than the farmer was.'

Amy felt her heart drop. The way Mrs Peterson had said this wasn't a denial of any blame being on her shoulders. Did she really believe she was guilty?

48

'So, to give you a little information, this family haven't any daughters, so that might be a good thing as I believe the daughter of the Millers instigated a lot of your troubles. They have two sons. One is seventeen and the other the same age as you, going on for fourteen.'

'Will they take Ivan, Mrs Peterson?'

'Well . . . look, Amy, it is difficult and very rare for a family to take two of my children on . . . I'm sorry, but I'm not hopeful.'

'Then I don't want to go!'

'Sadly, the choice isn't yours, dear. If they want you, I have no right to stop them having you unless I know of anything which would mean you wouldn't be treated properly. And I don't know of anything, Amy. They seem perfect. They want someone to help in the house and to assist the wife as she can't do a lot and spends quite a lot of the day in bed. They don't need help on the farm as the sons do that work alongside their father.'

Amy's nerves jangled at being at the mercy of so many men. She would never trust another man as long as she lived. She vowed to herself that as soon as she could, she'd find, and squirrel away, a thick stick to defend herself with. But for now, she felt the heavy disappointment of having to part with Ivan and not being able to do anything about it.

She felt a little better when she entered the hall and was introduced to Mr Timblay and his son, William. William had thick, blond hair that flopped over his face, and a ruddy complexion from working outdoors a lot. He smiled a friendly but shy smile which made her think he wanted to be friends. She assumed he was his younger son.

As they greeted her, they seemed all right. They didn't give her any snide remarks as Mrs Miller had done on their first meeting.

Encouraged by this, she felt able to ask, 'Would yer take me mate too? He's strong and would be a good help on the farm.'

'We can't, I'm sorry. We only have one attic room for whoever we take today. But I do have a brother who farms not too far away from me who would take him. Then you'd still be able to see him regularly.'

Amy warmed even more to this farmer and went to thank him when Mrs Peterson interrupted. 'I would have to meet him, Mr Timblay, and he would have to make an application.'

'I can vouch for him, ma'am, only he did ask me to ask yer and to try to bring him a lad as he can't get away from his farm. He's struggling. He's a good bloke. He lost his wife in childbirth and I can tell you that he'd be good and fair to anyone you send.'

Mrs Peterson hesitated. 'I'll ask Ivan if he wants to go. If he does . . . well, I'll take a chance this time, seeing as it is your brother. But with the proviso that my inspector will make a visit in the near future to check up on him. I will need all of his details and will send a letter with you regarding his responsibilities — the provision of adequate accommodation and food for the boy's needs. Days off, et cetera . . .'

'He knows all of that. I told him the terms. And I will keep my eye on things — not that I need to as I trust my brother. But no doubt Amy will be watching too, by the sounds of things.'

Mr Timblay grinned at Amy.

Something in her relaxed as this was a friendly, kind grin and didn't ring alarm bells. She smiled back and

50

felt emboldened to say, 'I will. I ain't standing for no one treating Ivan badly again.'

'Again?'

Amy could have bitten her tongue off. But Mrs Peterson saved the day. 'All the children have had a bad start in life — extreme poverty, abuse, orphanages that were less than savoury. This is what they refer to as being treated badly. Here, they have received nothing but kindness.'

'Oh, I see. Well, nothing bad is going to happen to either of you, Amy. I can promise you that. Mrs Timblay is a kind soul and wants to take care of us, but her health prevents her from doing too much. You're going to be our saviour. Can you cook?'

'A little, but I'm a fast learner. And I can do the hard work while Mrs Timblay watches me and tells me what to do next.' Suddenly, Amy wanted them to take her. She couldn't stay here and getting back to London wasn't anything she could do soon so, to her, Mr Timblay was offering the next best thing and she would repay him by doing her very best for him.

★ ★ ★

Once in the back of the truck, which she and Ivan found was already an improvement on Mr Miller's and had been thoughtfully lined with sheepskins and a pile of blankets provided for them, besides a flask of water each, they were told, 'Now, you make yerselves comfortable. You've a long ride ahead of you. Two days it took, and it gets colder as we get nearer. So, keep warm. We'll be stopping every now and again, but we will travel through the night to get home as quickly as we can. Does that suit you both?'

Ivan had hardly spoken up to now, but he said, 'It does, ta, mister. We won't be any trouble to yer.'

'Good. Well, let's get going and get as far as we can while it's light. If you look to your left as we go, you'll see the bluest water ever of Ontario Lake. There ain't none in the world like it, and if yer look to yer right — except when going through towns — yer'll see mountains with snowcaps. They're the Blue Mountains.'

'Ta, Mr Timblay.'

'You're welcome, Amy.'

The journey seemed endless. They slept some of it and just gazed in wonder at the scenery for the rest of the time, except when they made stops for food and to visit the lav. But they were happy as Mr Timblay and William were nice to them and made them feel special.

It was early in the morning of the next day, after Amy had slept like a log snuggled up under the blankets with Ivan, that they stopped for breakfast. On offer were hot pancakes and fried eggs. Amy tucked in like she hadn't eaten for weeks and found it delicious. Hot mugs of coffee swilled it all down and left her feeling full and as if the new life she'd been promised was finally beginning.

'I'll come and sit with yer both for the rest of the journey, Amy.'

William surprised her, but pleased her too, as it was a mark of being accepted as one of them.

As he climbed up, he said, 'Call me Will. I don't like my formal title.'

They sat with blankets wrapped around them and leaning against the side of the truck to give them a bit of stability as the vehicle swayed and bumped over the deep ruts in the ground it travelled.

'Have yer been to school, Amy?'

'Yes . . . well, I mean, we had lessons at the orphanage. I can read and write.'

'Can you add up?'

'I can if it ain't complicated.'

'My ma and da taught me all I know as we ain't got schools where we live. I can add any amount up and quickly, but I ain't a lot of good at reading.'

'I can read to yer if yer like. Have yer got some books at home?'

'Yes, loads, but they're old. I'd like yer to read to me, though. My ma can't read, so she'll like that too.'

'What's wrong with your ma, Will?'

Will looked down at his hands.

'It don't matter if yer can't tell me. It's not important.'

'It . . . well, it was when I came into the world. Something happened to her, and it left her weak. Her legs don't work. She has a bath chair and my da carries her from room to room and helps her to wash and dress. But he's hoping you can do all of that. Not carry her but wash her and everything.'

Amy decided that she would do all she could for his ma and said so. 'I'll make sure she is all right. Well, at least, I'll do me best.'

'That's good, as my da wants to build the farm to its full potential. There's fields that he's never cultivated yet. They stretch to my uncle's land and they want to join forces and cover it with an orchard and grow fruits and have grapevines so if the three of us and my uncle and Ivan can get on with that, it'll make a big difference to the future of both farms.'

Amy felt as though she was going to be an important part of this new family and she looked forward to it happening. She liked them a lot and wanted so badly to make things easier for them. She made her mind up to do her utmost to make that happen.

6

By the time winter crept up on them, Amy was settled and very happy. Ivan was doing well at the brother's farm, which, though attached to theirs, was about four miles away by road. Ivan had found shortcuts across the land, and they had met up most weeks. She loved Mrs Timblay, who'd asked her to call her Grace when they were alone.

Beautiful, with long black hair that reached her waist, Grace had a gentle nature and hated to put too much onto Amy. But Amy worried about her. She reminded her of Lucy in how delicate she was. At times, it seemed that her skin was see-through and it appeared paper-thin.

The eldest brother, Edward, who was affectionately called Teddy, was the only problem — not that it was his fault, he was polite enough. It was just that, somehow, he had an effect on Amy.

She blushed in his presence and said, or did, daft things, and yet he didn't seem to even notice her. If he did, he probably thought her as daft as a brush and not worth bothering with.

'You're daydreaming, Amy, you often do that. Are you thinking about the friends you told me about?'

Not wanting to admit the truth, Amy put the mixing bowl she'd been washing on the draining board and nodded. 'I was. I miss them and wonder how they are. They're the world to me.'

'Didn't you say you had an address? Why don't you

write to them? At least you would have news of them, though the post isn't that reliable, and I don't know how long it would take to get to England, which is a long way from here.'

'I know. It took weeks for us to get here.' Amy shuddered as the first week of the journey came flooding into her.

'Are you all right, dear? I often detect that you've things going on in your mind that disturb you. If ever you want to talk about them, it might help.'

Amy shook her head, in a gesture to dispel the thoughts about all that had happened to her as much as to say she didn't want to talk.

'I have things stored away inside me, Amy. Things that aren't nice to visit so I know how you feel. I can't talk about them and hate thinking about them, so I understand. But I just wanted you to know I will listen. I won't judge you.'

'Ta, Grace. I — I wish I could. It might make sense then. But if I started, I'd cry from now till kingdom come!'

'Oh? What is kingdom come?'

'Ha, it's a saying — till the end of the world then.'

'Oh, I see. That long? Well, I bet I would beat you and make my tears a river all the way to heaven. But, well, for now we're coping so probably best to let it all lie.'

'I would like to write that letter, though, Grace.' Amy started to dry the dishes as she said this. Together they'd prepared a huge pan of stew and it was now on the stove simmering for when the men came in for supper. After this, Grace had talked her through making a bread-and-butter pudding. They made their own bread and mostly it was wolfed down before it had cooled, but Amy had made one that hadn't risen and this was Grace's solution for using it up.

'Worth a try. Look in the bureau over there, you'll find paper, pen and ink. But you won't be able to post it till Mr Timblay next goes into town.'

'Ivan sometimes goes in. Uncle Cirrus sends him for supplies. He drives the cart in.' Amy had been told to call Mr Timblay's brother 'Uncle Cirrus' so as not to muddle the two brothers up, but Mr Timblay was always to be called by his formal name. Not that he was a very formal person, or off-putting, as she'd never met a nicer man. Like his sons, he had a shock of blond hair and a rugged complexion. His strong frame mirrored that of Teddy's and yet, Will didn't take after them. His features and make-up were much more like Grace's — slim and delicate-looking, though he surprised you with his strength.

Grace brought Amy out of these musings as she said, 'Well then, you might be lucky and get your letter off sooner. Aren't you seeing Ivan this afternoon?'

'Yes, I am.' Drying her hands, Amy went over to the bureau. Like all the furniture, it shone from the many times she'd polished it. Plain with ornate legs, she loved it more than anything else in the comfortable, if a little shabby, tall wooden house.

It was the shabbiness that gave it its homely feel. The covers on the huge sofa and two upright armchairs were a faded green. The rose-coloured rug was threadbare in parts, and the huge brick fireplace blackened where billows of smoke had blown back down the chimney over the years. Amy loved it all. And most especially her bedroom. Accessed by a wooden ladder on the landing, it was like a haven to her. Not that it housed much furniture — a small but comfy bed with a feather mattress that occasionally stabbed her as a feather escaped through the tick. The quilt had been made for Grace when she was a girl by her mother, its patchwork fashioned from pieces of material that held memories for Grace — a skirt she wore as a little child; a piece of her mum's apron she remembered rolling herself into if she had a shy moment when her ma was speaking to a stranger; a square from a tablecloth that had seen better days but had yielded enough to sew into the quilt to be remembered by; and on and on the memories went, making Amy feel as though she'd always known Grace when told of them.

Though her bedroom floor was polished wood, there was a sheepskin rug that she loved to curl her toes into. There was also a cupboard for her few clothes, though Grace had said that once the summer came, they would go to the market and buy some material and set about making her some more. And her favourite thing of all, some shelves. On these she had the few books that Grace had said she'd bought because she liked the look of them. These were Amy's solace when she felt down, though reading them was hard-going as the language was what she would call highfalutin.

The book she liked the most and was least like that was *Middlemarch* by George Eliot. She couldn't believe that a man could write such a good story. To her, Dorothea and Celia were posh versions of herself, Ruth and Ellen, as they, too, were orphans. But there the similarities ended and Amy found she could lose herself in their world which was different to any she had ever known.

'I wish I knew what went on in your head, dear Amy. You do go very quiet at times.'

Amy told her about the book. 'I think you would like it. I'll read it to you if you like.'

'That would be wonderful. But I'm tired now. Will you help me to go and lie down, dear? Then you can write your letter in peace, and then go and meet Ivan. I will be fine.'

As she helped Grace through to the downstairs bedroom she shared with Mr Timblay, Amy worried at how thin Grace was, and how tired she became. She didn't get as far as the bed but collapsed into the chair just inside and next to the window. 'I'll sleep here a while, Amy. I'll be fine. Oh, and you'll need to pay for the postage of your letter. Hand me my purse, dear. It's in that top drawer.'

'Ta, Grace. If yer sure? I do really want to write to me mates.'

Grace just smiled a weary smile.

Once Amy had the money in her pinny pocket, she was about to leave the room, but hesitated. The worry inside her wouldn't let her leave things as they were. 'Grace, I think yer'd be better lying down. I'll fetch yer bath chair, eh?'

Grace didn't object. It seemed to Amy that she didn't have the strength to.

With a struggle and determination, Amy managed to make Grace comfortable on her bed. She fell asleep almost immediately.

Going back to the bureau, Amy found paper, pen and ink and sat down to write.

Dear Ruth,
    This is Amy. I'm all right. I live on a lovely farm with a lovely family. I have had it rough, but that's all behind me now. I hope this letter finds you well,

and that you have found Ellen. I like to think of you both together. My address is, Care of Mr Timblay, White Gate Farm, Niagara on the Lake, Ontario, Canada. Please write to let me know how you are. I will write often, but for now, this will only be a short note, as I need to get out to meet me friend, Ivan. He'll take it to the post office for me.

I love you, Ruth and Ellen.

From Amy xx

Hurrying up the ladder to her room, Amy grabbed her cloak and boots and was out of the house and in no time walking at a fast pace to meet up with Ivan.

She'd come to the small clump of trees that began the border of the land between the two farms when she heard a loud crack. Freezing, she looked in the direction the noise had come from and saw a figure dash behind the tree.

Terror gripped her. She couldn't move. The shadow that the low sun threw across the grass looked long and scary. Finding her voice, she called, 'Who's there?'

A young man came out. He didn't look like any man she'd ever seen. His hair was jet black and braided into two long plaits, his clothes were ragged and he had an even ruddier complexion than the Timblays. He held a colourful blanket around him with one hand, and in the other he held a knife.

Amy watched the blade glint as he moved. Her heart stopped.

'I am Maskwa, son of Mistahi-Maskwa. I do no harm. I am hunting for food.'

Amy just stared at him.

He uttered a few more words she didn't understand then turned and ran faster than she'd seen anyone run in her life.

Shocked, she stood looking after him till gradually she calmed and sorted out her thoughts. Mr Timblay had told her of the Mississaugas, who lived not far away, and that she mustn't be afraid if she met one. Maskwa must belong to the tribe.

As her breathing steadied, she wished now that she'd spoken to him. Ivan had chatted to someone he said was from the Mississauga tribe. Amy now thought the young man could have been him.

Feeling she could go on as her fear left her, Amy pondered on Maskwa. His strange clothes, his accent. Suddenly she had a desire to know more about him and his people.

As soon as she met with Ivan, she told him, 'I met him, Ivan!'

'Who?'

'Maskwa, the young Mississauga man yer told me about.'

'Oh? Was he all right with you?'

'Yes, he seemed to want to be friends, but I was scared.'

'That would scare him then as not many treat them right and he'd be afraid yer'd tell someone that he attacked yer or something.'

'I wouldn't do that unless he did.'

'I know, but he's not to know that.'

'Where do they come from?'

'Here. This was all their land till settlers came from France and England. They tried to fight for what was theirs, but in those days they didn't have proper ammunition, only bows and arrows and hatchets. Cirrus tells me a lot of tales as all the wars were still going on when he was a lad. Anyway, what's that yer carrying?'

'It's a letter, to me friend. Will yer post it and then I'll write one to yer mum for yer if you tell me what to say?'

'Will yer? Ta, Amy. Yer a good mate and I'll post yer letter the next time I go to town.'

Amy held on to the letter while they stood in silence. She guessed Ivan was thinking about his family. When he spoke, he said, 'Tell me mum that I'm all right. Tell her I'm 'appy and that when I'm older and get a wage, I'll save up and get 'ome to her. And . . . tell her that I miss her and all me brothers and sisters.'

They sat down on the grass without telling each other they were going to. Amy knew that Ivan had felt the despair that had descended on them. He'd looked away but Amy didn't miss the sound of a sniffle and saw him wipe away a tear.

She didn't comment on this but asked him, 'What do yer miss most about home, Ivan? I mean, apart from family.'

'Me mates. We stuck together, yer know? One would nip into the shop, then another would cause a distraction, then the one who'd been in the shop came out with some buns, or anything they could get 'old of and we'd all run like the devil. And going behind the coalman's yard and all of us filling buckets with slack . . . It were always a giggle, and yet scary at the same time. I miss pie and mash too. Me mum used to make the best. Me and me mates would go to the allotments during the night and dig up buckets full of spuds, and me mum would get the meat. I never knew 'ow as she hadn't two ha'pennies to rub together. She made a lovely crust and liquor . . . I can taste it now.'

'I'll have a go at making some and I'll see if yer can

come to supper when I do, eh?'

'Do yer know 'ow?'

'No, but when I tell Grace what it is, she'll know and guide me. She says I'm turning into a good cook, as often I've all the preparation done in the afternoon while she sleeps and I'm learning how much time everything takes till it's done right too.'

'That'd be lovely. I love pie and mash . . . So, what do you miss about London?'

'Only me mates. I didn't have anything else other than . . . Anyway, there's nothing for me to miss other than them.'

Ivan didn't speak and to Amy it was funny to think that even though he came from poverty and suffered hunger and cold, he had things he missed — good times he could look back on, a mum who'd loved him, and freedom. Amy sighed; she'd never known a mum to love her, though she would never forget her time at the workhouse and the motherly love Ethel had given her.

She shivered as memories came to her of what life had thrown at her since then.

'Are yer cold?'

'No. I'm all right, but I'd better get back. Yer will post me letter, won't yer?'

'I ain't got any money to pay for it.'

'Oh, I forgot. This should cover it.'

Amy went to hand him the letter and the money, but then kissed the envelope and held it to her heart. *Please let it get to me Ruth.*

Ruth's Holy Mary came into her mind, and she added, *Do this for me mate who loves yer, Holy Mary.*

'Yer'll 'ave to let go of it for me to take it, yer know!'

Amy giggled. 'I was just trying to help it on its way.'

Ivan grinned. 'You were praying! Ha, that'll do yer a fat lot of good.'

They said their goodbyes, always a sad moment for Amy as though she felt safe, she never felt safer and more at ease than when she was with Ivan.

Suddenly the walk that she'd done many times seemed daunting and a little scary. Ivan had said that Maskwa wouldn't harm her. He had become a strapping lad whose appearance alone would intimidate any would-be attacker. But she was just a girl who, yes, had the curves of a woman, yet she had a small frame that would be no match for anyone.

With these thoughts, she jumped out of her skin when she heard the same sound of dead wood trodden underfoot by someone nearby. Once more she froze, her eyes pinned on the bushes ahead. Her fright was such that she couldn't even call out.

Then suddenly a drawling voice said, 'You been to see your boyfriend then?'

'Teddy! Yer scared the life out of me. I thought yer were Maskwa.'

'Oh? Has he been bothering you?'

'No! I'm just not used to . . . well, I ain't ever seen a native before and he made me jump, but he said he was sorry and ran off. It's just me, me nerves are on edge now.'

'I don't trust them, and you shouldn't. Come on, I'll walk the rest of the way with you. I'm finished doing what I came for. We're measuring up to see how many trees we need to cover half of this land.'

Amy thought of how the land stretched for miles towards the mountains. 'A bloomin' lot, I'd say.'

Teddy put back his head and laughed. 'You're not wrong.' He became quiet then and looked at her as if

64

seeing her for the first time. 'You know, you shouldn't walk these lonely paths on your own. It ain't that long back that the natives took young girls to be their wives.'

Amy didn't like the sound of being taken.

'I have to. Ivan don't get a long break, so I meet him halfway.'

'Well, it's not safe. I'll speak to Da about it.'

'Yer won't get him to stop me, will yer, Teddy?'

Once more he was quiet and just stared down at her. After a moment, he said, 'You really are that close to Ivan, aren't you?'

'He . . . he's like me brother.'

'Well, I hope he behaves like one and doesn't take advantage of you.'

Colour flooded her cheeks. Her temper rose. ''Course he don't. Ivan would never do that to me. He's decent, not like most men.'

'So, you know what I'm talking about and have no doubt had experience, by the sounds of it?'

Feeling trapped for a moment, Amy snapped, 'No! I ain't.' With this she flung herself around in a defiant way and stormed off.

'Amy! Amy!'

His hand caught hold of her sleeve, and then his fingers wrapped around her arm pulling her, forcing her to turn till she stood facing him. He towered over her. His steely blue eyes stared down at her. It was as if he could read her soul.

'Amy, I . . .' He let her go abruptly. Turning away from her, he took off.

In a daze, Amy stood a moment watching his disappearing back. *He was going to kiss me!*

The thought didn't repulse her; instead it made her heart sing.

7

1914

As Amy pummelled the sheets in the huge dolly tub in the yard behind the house, she didn't feel the bitter cold. The sky looked full of snow and Christmas was just a week away. Every day seemed to roll into the next now as her workload had increased.

The sound of Teddy whistling as he sorted sacks from a pile that was left outside each time the grain stored in them had been emptied out made her look up from her work.

Will stood not far away. She'd felt his eyes watching her every move — 'feeling the stirrings of becoming a man', Grace had described him as being. 'Don't break his heart, Amy, dear. Let him down gently if he makes a move.'

She'd just giggled, but had prayed that would never happen. She didn't want any boy or man to make a move on her . . . Though . . . She sighed. It may have been three years ago since it happened, but she had never forgotten the encounter in the woods with Teddy.

Sometimes she longed for it to happen again, and at others she was afraid it would, and so kept out of his way as much as she could.

Straightening and wiping her brow, she caught a glance from him. He grinned, then looked over at Will. 'Come on, you love-struck fool, we've work to do.'

66

Amy avoided looking at Will, trying to appear as if she hadn't heard. She'd hate for him to be embarrassed. If only the stained sheets would come clean so that she could move away, but that wasn't happening.

Poor, lovely Grace had deteriorated a lot with the passing of time. Amy worried that she was near to her end. She hardly moved from her bed now and had little control over her bodily functions. Even talking was a strain for her, but Amy patiently stood by her as she tried, letting her get out what she had to say, even if it did take an age and she had umpteen things to do.

With Will and Teddy leaving the yard, her thoughts turned to Ruth. She'd never heard from her even though she'd written a few times. Maybe Ruth had moved, or the letters had never reached her address. There could be no other reason as Amy knew in her heart that Ruth would have written if she could.

And now, a lot of the world was at war and the man who ran the post office told her that he didn't think letters would get through to foreign countries or, if they did, they would take a long time. 'There's many a ship in peril now, Amy. And England is too engaged in France to give heed to post of any kind.'

War was all that the menfolk talked about these days, leaving Amy to wonder about the fate of the young boys who she'd been at the Bethnal orphanage with — had they gone to war? And Ruth too? Ruth was the sort to find some way she could help to fight off the Germans, even if she had to make her way to Sheppey and stand on the beach and throw stones at them as they tried to land.

She smiled at the image, denying the fear it planted in her and the feeling of being cut off again from Ruth and Ellen now that it was futile to write letters.

67

Of late, to fill the void this had left in her, she'd taken to writing in her diary — a notebook that Grace had had sent away for and given her last Christmas — recording life on a day-to-day basis. The highlights were the days when she met up with Ivan.

But now, even Ivan could talk about nothing other than war and how, as soon as he could, he would volunteer. 'But I wouldn't come back here, Amy. I'd stay in England after, and I'd save and send yer the money to buy a ticket to get home as well.'

Amy dreaded him going.

'You look deep in thought, Amy. Those sheets will be threads in a moment.'

'Oh, Mr Timblay, I — I didn't see you there.'

'No, you were miles away. I need a hand a minute. I'm trying to get the chickens in the run as we're going to move them to the orchard, but the boys are busy elsewhere. Can you give me a moment? I know you're busy.'

'Well, as yer say, I think these sheets are done. I'll let them soak while I help yer.'

'They're behind the barn. I got them that far from all the various places they'd found to nest. It's a day's work collecting the eggs with them running wild, so the plan is to keep them in a pen that's big enough to give them freedom but contains them. There's good business in sending eggs to market.'

The next half an hour was a real respite for Amy as they chased chickens, caught them and held the squawking birds till the other could help to get them into the pen. Their giggles broke into laughter at times, and there were shouts of 'Hold her, she's getting free' and 'Run! she's off!'

Until the moment when they collided. Both were

running after the same hen which suddenly decided to double back. As Amy turned, she ran straight into Mr Timblay. His arms came out to catch her from falling, but he didn't let go when she was steady on her feet.

Looking up at him, she saw the look in his eyes that she'd seen so often in Belton's. 'No! Let me go!'

'Amy . . . Oh, Amy. I — I . . .'

He pulled her close, his strength too much for her.

'No . . . please . . . please don't.' Her stinging eyes released the tears held in them. She could hear her own voice begging, but still he held her. When his grip tightened even more, she could feel his need. Memories of Belton assailed her. Disgust made her beg, 'Please, please don't . . . Please let me go!'

When he lowered his head, and his gruff voice uttered the words, 'Let me, please let me, Amy. You drive me wild. I — I want you,' Amy's fear and heartache were such that she jerked away from him and kicked out. Her foot landed between his legs. His holler sent a deeper fear zinging through her. She turned and ran back to the house.

Not heeding the noise coming from Grace's bedroom, which she knew meant she needed help, Amy ran upstairs and then scrambled up the ladder.

All she wanted was her diary, her coat and a scarf. She had to get away from here! Mr Timblay had turned into a monster.

Hurrying down again, she made for the door, once more ignoring the cries from Grace. It broke her heart to do so, but she had to go before Mr Timblay recovered and stopped her.

★ ★ ★

Three days later, Amy lay on the side of the road exhausted. She'd walked, rested and walked again. The miles had meant nothing as she'd crossed fields, run through woods and finally come to a highway.

There'd been times when she'd heard a vehicle, or a horse-drawn cart, and had dived into the ditch. Now, filthy and stinking, she could hardly put one foot in front of the other before her legs gave way.

Hunger gripped her stomach. Thirst dried her tongue and made it feel twice as big as it stuck to the roof of her mouth. She couldn't go on. Her eyes closed.

★ ★ ★

'You drink!' A voice came from nowhere.

Someone had hold of her head, and a strange smell was tingeing her nostrils. Cool water dripped into her mouth and soothed her.

Opening her crusted eyes, she could just make out Maskwa. Fear shot through her; she hadn't seen him since that day three years ago. But stories were always being told of his tribe carrying out raids on the farms — not to harm but to steal — and relations between them and the farmers weren't good. She tried to move away but couldn't.

'No. I not hurt you. I help you.'

Remembering what Ivan had said many times, that they were a misunderstood people, that they were starving while the settlers were getting rich on the land they considered theirs, Amy relaxed. She, too, would steal to eat.

'Drink more.'

'Ta.'

She could think of nothing more to say.

'Why have you run away? Was Timblay bad to you? The young bucks? Did they mess with you?'

Amy nodded. 'Mr . . . Mr Timblay . . .'

'I kill him!'

Amy woke fully now. 'No! No, you mustn't. He — he's kind usually. His . . . his wife, well, she hasn't been a wife to him for so long.'

'These things not give him a reason.'

'Please don't hurt him.'

He didn't answer this.

'You recover enough to walk?'

'I don't know.'

'I take you to my tribe, they take care of you.'

'No. No, I — I can't. I have to go further away.' Sheer terror had gripped Amy. Her stomach clenched. She felt as though she would be sick.

'You cannot stay here . . . I track you to care for you. Ivan, he tell me, but he could not come. Ivan has had to go far away to war.'

'What? How? When?'

'He tell me it has been a plan for a few weeks only he couldn't bring himself to tell you. Then he had letter. He went to the farm to see you, but Mr Timblay say that you were bad. That you tried to lead his son astray, but when he not have anything to do with you, you ran away.'

'That didn't happen! Mr Timblay . . .'

'I know. Ivan asked Will, son of Timblay. He told him they were in the fields and when they came back you were gone. Their father not tell them why.'

'Oh, Ivan . . . did he believe them?'

'Yes. He knows something bad happened to make you go in such haste. I promised I would find you and

71

take care of you.'

Amy's heart felt as though it would break. Ivan, her lovely Ivan had gone.

'You stand now?'

'Maskwa, I cannot go with yer. I — I just need food and rest, then I will go on. I want to get to Belleville to Marchmont Home, they will care for me. Will yer help me?'

'You're cold and wet. We must get you warm.'

'Please, Maskwa, please.'

Maskwa straightened. He looked around him. 'There's a barn over there. I knows it is not used. I get you to it and take care of you till you can travel again.'

'No! Just help me there, then yer can go.'

'I'll not leave you. I know you're afraid of me, but you have no need to be, I will not hurt you. You are Ivan's woman.'

This shocked her. Had Ivan said that? Is that what he believed? She'd never thought of him in that way, and he'd never, ever treated her in any other way other than as a sister!

'I'm not Ivan's . . .' But suddenly, she wanted the safety of him being with her. A sob escaped her. 'Ivan, oh, Ivan.'

With this, Maskwa bent over her. His strong arms lifted her as if she was no more than a feather. The warmth of his body eased a little of the cold in her. Her fear left her.

★ ★ ★

Amy didn't know how long she'd slept. Since Maskwa had come across her it seemed like no time had passed, and yet her clothes were dry and she was wrapped in a warm sheepskin, the smell of which she recognized from the first time she opened her eyes and saw Maskwa towering over her.

As memory flooded her, her heart hurt. *Why? Why? I was so happy. I loved them all, I cared for them, cooked for them, washed their clothes. And I took special care of Grace. Poor, poor Grace, what does she think of me?*

'You awake?'

Amy looked up. For a moment she felt fear again, but then shame as she realized that not only were her clothes dry, but that they were clean too. And she was clean. She felt her hair. It was soft and braided. Had Maskwa done all of this? Had he stripped her and washed her clothes?

As if he read her thoughts, he said, 'I fetch Catori. She is to be my bride. She come to care for you. Come, there is a fire. Catori, she make broth to feed you. You drank even though you not open your eyes.'

'How long have —'

'Three days. Catori give you plant juice to keep you resting.'

This shocked Amy, but she was grateful as she felt better and that was down to them. 'Ta, Maskwa, and tell Catori that I thank her.'

'She hears you, but she only speaks in the tongue of the Mississaugas. Come.'

Amy found that she could stand easily and was surprised by how strong she felt. As they left the barn a delicious smell hit her.

'Sit. Eat.'

Amy sat crossed-legged, as did Catori. She smiled at the slender girl, who wore a colourful shawl over a brown tunic-type frock, which was pulled in at the waist by a patterned belt made of the same rainbow beads that hung in strings from her neck and were entwined in the long black braids that her hair was fashioned into.

Catori said something.

'She is greeting you. She says you are welcome to her help and she is happy to see Ivan's woman get better.'

This annoyed Amy as she'd told Maskwa once that she wasn't Ivan's woman, but she stopped herself from repeating it as they might take it that she was insulting Ivan and they obviously thought a lot of him. How come he hadn't talked about them? She'd thought Maskwa had disappeared. But then, Ivan may have been afraid of being found out to still be associating with them.

Thinking of him, she felt again the pain of loneliness that he had gone. Would she ever see him again? Would he be safe? *Oh God, keep him safe. Keep me Ivan safe.*

After they'd eaten a delicious stew, Maskwa suddenly stood and looked around him. He sniffed. Then he said, 'Catori and I must go. There are men from the farm coming. Hurry . . . Please, you come too, woman of Ivan.'

'No. You go. I will be all right. I'll tell them I got lost. I'll ask them how to get to Belleville.'

'You follow the water, that way.'

Amy looked to where he was pointing. For the first time she saw the beautiful lake in the distance, gleaming in the winter sun like a sheet of diamonds.

'Make your way there, but it is a long way to Belleville.'

'I'll be all right. Just go. And Maskwa, ta. When I get Ivan back, we will both thank yer.'

74

Maskwa hesitated. Catori spoke in an urgent voice. And then they were gone as if the earth had swallowed them.

Amy stood shielding her eyes. In the distance she saw clouds of dust — horse riders. As the cloud came nearer and nearer, Amy's heart thumped. *Please let them be kind to me. Please, please.*

But as they came near enough for her to see their faces, she had the feeling that she should run and run.

'Hey up, what have we here, then? So, you're the one lighting fires then?'

Amy looked up into the swarthy face of a man of about forty. He spat out something black. 'Are you alone, girl?'

'I know her! She's Timblay's home child. She ran away. Ha! She tried to get her feet under the table by making eyes at Teddy, but he was having none of it.'

The man who'd first spoken looked her up and down. Amy felt her skin crawl.

'Well, we'd better take her back to the farm and let Timblay know we have her.'

'No! I don't want to go back. I want to go to Marchmont Home!'

'Oh, yer mean that place that yer first came to up in Belleville? Well, yer a long way from there, girl. Better that yer come with us. My old woman'll find yer useful till we can return yer to where yer belong.'

With this the man in his forties jumped down, picked her up and almost threw her over the horse's back. In one movement, he was in the saddle leaving her dangling over the horse. As he geed the horse up, Amy's stomach felt as though she was being kicked. But despite her cries, he didn't slow the horse, or take heed of her.

When they reached white fencing, not long after that, Amy had never been so glad in all her life, as here they halted, and slid her off the horse. Now she could see ahead, she caught sight of the farmhouse she assumed they'd come from.

A stout woman with an ugly expression came out of the black-painted door. 'What yer got there then, Mickey?'

'Timblay's home child. She ran away. We can keep her in the barn till he comes for her.'

The woman snapped the cloth in her hand as if it was a whip and turned to go inside. As she did, she shouted, 'Yer should have fetched me one of them. I can't cope with looking after you lot.'

The man who now had hold of Amy shouted back, 'Yer should have kept the daughters I put into yer, instead of shedding them before their time!'

Amy cringed at this. Her own child came to mind. Though she'd named her Ruth Ellen, she'd long wondered if she truly had been a girl. But with the thought came the pain of her loss and she heard that now in the woman's moan as she slammed the door behind her.

'Right, get her in the barn, Joe, and none of yer tricks. She belongs to Timblay.'

Joe, a dirty-looking young man she guessed was the same age as Teddy, spat on the ground before grabbing her arm. Amy yelped in pain.

But that pain increased when he opened the barn door and shoved her inside. 'Dirty home brat!'

Then he was gone, and the large doors of the barn slammed shut.

Amy sank down onto a bale of hay. Her head flopped forward. Tears ran down her face and mingled with her snot as she sobbed her heart out.

8

Amy had no concept of how long she'd been here in the barn till she heard a noise at the door. Darkness had fallen and she shivered as the freezing cold bit into her.

When the door opened, she squinted against the brightness coming from a lamp held high.

'I've brought yer some grub.'

As she got used to the light, she saw through the lingering blue flashes in her eyes that it was Joe. There was something about him she feared.

'So, yer ran away, did yer? Tried it on with Teddy and upset them all? Ha! Teddy don't know what he's got a cock for. Never has. Them Timblays don't farm proper like us or he would know then all right — the animals are always at it. But the Timblays tend to trees. Ha! Anyway, they don't want yer back, so Ma's going to keep yer here. Yer'll be a help to her.'

Amy nodded, unsure of what to do. Hating the idea and the crude way Joe spoke, but having no choices open to her, she had to submit. But the first chance she got she would run away and get back to Mrs Peterson.

'Eat that, then come to the kitchen door. Ma has blankets there for yer. Yer to sleep out here. There's a well out the back. Get water from it for yer wash, and there's a bucket for yer to use as a lav over there. I'll leave this lamp with yer, but don't run out of oil before a month's up, or yer'll be in the dark.'

With this he left her.

Amy looked at the bowl of greasy stew he'd put on the floor in front of her. She wasn't hungry as Catori had fed her well, but instinct told her it wouldn't be a good thing to leave it.

A vision of the ugly woman came to her. She shuddered but picked up the spoon and took a sip of the stew from it. She grimaced as the salty taste dried her mouth and left her wanting to wretch. She just couldn't eat it. All she wanted was a drink.

Thinking of the well, she picked up the lamp and ventured outside. She was met by laughing voices. From the side of the house, light splashed across the ground, but left the part of the yard that she was in in darkness. She could see the light was mainly coming from a balcony and guessed the menfolk would be swilling beer down them, something Mr Timblay and Teddy had liked to do after a hard day in the fields. For the first time, Amy felt a pang of regret at having run away. Mr Timblay had behaved badly, but it had been out of character for him. Something must have made him behave in that way. A need that had been too great for him to fight. Maybe if she'd stayed, he would have apologized and never approached her again. But with running away, he'd had to find some excuse. Why he'd thought of saying that she'd tried to seduce Teddy she didn't know. Had Teddy complained about her?

Suddenly a voice shouted over to her, cutting into her thoughts. 'Where d'yer think yer going, eh?'

'I — I need water.'

The man who'd treated her roughly by throwing her over the horse let out a laugh. 'Well, come over here and yer can have a beer.'

'No, ta, I don't drink beer.'

Joe joined his father in leaning over the balcony fence. 'We'll soon teach yer how, and give yer what yer craved from Teddy, if yer want it.'

His father laughed out loud. 'All three of us, as I'm sure one of us wouldn't satisfy yer.'

Amy couldn't swallow for the fear that had risen up in her.

The third, who she guessed was the younger son, hadn't spoken till now but piped up, 'Leave the girl alone. She ain't a plaything for you. She's scared, can't you see that?'

'She's ripe for it, she's like a cow on heat. I bet she heard us and came out to tease us. Ain't that right, girl?'

'No! I just want some water . . . Please don't touch me.'

The one who'd spoken in her defence came down the steps towards her. 'They won't. I'll make sure of that. Come on, I'll take yer to the well.'

Feeling she could trust him, Amy walked with him.

'I'm Josh. I'm sorry about my folks. They're harmless usually but when they're drinking, well, I would put the bar across on the barn door if I was you. Ma long ago put a bar on my pa going to her bed and that leaves him looking elsewhere and Joe's unruly and uncaring of women. He thinks they're all his for the taking.'

Amy's stomach clenched at hearing this. 'Will . . . will yer help me to get away? I know I'll be safe if I could get back to Marchmont Home . . . only, yer see, it ain't true that I was after Teddy, or any of them, but what you just said about yer pa happened to Mr Timblay . . . I mean, he was the nicest, kindest person, but with Grace — Mrs Timblay — being unable to . . . well, yer know, I think he got tempted and tried it on with me. That's why I ran away.'

'Timblay! What? Are you telling the truth as that's a rotten thing to say about a decent man?'

'I am. Honestly, it happened. I just ran. I — I shouldn't have as I reckon he would just have apologized and not done anything like it again, but I was scared. I don't know why he said what he said about Teddy.'

'Well, if what yer saying is true, it would be to save face. I'll think about helping yer, Amy, as I can't see yer being safe here.'

'Ta, Josh.'

'Now do as I say and bolt the barn door . . . and . . .' He looked around him. 'Ah, that'll do.' He strode away from her then returned with a metal bar. 'Use this to defend yerself but avoid hitting whoever comes for yer across the head. Keep it by yer bed.'

'I ain't got a bed.'

'I know. Well, by wherever yer choose to lie in the barn. If it were me, I'd climb into the loft and spread some hay out.'

Amy gasped.

'What? Have I said something out of order?'

Without thinking, Amy told him what had happened to her and Ivan at the Millers' farm before they came to the Timblays', and how the mention of sleeping on hay had suddenly brought it all back to her. She was shocked at his reaction.

'God! I heard of that. We were told it was . . . So that was you! You did it to Ralph Miller too?'

'No! No, Josh, I didn't. It wasn't me that were

involved. It was . . . I didn't do anything, I swear.'

Josh turned abruptly. 'Once I could believe, but twice? And now yer saying that a decent bloke like Timblay did . . . God! Yer evil!'

'No. Please believe me, Josh. I never did anything to either of them . . . It were me mate, me lovely Lucy, who Miller went after . . .' Letting the whole sorry story tumble from her ended with her sobbing as frustration burned her insides.

Josh had stopped in his tracks. He turned. 'You mean . . . but we were told . . . Look, I'm sorry . . . Yer've had it rough, but we're not all like that. Miller's a bastard, but Timblay's a decent bloke really.'

'I know, I told you, all the family are good. They treated me like one of them. I was happy and loved Grace and taking care of her . . . It just came crashing down when Mr Timblay tried it on.'

'I'm sorry. I believe yer. Now, get into the barn before —'

'Ha! So, have yer done the deed then, brother? Yer've took yer time.'

'There's no deed to be done, Joe. Leave Amy alone. Go back to yer drink.'

'Amy, is it?' Joe turned to look at Amy. 'So, yer've made yer choice, eh? Another one who'll not give you any satisfaction. Yer can pick 'em, I'll say that for you.' He smirked and looked at Josh. 'So, is this going to be yer first then, Josh?'

'Shurrup and leave us alone.'

Joe pounced on Josh, shoving him till they both landed on the ground.

Amy heard her own scream, but it died as it seemed all hell let loose. The young men hit out at each other and rolled around the yard. The older man came swaggering down the steps, took one look and went over to the well, but it was the ugly woman who gave Amy the biggest shock — she came out in her nightie, her hair pinned hideously in pipe cleaners, and wielding a cane rug beater.

Amy looked this way and that, trying to find a place to hide. The sight brought back horrifying memories to her. Her instincts told her that the demented woman was coming for her.

Running as if the devil was after her, Amy made for the barn, but as she passed the fighting men, Joe stuck his foot out and sent her flying.

The first blow stung her buttocks.

'Yer nothing but trouble. All you home children are the same. Yer come here to take, take, take, take!'

With each time she said 'take', she whipped Amy till her bottom stung and her screams turned to sobs.

Just as suddenly as it had erupted, it calmed as the older man threw a bucket of water, firstly at his sons, and then at his wife. 'Have yer all gone mad? Pack it in! A man wants some peace after a bloody hard day's work!'

Amy shivered with the shock, the pain and the cold water that had hit her too.

From where she lay, she saw the young brothers get up and slink away, still arguing as they went. Then she heard the sobs of the ugly woman. 'She's set them against each other already! I don't want her here. I'd rather cope on my own! Get rid of her!'

With this she ran towards the house.

The father turned to Amy and on a deep sigh told her, 'Get yerself into the barn. I'll see yer in the morning and decide what's to do with yer.'

Amy stood. Her bottom smarted from the onslaught,

but she was glad to see that her lamp was still lit and stood on the ground not far from her. Feeling the need to hurry to safety, she grabbed it and ran into the barn, bolting the door behind her with the big iron bar that slotted into two hooks.

Shivering, she placed the lamp in a safe position and began to peel her wet clothes from her sore body, crying in pain when she got to her bloomers.

As she wrapped herself in the blanket, she dared not douse the lamp. Her body still shook with terror, and she couldn't face the darkness.

Her sobs exhausted her. Blessed sleep took her and eventually brought her some respite, but it felt as if she'd only just dropped off when she was awoken by the barn door rattling.

Catapulted to a sitting position, Amy stared at the door and saw it shake. She couldn't speak or cry out. But then a familiar voice came to her. 'Amy, Amy, are you in there? It's Teddy. Let me in, Amy, I've ridden through the night.'

'Teddy?'

'Yes. I'm here to help you, Amy. Open the door before we wake the household up.'

Wrapping the blanket around her, Amy tentatively got up, gasping in pain as she did. Was she dreaming? Was Teddy really at the barn door?

'Amy!'

'I — I'm coming.'

The removal of the iron bar sounded like thunder in the still night. As soon as it gave, Teddy stepped inside and closed it behind him. Holding the blanket around her, Amy could only stand and stare at him.

'I saw the light in the barn and guessed you might be in here. I've come to take you back, Amy. My pa's sorry. He don't know what came over him, and then to blame me!'

'Has he admitted it?' Amy couldn't believe what she was hearing.

'Not at first, but earlier tonight . . . well, Ma's gone into a coma . . . and I went downstairs to check on her. When I got to her bedroom door, I heard Pa. He was sobbing. He was telling Ma how sorry he was and how he didn't know what got into him. That you suddenly seemed to be her. And how he'd longed to lie with her . . . I couldn't believe what I was hearing. My temper boiled and I waited. When he came out, I was ready to punch him, but he looked like a broken man. He fell into my arms and begged my forgiveness . . . He ain't like he appears, Amy. He ain't a man who would ever have done what he did, and he wouldn't have gone through with it . . . it was the circumstances. Please believe me, Amy.'

'I — I do . . . but I don't think I can face him. Will yer take me back to Marchmont Home . . . Please, Teddy?'

Teddy seemed to fold. 'I — I want you back with us. I have feelings for you . . . and, well, I'm going to war and I want to think of you at home waiting for me.'

Amy's heart filled with joy and yet flooded with sorrow.

'I ain't said, because you're too young yet, but I love you, Amy. I know I haven't shown it because I had to keep my distance as you were driving me mad. But now that I'm going, I don't want to lose you. If you go back to Marchmont, they could send you anywhere and I may never find you. I promise you, my pa won't ever behave like that again . . . he . . . he knows how I feel about you now.'

'Oh, Teddy. I love you too. I know I'm young, but I don't feel like I am. But there's so much yer don't know about me.'

'Let's get on the road and you can tell me, eh? Have you got a coat?'

'Yes. But all me other clothes are filthy and torn.'

'Joe Wanderman didn't cause that, did he? He hasn't touched yer, has he?'

'No. Josh looked after me, so he didn't get the chance.'

'Josh is a good bloke. He's like Johnny the older brother who's fighting somewhere in Belgium. Anyway, we'd better hurry. Just put your coat on and keep the blanket to wrap yourself in.'

Outside they held hands while they walked. Amy winced a couple of times.

'Are you hurt, Amy?'

'The woman beat me.'

'No! Oh, Amy, I'm sorry.' Bending, Teddy lifted her as if she was a feather and carried her for the rest of the way across the field where he had tethered his horse to a fence.

'Don't put me over the horse on me stomach, will yer, Teddy?'

'What? No, that would hurt you, why d'yer ask that?'

'The man back at that farm did that. I'd been with Maskwa and Catori, his bride-to-be. They had helped me and fed me but had to run away when Joe and his dad came across us. The dad slung me over his horse like I was a piece of meat. It hurt me so much.'

'The swine! So Maskwa helped you, did he, eh?'

'Yes. He's a good man, Teddy. Yer shouldn't mistrust him.'

'Too much history with the Mississaugas, I suppose. But I'm grateful to him and will acknowledge that if I come across him before I leave.'

They didn't speak again until they were sat on the horse, Amy in front of Teddy and snuggled into him, the feeling of being so close to him more than making up for how the movement of the trotting animal hurt her bottom. It was Teddy who broke the silence between them. 'So, you say you've something to tell me?'

'I'm afraid yer won't want to know me when you hear it.'

'Is it that bad? What is it you've done, then?'

Amy felt her temper rise. 'I ain't done nothing, mate! It were what was done to me.'

'Ha! I've got myself a fiery one in you, Amy. And I like you calling me 'mate'. But what has been done to you that I might not like?'

'I — I was raped as a child, over and over.'

'No! No, Amy, tell me it ain't the truth!'

'It is . . . I — I couldn't help it, or stop it, and . . . and I had a baby. I was twelve at the time. It — it happened when we were coming over . . . I did nothing to make Belton rape me . . . I didn't.'

Teddy didn't speak.

Amy's heart felt heavy. She'd vowed never to have another man near to her and yet, she didn't want her telling of the truth to make her lose Teddy. Feeling unsure, she stiffened and eased herself away a little from his warm body, but then felt bereft as she did. He didn't manoeuvre her back towards him.

Tears pricked her eyes, and as she took a deep inhale she heard a sob. 'Teddy? Oh, Teddy, I thought yer hated me.'

He let go of the rein with one hand and drew her back into him. Into her hair, he whispered, 'No . . . No, I — I just cannot take it in . . . How? Where?'

'It was at the orphanage back in London, that I were taken to from the workhouse. On me first night there, the night warden fetched me . . . He hurt me, Teddy.'

Teddy stopped the horse. He slid off and gently pulled her off too. His arms came around her. His head leaned on hers. 'My poor Amy.'

His crying triggered her own. She put her arms around him. It felt strange — she'd never held a man in her arms in a loving way. Feelings she hadn't experienced before tightened her throat as the muscles in her groin contracted, sending a sensation through her that quietened her repulsion of ever being close to a man and left her feeling confused.

'And after all that you come to my country and suffer more abuse. Even at the hands of my own pa! How can you ever forgive, Amy? How?'

She couldn't say that she could at this moment.

'Talk to me, Amy. Tell me that you will be all right.'

'Take me home, Teddy. Take me to London. My friends Ruth and Ellen will look after me.'

'I can't, Amy. I have to report for training in the next few weeks. But I will, I promise you. When I come back from the war, I'll take you home.'

A happiness that Amy hadn't felt for a long, long time lifted her. She looked up at him. In his eyes was the confirmation of all he'd said. Her heart healed in that moment as she closed her eyes and leaned her head on his chest. *Teddy loves me! He truly loves me and one day he will take me home.*

9

1916

Two years later Amy stood by the gate with Mr Timblay, ready to wave Will off as he was to join the same 2nd Division Canadian Battalion Teddy had. She wished with all her heart that this wasn't happening but that instead they were waiting to welcome Teddy home.

Her mind went back to that night when Teddy had declared his love for her. It seemed to her that everything had changed in her life from that moment.

On their return to the farm, she'd gone straight to Grace's room, mortified that she had left her alone and wanting to be reassured that nothing untoward had happened as a result, but the sight that had met her when she'd opened the bedroom door had stopped her in her tracks.

Mr Timblay sat with his head on the bed next to Grace.

Amy had stood gazing down on them and it had seemed to her that the picture they made spoke of love — a love strengthened and yet damaged by Grace's ill health.

Without her knowing how, or why, she'd become aware of a feeling of forgiveness of Mr Timblay's actions towards her, borne from the understanding that had come to her of how deeply a person can feel for another, and how devastating it was to have that taken from you. She remembered thinking that she couldn't ever see a time when she would seek solace with another after Teddy had left and feeling fear that he might, as it seemed to be that men had this great need that drove them to do such things.

But that had passed when Teddy had come quietly into the room and taken her into his arms. After a moment he'd woken his pa and persuaded him to go to bed.

As Mr Timblay had passed by Amy, he'd whispered, 'I'm sorry, so very sorry.'

It had been enough.

After a short while Teddy had told her that he would stay with his ma, but she should go to bed to get some rest, as his ma would need her the next day.

The next morning a dreadful howl had woken the whole household; Teddy had found Grace had died in the night — he'd been unable to keep awake.

It had been the saddest day when Grace was lain to rest. It was hard saying goodbye to her, but then more heartbreak followed. That same afternoon, Teddy left to go to war.

★ ★ ★

'Take care, son.'

The words Mr Timblay spoke brought Amy back to the present. She watched his eyes fill with tears as he continued. 'And when you see Teddy, tell him we love him and his bride is awaiting him, so to keep safe and come home, and you do the same, my boy.'

'I will, Pa. You both take care too, eh?'

Amy smiled at him through her own tears. She'd come to love Will like a brother.

As he came forward and hugged her, she managed to say, 'Yes, take care, and if you see Ivan, tell him his best friend will come to London to see him when all this is over. And . . . and give all me love to Teddy . . . I've written a letter for him and knitted him some socks. Can yer give those to him too, luv?'

'I will, and I'll wear the pair yer knitted for me with pride, Amy.'

As he disappeared into the dust cloud made by the truck that had picked him up, Amy prayed to Ruth's Holy Mary to keep him, Teddy and Ivan safe.

She'd never heard from Ruth but knew that one day she would find her and Ellen. She and Teddy would make it their mission to do so when he took her to London as he'd promised to do.

The farmhouse wasn't empty when she made her way inside as Betty stood by the stove stirring a pot of stew and Ivy rolled pastry for a jam tart on the huge table.

As well as these helping hands, there were two lads working in the orchard, Jack and Rodney. All four had come to them from Marchmont Home.

Amy had known of them as they'd been the same age as her when she'd first arrived there in 1910, but none had ever been placed until Mr Timblay went to see about more help. She'd suggested he ask for them, telling him how nice they were and eager to please but were never chosen because each suffered a disability.

Betty, a pretty girl with long golden hair and a dainty figure, only had a stump for a left arm. Ivy, dark haired, with small but twinkly eyes, was taller than herself and Betty and on the plump side, had a wheezing chest and many days when she couldn't do a full day's work. Rodney, a lad who had a pimply face and a condition that made him pigeon-chested and left him with a hump on his back, and Jack, who but for his thick glasses would be a handsome young man, but his eyesight was poor to the point that he was almost blind and would never manage to do what he did without the guidance and help of Rodney, who they all called Roddy.

Each of them was a joy, bringing love and laughter into what had been a sad home.

'Well, that's another brave one gone to war. But they'll both come back, you'll see, Amy.'

'Yes, they will, Betty. We have to think like that, luv. So, how's that stew coming along, eh?'

'Pity Will couldn't stay for some.' Ivy's voice sounded wistful.

Amy glanced over at her. She'd seen how, in the short time she'd been here, Ivy had fallen for Will. Sadly, he'd hardly seemed to notice her, his mind being preoccupied with what he had to face.

Not to be daunted for long, the ever good-humoured Ivy said, 'So, what d'yer think of me pastry then, Amy? I've made it an oblong as I've a mind to roll it around the apples like a strudel.'

Betty piped up, 'Ain't that a musical instrument?'

Ivy burst out laughing which set them all off and the atmosphere lightened until Ivy began to cough and then to gasp for breath. Betty ran to what they called the medicine chest — a tin with various healing potions in it — and retrieved the Friar's Balsam. Mrs Peterson had told them to always keep some in and how to mix it with hot water.

'Come and sit down, Ivy, luv.' Amy led her to the edge of the table and sat her down and bent her head over the steaming liquid Betty had prepared.

'Best if you put a cloth over her head, Amy. Then she just breathes the vapours in.'

Amy did as Betty said and within a few minutes, Ivy was feeling better. Amy sighed with relief. These girls and the two lads had become like a family to her. Despite their ailments they were cheerful and worked hard, between them managing the work that two would do normally, but although it cost more to keep them, Mr Timblay didn't grumble. He'd done all he could to make up to Amy for his mistake and had tried to please her in everything she needed. It wouldn't have been his choice to take four instead of two, but it was what she'd wanted.

It had meant that she had often had to help out in the fields and orchards, but she didn't mind that. She wanted to work every hour she could to keep her from constantly longing for Teddy.

Teddy's letters were few and far between, with a total of three so far, but each spoke of his love and how much he longed to be with her. None spoke of what he was going through, though from what news they heard, the war was taking its toll in human life and injuries.

But mostly, she never wanted to be alone with Mr Timblay again. For though he was sorry and tried to make it up to her, he was still a man, and in her eyes, they weren't to be trusted.

'I'm all right now, Amy. Can I come out from under here?'

Amy smiled. ''Course yer can, mate. I ain't got yer as a prisoner, but take it easy, eh?'

* * *

92

It was later that evening when they were all sitting on a bale of straw drinking hot milk outside the barn that Mr Timblay had converted to house the four helpers that Amy heard their stories for the first time after having been living with them for six weeks. She'd never asked, but now, once more, felt the pity of the 'solution', as she saw the getting rid of all the poor and troublesome kids. Now their own country didn't have to care for them — not that it did before, from all she'd heard from other home children and from her own experiences.

It was a statement from Ivy that began it all. 'You know, Amy, when I had a bad bout, me mum used to rub me chest with this oil that stank — cambert oil, or something it was called.'

Betty laughed. 'Camphorated Oil, you mean, you daft thing.'

'Oh yes, that was it . . . I liked it when it happened as I felt me mum's love and felt cared for by her, but . . . well, now I can't remember what she looked like any more.' This was said on a sob. Amy knew what she meant. It happened to her at times with Ellen and it pained her that she couldn't always bring her face to mind. She could Ruth's. Ruth was in her heart all the time; she was special was Ruth.

'I never knew mine,' Amy told them. 'I sometimes think that's better than being taken away from her. Though I still long for her. So, did yer mum die, Ivy?'

'No. But there were a lot of us, and she couldn't cope, or so they told me when they come for me . . . it felt like . . . well, she didn't want me. But why? I loved her. Even though I can't remember her face, I still know that I loved her.'

Amy sighed. 'That's the same as me mate, Ivan.

93

You remember Ivan, don't yer? He was taken away because his mum couldn't cope.'

Betty sighed. 'I didn't have a mum or dad. Mum weren't married and she died giving birth to me. Me gran took me in, but when she got ill, they came for me . . . I screamed that I wanted to carry on caring for me gran, but they didn't listen to me. Next thing, I was on a ship and came here. I don't know if me gran's alive or not. She never answers me letters.'

A tear glistened on Betty's cheek.

Amy put her hand out and took Betty's only hand. 'You have us, luv. We're yer family now, eh?'

Jack, usually one to never utter a word, surprised them then as he squinted through his thick glasses and looked at Betty. 'Yes, we're all here for you, Betty.'

'Ha! You more than most, Jack. He's got a soft spot for yer, Betty.'

Jack blushed as he playfully hit out at Roddy who'd teased him with saying this, but Betty beamed. 'Ta, Jack, that's a lovely thing to say.'

A look passed between them that warmed Amy's heart. But then Betty said, 'You've never said why you're here in Canada, Jack.'

Jack lowered his head. 'Me dad beat me a lot because I couldn't do things like other kids. He called me names . . . Me mum tried to defend me, but he used to hit her and tell her that I was her fault. That she'd given him a blind-as-a-bat son who'd never do any good . . . One day . . . he hit her too hard and killed her . . . He's in prison . . . well, I think he is . . . only, don't they hang them as commit murder?'

No one answered this.

'Anyway, I had an aunt, but she wouldn't take me, and so I was put into a home.'

A shudder went through Jack; Amy opened her mouth to change the subject, but Roddy didn't give her the time to. 'Well, at least you've all had the love of a mum. Mine hated me at birth. She told me so, many times. She called me ugly . . . deformed . . . the devil incarnate . . . besides other nasty things. I never knew me dad, but me gran were no better. She used to keep me inside while me mum were at the factory working. She'd tell me she was ashamed of me. Then, one day this woman came for me and that was it, I never saw either of them again. I was taken to the same home as Jack. We looked out for one another, didn't we, Jack?'

Jack managed a weak smile.

It was Ivy who cheered them. 'Well, it is what it is and it's up to us to make good. We all can, there's nothing to stop us now. We're happy here, ain't we, eh?'

They all nodded.

'Well then, let's cheer up . . . I know, let's have a sing-song. That's what me mum used to do when things were rough. She used to make us all laugh with the jig she used to do.'

Ivy got up then and began to dance, but it ended in a fit of coughing and laughter and then tears. 'I — I miss me mum, Amy.'

''Course yer do, luv, but yer must never think she didn't want yer. She sounds like a lovely mum, dancing and singing to keep yer happy, and trying to make yer chest better. They ain't the actions of someone who didn't love yer, are they?'

Ivy cheered up. 'No . . . they ain't. Ta, Amy, I feel better now.'

'Come on, let's have that sing-song, but no dancing, eh?'

Ivy nodded. 'Me favourite is 'Down at the Old Bull and Bush'.'

It was Roddy's turn to surprise them then as he leaped up and began to sing in a broad cockney accent, while holding his braces with his thumbs and performing funny actions that mimicked a clown.

'*Come, come, come and make eyes at me, down at the Old Bull and Bush!*'

They all joined in: '*Da la la da da . . .*'

All five of them were singing and laughing at the same time, and Amy thought it a lovely moment, though her heart was still heavy with the pity of what had happened to them all. Five innocent children, hurt, abused, taken from their homeland and dumped in a far-off country. It was unjust and all of it so unfair.

This feeling lay heavy on her as she left them to go to bed, as did fear as she realized she would be in the house on her own with Mr Timblay for the first time. She decided that she would use the outside lav and then get to her room, forgoing a wash, and she would shove the chest of drawers up against the door.

But she needn't have worried as when she got inside, he sat at the kitchen table drinking a hot coffee. 'Amy, I — I, well, I wanted to say that I don't want you worrying about anything. I've decided that it will be best to bring Jack, Rodney, Betty and Ivy inside. We could put another bed in the downstairs bedroom, and you could share that with the girls. They're used to sleeping together and you can have the single bed and Jack and Rodney can share the boys' room.'

She didn't speak. This had taken her aback.

'Well, it ain't right you being in the house on your own with me. Tongues'd wag and you don't deserve that. So tonight, I'm going to sleep in the loft of the barn.'

'There's no need for that . . . though ta for thinking about me. But the bed in the downstairs bedroom wouldn't take a minute to make up and the girls could come in tonight, as could the lads . . . But, well, I'd like to keep me bedroom if yer don't mind . . . It's like me own little place, and it's what I'm used to.'

'Right, if that's what you want. Go and fetch them in then, girl.' He smiled, and the smile showed his relief.

Amy realized that he was battling with himself. That he did still have needs but was doing all he could not to give in to temptation where she was concerned. Her admiration for him grew, and she felt a little healing of her feeling about all men being the same.

'You should go out, yer know,' she told him. 'Go to the local bar and meet with yer friends, it would do yer good. Then when yer come back, we'll be all be settled and yer won't have to witness Grace's room being taken over.'

'That's a good idea. You've a good heart, Amy.'

With this, he rose and walked towards the door. She watched him lift his hat off the hook — the kind of hat she'd always associated with cowboys since she'd seen an article in one of Mrs Peterson's magazines that had a picture of them rounding up the cattle. The article under the picture had said they were the backbone of the country.

Turning to her just before he went out, Mr Timblay said, 'Everything will be all right, Amy. You need never fear me again.'

She didn't have time to reply as he went through the door.

How he'd handled the situation made her feel so much for him. Her instincts told her that he still desired her, but she knew she really didn't have anything to fear and that he would do what she knew he'd done over the last two years as she'd heard a rumour once when visiting the store — go to the bar and lie with one of the prostitutes.

Sighing, she gathered her skirt and ran out to the barn. 'Ivy, Betty, Jack, Roddy, you can come and sleep in the house!'

This was met with an excitement that swept her along with it and with the work they all undertook to make it happen, any thoughts and doubts surrounding Mr Timblay left her.

Everything was going to be all right; they would get through this wartime and Will and her beloved Teddy would come home. Maybe Betty and Jack would get together, and she would pray that Ivy got better and that, one day, Roddy would find happiness.

Eight weeks later, all this hope was shattered by the arrival of a telegram.

10

KILLED IN ACTION.

'Oh, Teddy . . . No! No!'

Mr Timblay's arm came around her, his head leaned on her shoulder, his tears wet her frock. Amy didn't reject him but turned into him and held him as they sobbed.

It was then that his legs gave way. She couldn't hold him. He sank to the floor.

The gasps, amidst the crying around her, put a new fear into Amy. For a moment it took away the pain that had ripped at her heart as Roddy whispered, 'He's dead!'

It felt to Amy as though the world had gone mad. She wanted to scream and scream, but the frightened sobs around her made her strong. She had to care for them all.

'Roddy, run and fetch Uncle Cirrus. Hurry!' She looked up. Jack was holding Betty. Ivy just stood there, her breathing laboured.

Realizing the shock had done this, Amy grabbed her and sat her down. 'Ivy, calm yer breathing, luv. I know yer can't fill yer lungs, but take it slowly, yer know that's always the best way. We'll sort everything, I promise . . . That's right, slowly . . . Now, Betty, get the Friar's Balsam and see to Ivy, and Jack, get a blanket to cover Mr Timblay.'

With everyone doing something and Amy left in limbo, she realized that despite helping Ivy, she still held on to the crumpled brown paper that held the news that had sliced her heart in two.

Lowering herself into a seat, she stared into space. In this place of loneliness, she could feel Teddy by her side. Feel his arms holding her as he always would have.

She didn't know how long she sat there, but when the door opened, her conscious mind came to know that it was Jack who was holding her, not Teddy.

She looked up to see a shaking and pale Uncle Cirrus staring at her in disbelief. His eyes went to the body on the floor. Without a word, he crossed the room and sank to his knees beside his dead brother, sobbing as he lifted the blanket and looked down at the still, waxen face.

Seeing that Ivy was doing all right now, Amy told Betty, 'Put the kettle on, luv, and make a pot of tea. Oh, and brew a coffee for Uncle Cirrus.'

Jack moved from her side and went to help Betty, telling her he'd fetch some water up to the kitchen from the well. He was good at getting around the house and farmyard and rarely needed a guide to do the simple chores, but still Roddy jumped to help him. 'I'll give yer a hand, Jack.'

As they went out the door, Amy heard Jack say, 'What do yer reckon'll happen now, Jack?' and for the first time, the situation really hit her.

My God! This could mean . . . No. Oh God! What will happen to us . . . to me? I couldn't go anywhere else other than home, but now my chances of doing that have gone . . . Oh, Teddy, me darling Teddy. How am I going to live without you?

From a long way off, she heard a moan. A painful sound that filled the space around her. Two strong

100

arms grabbed her. An unfamiliar smell tinged her nostrils, that of stale tobacco. Uncle Cirrus was holding her. The moan, she now realized, had come from herself. She clung on to Uncle Cirrus. She heard his cries.

This man was little more than a stranger to her even though she'd seen him in the fields and worked alongside him, and yet in her deepest hour of need he was the one who saved her from falling.

It was hearing his loud sobs that gave her strength once more. She patted his arm. 'Sit down, Cirrus' — the use of his first name without his title rolled off her tongue with the familiarity of use, not because she had any affection for him.

He sat heavily on the chair next to the fire. 'What should we do?' He shook his head. 'I just don't know what to do.'

'We need a doctor and an undertaker.'

Roddy and Jack came through the door at that moment. Between them they carried a bucket full of water.

'Roddy, yer'll have to take the trap and ride into town, luv. Bring the doctor and Mr Jacobs the undertaker.'

This seemed to help Uncle Cirrus as he straightened his back. 'We can't leave Danny on the floor. Give me a hand, Jack.'

When Jack couldn't lift the body, Cirrus went outside and blew on a horn, a way of communicating over a distance too far to call anyone. When he came back in, he said, 'Maskwa will come. Don't worry, Jack . . . Ta, Betty, yer make a good coffee.'

He managed a smile. 'Don't fret, all of you, I'll still need your help . . . more than ever now.'

Though Amy had often seen members of his tribe in town, she hadn't seen Maskwa since he'd run away and left her to the farmers who'd taken her to their farm. She shuddered at the memory but felt glad she was seeing Maskwa again. She'd often thought about him and Catori and hoped they were all right.

A relief had entered her at Cirrus saying he would still need them all to stay. She took it that he meant they could help to keep both farms going, but she felt even more pleased when he said, 'I've spoken to Maskwa lately about helping out on the farm. He seems keen as he's a married man now with a baby.'

It was good to know that Cirrus liked and respected Maskwa. Amy had never been able to ask Mr Timblay or Will why they both spoke badly of the Mississaugas when Cirrus seemed to get on well with them.

★ ★ ★

The next few weeks passed in a haze of grief and work. Maskwa had agreed to employment on the farm even though he said he felt trapped by the commitment and missed his life of freedom.

Jack and Roddy admired him greatly and loved learning many skills other than those needed to farm the orchards and the fields. And so, despite the changed circumstances, the farm had continued to tick over more or less as usual.

But now the day was on them that Amy had waited patiently for, and yet had dreaded. Will was coming home. He hadn't left the country but hadn't been able to be released on compassionate grounds until now.

Amy wondered how he would be. His grief would

be immense in losing both his brother and his father. Would it affect him? Would he be fine with having them all there still? And what of Maskwa?

In preparation for his return, she'd moved Jack and Roddy out of his room and back into the barn. And between them, they had made a section of the barn even more comfortable for Betty and Ivy. None of them had minded, understanding that Will would need his home to be like always as much as possible and that them coming back inside had to be his decision.

With her mind going over all the details of these goings-on and checking that she'd thought of everything so that Will didn't think they'd taken over his home, Amy stood on tenterhooks by the gate as she watched the cloud of dust come nearer and gradually clear and become the horse and trap driven by Roddy. Her heart pounded with anxiety.

But when the trap pulled up and Will jumped down, he dropped his rucksack and ran towards her with his arms open. She went willingly into them. They clung together. Both sobbing. Both lost.

Amy patted his back. 'We'll get through this, Will.'

He straightened. 'I don't know how . . . Teddy . . . Pa . . . Why? Why?'

She had no answers. Her heart was broken. It was as if the deep lonely chasm inside her had opened wider and left her empty, leaving her feeling that all her strength had been sucked into the dark hole of where her soul should be.

★ ★ ★

It took a few days for Will to gather himself. He spent long hours just lying on his bed, and then going for walks for hours more. It was a surprising turn of events that pulled him out of his morose state.

Amy was accompanying him on his walk that day. They talked about Teddy, they laughed, and they cried, but when they came across Maskwa working in the orchard, Amy held her breath. Fear gripped her. Will had always kept his distance from the Mississaugas but hadn't been as verbal of his hate for them as his pa or even Teddy had been at times.

But to her surprise, Maskwa came forward and greeted Will. 'Me and the Mississaugas are very sorry for your loss.'

Will eyed him.

Maskwa ignored this and greeted Amy, smiling and saying it was nice to see her.

Finding the moment awkward, Amy found herself replying, 'Hello, Maskwa. We're on our way to see Cirrus.' It was obvious they were so this sounded odd even to herself, but it was all she could think to say.

'He up at the house.'

Will still hadn't spoken. They walked by, then suddenly Will turned. Amy caught her breath again, but she needn't have worried. Maskwa said, 'I can offer you healing, Will. Part of that comes in making peace. My people have nothing but respect for you.'

Will showed no aggression but went up to Maskwa with his hand out. 'I'm sorry for all the bad feeling, Maskwa. My pa handed it down to us. He'd had it handed down from his father, who had heard from his grandfather how your people took his daughter. The bitterness came down the generations.'

'Their actions were no worse than those of your people.'

'Yes. I have read a lot about those times and you are

104

right. It was wrong of my people to take your people's land and they did bad things to your womenfolk too. I've thought for a long time the land should have been bought, not taken. It must hurt to now be working on it when you should be the owner of it?'

'No, I too know our history. We both have things to be ashamed of in what our forefathers did.'

'But your people had no choice, Maskwa. They thought of themselves as honourable, and defending what was theirs. They only had the methods they used as their weapons against those who had greater power. But it is in the past, there is no need for us to hate each other.'

Maskwa nodded and then a surprising thing happened. Maskwa and Will hugged.

'You are my brother, Will.'

'And you are mine.'

Amy had tears running down her face as she heard Maskwa say, 'A brother is always by the side of his kin. I am by yours.'

The two men embraced again, and Amy's heart filled with joy.

★   ★   ★

Life fell into a pattern after that incident. For Amy, it was as if she wasn't whole for a long time but gradually healed until she could talk of and think about Teddy without her heart breaking. He'd become a lovely memory and an 'if only' as she often imagined being married to him. In her imagination, she'd also seen herself going to London, finding Ruth and Ellen and then returning to be a wife and mother, but always having them back in her life, writing to her and even visiting her. Now, she didn't know what the future held, or if she would ever get home or not.

11

1918

It was Christmas Day 1918 when life changed once more. By now all were living in the house, and life had settled into a routine, but it was not a surprise as they sat eating a lovely dinner when Ivy and Will announced that they would marry in the spring. Amy had known it was only a matter of time as the pair were besotted with each other.

But it did surprise her and warmed her heart when after the announcement, Will said, 'And we would like you, Jack and Betty, to make it a double wedding!'

'What?'

Betty looked astonished. She looked at Jack. Jack shrugged. 'I've asked you many a time, Betty, luv.'

'Well, the answer's yes now, me lovely Jack. I just didn't know what would happen to us if we married.'

Will winked at Jack as he told him, 'The way I see it, you've got three months to convert the barn into a house to live in. It's yours. I will sign the deeds over to you, and a plot of land around the back of it so that you can have a garden too. We don't want to lose either of you, and the barn hasn't been any use to the farm for years.'

Amy looked at Roddy. Saw that he looked as confused and worried as she felt. Suddenly, things were moving at a pace and, like her, Roddy must wonder where they both stood.

She heard Will take a deep breath. She waited.

'Now that's settled, what to do with you two?'

Amy felt her temper rise a little. She was happy for them, but they hadn't consulted with her over anything, nor prepared her, or given her a chance to make plans for herself. 'Oh, don't bother about us!'

Will laughed. 'I love to make you cross, Amy. You look so funny trying to raise your height and look all hoity-toity!'

Amy huffed.

'Nothing will change . . . well, a few things, but yours and Roddy's position here will just be the same. You're family, Amy. You're like a sister to me, and to all of us. A bossy sister, but we all love you and we can all carry on as always.'

Suddenly, Amy didn't want that. It wasn't right. Ivy should be mistress of her own house. Over time, her chest had improved, as had her general health, which Amy had put down to her being happy and settled and having put many demons to rest, though she still talked about her mum and one day going home.

'Thanks, Will, I feel the same about you all, but no. I'm so happy for you all, but suddenly, I really do want to go home. It's time for me to make me own way in life. After the wedding, I'd like to go back to London.'

There was a silence. 'I — I know I haven't said anything about doing so for a long time but talking didn't bring it any closer, it just made me yearn day and night, so I put it to bed and accepted me lot. But now, I think the time is right. I've got a bit of money put by, but I'd need a loan to top it up.' Feeling bad about asking but not able to deny her heart any longer, she looked at Will. 'Would yer help me out, Will?'

'If I can, and I can ask Uncle Cirrus to help with what I can't. But I don't want yer to go, Amy. I was going on to tell yer that I was planning to build a shack for you with living accommodation at the back. Maskwa and I have talked about it. There's plenty of trees we could take down to build it with and we thought to put it on the edge of the field that slopes down to the lake. I was going to put it to yer that with your baking skills yer could open a sort of English tearoom. Ivy's been telling me about them, and I reckon one would do really well by the side of the lake.'

'Oh, Will, that sounds wonderful . . . but, well, I need to see me mates . . . Maybe if I don't settle in London, I could come back and take up your offer, eh?'

Will looked downcast.

'I'll pay yer back every penny, Will, I promise. I'll find work in London and send something back to yer every month.'

'It ain't the money, Amy . . . It's . . . well, I don't want yer to go. Life won't be the same without yer here.'

Amy wanted to hug him but thought it wouldn't be appropriate, but without warning, Will stepped forward and held out his arms and Amy went into them.

'I'll write often, and I want yer to write to me and to tell me all yer news. Now, let's get on with Christmas, shall we?'

★ ★ ★

A week later, Amy was busy making Ivy's wedding cake when the kitchen door suddenly flew open, letting in a huge wind that carried snow into the kitchen.

'Amy, Amy!'

'Roddy, for goodness' sake, put the wood in the hole, will yer!'

'Sorry, Amy, but I've something for yer . . . Oh, Amy, it's a letter! And it's from London!'

'What?' Amy stood and stared at Roddy.

'Here, look. It's a bit crumpled.'

The envelope was more than crumpled, it was dirty and looked as though it had been in the dustbin, not come through the post. It was also open. 'Where did it come from . . . I mean, how did yer get it, Roddy?'

'I went in the bar for a drink and this fellow came up to me. He asked if I worked on the Timblay farm. He said he was from a farm a few miles from ours and was just home from the war. He was injured and said his name was Johnny Wanderman.'

Amy gasped. 'Teddy told me about him. I thought he was at war, but how come he had a letter for me?'

'He said that when he got home, he found that his dad had been killed during a drove of his cattle — they stampeded. I remember talk of that happening and how the brother, called Joe, had become a drunkard and had been kicked out of the army after serving time in a military prison.'

'Yes, a nasty piece of work. But none of that explains the letter. Let me see.'

When she took the letter, her heart jumped to see it really had been posted in London! Her hands shook. She stared at Roddy who was telling her, 'Johnny said that he found it amongst his dad's things. He imagined that he meant to deliver it to you but didn't get the chance. His younger brother Josh had never gone through the papers his dad kept as he's been too busy trying to keep the farm going on his own.'

110

'I — I think it's from me friends. Oh, Roddy. I'll have to sit down a mo, mate.'

Roddy hurried around the table to her and supported her arm till she was sat down by the fire. Her fingers trembled and prayers tumbled through her mind asking Ruth's Holy Mary to make it happen that this letter was from Ruth.

The first thing she saw was July 1915!

'My God, this was written more than three years ago! Oh, Roddy, it's from Ellen and Ruth!'

Tears flooded her face. She swallowed hard.

'That's a good thing, ain't it, Amy?'

'It is, luv . . . Oh, it is, but if only I'd have got it before! It gives an address in London . . . and another at the bottom of the page . . . in Leeds. Ain't that somewhere up in the north of England?'

'Yes, I think it is.'

'I don't understand, why Leeds?'

'Why don't yer read it, eh? Go on, luv. I'll put the kettle on the hob, and we'll have a cuppa. Will told me to have the full day off after I came back with the supplies. Him and Jack can manage . . . only, well, I'm finding it difficult lately.'

'Oh, Roddy, luv, I hadn't noticed. Why didn't you tell me? You sit down, and I'll make the tea. It'll steady me and make it so that I can tackle reading what me mates have to say.'

Amy knew she was putting the moment off, but it was all such a shock to her after such a long time without news that she hardly dared find out what had happened, or how they had found her — and why at the Wandermans' farm? She'd only been there for a short time. Not even overnight as Teddy had fetched her home . . . *Oh, Teddy, how I wish you were here to help*

111

and to guide me. I love and miss you so much.

With the tea made and a sip of the hot liquid helping her, Amy steeled herself to read the words she'd wanted to receive for so long. She lifted the letter.

Dearest Amy,

Tears misted her eyes at these words, but she read on:

> *We hope with all our hearts that this letter finds you. We are nurses now and have been working in Ypres. We nursed the son of a farmer in Ontario who had heard of you — he described you so well. He says you are on a farm close to his father's, but he thought you may have gone to another place by now.*
>
> *Ruth, who sends all her love, stole his address so that we could write and appeal to his father to get this letter to you, or to tell us where you are.*
>
> *At the end I have put two addresses. One is mine. I own a little cottage in Leeds now. The other one is Ruth's but she may not stay there as though we are home for a while, we will be posted again. Oh, Amy, there is too much to tell you in a letter that we don't even know will reach you, so until we hear from you, we won't try. We just want to do all we can to find you and to tell you that we are well, we are together and when the war is over, we will come to bring you home.*
>
> *We think it better that you write to my address in Leeds (Rose Cottage) as my solicitor deals with all my post. I will instruct him that wherever I am, he is to contact me and give me news of you, and if you*

*can, and want to, come home immediately. He is to
wire you the money, or pay for your passage. He is
also instructed to liaise with you on my behalf to get
you home and to see that you are taken care of and
settle you wherever you want to go.*

   *We love you, Amy, and have never forgotten you.
Your friends,
Ellen and Ruth x*

Amy sat stunned. How could this all be true? Ellen
and Ruth having enough money to get her home? And
to have trained as nurses? Ellen was younger than herself, how could she be a nurse? And having a cottage
she owned — but then, when she'd seen Ellen's dad,
he obviously had money. He'd fetched Ellen in a car!
But surely even money can't get you to be a nurse
when you are only . . . ? She quickly did the calcula-
tion. To her mind, when she wrote this letter, Ellen
was only fifteen years old — possibly sixteen, depend-
ing on her birthday. But still?

Suddenly, it hit her that this question didn't matter.
She'd been found by Ruth and Ellen.

Clutching the letter to her, she looked up.

The expression she caught on Roddy's face shocked
her. 'What is it, luv?'

'I can see from your reaction that you're really
going, aren't yer, Amy?'

'I am. Oh, Roddy, it's a reality now.' She told him
the contents of the letter.

'Amy . . . could I come with you? I wouldn't be any
trouble.'

'Oh, Roddy, I thought you were happy here?'

'I am, but . . . to lose you, Amy, I — I can't think of
doing that.'

Amy felt a strange feeling as she looked at Roddy. What was he saying? She didn't want him to see her as anything but a friend — maybe a sister, but nothing more. 'You're not getting ideas about me, are yer, Roddy? Yer know we're just friends — well, you're like me brother, nothing more.'

Roddy grinned. 'I ain't getting ideas, Amy. How can anyone who looks like me expect anyone to fancy me? I know that ain't going to happen.'

'Oh, Roddy. Me feelings ain't nothing to do with how yer look. You're you . . . I mean, you ain't how yer look and I think the world of yer, I just ain't ready to give me heart to anyone, that's all.'

'Will yer ever be ready, Amy?'

There it was again. There was something in Roddy's voice that was telling her a lot more than he was admitting to. She felt sorry that he felt his affliction would bar him from being loved, but then, he'd been told from a baby how ugly he was and had endured how those who were supposed to love him had hidden him from view because they were ashamed of him. But he wasn't ugly. His body was misshapen, yes, but his face was lovely. The pimples and weeping spots he'd been prone to when he first arrived had cleared up. His hazel eyes were full of expression and framed by longer lashes than men usually had. His hair, not dissimilar to her own mousy colour, lay in waves no matter how he tried to straighten it and often, especially if he sweated, would form curls that flopped around his face. And his kind and eager-to-please ways shone from him.

'Amy?'

She hadn't realized she'd been quiet for so long, or that she'd noticed so much about Roddy. Suddenly, she wasn't seeing his hunched left shoulder, or how his chest turned inwards, but a good man with a heart of gold and his love for her shining from him.

'Maybe . . . one day, maybe.'

'Oh, Amy . . . really? I dared not think of such a thing . . . I wanted to. I — I love yer, Amy, with all me heart, and cannot bear to think of yer going away.'

Amy didn't know what to do or to say. She was flattered he felt this way but wasn't sure how she felt about him doing so.

He leaned back in his chair. He looked as though a huge weariness had taken him and for the first time she noticed his breathing was laboured. Alarm sent her to his side. Going on her haunches next to him, she asked, 'Are you feeling really unwell, Roddy? Should I send for the doctor?'

Tears filled his eyes as he looked into hers. 'It's like a weakness . . . like someone takes me stuffing from me whenever I exert meself. I'll be all right in a moment.'

'You're shivering! Oh, Roddy, luv, yer must be sickening for something. I'll put another log on the fire and fetch a blanket to put over you.'

'Ta, Amy.'

Forgetting that the cake she was making was ready to go into the oven, Amy scurried through to the ground-floor bedroom that Roddy now shared with Jack. She hadn't given a lot of thought to them swapping with Betty and Ivy, but now, thinking about it, she wondered if that had been due to Roddy finding even the stairs difficult?

With these thoughts a worry set up inside her as to the real state of his health and she felt cross with herself for not noticing. But then, she'd been like that since the news of Teddy's death and the shock of his dad dying so suddenly. It was as if she was in this world but wasn't. Like she was watching life, but not taking part in it. Look how taken aback she'd been when Ivy and Jack announced their wedding when she should have been prepared!

But now her heart was heavy with fear that she might lose Roddy, too.

When she returned to the kitchen Roddy sat with his eyes closed. His hump prevented him from leaning back and relaxing, so he looked hunched over. Pity for him flooded Amy. But then alarm took over as now she could hear his breaths, and each one that he took seemed to gurgle as if he was breathing through fluid. She hurried to his side. 'Roddy, Roddy!'

He opened his eyes, but they were shielded by his lids not completely lifting, leaving him looking as if he was drunk.

'Roddy, Roddy, luv, I'm here.'

His gaze held hers and Amy had the sensation of being a lifeline for him, that if she moved, he would slip away. Her desperation took all reason from her. 'Roddy, don't go. I love you, Roddy.'

Hope filled his squinted eyes. 'Help me . . . Amy . . . I lo . . . love you.'

His eyes closed. Amy stood and fled from the room, shouting at the top of her lungs for someone to come. Then prayed, *Please, please let him hear me. Bring Maskwa to me, Ruth's Holy Mary, please bring him here to help me!*

Wanting to run towards the orchard, but not wanting to leave Roddy, she turned back towards the kitchen. As soon as she stepped back inside, she heard his watery breathing, saw his eyes were now closed. His body seemed to have shrunk, but he had the most wonderful expression on his face — a kind of peaceful, happy and accepting look.

But she didn't want him to accept, she wanted him to fight. He could get better but to do so he had to at least try.

Her own voice sounded sharp to her ears as she snapped out his name. 'Roddy! Wake up, Roddy! Yer have to fight this. Yer have to get well. You can do it, Roddy, you can!' She took the deathly cold hand that had flopped over the side of the chair into hers and began to rub it, trying to warm it whilst she pleaded with him. 'Roddy, please, luv. Sit up straight . . . I mean, don't try to lean back, yer hindering yer breathing. Give yer lungs a bit more room to expand, luv.'

Roddy responded to this and wearily sat forward. This position did seem to help him as he took a deeper breath, but then went into a fit of coughing.

Holding him, Amy felt her love for him sear her heart. She didn't try to analyse her feelings; she only knew that she didn't want to lose Roddy.

Desperation made her beg him to fight. 'Please, Roddy, please live.'

A sound behind her made her turn.

'I heard you shouting, Amy. I wasn't far away. What is troubling you?'

As she moved, Maskwa caught sight of Roddy. His face filled with concern. Striding forward, he scooped Roddy up as if he was a doll. 'I take to Hausis, she has many remedies and will make Roddy well.'

The muscles in his tanned arms rippled as he carried Roddy out of the door and laid him gently on a multicoloured blanket spread out on the back of his cart. Wrapping this around Roddy, he spoke in his native tongue. The words sounded unfamiliar to her.

Fear gripped her, but as Maskwa turned to her and told her, 'Roddy is my brother, I will care for him,' her confidence returned.

'Ta, Maskwa. Make him well, please make him well.'

'I believe that Roddy will bring you happiness, Amy. Never deny your heart for the repulsion of the disabled body.'

'I — I . . .'

Her protest was lost in the cloud of dust that covered her as, urging his horse, Maskwa drove away.

Shock at what had happened and at what Maskwa had said kept Amy rooted to the spot. Had she been put off by Roddy's disability? He'd just been 'poor Roddy'. But now, she felt desperately that she wanted him to live — to be the man he was. Wanted him to come with her to London, wanted him by her side for ever.

Tears streamed down her face as she thought of Teddy. But then, a kind of peace came to her. It was as if Teddy was releasing her, allowing her to go forward towards the future without the extreme pain of missing him. He would always have a place in her heart, but she also knew there was room in her heart for love to come into her life again.

Sighing, she turned and went inside. Picking up the letter once more, she held it to her breast and despite everything, the joy of what the contents offered her lifted her and lit up her soul. She was going home.

12

August 1919

As she stood with her case waiting to board the huge ship, Amy reflected on how the last eight months of her time in Canada had been peppered with sadness and joy. The sadness had been when Roddy had died within hours of declaring his love for her.

Amy knew again the pain of his loss to visit her as she remembered his burial deep in the heart of the orchard he'd loved.

Maskwa and Catori had stood each side of her giving her support. As they'd turned to leave, Maskwa had comforted her by saying she had given light to Roddy's soul and that his last words were, 'Amy loves me.'

As she thought of this, she realized that everyone was moving ahead — they'd begun to board the ship.

There was no time to think of anything for a while, but once all her documents had been checked and she stood waiting for her cabin to be allocated, she found she was able to think clearly about her feelings for Roddy and realized that she'd long concluded that it was as a brother that her love extended to him. She smiled, happy in the knowledge that Roddy had thought otherwise and that had mattered a great deal to him and, so, to her too. She would always miss him, but knowing he was at peace helped.

It had been the double wedding of Will to Ivy and

Jack to Betty that had brought joy to her. Held in the garden at the back of the farmhouse that had been her home for so long, the setting had been made even more beautiful than it already was by the wooden arch that Will had constructed as a focal point for the ceremony to take place, and which she and the girls had decorated in multicoloured paper flowers that had taken weeks to make.

But above all of the work it had taken, what would stay with Amy was the happiness as four of the people very dear to her heart cemented their love.

One of the highlights for her, which hadn't been to do with the happy couples and had set her on this journey with more than hope in her heart, was the meeting of herself and Johnny Wanderman — the soldier she knew Ruth had nursed and who had led Ruth to find her — though not willingly it seemed.

At first, he'd been curious about them — how she had landed here but Ruth hadn't. As she'd told her story, he'd understood how it had made her shudder to recount it, telling her the war had left him with memories that gave him nightmares. She'd wanted to hear more, but had stopped herself asking, afraid to know the circumstances under which her beloved Teddy had died.

Johnny had moved on to apologize for how he'd looked on home children and for his family's behaviour to her.

It was then that he'd spoken of Ruth and she realized that he'd thought a lot of her and had surprised her by telling her that Ruth was engaged to be married!

As she'd been trying to take this in, she heard how Ruth had asked a lot about the home children and herself in particular.

It appeared he hadn't offered to help Ruth to find her, but that she had stolen his address from the records when he'd indicated that he knew of her whereabouts.

The loud blast of the ship's hooter made Amy jump and brought her out of these thoughts as the sound filled her with excitement and anticipation.

Despite the Wandermans and the Millers of this world, she truly was on her way home.

Casting off from the shores of Canada wasn't without its sadness, though.

Saying goodbye had been a tearful event. Will had held her longer than all of them. When he released her he'd had tears in his eyes. She'd looked up at him and told him, 'I'll never forget the kindness of yer family, Will. Yer lovely ma, me special Teddy, you and, yes, even yer pa will always be in me thoughts.'

As she'd uttered these last words, she'd wanted to swallow them back, but Will nodded. 'Teddy told me what my pa did.'

'Don't worry about it,' she'd told him. 'He made up for it. It was a lapse, we all have them. I'll think of all the good things about him.'

Will had looked relieved. 'Thanks, Amy. The knowing of what he did to you has always tainted my memory of my pa.'

She'd brushed a fleck off his collar and swallowed hard as she'd said, 'Take care of yerself. I'll write, I promise,' and then had added, 'And, Will, be a good husband to Ivy. Her life till coming to your farm was hell. Never let it be so again, luv.'

He'd promised it wouldn't.

They'd hugged again and then parted. More hugs had followed from Betty, Ivy and Jack before she'd at last left them on the quayside as the queue she was in had moved to where they could no longer follow.

Now they were little dots far below her.

She'd thought she'd feel torn, but she didn't. They were all settled and happy. Jack and Betty had made a lovely home, reminiscent of an English countryside cottage, or it would be when the rambling roses they'd planted covered the wedding arch which now shaded their door. The mock leaded windows that Jack had made and had replaced the old ones with added to the effect. And Ivy was well and truly mistress of hers and Will's home, as all traces of how it had always been had been replaced — newly made curtains were hung at the windows, chair covers to match were added to the chairs, and more than a lick of paint had been given to the doors.

It was lovely to see them all happy. She would miss them, but the pull of Ruth and Ellen was a far greater urgency in her life.

* * *

The journey seemed endless, even more so than it had on the way to Canada, though Amy was glad of the comforts she had which were a million times better than on her outward journey as a child. She had a cabin to herself with a window to look out of and the run of the long decks for walks, which broke the monotony.

It was when it was announced that they were nearing

122

London and expected to dock on time that her heart lifted and she once more filled with excitement. From then on, her walks along the deck were enhanced by seeing the land that began as a haze in the far distance but gradually became clearer and clearer until she could make out some buildings and see smoke churning out of high factory chimneys. Such a different landscape to greet her from the one in Canada, but one that was so welcome, she thought she would burst with anticipation.

Suddenly there was a rush of passengers as the loudhailer announced from the deck that they would be docking in forty minutes!

For Amy, there was no need to dash back to her cabin — she already had her small suitcase by her feet. She had very few clothes — what she stood up in, a cotton navy and white gingham frock she'd worn for the wedding, on top of which she wore a navy box-shaped jacket. Her mousy, almost untameable hair was kept neat by a white crocheted bonnet, and in her case, a skirt and three jumpers, which had been Grace's. Will had given them to her for her journey. Besides these, she had two sets of underwear, one she wore and one clean in her case. A nightly routine of washing them out had kept her going and lying on top of her case, her long grey coat that she'd picked up at a bargain price especially for her journey.

With the wind coming off the sea and seeming to use the Thames like a tunnel, Amy donned this now and was glad of the extra warmth it gave her.

Pulling it around her, she swallowed hard, unable to contain herself. Was she really going to see Ruth and Ellen very soon? Would they be at the dock to meet her?

The letter she'd received in reply to the one she'd written to Ellen's cottage had been very formal, informing her that if she would like to wire the approximate date she could travel and where in England she would like to travel to, arrangements for her journey would be made and the details wired back to her.

All of that had gone very smoothly, but what was to happen from now on she did not know. She only knew that she would be met at the quayside but not by whom.

Scanning the crowd, who were all looking upwards but were too far away to discern, Amy felt like shouting out, 'I'm here!' But instead she filed in the orderly trail of people making their way towards the gangplank.

She was halfway down when a voice very dear to her shouted, 'Amy!' then screamed, 'Amy. Oh, Amy!'

Her own voice hurt her ears as she shouted, 'Ruth! Ruth!'

Tears flooded her face. She wanted to shove the lady in front of her to hurry her along. But then it happened. Her feet were on British soil again!

Around her nothing much had changed. The docks were almost as she'd left them with a gang of men and boys, looking poverty-stricken, standing waiting to be chosen to be the ones to work on unloading the ship. Cranes and piles of crates abounded, and there were the same smells and sounds — a mixture of exotic spices and the stench of the stagnant Thames, banging and clanging and folk shouting to one another.

Nine years had passed — she'd left these shores in September 1910, and now, all she was surrounded by seemed to be saying, 'Welcome back, Amy.' And none more so than finding herself in Ruth's arms.

They clung to one another, uttering each other's name. At last, they parted. Their eyes locked and Amy thought she never wanted this moment to pass. She needed to stay like this, her soul joined to Ruth's — her life feeling complete.

'I can't believe this. Oh, Amy, Amy, yer home, luv!'

Amy couldn't answer. Her vision of Ruth blurred through her tears, and they spilled over when she nodded her head.

Ruth wiped one away with her thumb. 'Don't cry, luv, it's over, it's all over. We're together again and no one can hurt us now.'

They hugged again, then Ruth told her, 'Ellen is waiting in a cafe just outside the dock, and so is someone else I want you to meet.'

'Ellen! Really? Oh, Ruth, I've so many questions, luv, but first, who is the someone?'

'Hold on to yer hat, luv . . . It's someone yer wouldn't guess in a million years! Me son!'

'What? You have a son! Oh, Ruth, so much of our lives have passed us by, mate. A son! I can't wait to meet him. And to see Ellen. Is she all right? It sounded as though she'd landed on her feet when her dad fetched her out of the orphanage.'

'She didn't. Well, not altogether. He didn't want her. He wanted her out of there as he could do that once his wife had died, but he took her to her gran in Leeds. For the most part she was happy, but bad things kept happening to her.'

'Don't tell me yet, luv, I can't take it all in. But I do want to know how the 'eck she came to be a nurse at fifteen years of age!'

'Ha, she duped everyone. And easily. We both did. Our Ellen's a genius. She knew more than most

125

doctors by the time she was thirteen, and by the time her gran died, I reckon she could have passed the exams to be one! Anyway, she found me, and I was training with the Red Cross as I wanted to do me bit, and she just tried her luck. They didn't guess her real age and neither of us have birth certificates, so we lied and got in!'

'Sounds amazing, and that's where you met Johnny?'

'The Canadian that led us to you? Yes, we met him all right, mate. The rotter. He talked about you as if yer were scum. But we had the last laugh as we stole his address . . . and, well, yer know the rest.'

'He apologized, Ruth.'

They came to the customs entrance at this point and Ruth had to go through another exit, but Amy didn't miss Ruth's expression as her mouth dropped in surprise.

When they met up again, she asked, 'You know him? . . . Here, luv, give me yer case for a bit as we've still a little walk to get out of here and to the cafe.'

Grateful to get rid of the extra weight, even though it wasn't heavy, Amy handed the case over.

'Yes. I know Johnny, he's a good bloke really. He told me it was his pa who'd filled him with all that stuff about us kids. He told me to tell you he was sorry for what he said and that he's grateful to yer for saving his life and that he thought yer beautiful.'

'He said that?'

'He did, luv.' Amy found Ruth's free hand and squeezed it. 'But he also said he knew yer were engaged, but here yer are married, so he ain't got a chance, though I think he's hoping to have.'

'No, I ain't married, Amy . . . I — I lost me man . . . He died of an asthma attack before we could wed.'

126

'Oh, luv. I'm sorry . . . Ruth . . . I — I know how that feels . . . Did yer ever come across a bloke from Canada called Teddy . . . Edward Timblay?'

Ruth was quiet for a moment. 'No . . . no, I can't recall anyone with that name. Is he a friend of yours, luv?'

'We were in love, but he was killed in action.'

'No! Oh, Amy, me and you go through it, don't we, eh, luv? I'm sorry.'

Ruth dropped Amy's hand and put her arm around her shoulders. 'We'll get through, luv. Now that we have each other again, we'll be all right . . . I love yer, mate.'

Though more tears prickled her eyes, Amy wouldn't let them fall. Ruth had as much to cry about as she did, maybe even more, who knew, but she was being brave, so that's what she'd do too.

'And I love you, Ruth. It's been hard living without yer and not knowing where yer were. I wrote, yer know. I wrote to that address yer wrote down.'

'And I didn't get your letters! Oh, Amy, I made arrangements to get any post with the people that moved in, they knew Bett . . . I'll tell you about Bett another time. Anyway, they promised if anything came for me, they'd give it to Bett.'

Amy snuggled into Ruth. Her heart was breaking. She wanted to cry huge sobs, for all they'd missed, for all they'd been through, for Teddy and for Ruth's man, but she dared not let go. If she did, she had the feeling that she would never stop.

After a moment, they walked on, hand in hand. It all seemed surreal to Amy, and she was glad of the distraction when Ruth suddenly said, 'We're here! Oh look, Ellen's at the window. She can't wait to see yer, luv.'

Amy gasped as she caught sight of the young woman in the window. She'd recognized Ruth immediately, but Ellen looked so different to how she remembered her, but then, of course she would do. She looked so much more like Ruth than Amy remembered, and, well, older than herself even, when she was a year younger and would be going on twenty.

Ellen put her hand up and waved.

This was a more confident Ellen. At the home she'd been the shy, quiet one. Probably more out of her depth than she and Ruth as Ellen had been brought up in a posh home, but her father's wife hadn't wanted her. She'd treated her cruelly and called her 'her father's bastard'.

To Amy, what happened to Ellen was far worse than what she and Ruth endured. They'd known no different since birth, but for Ellen, the orphanage must have been a massive shock. No wonder she'd clammed up.

Amy followed Ruth inside the cafe. The warmth of the place hit her, as did the curls of smoke from the fags the women sitting at the tables were smoking. Her eyes began to smart.

It was then that it hit her. The difference between Canada, with its beauty, its fresh mountainous air and peacefulness, and London, grimy, smelly, noisy and with smoke pouring from chimneys, or people's mouths as they all seemed to smoke fag after fag. And the people. Hundreds and hundreds of them, bustling, for no one seemed to be walking, all were in a hurry. A repulsion came over her. Never in a million years did she think she would feel like this about her beloved London. The place she'd longed to be. But now, she'd give anything to gather up Ruth, Ellen and the adorable little boy she could see staring at her and whisk them to Canada!

'Are yer all right, luv?'

'Huh? Oh yes, Ruth . . . I'm sorry, Ellen, I were just a bit overwhelmed.' She went into Ellen's open arms.

'You're bound to be. Don't worry, take your time to get used to it all — to us again. Nothing need be done in a hurry.'

Ellen sounded posh. She couldn't remember her speaking like that. She must have had a good education; Ruth had said she was clever.

Ruth nodded. 'Yes, we've all the time in the world, Amy, luv.'

Ruth's little son had grabbed Ruth's skirt and now hid behind it. Amy understood how he felt as a sudden shyness had come over her too. It was as if she had closed down — an empty shell. She didn't want to feel like this. She wanted to feel the excitement she'd felt at seeing Ruth. She was home, wasn't she?

13

Ruth

As they walked in silence, Ruth was at a loss. This wasn't going how she and Ellen had thought it would. But then, all of it must be overwhelming for poor Amy.

She decided they must take things gently but was mystified as to how to break the ice, to even begin to smooth what to Amy must seem like a very strange experience.

Ruth looked around her, but nothing helped. She couldn't point out places Amy might remember for as far as she knew, Amy had only left the workhouse where she'd been as a child to walk to the orphanage where they'd met each other. Maybe if they went to Bethnal Green, she would feel more at home.

There, she could tell her about her own life after she'd run away from the home. That was their first parting. Everything that had happened to her since had happened there and had shaped her life.

She hailed a cab and asked the driver if he could put the pushchair she found she still needed to use at times into the back and they would all sit in the front with him.

''Course I can, luv. 'Op in, I can't 'ang around.'

Amy still looked in a daze.

'I thought I'd take yer back to the beginning, Amy, luv. That's if yer not too tired?'

'No, I ain't tired, but yer don't mean the orphanage, do yer? I don't ever want to see that place again.'

'No, just to Bethnal. We might see something that's familiar to yer.'

Still there was no reaction from Amy.

When they alighted, Ruth pointed over to the market stalls. 'See that, Amy? That stall used to be run by me mate, Ruby. And the hot potato stall by me second mum Bett — well, me third if yer count me real mum. I lost both Ruby and Bett from the flu last year. Anyway, it's that stall that I hid under when I ran away.'

'That very one? So, nothing's changed in all these years?'

'No, very little changes in the East End, luv. The folk are still poor — maybe poorer as the war took its toll and many are grieving and have lost their breadwinners. But they're still the salt of the earth and still looking out for one another . . . Anyway, the stall next to it I had with Rebekah, the lovely lady who took me in and taught me how to make hats, and to dance and love the life that we have. She were me first mum and I loved her — we sold our hats on that stall and now I'm about to open a milliner's shop!'

Amy looked flabbergasted, then burst into tears.

'Amy, luv . . . Oh, Amy. What's wrong? Come here, girl. Let it all out, eh? Look, let's cross the road and sit on that bench in the park. It's mine and Robbie's bench. Robbie's me mate. He saved me really. Do yer remember him? He was with me when I came to the orphanage gates that time and yer told me Ellen had been taken out by her father . . . anyway, yer'll meet him later, he's adorable.'

Ruth wondered to herself what Amy would think of Robbie. A theatrical person, who made his living on the stage, he and Abe lived together in a loving relationship. They had a flat in the downstairs of the house that Ruth owned. She and Ellen had a flat upstairs.

When they sat down, Ruth held Amy close as her tears flooded her.

Always the one to have insight, Ellen went down on her haunches in front of them and held one of Amy's hands. 'Is it all too much for you, Amy? Would you like me to go and take little Archie with me? You can sit with Ruth and go and have tea together and do a little catching up. I think that would be best for you.'

Amy nodded, then bent forward and grabbed Ellen. Between sobs she said, 'Oh, Ellen, I luv yer, mate, and I've missed yer so much, but . . . it's like, well, as if yer both so different.'

'We are, dear. As you are. We've lived in your memory as the young girls we were, and you've lived in ours in that way too. Now we're together and we couldn't be happier, but everything's changed. Oh, we knew it would be, but still, it's a shock.'

Amy nodded; the gesture dislodged more tears.

Ellen continued: 'Ruth and I have changed together, been through a lot together, so we haven't got to adjust to each other, only to you. But you, dear Amy, you've come home to two virtual strangers, whose lives have carried on and developed in different ways to your own. We understand as we were separated again for four years after finding each other and being at war together. Ruth stayed home to have Archie, but I went back to France to carry on nursing, and I haven't been home long — just a few months. The one thing we said when I arrived back was, that though we had catching up to do, we still loved one another, and we were still those two little girls from the orphanage.

Now, we are those three little girls from the orphanage, Amy, and though things have changed, nothing can change our love for one another.'

'Oh, Ellen, Ellen, yer right. Nothing can change that.'

Ruth felt her own tears sting her eyes as she watched Ellen and Amy hug, but a relief settled in her. Amy would be all right. She would.

'Lady cry, Mummy?'

Ruth smiled down at her son. 'You remember when Aunty Ellen came home a few weeks ago and we were crying? Well, we told you it was because we were happy. We women do that. We cry because we're happy.'

'Like taps!'

Ruth laughed. 'That's your Uncle Robbie talking, isn't it? I bet he told yer we turned the taps on when we're happy as well as when we're sad, eh?'

Archie giggled, but Ruth could see he was a little unsure. Swallowing her own need to cry, she bent over his small carriage — a basket woven chair that resembled a crib on a slant. It had four wheels and was half the size of the huge pram she'd used for him when he was a baby. Lifting him out, she told him, 'Let's pick some buttercups and yer can give them to Aunty Amy . . . She's a lovely new aunty who's come a long, long way to meet you and is feeling overwhelmed. You will love her. She just needs time to cry all her happy tears at being home with us.'

Archie looked up. His quizzical frown reminded her so much of her beloved Adrian, Archie's father. Adrian, who would have been proud of his son and would have loved him so much. *He's going to be clever, Adrian, luv, just like you . . . Oh, I wish yer could have met him. But I'll always make sure he knows of you,*

133

I promise.

Sighing, Ruth succumbed to Archie's pulling of her skirt. His face, eager and adorable, looked up at her. 'Bu-her cups, Mummy.'

Ruth laughed out loud as she followed him. 'No, butter! Ha, yer'll sound like a cockney dropping your Ts! Come on then.'

When they went back to the bench, Amy and Ellen were laughing together. Archie, without a trace of shyness, presented Amy with a little bunch of buttercups with their heads drooping and their leaves bruised, but Ruth could see that none of that mattered to Amy. As she took them, she held out her arms. 'Hello, Archie, mate. Are these for me?'

Archie nodded, his eyes not leaving Amy's face. Ruth held her breath, but after a moment's indecision, Archie giggled as he went into Amy's arms. Amy held him tightly to her, but Archie didn't object. When he came out of her hug and saw tears still flowing down her face, he reached out his finger to touch one that glistened in the sunlight. 'Like taps!'

This made them all laugh and Archie, sensing he'd been the cause, squealed with delight.

Amy looked up and smiled. 'How old is he, Ruth?'

Archie held three fingers up as he said, 'I'm three. I had a birthday. I like making numbers.' He bent one finger and pointed to each of those he held aloft. 'Ellen and Amy.' Then counted them, 'One . . . two . . . two aunties.' His grin broadened as he clapped his hands together.

'That's right. I am your aunty.' Amy looked up. 'I am home, Ruth. Archie just made me belong. I'm truly home.'

'Oh, Amy, you are, me luv. And your being so makes

134

it feel as though at last we're all home — back where we started, and yet not. We've all grown and become strong, Amy. Our story didn't end in that horrible orphanage, we've a lot of it to live yet, but we've made a good start, girl . . . A bloomin' good start!'

'Blimey, Ruth, you sounded like a preacher!'

At Amy saying this, their giggles became belly laughs and their happiness bubbled over as they bent double with the pain of their laughter. They hugged, they cried again, and they hugged some more, and Ruth knew everything was going to be all right.

'Well, shall we go home? Home is me own house, Amy, another tale, but now it is your home, me darlin', and it's where yer should be with me and Ellen.' Ruth held out her hand as she said this and it was a stronger Amy who took it and walked with her, following Ellen and Archie, who wanted to push his carriage and not sit in it.

'Do yer think yer up to knowing the most astounding news of all, Amy, luv?'

'I am, Ruth, and to telling yer of me own life too.'

'Well, this will come as a shock, but me and Ellen have found out that we're half-sisters!'

'What! No! How . . . ? That's wonderful — real sisters?'

'Half. We share the same mum, who we're hoping to find, but not the same dad.' Ruth told her how they had come to this conclusion. How Ellen had been with her father when she was eleven and a woman who looked exactly like Ruth confronted him. 'It seems she was Ellen's dad's mistress. She had her son with her, who she handed over to Ellen's father.'

'But that don't make her Ellen's mum and Ellen your sister . . . I don't understand.'

135

Ruth explained how during the conversation between the woman and Ellen's dad, the woman became upset and said that she wanted to keep her child. 'Ellen's father accused her of not being capable as she'd already put one child in the orphanage.'

'Well, so did he. He put Ellen in an orphanage. Why did he do that?'

'I know. It seems his wife couldn't accept Ellen and treated her badly to the point where she wanted her out of the house.'

'Poor Ellen . . . So, you think this other child was you?'

'Yes, because the woman said that she hadn't put her child into the orphanage but had left her with a priest who she thought would find a nice home for her. I was left with a priest and the woman looked like me. And the time when they said this happened also fits with when it happened to me. Then the woman told Ellen she loved her and would always love her. After that, Ellen's father took her to her gran's in Leeds but on the train, he admitted that the woman had been Ellen's mother.'

'Yer mean, he didn't keep Ellen this second time?'

'No. Like I said before, he'd found himself another woman — must have been having an affair with her on the side as his wife hadn't been dead long. So, he wanted rid of Ellen again and told her that she had a gran all the time, but he'd been ashamed till then to tell his mother of her.'

'Oh, poor Ellen.'

'Well, it turned out well for her. She was loved . . . though she did have some problems, but on the whole she had a good life. And she had a good education . . . Her tutor was the loveliest man. Adrian.

When Ellen found me, she was with Adrian — he was her chaperone . . . Adrian and I fell in love and . . . well . . . Archie is his son.'

'Oh, Ruth. I'm sorry that you lost your Adrian.'

'Ta, luv . . . It all seems a long time ago. I'm all right now. Oh, Amy, luv, there's so much to tell yer.'

'And me you. But though what you've told me was a sad story, Ellen actually met her own mum and now you both know who yer mum is . . . Oh, Ruth, luv, I so want to do that.'

'I know. When I was told, it made me yearn to meet her. Me and Ellen, we want to take care of her. Stop her need to . . . well, it seems that she's a prostitute, Amy, but they ain't all bad, yer know.'

'I ain't never thought of them as bad, Ruth. We had some of them in the workhouse. Lovely, they were. There was one that I loved dearly, Ethel, and I've never forgotten her. She used to take special care of me.'

'Ah, yer were happy in the workhouse, weren't yer, Amy?'

'I was. It was like one big family. Not that I can remember it all, but what I do gives me a nice feeling. And Ethel was like you said Rebekah and Bett were to you. She were like a mum to me. And nothing bad happened to me, or to the other kids in there . . . until one day, someone decided that as I wasn't with a mum of me own, I should be in the orphanage . . . But, well, I've wondered time and time again about Ethel. The night before I were going, she held me to her and told me, 'Yer do have a mum, but she can't take care of yer, but she loves yer, never forget that.''

Ruth squeezed Amy's hand. All she could think to say was, 'Well, we wouldn't have met if yer hadn't been taken to the orphanage, girl. So, something good come of it.'

'They say it does of all bad, but I ain't so sure. Though meeting you and Ellen was a good day.'

'Right, luv, we'll get a cab from here.' Ruth thought to nip any sadness or bad thoughts in the bud as she looked around. But as much as she'd tried to avert Amy from going over the past, she found herself doing just that as memories assailed her.

She glanced back at the stalls that had meant so much to her life and a vision came to her of Rebekah, the beautiful, older lady who'd taken her in after she'd run away from the orphanage, a bruised and battered child who'd been repeatedly raped.

Rebekah who had given her a loving home, cared for her and taught her so many skills now seemed to be standing by their old stall nodding as if to say, 'Yer doing good, Ruth, girl, Rebekah am proud of you.'

Ruth smiled and almost lifted her hand to wave. Instead, she looked skyward and sent a little plea up to Rebekah. *Help me, Rebekah, help me to get this right. Amy needs careful handling for a while.*

Then for good measure, she asked the same of the Holy Mary, her special lady in heaven who she'd always loved and prayed to since a kindly vicar visited the orphanage and told them wonderous stories about baby Jesus and his mother, Mary. He'd shown them pictures. Mary had a lovely smile that seemed to say she understood you, and she had a peaches and cream complexion and wore a blue cape which was the same shade as her eyes. Always when she prayed to her, Ruth pictured her like this, though she now knew this could not have been a likeness as Mary was a Jewess and would most likely have had lovely olive skin and a beautiful, chiselled face with big dark eyes and black hair.

When they arrived, Amy was in awe as she looked up at the three-storeyed house in Southampton Way. She turned and looked at Ruth. 'This is yours? Your very own?'

'It is, me darlin', given to me through the heart-break of losing me Adrian who I told yer about, and yet making me feel that he is taking care of me, how he vowed to do once . . . once we married.'

Amy's arm came around her. 'I know. It always pains yer to remember, and yet fills yer with joy too. For me, me man didn't have time to do anything like this. He told me he loved me when he rescued me and then was gone to war.'

'Me poor darling. When yer feel like it, yer can tell us all about it, eh? It sounds frightening having to be rescued, but all that is behind us. We can go forward, and we will . . . Oh, Amy, I've such big plans. Yer going to learn to make hats, girl! And me and you are going into business with Ellen — only, she'll just be a sleeping partner as she has plans.'

'Come on, you two. Let's get in and get Amy settled, and then later, we can sit together and tell all. Nothing left out as there's a theory that if everything is shared, it helps you — like halving the burden.'

'Yes, Doctor Ellen.'

Amy giggled at this, but Ruth told her, 'There's truth in me calling her that. At least, there was. Now it's going to be Ellen, the doctor's wife! . . . Anyway, she's right, let's get inside. We've prepared a lovely bedroom for you, but you can share with any of us in the beginning if you want to, till you've got yer feet well and truly under the table . . . Oh, Amy, luv, I can't believe you're here at last!'

With how Amy had been, Ruth decided not to knock on the door at the bottom of the stairs leading to Robbie and Abe's flat and introduce her to them, but to take her straight upstairs and get her settled. She could explain their relationship first then.

Her heart skipped a beat at the thought of doing so as she was unsure of what reaction Amy would have, but she hoped it would be a good one and thought that more likely. Those who had been through a lot were always more tolerant of others, she found.

But then, she might not go into anything at all about them and let it just be a natural process that Amy would find out about in her own time.

After all, to all intents and purposes, Robbie was Abe's live-in nurse and companion and she might just accept that.

Poor Abe had been badly injured in the war, losing both legs, but he got around in a wheelchair. For all that, he was active, happy and a lovely and loving man.

With this, Ruth blushed as she remembered being so in love with him in the past, and he imagining he was with her too! They'd met when she was the maid in his house and he a young man waiting to go to university. It had all happened by accident — the maid, bumping into the son on the stairs, but in that moment, something had clicked for them both. They'd been through a lot since then, but as for love, Abe had given that to Robbie from the moment she introduced them. Both men had known in a glance what their lives were truly about.

Ellen brought her out of these thoughts as she said

140

to Amy, 'In here, Amy. This is our sitting room. We'll have a nice cup of tea first, eh? You must be ready for one now.'

'I am, Ellen. All the crying has worn me out. It all still feels so strange. I can't take in how this beautiful house can belong to Ruth! I can understand you having a cottage, yer dad was rich. But Ruth! I'm so glad, though. There've been times that I've worried about yer, Ruth. I used to think of yer maybe living on the streets, or in the workhouse. Never in me wildest dreams did I see yer having anything like this. It's beautiful.'

Ruth glowed with pride. Over the last four years she'd gradually made her flat at the top of the house just how she liked it — comfy and homely, with big armchairs and a sofa with cushions stuffed with feathers that welcomed and hugged you. And polished, dark wood furniture that gave a feeling of elegance. And the colours — maybe a little theatrical reflecting her acting and singing days, and also from having Rebekah's influence in her life as she had always been surrounded by vivid colour.

This bright and airy room which was a pallet of blues — light shades of the turquoise velvet cushions, royal blue for the suite, but with some red cushions too, giving a striking contrast. These were picked up in a huge cream rug that covered most of the polished oak floor as that, too, had hues of blue, soft green and then a rich red from the roses woven into it.

But for all its grandness, it was welcoming and it warmed Ruth's heart to see Amy relax into the sofa and look as if she was at home.

Archie toddled up to her, leaned his arms on her knee and gazed up at her.

'Well, young man, will I do?'

Archie nodded. 'Aunty Amy.' Then giggled as if he found something amazing about having another aunty.

Ruth looked at Ellen and smiled. She'd paved the way for Amy in many ways as she was a lovely aunty to Archie, always having time for him and taking over a lot of his care. And now, she seemed only too pleased that Archie was helping to smooth Amy's homecoming and make it how they had planned — a joyous occasion, a uniting of them all once more and the beginning of a new life for them. Because that, Ruth thought, would complete her and bring all her worlds together — well, almost. She still had a longing to find hers and Ellen's mum and to one day be reunited with Christopher, the little boy who Ellen had witnessed their mum hand over to her dad. After all, her mum was his mum, so he was her half-brother too!

Before the war, they'd both visited the house Ellen had been banished from and had seen Christopher but hadn't been allowed near him.

So much had happened to them since that day.

Together, they had pretended to be older and to be twins so that they could go to war as Red Cross voluntary workers. Ellen had fallen in love with Bernard, a doctor working in France alongside them. She had always wanted to become a doctor and a lot of her education had been along those lines, but now, all she wanted was to be Bernard's wife — that would happen soon.

In a way, Ruth dreaded it doing so as it would mean everything would change, but life had to move on and, no matter what, she and Ellen would always be sisters — sisters in the love that bound them together.

And now, Amy was home. Truly home. Oh, how they'd all so longed for this moment.

14

Amy

Though she felt tired, Amy was loving being home and felt that she truly was too. Her welcome had been wonderful and now, as she looked around the bedroom with its single bed in the centre covered in a patchwork eiderdown with a matching pillow, the lovely polished wardrobe and dresser and the basket chair with a patchwork cushion and pretty flowing curtains that picked out the apple green in the patchwork, she felt she could believe that it really had happened — all had come right and she would never leave Ruth and Ellen again.

'It's lovely, Ruth, ta, luv . . . I can't thank you and Ellen enough for never forgetting me, as I ain't never forgotten you.'

'We know, luv. We're all going to be fine now, I promise. Let's get yer unpacked and then yer can freshen up. We've got a bathroom with a bathtub, yer know.'

'Yer haven't! Yer mean, no bloomin' getting the tub in and filling it!'

'Ha, no, none of that. Mind, the boiler's a bit dicky at times and means we have to put a lot of pans on the stove to get the water hot enough, but then, it wouldn't seem right if we didn't.'

They both laughed.

As Ruth opened Amy's case, she looked over at her. 'Well, yer've travelled light, girl!'

'I didn't need many clothes. Just housework ones and a Sunday best. Ha! I'm wearing that!'

'And lovely it is too, me darlin'. But this is nice, I like this blouse and skirt. Why don't yer have a nice bath and change into them, eh?'

Ruth held up the cream blouse that Amy loved — plain, with a navy-blue velvet ribbon threaded through and around the stand-up collar. It looked lovely with the long navy skirt in Ruth's other hand.

'You could take a few inches off this, yer know, Amy. Women are wearing their skirts just below calf-length now. We no longer sweep the floor, luv.' Again, they laughed, and Amy felt the last of the tension leave her.

A voice came to them from downstairs. 'Shall I get the tea made yet? Are you going to be long? Only there's a note from Robbie. It was standing against the teapot.'

Ruth went to the door and called out, 'Keep the tea for a moment, luv. What does the note say?'

'Robbie would like us to go down to their flat and he will cook tea for us, he says he's dying to see Amy again.'

Amy thought that Ruth's look held a question as she turned back towards her.

'I'd love that, Ruth. Be good to meet Robbie again, though I can hardly remember him as I was so young when you brought him to the gates of the orphanage that time. And I'd like to meet his flatmate ... Did yer say his name was Abe?'

'Yes ... well, Robbie's his nurse ... and, well, much more. They are a loving and lovely couple, Amy.'

'Oh? Well, I didn't expect that but ...Well, as long as they're happy ... I'm wondering when the surprises today are going to end, though, mate. Is that

145

it now?'

They giggled and Amy thought that Ruth looked relieved as she said, 'I know. So many changes for you to take in. And yer haven't said much about yer own life yet, luv. Are yer up to it? Or would it be best if yer get yer bath then come down for a cuppa, eh? I'll put Archie down for his afternoon nap.'

★ ★ ★

Feeling fresh after her bath and change of clothes, Amy felt she was able to face telling Ruth and Ellen her story, so opened her heart as she sat drinking what she thought was the very best cup of tea she'd ever had.

Everything tumbled out, though at times she had to stop. When this happened, Ruth, who was sitting on the sofa next to her, held her hand or put her arm around her.

Lucy's story had shocked and saddened them, as had Grace's, though they were glad she'd met Ivan and together they'd eventually found a good place to live and work. Telling them of Teddy and how she and he had at last declared their love brought tears, but then her time with Will, Roddy, Jack, Betty and Ivy cheered them. Though they were sad once more to hear of poor Roddy dying.

Now, with it all told, a clear mission came to her. She would find Ivan.

She'd hardly thought this when Ellen said, 'Have you any way of contacting Ivan? Do you know if he came through the war?'

'Yes, I do, Ellen. You see, he registered as living on the farm so we would have heard if he'd lost his life

146

or been injured. But he was determined to somehow stay in England, and I have his address.'

'Could he get into trouble for that? Won't it be considered that he has gone absent from the Canadian army?'

A glance passed between Ellen and Ruth that sent a shiver down Amy's spine. 'What? Is there something bad that can happen to Ivan?'

'No! It's just my concern for him . . . for you.'

'I'm thinking, I could get one of those cabs to take me to his house. I had his address as I wrote a letter to his mum for him and I've remembered it.'

'Oh, that's good. We'll come with you, won't we, Ruth?'

'Yes, we'll be by yer side, luv.'

Amy's worry deepened; it was as if they knew something she didn't. 'Can we go tomorrow?'

'In the morning we could, luv. I have to look at a shop just along this street in the afternoon and hoped yer'd come with me. I want us to get up and running with the milliner's soon, but yes, we can do both, I can leave Archie with Robbie.'

'And I am seeing Bernard in the afternoon, so, yes, we could go to Ivan's in the morning.'

'Ta, Ellen, and you, Ruth. So, yer've a shop lined up?'

'Yes, though I'm hoping to find something in Bethnal. I did well on the market there.'

Amy couldn't think how, as to her the streets she'd walked through in Bethnal spoke of poverty and overcrowding. Except the park — well, more of a green patch with a bench, really. But it had been a welcome respite.

It was Ellen who voiced this concern. 'Yes, but you

147

had to sell your work so cheaply, Ruth. You would never progress like you could selling from a shop in this area.'

'I know, but what I did think was we could have both! I could run the market stall once a week and, on that day, Amy could run the shop!'

'That's an idea. I know how you feel, it's difficult to give up your roots. You're a cockney through and through, Ruth.'

'I am . . . and, well, I think that if ever we're going to find our mum, it will be in that area.'

'Talking of finding mums, is the workhouse still on Waterloo Road?'

'It is, Amy, luv . . . but, well, your Ethel may not be there now. There was a lot of work created for women during the war and workhouse women were part of that. Ethel might be able to rent somewhere. But we'll find her, no matter what it takes, luv.'

'We will, and the workhouse is a good starting point for me, Ruth. Even if she has done what you say, there might be someone who knows where she is . . . I — I'd just like to know that she's all right.'

'We'll do that, luv, I promise, but now if you're ready, we'd better get downstairs.'

A cry of 'Mummy' came loud and clear.

'Oh-oh, someone thought we were going without him!'

When Ruth disappeared, Ellen made Amy's heart sing by asking, 'Will you be my bridesmaid, Amy? I want you and Ruth, and for Archie to be a pageboy and Robbie to give me away.'

'Oh, Ellen, luv, I would be honoured, me darlin', ta. When are yer planning yer big day?'

'Bernard wants us to get married tomorrow!' Ellen

laughed the grown-up version of the laugh that Amy remembered so well. Not that they laughed often in the orphanage, but when they got to sit on the landing of the stairs that led to the playground the three of them did have some giggles together.

'But he has so much to do.' Ellen explained how he wanted to set up his practice in the East End as he felt the people there needed him the most.

'Ruth told him about a doctor who had a penny scheme. Those that could afford it paid a penny a week and then he tended them whenever they needed him to. Those who couldn't gave this doctor whatever they could — a slice off a freshly cooked meat pie, or a jar of jam they'd made from produce they'd bought from the market. Or they offered a service, like sewing or knitting, to him. And this kindly doctor took care of them all. Bernard wants to do something like that and so do I. I could deliver their babies — not that I've done that yet, but I know from books what to do . . . What is it, Amy?'

If Amy could have taken back the involuntary gasp that had come from her, she would. She hadn't told of her baby and had vowed she wouldn't.

'I — I . . . nothing.'

Ellen came to her and went on her haunches in front of her just as she'd done when they had been in the park. 'Nothing is nothing, Amy, dear. Don't keep anything in as it can fester inside you and make you ill. I know. I was very ill — mentally so, because I had so much inside me.'

'I — I had a baby, Ellen . . . Belton put a baby in me . . . It . . . she died. I — I called her Ruth Ellen . . . It was dark, I were on me own . . . It's like it didn't happen . . . she didn't happen, but I — I loved her,

149

Ellen, I loved her!'

'Oh God, Amy!' Amy collapsed into Ellen's arms. The tug of this made her slide off the sofa. They lay together. Amy felt herself cocooned in love; Ellen could make everything right.

The door clicked open and then closed again, and she heard Ruth say, 'Oh, I forgot your bunny, Archie. You like to have your bunny with you in case Uncle Abe tells yer a story, don't yer?'

'It's all right, Amy. I've got you . . . Your baby did exist, she did. We'll honour her, dear. We'll have a service for her and make her a garden. You can plant a rose for her, eh?'

'Oh, Ellen, yes. That would make me happy. 'Cause she had a soul, didn't she? All babies have a soul. And so that she didn't go to that limbo place, I christened her in me head. God would have known that, wouldn't He?'

'He would. Oh, my Amy, why did we go through so much?'

They lay their heads together and wept.

This bonded them once more as she hadn't felt quite as close to Ellen, with her talking posh and seeming to be more changed than Ruth was. But now all the love she had for Ellen came rushing into her and she understood that it wasn't how a person spoke that made them. Ellen was still Ellen, the lovely kid she used to be.

'Oi, you two, can yer turn the taps off, please? I've a young son here who can't wait to come back in to see yer both. I think he's had enough emotion for one day, me darlin's.'

They both sat up. 'Sorry, Ruth. Something came up and made us both cry.'

'Well, it will keep happening. Yer can tell me about it later, eh? I'm always here for both of yer.'

With this they both dried their eyes and got up off the floor with Ellen saying, 'Taps are off, Ruth!'

They both giggled.

But though they did, the ache in Amy didn't go away. It was soothed a little by Ellen's suggestion, though, and she couldn't wait to do that. It would be like honouring her little Ruth Ellen and putting her soul to rest.

★ ★ ★

Robbie hugged her like a long-lost friend, which surprised Amy, but pleased her and made her feel welcome.

'I've cooked a good old cockney favourite, Amy. Pie, mash and liquor!'

'And he makes the best liquor — yer'll not have tasted any better, luv.' Ruth smiled as she said this and, in the words, Amy could hear her love for Robbie and see it in the hug he gave her.

Archie had run to Abe and sat on his knee. 'Read to me and Bunny, Abe.'

'Not yet, Archie, that's later. I've brought your nightshirt down with me, so I'll bath yer after tea and then yer can have a story and go to sleep on Robbie's bed.'

'And Abe's bed!'

Ruth glanced at Amy. Amy nodded.

'Yes, and Abe's bed. Now, can I give yer a hand, Robbie?'

Robbie had smiled a relieved smile at Amy. 'No, but Amy can. Come on, luv, this way to the kitchen.'

As much as the living room they'd been in was very masculine with two tan-coloured leather wing-backed chairs and a dark brown sofa, with a cream rug in front of the fireplace, in contrast, the kitchen was cosy, with a range and a deep pot sink with a yellow gingham curtain hanging around it, and matching ones at the window above it. Through the window above the sink, she could see a courtyard with pots that held flowers and bushes. There was a vase of flowers on the scrubbed table, and a matching enamel bread bin, tea caddy and biscuit barrel on the sideboard, with a lovely flowered teapot, sugar bowl and milk jug standing next to them. Amy loved it.

As she did the delicious smell coming from the oven.

'I've mashed the spuds and they're in the oven, keeping warm with the pie, luv. So it's just the liquor to make now.'

'Not gravy?'

'No! Call yerself a cockney! Bloody gravy . . . Never heard of pie, mash and liquor, dear?'

The way he said this made Amy giggle. 'Heard of it and nearly made it once, but never had it.'

'Well, yer ain't lived at all, luv, but that'll soon change. Oh, I know we live in this posh area now, but we ain't left our roots behind. This house is little East End as me and Ruth have kept it so. We love our pie and mash and go to Bethnal as often as we can . . . though we've lost most of our mates from there now. They were all getting on, but they were family: Rebekah, Bett, Ruby, Reg, who was killed at the Somme, Irish Mick — he died a long time ago — and Ted. He was in the orchestra at the theatre. He rose from playing on the streets and begging, but the flu got him, poor

152

bloke . . . But we've got each other and now you're back with us, and that's all that counts.'

'It is . . . Yer know, I can't remember much about yer, Robbie, and yet I feel as though I've known yer all me life.'

Robbie turned towards her and opened his arms. She went into them. 'That's good, Amy, luv, as we orphan kids have to look out for one another. Yer've got a friend in me, mate.'

'Ta, Robbie, and you in me.'

As he released her, he said, 'I take it yer know about me and me Abe?'

'I do, and I'm happy for yer both. Happy that yer've a safe place to be and that yer can be yerself here.'

With this he flapped his arm. 'We can that, darlin'.'

This made her giggle again. Robbie laughed with her as he set about making the liquor, a kind of parsley sauce.

'You stir that, Amy, while I dish up the pie and mash. We've a dining room through that door. I've set the table, so I'll just give the rest of them the nod to make their way through and sit down.'

The dinner was delicious, and the easy chatter helped Amy to relax and to just see Robbie and Abe as friends, lovely friends she felt comfortable and happy with.

This changed as Abe asked, 'So, Amy, was Canada an adventure?'

The room hushed. As Abe looked from one to the other, his face coloured. Amy hated seeing him uncomfortable, so answered in as normal a voice as she could muster after suddenly being put on the spot. 'You could say that — it had its ups and downs, but a lot of it was all right . . . It was just me yearning

153

to be home with me mates that marred it and how we were looked on as nothing more than servants, either of the land or domestic type. Though I dropped lucky in the end and made some good mates among other home children.'

'Home children? Is that what they called you? It sounds rather nice, like children of the motherland.'

'Put like that, it does, but mostly we were looked down on and well . . . sort of clumped together as being of a type.'

'Oh, I see. That puts a different light on things. What was the country like, though, all snow-capped mountains and farms?'

Amy thought for a moment. In a way, this did sum up Canada, but didn't give a picture of its breath-taking beauty. 'Where I was, almost every way you turned the sight took your breath away — towering mountains, shimmering, huge lakes, dark green forests, patchwork fields, gold with wheat, or white with the blossom of the fruit trees. It were like a painting. I never got used to it as it seemed to be forever changing. What were sad was that it belonged to the original tribes of Canada — the Mississaugas were the ones in Ontario — but was taken from them by settlers. The young Mississaugas, like Maskwa and his wife, Catori, now have to eke out a living by hunting and selling the beautiful blankets woven by the women, or jackets made from the hide of animals. They also work the land, but for a pittance from the settlers who have built up rich farms.'

As she came to the end, all were staring at her in wonderment. For the first time, she could look on her being taken to Canada as an experience, something none of these had had, or probably ever would have.

154

Somehow, she felt privileged, and it was a nice feeling — much better than the way she had looked on it all till now.

'Wow, yer met Red Indians, like them in the western films?'

'I did, Robbie, but they ain't red and they think of themselves as being native Canadians, not Indians.'

'What are they like?'

Amy told them all she knew of Maskwa and in the telling found herself missing him and Catori. All were amazed at how they helped her and took care of her when she found herself adrift, though she didn't tell the real reason she'd run away, just that she'd become very unhappy, and that her problems were sorted out when she returned to the farm, and how happily they were. 'Only, I lost me Teddy to the war.'

This made the mood a little sombre, and Amy felt sad about this. She sought to lighten it by saying to Robbie, 'Anyway, yer've a tale to tell that beats mine. Ruth tells me yer famous on the stage. I'd love to go to see yer one day.'

'Yer can, and as me guest, Amy.'

Ruth, who hadn't spoken for a long time, piped up, 'Let's have a good old cockney sing-song now, eh, Robbie?'

It was a scurry then as they all pitched in to clear the table and wash the pots. Even Abe and Archie helped. As knives and forks were put on a tray in front of Abe, he dried and polished them then handed them to Archie who put them in the bottom of a chest of drawers. Amy thought for a moment that this was a funny place for the cutlery, but then realized that it had been especially planned that way so that Abe could get to them if in on his own.

Back in the living room the singing started with a song from Robbie, and then one from Ruth, which sent Amy's heart soaring, then they were all singing, 'Down at the Old Bull and Bush' and Amy felt her cockney roots seeping back into her — pie, mash and liquor, and then a good old sing-song. She smiled to herself as she thought, *Nothing speaks more of the East End than this!*

15

Ellen

Ellen felt more and more at peace as the days went by. Amy was settling in so well, though had postponed finding Ivan. She and Ruth hadn't questioned her as to why. This mission she had to find him was personal to her, and they thought to leave the timing to her, but to support her when she did decide to go.

It had concerned Ellen that whilst at first Amy had seemed to fall into an easy rapport with Ruth, with herself it had seemed she found it more difficult to relax and relate. But she'd been patient about it. After all, Ruth had been like a big sister and mum rolled into one for both her and Amy.

But now, she and Amy were as if no time had passed with them being parted. They had sat together chatting for long hours — Amy had even come into her bed one night after she'd been woken by a nightmare. They'd squeezed up close as if they were still kids, but grown women or not, this had sealed them back into being how they had been with each other in the orphanage.

Amy had asked Ellen to tell Ruth about her child. She felt the emotion of doing so herself would be unbearable.

Ruth, as only Ruth could, had helped Amy with her presence and her love and kindness. She'd prayed to Holy Mary with Amy and had taken up the idea of

157

having a service for the soul of Amy's little lost baby, Ruth Ellen, saying, like Ellen had, that she was honoured the baby had been named after her.

Ruth planned to ask the preacher of the chapel that had become a big part of her life when she lived with Rebekah and was now part of Ellen's too if he would hold a service for Ruth Ellen.

The chapel's preacher was a priest from St Nicholas the Great Church. He conducted special services that were very lively with the congregation mainly made up of the African community, interacting, singing, clapping and dancing in the aisle. Ellen found her spirits soared whenever she attended as the joy everyone showed in celebrating God swept you along.

And for Ellen to have been able to be the main benefactor of a soup kitchen in the chapel that had started up during the war and was still needed today made her feel proud. She and Ruth had both been involved with the practical running of it at different times with Ebony, a niece of the late Rebekah.

Ellen sighed. It would seem strange to go there and not to see Bett. Bett, who Ruth had looked on as a mum, and who'd been very kind to Ellen, had been the organizer of the volunteers, whilst the lovely Ebony, an amazing cook, had overseen the kitchen. Her stews were famous among the needy, but then it wasn't surprising as Ebony did run a successful restaurant with her husband, Abdi. The sound of a car hooter interrupted these thoughts. Ellen's heart raced as this meant Bernard was here.

She stopped on her way to the door to check her appearance in the mirror, tucking a stray curl under the lovely silver-grey silk hat Ruth had made for her. It matched the leaves of the same colour that formed a pattern on the collar of her dark blue wool coat, which she put over her arm for now, knowing she was bringing Bernard in to meet Amy before they went out to dinner.

One last check in the mirror and she was happy. Her light-blue frock, which had a baggy bodice, three-quarter sleeves, a belt that pulled in her waist, and a pleated skirt, looked just right for their dinner date.

The frock was one of several items of clothing she'd bought on a shopping trip after being home from France for a week as all the clothes she had suddenly seemed dowdy and dated against the new fashions seen everywhere.

Ruth had encouraged her, telling her that she'd done the same once she'd regained her figure after having Archie. To Ellen, Ruth always looked lovely — elegant, with her long dark hair held back behind her ears with hairpins and her beautiful big brown eyes. It had always pleased her that she and Ruth had easily passed themselves off as twins during the war.

Running downstairs, just as the door knocker rattled, Ellen opened the door and almost jumped into Bernard's arms. He held her to him.

Happiness zinged through her. She loved everything about Bernard: his lovely thick fair hair and hazel eyes and how handsome he looked when serious — which often he was, being a dedicated doctor. And yet how boyish he appeared when he grinned. She'd fallen for him the moment she'd first set eyes on him when she and Ruth had arrived in the Ypres hospital in 1915. Together they had all been through so much — saved lives, lost many, but always doing their best for the wounded no matter if they were friend or foe. And

159

with the other medical staff, they had always honoured the dead as they made sure that someone from the hospital attended the graveside to represent them all.

A shudder went through her.

Bernard's hug tightened around her. 'I know. It happens to me every time I see you too, darling — memories flood me.'

Wanting to reassure him, Ellen told him, 'They will fade, I promise, my love. The main thing is that we remember we did all we could, and now we deserve the happiness we have. We will never forget them.'

'We won't, darling. Especially when the poppies bloom. Do you remember the beautiful sight of them covering the fields in Flanders and growing over the soldiers' graves? And now next month on November the eleventh it will be the first Remembrance Day and the poppy is to be the emblem.'

As they came out of the hug, Ellen told Bernard that she thought that a wonderful tribute. 'Changing the subject, darling, Amy is a little nervous at meeting you, but cannot wait.'

'I feel the same. I'm really looking forward to meeting the last of the girls from the orphanage who have all meant so much to one another. I think it is an amazing story how you were all determined to be with each other again and now you are, my darling.'

'It seemed impossible at times. Even me finding Ruth. But Amy! When I knew she'd been shipped to Canada, I didn't ever give up hope of finding her and bringing her home, but never thought it possible to do so.'

They were at the top of the stairs when Ellen felt her own nerves kick in. She so wanted Amy to love

160

Bernard. She needn't have worried. Amy was changing by the day, growing in strength and confidence and it was lovely to see her smile as she told Bernard how much she'd looked forward to meeting the man who'd made Ellen so happy. She even offered her cheek for a kiss. Ellen's heart warmed. She wanted all the people she loved to love each other too.

After a chat and Bernard playing for a little while with Archie, Ellen donned her coat.

'Now your hat makes sense, Ellen. You look lovely, darling.'

Ellen did a twirl for Bernard and giggled as she did. 'I have the best hatmaker in the business at my beck and call!'

Ruth giggled at this. 'There'll soon be two of us, as I just know Amy will take to it.'

'Have you found your shop yet, Ruth?' Bernard asked.

'Yes. We looked at one the other day. Just up the road, which is very convenient, and it doesn't need a lot doing to it. I need to put up shelves, and buy hat stands for the window display, but mostly I need to get all of my hat-making kit fitted into the back room, which is a good size to take it all. And there's a kitchen next to it and another room which will be useful for storage.'

'I'll give you a hand with any lifting and would enjoy doing it. I'm at a loose end at the moment.'

This surprised Ellen as she'd thought him to be really busy looking for somewhere to set up his general practice surgery and taking the necessary exams to gain his registration. But she didn't take him up on it as Ruth gratefully accepted any help he could offer.

'We get the keys next week and'll be glad of your

help, mate, ta. Mind, it won't be easy with me treadle machine, so I'll arrange to move it when Robbie's about to help you. He don't usually go to the theatre till midday.'

Outside in the car, Bernard leaned forward to tuck the blanket he always kept for her around her knees. 'I — I have to talk to you, darling. There's been a hitch to me starting up my practice.'

'Oh, Bernard, no! I thought it was all going to be so easy and we could soon plan our wedding.'

'I know. Let's get to the restaurant, darling, then I'll put you in the picture.'

* * *

Once they'd ordered — a Parma ham and melon starter, salmon en croute with new potatoes for their main course and a crème brûlée for sweet, they sipped the lovely crisp, cold French white wine.

Bernard's actions seemed precise as he took his napkin and shook it out, and then placed it on his knee. A sign that he was nervous too. 'What is it, darling? Are your plans not working out?'

'No, they're halted in a big way. Frederick is proving to be very difficult.'

Ellen tensed even more. She'd never liked Bernard's brother Frederick. She'd met him before she'd met Bernard. He was a womanizer and, not knowing how young she was, had made a play for her assuming that she would fall at his feet as every woman he gave the eye to seemed to. He was arrogant too. 'Frederick? How can he affect your plans, darling?'

'It's our father's fault. He left Frederick the power over me where finances are concerned. He never got

162

over me wanting to become a doctor. He funded my training, but with great reluctance as he wanted us both to go into the family law firm. It seemed almost spite when his will was read. Though he'd left us both equal amounts, Frederick was to be in charge of the purse strings and I to go cap in hand to him whenever I need funds — that is until I am thirty-five, when my share, or what is left of it, is to be handed over to me to use as I wish.'

'And Frederick is refusing you your own money, why?'

'He says that whilst father was reluctant about my chosen profession, once he gave in, he had ambitions for me becoming a top surgeon of repute. Frederick believes that I should pay father back by doing that . . . but I don't want to, darling. I've had enough blood and gore during the war to last me a lifetime. I just want to help those who cannot always get medical help. I want to be that doctor who has a penny insurance going for poor families, or accepts a pot of jam for treatment, and yet charge the rich a good amount for my services to compensate. I want to relieve the pain of earache, or tummy bugs, not cut people up — but recognize when they need operations and help them to get them from those who want that kind of career and will give their time to the poor amongst us . . . You understand, don't you, Ellen?'

'I do. Oh, I do, darling. Look how my own ambition to be a doctor has changed. Now I just want us to be married and for me to assist you.'

'We will be like two doctors working side by side, but if ever you change your mind and want to become qualified, I will support you all the way, Ellen.'

'I know that, and it is what helps me so much with

163

my decision — that the door isn't closed. But like you, I just want to help those who are so often left to fall ill and die when they could be saved.'

Bernard looked downcast. 'Well, that seems to be a non-starter with Frederick's present attitude.'

'It needn't be. I have my house in Leeds. I am going to put it up for sale, and with the proceeds and what I have in the bank, we can still do it, darling, we can!'

'I couldn't ask that of you, Ellen, my dear. That is your future security . . .'

'I want no other security than to be with you. To work alongside you and to make your dreams, and so my own, come true. Please say yes, Bernard . . . We are as one. None of us have anything that doesn't belong to the other. But will it be enough? How much does it take to set up a general practice?'

'Not a great deal. But I need to buy or rent a house to register the practice to. I have my flat of course, I could sell that too. Even in the East End houses are a lot more to buy than you would get for a cottage up in the north, or if we rented, we would still need lots of capital to keep us going till we got on our feet.'

'But if we combine our assets, and maybe get a loan?'

'I don't think we would get a loan. You see, you need a job, or collateral. I won't have either until I set up the practice and then it will be me employing me. That's not security for a bank.'

'Maybe take a hospital job . . . I know you don't want to, and I don't want you to, but we could marry still and live in your apartment for a while. I could sell my cottage and get a job. We could then put all our assets in a bank as a joint account, and when we have a hefty deposit, apply for a loan to buy a house with.

164

After we have, we can then register it as a doctor's practice.'

'Oh, Ellen, I don't know where you get your amazing brain from . . . but would you do all of that for me?'

'For us, darling. For our future. And I owe all my knowledge to the wonderful Adrian . . . I miss him so much. He was a tutor in a million, Bernard. I so wish you could have met him.'

'I do too, though I did know of him. He and Frederick were at school together and were friends so I met Adrian, and I am knowing more about him through Archie. Everyone says he is like his father.'

Of course, Ellen had forgotten that it was Adrian who introduced the horrid Frederick to her but she didn't say so.

'Talking of Archie, Ellen, we must make sure to help and encourage Ruth to see that Archie gets the best education to bring out the potential he is showing.'

'Oh, she will. She has this fund that's for Archie's education. Adrian's aunt — the one who gave the house to Adrian — started it with a good amount she left in her will for him, but Ruth adds to it whenever she can.'

'Does she have enough income to do that?'

'She does. She has a good rent from Abe and Robbie, who both insist on paying the going rate, as do I as a lodger. Well, I know I am her sister, but I wouldn't let her refuse to let me contribute to the household costs. And she has what she has been making from selling her hats to various outlets.'

'I'm so glad you're helping her to set up for herself, she will make so much more money doing that and it's well deserved as her talent is amazing . . . Oh, that

165

plan won't be jeopardized if I agree to your ideas for our future, will it?'

'No. I have already put the money into an account that is held jointly with Ruth for our business venture, though I am only to be a sleeping partner. I can stitch humans, but hats, no good at that!'

This made them giggle and Ellen was glad it did. She wanted tonight to be a happy one. She'd thought they would finalize so much — their wedding, the starting of the practice — now it all seemed up in the air.

'You're wonderful, darling.'

'So, you think my ideas for us could work?'

'I do. It will delay things and put me back into the blood and gore situation, but we all have to make sacrifices for what we want.'

'Your sacrifice will mean you are saving lives, Bernard. You are a brilliant surgeon and though I agree that your future lies in general practice, you will be a big loss to that field.'

Bernard pushed his empty starter plate away — they'd both finished the course but, Ellen thought, without really tasting it.

She took his outstretched hands and thrilled at the look in his eyes as he said, 'Marry me very soon, my darling. I need . . . I want to make you mine.'

Ellen quashed the fear that lit inside her. Prayed that the moment would be like Ruth said it was for her — a final goodbye to the horrific memory of being a child and of being used by the depraved Belton.

'Darling? Are you all right? You want that too, don't you . . . Oh, my darling, I didn't think . . . what you told me . . . I — I . . . It will be all right, Ellen, my love. We need never be intimate, or, at least, not until you are ready. I will never demand anything from you. I just want us to be together, my darling.'

Ellen shook the thoughts from her. 'I do, I do want you so much, Bernard, my love. It will be all right. I know it will. You may just need a little patience . . . Ruth . . . Oh, I shouldn't say . . .'

'Only tell me what you are comfortable telling me, Ellen.'

Suddenly she felt she could tell him — wanted to, wanted to give him and herself hope. 'Ruth told me that what she experienced with Adrian wasn't anything like what happened to us as children. She said it was so wonderful it took away all memory of that time, like wiping a slate that held dirt and filling it with beauty . . . I want that for me . . . for us, Bernard.'

'It will be like that, I promise. But we can take our time. Let's plan the wedding and leave all of that to take its course. Don't let it be a worry to you. It will never be something to fear. It will bind us together in the same beauty that Ruth told you of, I promise.'

Ellen felt all doubt leave her. 'I want to marry now, right here!'

Bernard laughed, but as soon as the waiter had taken their plates and delivered their meal, he leaned forward and took her hand. 'Ellen, I marry you. I give myself to you. I will be faithful to you until death do us part. You are my wife, my love, my everything.'

Tears came into Ellen's eyes. She smiled into his and saw they too were watery. 'I love you, Bernard, and from this moment on, I am your wife.'

With the words, her heart, her soul, her very being, had a purpose much deeper than it had ever had. 'May I come back to yours to begin our honeymoon, darling?'

Bernard looked quizzically at her, then a smile lit his face. 'You may, Mrs Holbeck. For that's who you are now, darling.'

For a moment she gazed deep into his eyes — a moment that gave her the knowledge that she could trust him to be the mainstay of her life — the person who was going to take her away from the horror of her childhood memories. Her saviour — *the love of my life.*

✱ ✱ ✱

When they reached his apartment, a second-floor dwelling a few streets away from Ruth's house, Ellen had no doubts visit her. In the eyes of them both, they were man and wife. Yes, they would need to make it legal and have a proper wedding ceremony, but that was for others to justify them being together. They didn't need that justification, just the vows they had exchanged which were precious to them.

Ellen knew what they both needed was to put their demons out of their lives — their coming together would do that.

As soon as they entered the tiny hall, Bernard leaned the starter handle to his car against the hall stand and took Ellen into his arms. 'My darling, I love you. I love you so much.'

His passion alighted hers. Clinging together, they made their way through his large living room. There, he threw kindling onto the embers of a dying fire in the grate. It leaped to life, giving Ellen the thought that Bernard had done that to her — sent sparks of joy through her just as those of the fire spat out their joy too. Adding a log, he soon had a blazing fire that welcomed and warmed them.

168

Then his kisses rekindled her fire too, and seemed to burn into her soul as his hands undressed her, caressing each part that became exposed, telling her how beautiful she was.

Ellen rode the wave of her emotions. Kissed him back, pulled at his tie to loosen it, discarded it and began to undo the buttons of his shirt. They hugged, paused to help each other with difficult garments, wondered at each other's beauty, and whispered words of love.

When he lowered her onto the cosy rug in front of the flames and came down to kneel beside her and hold her, he whispered, 'Are you sure, my darling?'

Ellen could only nod. Her throat had constricted. Her breathing came in gasps. She reached out her arms and accepted his naked body to entwine with her own — accepted him inside her and knew in that moment the ecstasy of love. The wiping away of all hurts, the undoing of her, and then the building her once more and the completion of her. This joy, this burning desire had been given to her by Bernard, and she would give the same back to him.

Then it happened. A feeling took her that she almost wanted to deny — knew it would lay her soul bare. Heard her own hollers, felt herself give all she had as wave after wave of sheer elation took her to a place she had never dreamed existed as Bernard's moans mingled with hers, joining them for ever.

16

Ruth

'Well, did you make final arrangements for your wedding last night, Ellen?'

Seeing the blush that swept over Ellen's face, Ruth smiled at her. Only one thing could have made Ellen look even more beautiful at this moment than she already was. Ruth opened her arms to her. 'Oh, Ellen, I'm so happy for you.'

'You've guessed? And you don't think me wicked?'

'No. Did you think me wicked when it happened to me?'

'Oh, Ruth, I'm sorry . . . so deeply sorry that you lost lovely Adrian as soon as you'd sealed your love.'

'I know, luv, but don't let that mar your moment. I only hope it was all that mine was to me.'

'It was. Oh, Ruth, I feel as though I have been taken out of a dungeon and put down in a beautiful garden.'

'You have, my lovely Ellen. You have, luv. Everything will be all right for you now . . . Yes, I know you have been well in your mind for a long time after your awful breakdown, but this completes that healing for you.'

'It does. I'm whole again, Ruth.'

They hugged. Ruth couldn't deny the sadness that made her heart heavy. *Oh, Adrian, Adrian, you did this for me, but it was only to be the once. I love and miss you so much.*

Ellen pulled away. 'You sobbed, Ruth . . . Oh, my

dear, I didn't mean to bring your pain alive.'

'You didn't, luv. It has never lessened, I have just learned to live with it. The loss of Adrian is still very raw.'

They clung to each other for a moment, then Ruth held Ellen at arm's length and grinned through her tears. 'We'd better get yer wed, girl, and quick!'

They both giggled at this and for Ruth her world steadied again.

'We've decided on a register office wedding, Ruth. Bernard is applying for a licence today.'

This shocked Ruth as she'd dreamed of a church wedding for Ellen and had thought that was what she'd wanted.

'You're disappointed.'

'No, no, luv. I'm happy with whatever you and Bernard want, me darlin'.'

'Well, it isn't what we want, but a necessity. You see . . .'

Ruth listened as Ellen told her how their circumstances had changed and how they planned to make things happen .....

'You will still be my bridesmaid, Ruth. You and Amy, and you'll both be our witnesses, too. Abe, we hope, will consent to being best man. As you know, Bernard and he knew each other at school, and because of what his brother has done he doesn't want to ask him — not even to attend the wedding! And I'm going to ask Robbie to give me away.'

'Oh, Ellen, all the help you've given to others and now you have to scale down your own dream.'

'Only the trimmings of the first part, and only delay the second part. We will get our dream but we have to work harder to achieve it.'

171

'Look, I don't want you to even think about backing me in me shop. You keep all you have so that yer dream happens sooner, luv.'

'No, Ruth, I couldn't do that. You're so close to your dream. I couldn't snatch that way from you.'

'You wouldn't be. I can still get there . . . Robbie has asked me to consider going back on the stage. He's been offered a season at Canterbury Music Hall in Lambeth, if he has a partner, as they want a duo singing and dancing and comedy act.'

'And you want to do it?'

'Yes, I do, luv . . . Oh, I know, it's a complete turn-around, as I gave up the dream of being on the stage, but I can do both the hat making and the stage work! And the extra money will mean I can be independent of you . . . I mean, free your money up.'

'Ha, I know what you mean. But will you manage?'

'I will. I just know I will. But if I do have to have help, it will only be a loan. Yer have to agree to that, Ellen, mate. It's only right and proper . . . Look, the rent on the shop isn't much. I have the money I intend to invest in me business and that will pay for a year. I've enough stock in the attic to fill the shelves to begin with. And, with Amy's help — she tells me she is good at sewing — I can increase that stock to really keep us going. Me only problem might come if I get a lot of orders — special hats in colours I haven't got — then it will only be time that will be a problem as I have enough material to make every hat in every colour, even dowdy ones. But we can cross that bridge when, and if, we get to it. Me music hall commitment will be rehearsals for an hour a day and then three evenings a week. I have Amy to take care of Archie while I'm out in the evening, and he can come to the shop with us

172

during the day . . . that is, until he starts school.'

'Oh, Ruth, it all sounds doable, if a lot of hard work for you . . . So, you have thought about school for Archie, then? What plans have you, love?'

'I'm thinking of that kindergarten at the end of the road, the one in the end house on the corner. Have yer seen it?'

'Yes, it looks good.'

'That's just it, I know it looks good, and the kids all look smart, but that's all I know, and . . . well, with me cockney way of talking, I'm afraid to go along and ask about it . . . what their terms are, and what the kids need and even if I can get Archie in or not . . . Only, well, Adrian's son deserves a good education. I know he's a clever kid and can go far . . . I have the money too.'

'I know, love . . . Look, I'll go with you and open the conversation, eh? There shouldn't be any snobbery, but we both know it exists. If it does in this school, then it isn't the right one for Archie, it will stifle him . . . You don't think you have enough to engage a tutor, do you?'

'Yes, I think so. Adrian's aunt left plenty for Archie's education, but I don't want what happened to you — for Archie never to have the company of other children, only adults.'

'I don't think that will happen. Me and Bernard want a family.'

Ruth was shocked then to hear Ellen, the quiet and proper one of the three of them, come out with what she said next: 'We've made a start already!'

They both burst out laughing. This brought Amy through the door. Ruth greeted her with, 'Hello, sleepy head.'

Amy laughed. 'I've a lot of catching up to do. What's amused you both? You woke me up!'

'Hmm . . . I think I'll leave that one to Ellen.' Ruth grinned at Ellen as she said this, not feeling a bit guilty about putting her on the spot.

'I — I . . .'

'You've set the day and sealed it with a kiss . . . Oh, Ellen, it's more than that, ain't it? Anyone can see a mile off what yer've been up to, girl!' At Ellen's wide grin, Amy laughed. 'Naughty you, but I'm glad for yer. Love can heal a lot. I hope it does for you, Ellen.'

'It has, Amy.' Ellen opened her arms to Amy, who ran into them. Ruth felt her heart swell with happiness to see Ellen and Amy locked in a hug of love, when there were days she'd thought she'd never see either of them again. Now they were here, in her own front room.

And, she thought, it was a measure of their love for each other how they shared their most intimate of secrets. For Amy, it was still to happen for her to discover the real meaning of love, but for herself and Ellen too, it had happened and could never be taken away from them.

When they sat down to breakfast, they told Amy what they had been talking about.

'I think it will be fine, Ellen, me and Ruth will manage. You have to follow your dream, luv.'

'Thanks, Amy. I don't want to do it and it was Ruth's suggestion, not mine, but it would help. Every little thing will help, but that's to get the practice, not for my wedding. That's going to happen very soon. Bernard will tell me when tonight . . . So, ladies, we need to sort out wedding outfits.'

'We'll make them.' At her saying this, Ruth saw

Ellen's mouth drop open.

'What? I know you're talented at making hats, Ruth, and can make them for the wedding, but frocks?'

'Yes, Ellen. Frocks! I learned a lot from Rebekah. I've never been drawn to making them, but that don't mean I can't.'

'And I'm not bad, I'm a good seamstress as it happens. I reckon me and Ruth can save yer a lot of money making all the outfits.'

'And we can come back here for the wedding breakfast.'

'Oh yes, Ruth, let's. I've so many dishes yer've never heard of. Me flapper pie is a must.'

'Flapper pie, Amy, what's that?'

'It's a Canadian pudding, Ellen, like a custard tart but better and just lovely.'

'Well, that'll be grand, as my lovely Dilly used to say.'

'Dilly? Who's Dilly then, Ellen?'

'I'll tell you about her. She was a northern lady, from Leeds. So lovely. I miss her every day, though I like to think of her with my gran in heaven and the pair of them chuntering on.'

'Chuntering?'

'Ha, another northern saying, Ruth. It means having a chinwag . . . chatting.'

'Ah, that's a lovely thought. Dilly and your gran were lovely.'

To answer Amy's questioning face, Ruth told her, 'Ellen's gran. You know, Ellen told yer her gran looked after her since she was eleven, till she left Leeds to come to live with me? Dilly was Gran's companion-cum-housekeeper. They were such lovely, kind people.'

'They were, Ruth, thank you.'

'What's having a gran like, Ellen?'

Ruth felt the pity of this from Amy. She didn't know for herself what it was like to have any family until she and Ellen discovered they were half-sisters, so she knew how heartfelt the question was.

'A privilege is the best word for it, Amy. I knew a love that you and Ruth have never known ... but I also know what it's like to have a father who doesn't love you, and to know of your brother, but him not to know of you. All are as painful as not knowing who your family are.'

'Well, I think we should put all of that right.' Ruth saw the look of astonishment they both gave her at this bold statement, but she carried on. 'We've all talked of finding our mums — me and you share the same one, but yours is out there somewhere too, Amy. That woman at the workhouse, she might know who yer mum is. Yer were taken there as a baby — why? Why, when I were left with a priest like you, but I were taken straight to the orphanage ... Did the nuns know yer mum were in the workhouse? It's a possibility. And our mum, Ellen. We know what she looks like ... I know it's been almost ten years since yer saw her in that cafe, but she couldn't have changed that much. We also know she was a prostitute, might still be, and we know that Bett's sons knew where she was at one time. Maybe they still do.'

'But they're gangsters, Ruth, we can't go to them.'

'Robbie can. Robbie knows all sorts. He told me once that he'd met Bett's sons — he also told me the reason they'd never married. They're like Robbie and Abe. Robbie could approach them and ask for us. And what about our brother? Well, your brother, my

176

half-brother. Christopher. He'll be about twelve now. We could try to see him again.'

'Yes, you're right, Ruth. What do you think, Amy? We're all longing to know our mums, but do nothing about finding them . . . Oh, if only we could find ours, Ruth, and before my wedding day.'

Amy sat wide-eyed. 'Do yer really think Ethel might know me mum, Ruth?'

'It's a possibility. And what about Ivan? You haven't mentioned him since just after yer got here, and yet yer said he was like a brother to yer. Well, I know what that feels like, as Abe and Robbie are that to me, and my life is richer for having them in it.'

'Yer right, Ruth . . . Let's do it. Let's try to find our mums, and let's go and find Ivan. He may need care. What have I been thinking of putting off finding him when I promised him I would if ever I got home?'

'That's the spirit. But don't be too hard on yerself, mate, yer've had a lot of adjusting to do.'

'Yes, I have struggled at times. It's . . . well, all of it is overwhelming, finding you both, fitting into yer lives. I mean, it's been the best thing to happen to me, but it were like it was all I could cope with. But I am ready now — ready to find out who me mum was, and to find Ivan.'

'Right, now the three of us are of the same mind, let's make a start. I'll go and talk to Robbie about asking Bett's sons . . . Get yer coats, girls, and bring mine down. We're going to Waterloo Road workhouse as the workhouse is a good place to start.'

★ ★ ★

177

The workhouse building looked drab and daunting. Ruth felt a shudder go through her as she looked up at its three storeys. She glanced over at Amy. 'Do yer remember much about it, Amy?'

'Yes. I know it looks dingy and like it houses a lot of horror, but the folk when I were here helped each other as much as they could.'

'I'm glad it don't have bad memories . . . Well, what do we do now?'

It was Ellen who answered. 'Knock on the door, I suppose, and ask for Ethel . . . Do you have a surname, Amy?'

'I think it was Thomas, or Thompson, something like that.'

With no more of a to-do, Ellen went through the gate and knocked on the door. Ruth felt nervous now she was here and was glad Ellen was taking the lead. She hoped with all her heart that they would find Ethel. It would be lovely for Amy if they did.

'What do yer want? What yer doing 'ere?'

The man who poked his head around the door looked scary. His black eyes were sunken deep into his dark, wrinkled sockets. His hair was a bright ginger. His teeth, yellow and protruding, looked huge. He looked taken aback as he stared at Ruth. Then his expression changed to one of fear. 'Go away!'

'I'm looking for Ethel Thomas.'

'Ethel? What's the likes of you want with Ethel? Yer should leave 'er alone, she don't do no one no harm.'

Amy stepped forward. 'She's me mate. I were here when I were a youngster and Ethel looked after me. I've come to see her to see if I can help her.'

The man pointed his thumb at Ruth. 'What about 'er?'

178

'She's me mate. The three of us were in the orphanage together. Her name's Ruth and this is Ellen.'

'What's your name? I never forget a name.'

'Amy. I don't know me surname but were given the name Smith.'

The man opened the door wider. The rest of him was just as weird-looking, as his body was stick thin, his hands bony, with long fingers and over long, filthy fingernails. He had a slight hump on his back.

'I remember. So, yer don't know me too then?'

'No, sorry, I can't remember yer.'

'Well, I'm Cyril. Ethel ain't been the same since yer left. She fell ill and her mind went. She's been looking in every nook and cranny for yer ever since they made her take yer away.'

'Please let me see her. I don't mean any harm. She loved me and I loved her. I've never forgotten her, mate.'

The door opened with a scraping sound as if a stone had caught under it. 'It's not up to me, but as I know it will make Ethel 'appy, I could sneak yer in. Not all three of yer. Maybe two.'

'You go with Amy, Ruth. I'll wait here with Archie . . . We passed a park up the road, I'll take him there.'

Ruth could see the fear in Ellen. 'All right, luv. Don't worry. I'll go . . . Come on, Amy, luv.'

As they followed Cyril through what seemed a long dark tunnel, up some stairs and along a lighter and airier corridor, Amy and Ruth held hands.

Ruth could feel that Amy's was clammy in hers.

'In 'ere. It's what they call the infirmary. Most are sick in their minds. Ethel is, but she ain't bad enough to be in the loony bin. It will do her good seeing yer,

Amy. Be the making of 'er.'

The room looked like a hospital ward with rows and rows of beds. Women sat beside them, staring into space, or fidgeting or pulling at their clothes. Sitting next to the second bed was a woman with mousy-coloured hair, just like Amy's. She stared ahead of her, not even looking towards the door as they entered.

'Ethel, luv . . . Ethel, I've some good news for yer.'

Ethel looked up. Caught sight of Amy. Amy ran forward. 'It's me, Ethel . . . Amy. I'm back. Oh, Ethel, I'm back.'

Amy held out her arms. Ethel did the same. Amy flung herself into Ethel's. 'Oh, Ethel, luv, yer remember me!'

''Course I do, luv. Where yer been? Are yer all right? Yer look lovely. Not changed, just grown . . . Oh, Amy, me little Amy.'

Amy sat on the bed. 'This is me mate, Ruth.'

Ethel's face changed. Her eyes opened wide. Her body cringed.

'It's all right, Ethel. We were in the orphanage together, but then we lost each other as I were sent to Canada, but Ruth and me other mate, Ellen, they got me home again. You've no need to be afraid.'

Ethel smiled. It was a smile Ruth had seen on Amy's face many times. Instinctively, she knew Amy had found her mum.

'Oh, me Amy. Me Amy. I've looked and looked for yer . . . They think me mad in 'ere, but I ain't, am I, Cyril?'

'No, yer ain't, me darling, yer just had a broken heart. Well, now that can mend, luv.'

Suddenly, Cyril didn't seem strange to Ruth any longer, he looked kindly and had a gentle nature. His love for Ethel was plain to see. And now in her presence all the scowling left his face and Ruth knew, with his hair tidied up, and if he had a good hot bath and fresh clothes, he could look very presentable. Not to mention feeding him up. She wanted to take him right now and do all of this for him, as it was clear to her that he'd looked after Ethel, and Ethel was a very important part of Amy's life.

This bore out to be the truth as Amy said, 'Ethel, I'm going to look after yer. Somehow, I'll get you out of here, and Cyril too, as he means so much to yer, luv.'

There it was — that smile, lighting Ethel's face once more. 'That's because he's me brother, luv.'

'Well then, we ain't going to see yer separated, but I have to ask yer something.' Amy surprised Ruth then by getting straight to the point. 'I want to ask yer, Ethel, if yer know who me mum is?'

Ethel glanced at Cyril. Then she nodded.

'Oh, Ethel, I've longed to know. Is she all right? Where is she?'

Ethel stared at Amy for a long moment. When she spoke, her voice shook. 'I'm 'ere, luv. I'm yer mum ... I — I couldn't 'elp what 'appened to yer, luv. They made me walk yer to that place ... I've 'eard about it, Amy. I've been demented thinking yer were being ill-treated.'

Cyril stepped forward as Ethel broke down in tears. Amy hadn't moved.

'She were ill in her mind afterwards. She forgot where yer were for years. But I knew. I came to the gate once to see yer, but this woman told me yer'd gone. I was going to tell yer about yer mum and me, luv, and ask yer not to give up 'ope. But I just cried and then it all set me Ethel back.'

'Amy?'

'Oh, Ruth, Ruth, help me.'

Ruth grabbed Amy. The weight of her body almost pulled her over. 'Amy, Amy, luv, yer've found yer mum . . . and an uncle, luv. That's good news. We'll get them out of here, me darling. Come on now, yer mum needs yer.'

Amy seemed to find some strength. 'It were the shock . . . all these years apart . . . Oh, Ethel . . . Mum, I've found yer.'

Once more Amy was in the arms of her mum. Both were crying. Through misted eyes, Ruth looked up at Cyril. Tears streamed down his face.

'We'll take care of yer both, Cyril. Just give us a little time to sort something out, eh?'

'And I'll come every day, Mum. I'll bring yer some stuff — clothes, food. Yer need building up . . . Oh, Mum, I love yer. Don't worry about anything. I know it weren't your doing. Like Ruth says, we'll sort something out.'

'What's going on 'ere then? Who are these people, Cyril? Did yer dare to let strangers in?'

Amy stood up and faced the hawk-like woman who'd entered.

'I'm Ethel's daughter. I've been looking for her. Now I've found her, I'm going to soon take her out of here.'

Ruth felt so proud as she saw Amy's strength.

'Well! Well, I never! There's a lot of paperwork to fill in, girl. Inspections of where yer going to take her. Scrutiny to see if yer can keep her. Yer can't just take her. She ain't a well woman, she's a bit loopy — more than a bit as it happens.'

182

Seeing Amy's face take on a look of thunder, Ruth stepped forward. 'We will see to it that our solicitor takes all the necessary steps to have Ethel and Cyril transferred to our care, so please don't worry.'

Where that came from, Ruth didn't know, but she did instinctively know that she needed to assert herself with some authority, so that Ethel didn't bear the brunt of this woman's wrath.

'Well! A solicitor, is it?'

'Yes. We know Ethel ain't being kept here illegally. We know there will be stuff to do to get her released, so we'll go along the proper channels. In the meantime, Amy will visit Ethel daily and make sure she is all right.'

Ruth's words were having the right effect.

'Very well.' She turned to Ethel. 'Well, Ethel, I'm pleased for yer, luv. Yer've spent a lifetime 'ere, as I 'ave. Now then, miss, if yer could both come with me, yer can sign in — even though yer going out. Yer can do that next. We 'ave to do everything in the proper manner.' She glared at Cyril.

Just before they left, Amy hugged Ethel again. 'I'll come tomorrow, Mum. Keep well, luv, it will help our cause to get you out of here if yer all right in yer mind.'

Ruth watched as Ethel clung on to Amy. Her own heart felt heavier for the sight as she prayed, *Please, Holy Mary, let me and Ellen find our mum too.*

17

Amy

Amy woke late again. She couldn't understand this need to sleep since she'd arrived here. It seemed that with her mind at rest, her body rested too. Though the dark mornings didn't help.

As she stretched, mixed feelings assailed her at finding her beloved Ethel was really her mum. Elation, yes, but a niggly feeling that if Ethel had claimed her, she might have been able to stay with her and not go into that awful orphanage.

Why did that happen? One day she would ask Ethel. She had to know. It would eat away at her.

Shaking these thoughts from her, Amy swung her feet out of bed and grabbed her housecoat. She shivered as her bare feet missed the rug and landed on the cold linoleum. Shifting her feet around, she found her house shoes.

Sitting for a moment to adjust to the light filtering through the curtains, Amy looked around her. How different the heavy, dark wood English furniture was to the Canadian pine that most of the furniture there was made from. And how ornate the bedhead, the chest of drawers and the wardrobe were compared to the clean lines of those she was used to. And, to her, the patterned wallpaper seemed to enclose you, whereas the fresh bright paint of her Canadian home gave a feeling that lifted the spirits. But still, she wouldn't change anything. She'd never want to be without Ruth and Ellen again.

Ruth greeted her when she opened the kitchen door. She and Ellen were sat at the table and had seemed at first to be deep in conversation.

'Hey, you all right, luv? The tea's still hot in the pot. And we've got something to talk over with yer.'

'I thought the pair of you looked like yer'd been plotting, with how you jumped when I entered. What've you got up yer sleeves then?'

'Ha, caught red-handed! Come and sit down, Amy, dear. We do have a plan, which we think you might like.' Ellen beckoned her over to the table. Ruth was already pouring steaming hot tea into a mug for her.

As soon as she sat down, Ellen said, 'Right. I've rung my solicitor. He has recommended one nearby to us, just a couple of streets away, and will make an appointment with him, giving him a rundown of what we need. And the good thing is, he said it will be a simple matter as the authorities are desperate to get people out of workhouses.'

Amy felt the relief of this as she had worried that they might not get Ethel out. But before she could express this, Ruth said, 'Here's yer tea. Get it down yer, luv, as there's more for us to tell . . . Ellen has good news. She and Bernard are to be married three weeks from tomorrow — this means her room will be free as they will live in Bernard's flat. And, Mr Busy Bee that Bernard is, he has already got some interviews lined up for himself!'

'Oh, that's good. I'm happy for yer, Ellen. So, are yer thinking that Ethel and Cyril can come here, Ruth?'

'Yes! It'll be perfect . . . Amy? You don't look as if you're sure, luv.'

'No, not altogether. I thought a lot about everything last night. I knew this is the way you'd think. But me mum ain't well, we could see that. And then where would we put Cyril? I don't think it would be right to separate them. Besides, I thought about little Archie too. We can't subject him to living with them. It wouldn't be fair.'

'But what are yer going to do, luv?'

'That involves Ellen.' Amy turned her head to look at Ellen. 'I think yer've got an idea how to put me mum together, Ellen. You have a way of helping people with what yer say. I think me mum needs that help. I can't afford a proper place for her, like the one that helped you, but if yer could do that for me mum, she might stand a chance.'

'Of course I will. I'll do all I can, but you have to get her out of that place, Amy, and Ruth is offering you the chance to do that.'

'I know . . . Ruth, will you consider something? I'm thinking about them rooms at the back of the shop. I know yer were thinking of a workroom for one of them, and a stockroom for the other, but there's a little kitchen and, don't forget, another room off the kitchen and a yard with a lav.'

'Yer want to make a home there!'

'Yes. One room is really big ; . . Look, I've thought it all through. The shop is very big — in width rather than depth — and you said yerself it was going to be difficult to make it look well stocked. So, I thought we could divide the space with a curtain and use the side that doesn't show through the window as the workroom. There's a side window for light, it being a corner property.'

'Hmm, it could work. But that only leaves three

rooms and a kitchen for you.'

'I know. It won't be easy, but I could do it. Me and me mum could have one room for a bedroom, then Cyril . . . well, me Uncle Cyril as he is, can have the other room as a bedroom and we could easily fit a big wardrobe in there and a large chest of drawers for all our clothes and bed linen. The kitchen already has a dresser and a sink, and a gas cooker. Oh, and a pantry leading off it with a cold slab.'

'My, you had a good look around, didn't yer? I didn't notice half of that!'

'I know. I think I had the idea of it all along really. Not with me mum and an uncle — I never dreamed I would find them — but if it happened that you met someone, Ruth.'

Ruth burst out laughing. 'Me! There's no one going to take me on with me little Archie in tow, luv. Most men run a mile at the thought of the responsibility of kids, let alone one that ain't theirs!'

They all giggled with her, but Amy sensed Ellen didn't want to. And that she, like her, wanted to protest that that wasn't true.

'So, yer both will leave me . . . I'm not sure I can take that.'

'No, not leave yer. I will see yer most mornings at the shop. We'll work together there till yer go for rehearsals, and I'll still look after Archie when you need me to.'

'But . . . Oh, I thought yer didn't want him around yer mum and Cyril!'

'Of course I do, but I don't want him subjected to living with them . . . We hardly know them, Ruth . . . What if I find it difficult to live with them, let alone Archie, bless him?'

'Well, yes, if yer put it like that.'

Ellen butted in before Amy could go further down this road. She was glad of it as the thought of not being able to live with the mum she'd dreamed of for so long wasn't a good one.

'I'll have loads of furniture you can have, Amy. When I spoke to my solicitor, I told him to put my house up for sale.'

'Oh, Ellen, ta, luv. That'll be a big help. I was wondering about all me big plans and not having enough money to carry them through.'

'Well, I can give you a sofa and a chair, and two single beds for sure. Oh, and a table and chairs — they're the ones we had in the kitchen, but with a cloth over the table and cushions on the chairs, they'll be lovely. And I have curtains . . . a host of things. Though I won't know exactly what. Bernard has put his flat up for sale now and is looking for a rented place for us, so we might need some of it.'

'Right, girls, we'd better get busy! We've wedding frocks to make, houses to sell, a shop to stock, a workroom to sort out, a flat to make from three bare rooms, solicitors to deal with, visiting for Amy, rehearsals for me, and you, Ellen, must start to look for a job!'

Ruth plonked herself down on a chair as if the thought of all of this had exhausted her.

Amy laughed. 'It's about organization, girls. We write down all we have to do, then make a plan of action.'

'Yes, I agree. Until your show starts, Ruth, we'll all have the evenings. We'll sew then. In the mornings, we'll sort out the shop. I'll go up to Leeds as soon as I can to sort out my cottage and arrange for what you need, Amy, to be brought down here. It could take some time to get your mum home, but if everything isn't ready by the time of my wedding, you could take up Ruth's offer and bring your family here for a little while.'

'Me family . . . Oh, Ellen, that sounds wonderful . . . I've been a bit daft to tell the truth. I've let doubts in. But it will be all right, won't it?'

'It will. You love yer mum. All right, you knew her as Ethel, but yer've always loved Ethel.'

'I have. And I do. So much it hurts me heart and it's that what gives me doubts.'

'That's natural, Amy, dear. I know what you are wondering, but it is all down to remembering that even mums are human. They have choices to make. They may not always make the ones we would have liked them to, but then, we are looking back from where we are now. We aren't in their shoes as it was for them when they took the actions they did.'

'Oh, Ellen. Ta. Yer've made it all clear to me. I were putting blame on Ethel's . . . me mum's shoulders . . . Oh, I can't get used to it. I've found me mum! I really have . . . Oh, I hope you find yours too.'

'We will. Robbie might find something out for us.'

Amy prayed this was so.

But there wasn't much time to devote to prayers as soon the three of them were hopping on a bus that shook their bones as it rattled along, having them giggle like schoolgirls. They were off to Petticoat Lane market.

'I feel so excited! I've heard such a lot about the market but never visited.'

'Me neither, luv. And, Amy, you definitely ain't, luv. Have yer heard of it?'

'No, but with the way you two are over us going, I

feel the anticipation in me belly. It's a long way to go too, so it had better be worth it.'

'It won't seem so when we get to Charing Cross. We can get a train straight to it then . . . Oh, it'll be worth it, I've always wanted to go.'

Amy hoped Ellen was right. She'd travelled across the world, or so it seemed, and had never known this excitement.

The noise — stallholders calling out their wares, and street entertainers, some singing, some dancing and even one walking on his hands while juggling coloured balls with his feet — swept them along when they arrived. As did the sight of clothes in all colours and styles. But it was at the stall that sold material that they all exclaimed at the wondrous sight of cottons and silks in a rainbow of colours blowing in the breeze.

It didn't take them long to choose. A deep blue for Amy and Ruth and a cream for Ellen. With their purchases completed by the buying of thread, buttons and ribbons, they made their way around the corner where they had been told there was a cafe.

Amy drew in her breath as they entered the tea shop. Christmas hadn't entered her head, but here as the bell jangled when they opened the door, it came to her in a rush as she gazed at the decorations the little shop had around it — holly with what looked like cotton wool stuffed into the bottom of its leaves to look like snow, and silver paper cut into strands draped every branch. This caught the light of the gas lamp and made a shimmering effect. In the corner stood a doll dressed as Santa Claus with tiny boxes made to look like presents at his feet.

Ruth's and Ellen's gasps joined hers.

'I ain't given Christmas a thought! But it'll be here just two weeks after yer wed, Ellen.'

'Nor me, Amy. This is such a surprise. It's only the middle of November!'

The lady behind the counter smiled at them. 'It might be, but I love Christmas and can't wait a minute longer than the first of November to start to welcome it . . . What can I get you girls then?'

'We liked the look of your cakes in the window, and would like one each, please, with tea for three, too.'

As Ellen ordered for them Ruth found a table. Amy hadn't ever seen a place like this. All the tables were draped with starched white cloths. In the centre of each was a small rose bowl. Each of these had a sprig of holly stuck in with the flowers. At each place was a rolled napkin in a silver holder. The chairs were high-backed and a deep mahogany and the walls were hung with pictures of different flowers. She wanted to clap her hands with the delight she felt as this place more than any, with its beamed ceiling and red stone floor, made her truly know she was back in England.

'The cafe where I saw our mum was similar to this, Ruth. Only that was in Bond Street.'

Ellen's voice sounded wistful and made Amy realize that no matter what the problems she faced with her mum not being well in her mind and with getting to know Cyril, she was lucky to have found them. She wondered if Ellen and Ruth would ever have the same luck as the thought occurred to her that it seemed an impossible dream for them both.

Ruth didn't answer, just smiled. But Ellen seemed to want to pursue the matter. 'You know, we could get to where I used to live with my father when I was very young and then again for a short while when he

191

took me out of the orphanage, before he married his second wife.'

This time Ruth looked up eagerly. 'And try to see Christopher again, you mean?'

'Yes . . . Though he may be away at school.'

'It's worth a try.'

'Oh, but Amy needs to get back and go to Bethnal Green . . . Maybe some other time.'

'No, do it now, luv, while yer can. I know how much it means to yer and I know me way to Bethnal now. I can leave yer to it, if yer put me on the right train. I've enough to get one of them cabs back.' After a lot of 'are yer sure?'s and 'but we don't like leaving you's, Amy found herself on the train on her own. The experience was a little frightening, but she took a deep breath, knowing she'd have to gain confidence to do many things on her own once she left Ruth's house to live independently.

It was as she began to feel comfortable and everything felt normal to her that she spotted a sign through the window saying *Shoreditch*. Shooting forward, Amy felt her stomach turn over as Ivan came into her mind. Ivan's address was in Shoreditch — Old Nichol Street! That was it. Without thinking, Amy jumped up as the train slowed, and hurried to the door.

When she was standing on the platform, an attack of nerves hit her. She desperately tried to remember the number of Ivan's house in Shoreditch. It wasn't until the train pulled away that she realized what she'd done. Looking around her, everyone was hurrying towards a sign saying *Exit*.

Feeling lost, she spotted the guard making his way back to the building in the centre of the station.

'Excuse me. Can you tell me how to get to Old Nichol Street, please?'

'Old Nichol. What does a young lady like you want in a dirty 'ole like that, eh?'

'I — I have a friend who lives there.'

'Poor bugger. Well, yer'll have to get a cab, but then, I doubt one'll take yer, unless it's just to the end of the road, as they won't venture along the street.'

'Ta. Are they parked outside the station?'

'They are if they ain't all been taken, luv.'

Amy sighed with relief when she left the station and saw that there were two cabs outside. Jumping in one, she gave Ivan's address without faltering, amazed at how the number of his house came to her.

'I ain't going along that road, luv. Sorry.'

'Will yer take me to the end of it then? I can walk from there.'

'All right, but yer pay me first. A penny three farthings, please.'

Amy flinched. She only had sixpence altogether and she had to get home yet. But she decided it was worth it. She was sure the cab from Bethnal had only cost tuppence. She'd have plenty.

When she reached the street, she saw why both the guard and the cab driver had been how they had. Filth caked the street, and the houses, which were all crammed together, looked as though if one fell down then they all would, like a line of dominoes. Washing hung across the street from house to house, and kids — what seemed like millions of kids — played, fought, cried and laughed in the street. All to the background of screeching women, swearing and cursing, at what, Amy couldn't be sure.

She hadn't gone far when she felt herself heaving.

The putrid smell of the rotting rubbish in the gutters, and the stinking brown water that snaked its way towards her, turned her stomach. *Oh, Ivan, me poor Ivan.*

When she came to number twenty the door and the curtains — if you could call them that; they were more like ragged bits of cotton material — were closed. Her heart sank. After taking this chance, she hoped with all her heart that Ivan was in.

'Who are you? What yer doing knocking on the door of me 'ouse?'

Amy looked down into a face that was a younger version of Ivan's. Snotty-nosed, with scabs covering his mouth and chin, he looked half-starved.

'I'm Amy, I'm a friend of Ivan's.'

'Me brovver Ivan?'

'Yes. Is he in?'

'He's always in. He'll be lying on his bed in a drunken stupor, no doubt.'

This repulsed Amy. What had happened to her lovely Ivan?

'Will yer go and tell him that Amy's here, please, luv?'

'Ha, it won't matter whose 'ere, yer'll not get him to shift.'

'Please. I have a farthing yer can have.'

The boy's eyes opened wide. 'Really! A whole farthing!'

Amy felt the pity of this. She'd known that kind of poverty. She nodded. The boy, who she'd put at around six years old, scampered off.

He was out again with his hand open within seconds. 'I told 'im. He wouldn't believe me, so I told 'im to look out of the window . . . Look, there he is.'

194

Amy looked up. The man she saw was unrecogniz-able to her until she saw him wipe the dirt to make a peephole in the only part of the frame that held glass, the rest having a board over the hole. It was then that his expression changed as his mouth formed her name.

'Open the window, Ivan. I've come a long way, mate.'

'He can't do that; it'll fall out and smash the last bit of glass.'

At this, Amy beckoned to Ivan to come down. His brother ran off, shouting, 'I'm going or he'll 'ave me farthing off me to get more drink with.'

Amy felt the tears prickle her eyes. How did this come about? She thought of her Ivan, laughing, care-free, growing strong, being there for her, and her tears trickled over.

It seemed an age till the door opened and a bleary-eyed Ivan stood in the shadow of it.

'Ivan! Oh, Ivan, luv, what happened?'

Tears fell down his cheeks. Amy put out her arms. When he came into them, the smell of him made her stomach retch once more but she clung on to his sob-bing, stick-thin body.

'Amy . . . Amy, is it really you?'

'It is, Ivan, luv. Yer'll be all right now, I'll help yer, mate.'

'No one can 'elp me, Amy. No one can take away the horror, the nightmares, the hell that I live every day.'

'I have a mate who can. I promise yer, Ivan. Ellen . . . you know, I told yer about Ellen and Ruth? Well, I've found them, or they found me. Anyway, they got me home and I live in a lovely place with

195

them . . . And I found me mum, Ivan.'

'Oh, Amy, Amy, help me, Amy.'

'I will, luv. I will . . . Though first yer need a bath, yer bloomin' stink!'

Ivan giggled as he said, 'I can 'ave a wash, mate, but in cold water and no soap, which won't get me much cleaner. I shall just have to stink!'

His merriment and the old twinkle back in his eyes gave Amy hope as the sound of his laughter was something she'd kept in her head for a long time.

'Where's yer mum, Ivan, is she here?'

'She died.'

'Oh, luv, I'm sorry . . . and yer brothers and sisters? Yer said yer had a few.'

'Gone. All had gone except for Jeff. They took them all before I came back. Next door told me . . . Mum . . . she hanged herself, just after I came home . . . It was as if she could leave Jeff now I was back . . . But, oh, Amy, I ain't been good to Jeff. I've been lost, Amy. Mainly a woman he calls Aunty Peggy just up the road takes care of him . . . I've let him down, Amy . . . and you. I've let yer down, luv.'

Once more he leaned on her shoulder and wept. Amy held him, at a loss as to what to do. When he calmed, stood straight and looked her in the eyes, she told him, 'The first thing to do is to stop taking solace in beer, Ivan.'

'I know, but it blots it all out for me.'

'So, your nightmares go when you're in drink, do they?'

'No, they still haunt me.'

'Well then, it ain't helping. Stop now, luv. Clean yerself up. I'll come back tomorrow. I've got to go, I've to find me way to the workhouse.'

'What? Why?'

She told him where and how she'd found her mum. 'I promised her that I would visit her every day.'

'I don't want yer to leave, Amy, I can't get better on me own.'

'You won't have to, luv. Promise me yer'll not drink any more tonight. Get yerself cleaned up and take care of your Jeff, eh? I'll come back tomorrow. I don't want to see yer looking this filthy and stinking like a sewer, mate.'

Again, Ivan giggled. 'Yer don't change, Amy . . . Have yer had a letter from Will? . . . I don't suppose in a million years yer would have from Teddy, he were a dour bloke.'

Amy gasped. 'Don't say that, Ivan. Teddy . . . well, me and him . . . Anyway, he didn't come back from the war. Will did, and we had new home children come to help on the farm . . . There's a lot to tell yer, luv.'

'You and Teddy! I — I never dreamed. I'm sorry, I shouldn't have said anything. And I'm sorry he's gone. He was dour, but he was a good bloke . . . So many, Amy . . . dead bodies . . . the fields were covered in them . . . We trod on them, we couldn't avoid it . . . Oh, Amy, it were awful.'

'I know, mate. It's over now. We just need to help yer to cope with it all and yer'll be all right, I promise . . . I'll see yer tomorrow, eh? About this time.'

'All right, luv . . . I'll try me best not to drink.'

Amy kissed his unshaven cheek. When she turned from him, her face flooded with tears. She didn't know if she could get her lovely Ivan back, but she would try. She'd do all in her power to.

18

Ellen

Ellen hung on tightly to Ruth's hand as they walked along Sardinia Street.

Everything seemed so familiar, and yet strange to her.

Her stomach muscles tightened as she neared the house. She knew Ruth, too, was feeling nervous as her hand quivered a little.

Suddenly she stood still. The house was in view and a young boy had come through the front door.

'That's him, Ruth! Oh, Ruth, he looks so like you.'

'And you, mate. Don't forget yer me twin.' Ruth gave a nervous laugh. Ellen knew from old that Ruth dealt with most things by making light of them.

As they neared him, the boy glanced towards them. Ruth shocked Ellen by saying, 'Hello, luv. You off out, then?'

The boy grinned. 'I am waiting for my friend who's coming to tea. I'm not supposed to be out here really. Mother would say that I will catch my death, but I don't think I will.'

Ellen couldn't speak, but Ruth said, 'Yer might, it's a bit nippy today.'

Now they were closer, the boy looked at them quizzically. 'Do I know you?'

Ellen nudged Ruth, then quickly said, 'No. We . . . We're just visiting a house down the road. I'm Ellen and this is Ruth. Ruth's always chatting to strangers.'

'I think that's good. I like to talk, but I don't get a lot of chance.'

'Oh? Don't you go to school, Christopher?'

The boy looked shocked. Ellen felt Ruth's eyes on her.

'How do you know my name? Who are you?'

'I — I . . . I'm sorry . . . I shouldn't have . . .'

Ruth saved the day, though how she thought up what came out of her mouth, Ellen couldn't think.

'We came by here sometime last year and you were getting into a car . . . Well, at least yer should have been, but you were dawdling. We heard yer mum say, 'Hurry up, Christopher!' We're sorry, me mate shouldn't have called yer by yer name. We'll get on our way now. Have a good time with yer friend . . . Though it's strange as we've been past a few times and not seen yer. We thought yer'd be at school.'

The boy relaxed. 'It's all right. I don't know how you remembered me, but don't worry. You just startled me, that's all.'

Ellen felt relief flood through her. She held Christopher's lovely dark eyes for a moment. She so wanted to hug him, to tell him who she really was, but knew she couldn't. Maybe when he was a lot older. 'Thanks. I apologize again. And maybe we'll see you again when we come by. It's been nice talking to you.'

'Well, I don't know if you will. I go to boarding school next year. Somewhere in the middle of England, a place called Rugby. It's a very well-known school.'

'Oh yes, I've heard of it. Are you looking forward to it?'

'Sort of. A bit scared too, though.'

The door to the house opened. 'Master Christopher, what are yer doing? Come on inside . . . Who are you? What are you doing here?'

'Oh, we're just passing by. We just stopped for a chat. Yer should know it's what we cockneys do, being one yerself, luv.'

The maid was about the same age as themselves. She visibly relaxed at Ruth's words. 'I do. I miss a good natter.' She nodded her head at Christopher. 'Though this one can talk the hind leg off a donkey, given 'alf a chance.'

Christopher laughed. A lovely sound. Ellen once more had the feeling that she just wanted to grab hold of him and hug him as he turned, then looked back and said, 'Goodbye, I hope I see you both again.'

Then he was gone. The maid shook her head. 'He'll be better off at school. Poor kid lives a lonely life with just 'aving a tutor, his mother and us maids for company. We're not supposed to talk to him, but we do. He's a little love.'

Ruth grinned. 'Not so little, he's taller than you!'

'I know. They say he takes after his dad.'

Ellen drew in a deep breath as a picture of hers and Christopher's father came into her head. It still hurt that he hadn't loved her enough to keep her with him.

'I don't think so, though. I've seen photos of 'is dad, and he ain't like him at all. Nor like 'is mother, if it comes to that.'

Ellen wanted to scream out that the woman in the house wasn't Christopher's mother. But she bit her lip. 'Well, we'll have to go. If we're passing this way again and see you out, we'll give you a wave.'

'You do that.'

With that, she went inside and closed the door.

Ellen felt as though she'd lost something precious.
'Are yer all right, mate?'

'I am . . . At least, I will be . . . Oh, Ruth, wasn't he beautiful?'

'He was. I wanted to grab him. I feel a love for him. One he'll probably never know of as we can't do anything about him being our brother. I realized that as we were talking to him. He's happy in his own world. We can't upset that, luv.'

Ellen knew Ruth was right but at the same time, she thought to herself that one day, when he was older, she would find him. She could do no other. She wanted him in her life.

★ ★ ★

When they got home, Amy wasn't there. Ruth began to pace up and down. 'Where can she be? I thought she'd beat us home.'

Ellen knew a worry to niggle at her, but she didn't show it. Her mind was still with Christopher, as was the feeling that she so longed to hold him, to show him her love for him.

'Ellen, I'm worried.'

'I know. Amy will turn up. There's nothing we can do. Let's get the tea on, and then we'll lay the cloth out and make a start . . . Though how you're going to do that, I just don't know. I'd be scared to death to put the scissors anywhere near it.'

'Room is going to be the problem, luv.'

'I've been thinking about that. Why don't I move into your bedroom with you for these last few weeks? I'd love that. It will be like when we were little and again when I came to live with you in London. Then

201

we could use my room as our sewing room. We could set up your sewing machine in there.'

'That's a great idea, luv. Yes, let's do that first . . . though, I don't want Amy to feel pushed out.'

'Well, it can be Amy's room if she wants, but we do need somewhere so that we don't have to keep clearing everything away but can close the door on it and then pick up where we left off the next evening.'

'Right. We'll wait till Amy comes home and see what she thinks.'

Just as she said this, they heard footsteps on the stairs.

'Amy, luv, we were just talking about you. We've been worried, luv. Where have yer been till now?'

Amy walked to the sofa, sat down and burst into tears.

'Amy, love, what is it? Oh, my poor darling. I feel you have been through so much and then to come home and find more trouble. Is your mum all right, dear?'

Amy nodded and two tears plopped onto her cheeks. Ellen wiped them away with her lace handkerchief. As she did, she thought of Dilly and how she used to do the same for her.

'That's good then, isn't it? Did you get lost? Is that what's upset you?'

'I'll make a pot of tea, luv. There's nothing like a pot of tea when yer feel down.'

'Ta, Ruth. I'll be all right . . . It's . . . Well, I found Ivan.'

'Ah, I'm glad. But obviously all isn't well. Look, you get your coat and outdoor shoes off, and freshen up in the bathroom. By then, Ruth will have the tea made and you can tell us all about it, eh?'

'Ta, Ellen. That's just what I need. Me legs ache with all the walking I've done and me heart aches with all I found out today.'

Helping Amy up, Ellen hugged her to her. 'You don't have to shoulder anything on your own, Amy, love. Me and Ruth are here for you. We can't make everything right, but we can stand by your side and support you. And we will, always.'

When they sat down around the table in the kitchen — their favourite gathering place — Amy told them how she'd found Ivan, and how, when she'd reached the workhouse, her mum was in a flood of tears as she thought she wasn't coming. 'I don't know if I'm strong enough to help them both. I want to, I love them, but their demons may be too much for me to battle . . . Though I found that me Uncle Cyril is a diamond geezer. He takes care of Mum's every need. I could never separate them . . . but I think Cyril has difficulties of some sort — like the saying 'a penny short of a shilling'. You see, they wanted to know where we were going to live. When I told them, Cyril said, 'But I don't want to go to Southampton.' I tried to explain that was just the name of the road, but he couldn't grasp it, he just kept repeating that he came from Bethnal Green and that's where he wanted to die . . . I just don't know what I'm going to do.'

Ellen put her hand over Amy's. She could feel it trembling. 'How did your mum handle this?'

'She told him he would be all right, and that she was going, so he had to. He quietened then, but he looked confused and upset. He sat there wringing his hands as if really distressed about it.'

'Hmm, I don't know what to think . . . Maybe bring him and your mum over here a few times to visit?

That might settle his mind and ease him into the situation. Perhaps he can help with painting your flat? That will make him feel that it is him that has made a new home for you.'

'Oh, Ellen, that might work. Before I said where, he was saying that he would do jobs to make our flat nice . . . Oh, Ellen, you're a natural at seeing what people need . . . and, well, I know you said you'd help Mum, but Ivan needs help too.'

'Yes, from what you have told us, he does. Thousands of young men do. You see them everywhere, sitting in the street, lost souls, begging for money to get their next drink. I understand. I saw what they went through, and yet didn't, if that makes sense? I saw them in a hospital environment, broken, wounded and unable to stop the images of what they'd seen from visiting them. If they came home to supportive families, they may stand a chance, but if not, then they will fall deeper and deeper into mental illness.'

As if she hadn't spoken, Ellen was shocked when Amy stared ahead and said, 'Ivan's mum hung herself.'

'Oh God! Oh, poor Ivan. Oh, Amy, poor Ivan. My heart breaks for him.'

'And all his siblings have been taken away, except one. He doesn't know where to. I don't know why the little boy that I saw wasn't taken, but he's a nice kid. He's got a bit of a way with him, a sort of cheek, but it's as if he has learned to do anything to survive.'

'Poor kid. Oh, Amy, luv, I'm sorry yer've come home to all of this. But we'll sort it, mate. Something'll occur to us as to how we can help them all.'

'Ta, Ruth. I feel as though I've done nothing but bring down trouble on yer.'

'No, don't think that. Look, we've been through a lot worse. We all stick together. Nothing stopped us getting back to each other, and nothing will beat us if we tackle it as if we are one. Anyone who you love, we do. That's how it is. Yer mum, Cyril and Ivan and his brother'll be all right, I promise. We just need to figure it all out.'

'I can't leave him there, Ruth. It's — it's the worst place I've ever seen in me life.'

'I know it well. A slum area. We thought we had it bad being brought up in the orphanage, but Old Nichol area . . . Makes me shudder to think of the poor people trapped in such poverty.'

Ellen found all she'd heard hard to take it in or to imagine. She made up her mind that she would talk to Bernard about it. These were the people she wanted to help. The idea appealed to her. *What a privilege to be able to help those tormented, just as I was helped in the wonderful Miss Roland's clinic when I had a breakdown.*

A little pang of guilt entered her. Miss Roland had so wanted to become a doctor, but being a woman was a huge obstacle in her day. She'd made Ellen promise that she would become one for her. And she wasn't the only one; Ellen had promised her Gran too. *Gran fought my father — her son — to ensure he paid for my education to fulfil the dream I had then, but maybe if I studied psychiatry?*

'Yer've gone quiet, Ellen, are yer all right?'

Amy's words brought Ellen out of her thoughts. 'Yes. Just fighting an inner battle, love.'

'Right, what would yer say to us if we did that?'

Ellen laughed up at Ruth. 'I would say you should talk about it.'

'Exactly!' Ruth folded her arms.

'Well, I'd better as you look as though you'll not stand for less!'

Ruth giggled and relaxed her arms. 'Well, luv, yer help everyone else, but yer have to learn to accept help. What's bothering yer, eh?'

Ellen told them.

'Ah, the old guilt path. Rebekah used to say that promises are made to be broken, that they put you onto a route, but then something happens to turn yer in the direction of yer true destiny. Besides, a psychiatrist is a doctor, ain't it?'

'It is, actually, but I promised to be a medical doctor.'

'Oh, I can see your gran now, putting her hands up in the air and screaming, "You let me down!"'

Ellen burst out laughing at the thought.

'See, you're worrying over nothing! You know what yer gran would say. She'd be right behind yer all the way. And this Miss Roland you're talking of would too. She wanted to be a doctor but was sent along a different path because of being female. That's not the same as you choosing to change your mind. Why don't you write to her and tell her? I bet she'll be over the moon that she was such an influence on yer.'

'I will. No, I'll do more than that. I'll visit her. I have to make time to go up to Leeds to sort out my cottage. I need to pack all my personal stuff and bring it home. And to label everything as to what I want to happen to it — some to Amy, some I want to keep and the rest to be sold or donated to a charity.'

'Lord knows when yer can do that, luv.'

'I thought this weekend. I'll ask Bernard to take me.'

Ellen felt herself blush as they both gave her a knowing look, but she just giggled, as they did, and then changed the subject back to Amy's problems. 'But before then, we need to sort Ivan out . . . Any ideas?'

'He must come here. Or, if he won't, his brother must, then we'll support Ivan all we can, but, Amy, luv, if he stays in Old Nichol, he hasn't much chance of getting better. What do you think he'll do?'

'I don't know . . . but it ain't going to be easy, luv. Are yer sure?'

'We are, aren't we, Ellen?'

'We are. And it fits in with something we were talking about earlier.' She explained about moving bedrooms. 'So, what I suggest is that we all move into Ruth's room — it is a huge room so we could do it. We'd have to put one of our beds in there — probably mine as yours is a double like Ruth's — then two of us sleep in Ruth's bed, and then Ivan and his brother in your room, Amy, and use mine for our sewing room. Or, Ivan's brother might like to go in with Archie.'

The moment she said this, Ellen wanted to un-say it as Ruth looked alarmed. But she was saved by Amy.

'No, with Ivan is best . . . Jeff may be a bit of a shock to you all, let alone Archie!'

To lighten the moment, Ellen mimicked her beloved Dilly again. 'Nowt can shock us, lass. We've seen it all!'

They all giggled at this.

'Oh, Ellen, I'd have loved to meet your Dilly.'

'And she would have loved you, Amy. She was special.'

With this, Ellen had a yearning for the weekend. She so wanted to go back to her cottage one last time and to share it with her adored Bernard. She wished they could keep the cottage and go there now and again for a rest as she had a feeling with the life they were planning they would need somewhere like it. But needs must, she told herself. 'Well, let's get on with our plans. The day's going and we're not much further forward than talking about it.'

Rising, she thought her life would always be like this, caring for those whose lives had become unbalanced, as it sounded as though Ivan and little Jeff really did need caring for, mentally as well as physically. The thought was a good one as it was what she'd always wanted to do. She'd done it as a nurse, and that would continue as she helped Bernard, but she wanted to heal their minds too. The prospect of finding out more about training for this excited her.

19

Ruth

How her life had changed, Ruth thought as she and Ellen carried bedding across the landing to her bedroom.

Robbie had helped them unscrew the bed Ellen used and to move the frame, carrying the heavier spring base for them. He was now putting it together once more. He'd also gone to the stores the theatre used and borrowed a table which had been used as a prop in one of the shows. It wasn't a proper table, but a plank of wood laid over trestle-top legs, which made it easy to do a scene change quickly. But it was also ideal for them to spread the material on for cutting and then, when the frocks were almost made, for hemming and sewing seams.

'So, yer picking up waifs and strays again, luv?'

'I am, Robbie. But you and Abe weren't waifs and strays, and still aren't. I don't know what I'd do without yer, mate.'

Robbie grinned at her. To her, he was a stable influence she could always rely on and had been since she'd first met him the morning after she'd run away from the orphanage — a twelve-year-old, afraid, hungry and with nowhere to go. Robbie, who had been fifteen going on sixteen at the time, became her saviour.

The day Rebekah took them both in was the day

they became like brother and sister, and they still looked on each other as that today. He was everything to her.

He stood now and looked at her intently. 'Yer not taking on too much, are yer, luv? Those damaged from the war are not easy to handle.'

'I know, Robbie. I dealt with many of them in Ypres. As did Ellen. We know what we're in for. Though I don't know if Amy does, bless her.'

'Well, me and Abe will help, as we were there — well, he was but, like you, I was a bit on the sidelines working as a chef and entertaining the troops. But it didn't shield me from the reality of it — the fear, the awful sights, seeing men go over the top and half of them not coming back. The noise, the blood, the filth and the ailments like foot rot, with men binding their feet and carrying on regardless. The smell of the latrines and the unwashed . . .'

Robbie shuddered.

Ruth put down the pillows she was holding and went to him. As they had done many times over the years, they hugged.

'I'll 'elp yer all I can with Ivan, Ruth, and Abe has said the same.'

'I know you will, but I hate putting on yer. I — I, well, I was going to ask Abe to take Archie on and be a tutor to him . . . though he might have two of them now as it wouldn't be fair not to give Jeff the same.'

'Jeff's more than likely to be like me and you were, only tougher and rougher, Ruth. Life taught us all the lessons we needed. But I know Abe would take them on and be glad to. Please go ahead and ask him, mate, and as soon as yer can as I know he's bored. He needs a challenge. He often feels useless.'

'I can't understand his family abandoning him.'

'I can. What me and Abe are ain't acceptable and is classed as a crime. We're lucky that Abe's disability is a cover for us being together . . . I know that's not a good thing to say, but we both accept it is that that keeps us safe. Though I've wished a million times he was how he used to be before the war. I have mates in jail, Ruth. Lovely men, who wouldn't hurt a fly, but just want to be who they are — how they were made to be. Whether that will ever change, I don't know, but yer will be careful with this Ivan and his brother, won't yer? Some are dead against us and would think nothing of turning us in.'

Ruth felt her blood go cold. She'd almost forgotten that others wouldn't see them how she did. She'd been lucky that Ellen and Amy had accepted them and both loved them as she did, but what if Ivan wasn't all right with it? There was no way they could keep it from him . . . or Jeff.

'I'll be back in a minute, luv.'

'All right, I've only one more nut to tighten. I've enjoyed doing it, I've always loved this kind of work. I love working with the prop men.'

Ruth remembered how Robbie had made a handcart and her stall for her. He'd always been handy in that way, and he enjoyed the work.

'Amy! Amy!'

Ellen came out of her room, her arms laden with blankets. 'Are you all right, Ruth, you sound stressed?'

'Oh, Ellen, where's Amy? I need to make sure of something before we carry on with this.'

'Robbie and Abe?'

'Yes, how did yer know?'

'I thought about it and spoke to Amy before she left

211

just now. She doesn't think it will be a problem. Like us all, Ivan has been faced with much during his life. But she's going to make sure when she sees him this afternoon.'

'Oh, I didn't think. I'm so used to the situation that nothing about it isn't normal to me.'

'As is so. Everything is normal to those involved. The world is made up of many kinds, Ruth.'

'Oh, Ellen . . . I — I can't say that about Belton.'

There came an audible gasp from Ellen as if a knife had been stuck into her. 'Oh, luv, I'm sorry, I shouldn't have said that . . . Oh, Ellen, come here, luv.'

From hugging Robbie, to now hugging Ellen. How damaged they all were by all that had happened to them as children. But they had each other, and that would get them through.

Ellen breathed deeply several times. 'My coping strategy. Don't worry. I have triggers to my own mental frailty, but I can combat them. Don't ever be afraid of saying what you need to say, Ruth.'

Ruth nodded but thought she would be mindful in the future. Ellen tried to be brave. She tried to be all things to them all, but she needed care and understanding too.

'Let's carry on anyway. Obviously if there's any doubt about Ivan's reaction to Robbie and Abe, we won't have him here, but I like the idea of us girls being in one bedroom together for the last few weeks of you being here, Ellen.'

'I do to. Oh, Ruth, I know I won't be far way, but I will miss you.'

'And I you, luv.'

They both gave a deep sigh. Ruth knew that they would always need each other, but as they did when

Ellen went to France, they had to get on with life. They couldn't make decisions on the basis that they would always want to live with each other.

'Come on, you two, we'll never get this room done . . . Women!'

Ruth threw a pillow at Robbie. 'Cheeky devil!'

He ducked but scooped it up and threw it back. Before Ruth knew what was happening, they were all having a full-scale pillow fight. Their shouts brought Archie running from his bedroom.

'Come 'ere, Archie, yer on my side — boys against girls. Grab a pillow!'

Archie did his best, but the pillows were as big as him and every time he went to throw one, he landed on top of it. His giggles filled the space around them. Ruth thought her sides would split she was laughing so much.

Robbie called a halt. 'Hey, I've just had an idea. You won't want the whole of that room for sewing, will you?'

'No. Why?'

'Well, our spare room just has a lot of junk in it. Stuff we want but haven't got around to storing properly. So, why don't I bring that up here and stack it in that corner, and then our room will be clear, and you and I can rehearse there?'

'Oh, Robbie, that's a great idea. It will mean we don't have to leave Archie with Abe so much as he can play in the corner of the room.'

'Well, no, that ain't a good idea, luv. Some of our material'll be a bit raunchy for Archie's ears.'

'What's 'raun . . . chy' mean, Robbie?'

'Ha, yer'll learn soon enough, Archie boy, but it ain't time for yer to know now . . . I'd suggest, Ruth, that

213

you take Archie to the shop with you in the morning, then Abe teaches him in the afternoon. Then you'll only have to leave him with Amy in the evening.'

'Oh dear. Now that Amy is moving out, that means he'll have to go to hers . . . I don't want that, Robbie.' Ruth looked down at Archie. 'Go back to your room to play for a while, me darlin'. We've got to shift furniture around now.'

Archie went to protest but changed his mind when Robbie said, 'I'll come along in a mo and we can set that train set up. I think yer old enough to play with it now. But let me get to the stage where there's only women's work left first, only I can't do that with you under me feet, Archie.'

Ruth watched as her son obeyed and for the first time thought that Archie needed a man in his life, and thanked the Holy Mary for Robbie and Abe, but were they enough? Shouldn't he have a father in his life?

Dismissing the thought, she told Robbie what she didn't want to say in front of Archie. 'Amy's going to have a job on her hands as it is, and we haven't even talked about what we're going to do with Ivan and Jeff when she moves into her flat. It's not big enough for them all.'

'What about the flat above the shop? I thought that was empty.'

'It is, but I can't afford it.' Ruth sighed. 'I'm beginning to wonder how I'm going to even manage the shop and the music hall, and yet, I so want to do both, and the money will help me.'

'That's my fault, Ruth. I feel so bad.'

'No, Ellen, yer mustn't, luv. We've all got our lives to lead. It was my idea that you didn't back me after all.'

'Let's see what I get for the cottage, eh? I might be able to help out. But the flat above the shop is a good idea, I imagine it's big enough to take them all. Is the rent really high?'

'I think it adds at least two shillings a week.'

'Look, you said the music hall is only three nights a week. I'll fetch Archie on those evenings, and he can sleep over with us.'

'Oh, Ellen, ta, luv. That'd put me mind at rest. Besides having a lot to contend with, I don't think the environment at Amy's will be a good one for Archie on a regular basis . . . Oh dear, that sounded snobbish for a girl from the orphanage!'

'It did a bit, luv. Mixing with all kinds never did me and you any harm. Reg and Irish Mick used to drink like fish and sing songs and dance around the square in a drunken fashion, but they were good to us.'

'I know, I feel ashamed of saying it now.' Ruth let out a huge sigh. She felt it all getting on top of her and shame prickled her at Robbie's words. She just couldn't explain how it was that she felt so strongly about protecting her son from ever experiencing what they all had. She smiled wryly to herself. *I've certainly made a good start inviting all and sundry to me flat and me shop!*

By the time all the work was done it looked lovely and Ruth couldn't wait for bedtime to come. It really would be like old times.

She snatched this thought back. It would be nothing like that! They wouldn't be lying in fear of the dormitory door opening and hoping and praying they weren't the ones picked to be Belton's special little girl that night.

Making an effort to banish all this from her mind,

she said the only thing she could think of: 'Time for a cuppa, luv.'

'Good idea.'

While she and Ellen sat at the kitchen table, they were quiet, each deep in their own thoughts. It was the sudden sound of a child's glee that lifted them both.

'Choo-choo!'

Then the clapping of little hands.

They both went along to Archie's room.

'Look, Mummy, look!'

Ruth laughed, but then caught a wistful look on Robbie's face. She knew what he was thinking.

'Right, now that yer know how it all goes, the pair of yer can take it to bits again and go and set it up on Abe's table! He played with it as a little boy, Archie, and gave it to you, but I bet you a tanner he'd love to see it going again and to play with it with yer.'

'Ooh, yes, Mummy! Come on, Robbie. Let's take it to Abe!'

Robbie smiled. 'Ta, Ruth. You always know what's on me mind and I think yer always will.'

'I read yer like a book, luv. You should have thought of that in the first place. Go on with yer. Me and Ellen'll come down in a bit to watch yer.'

By the time they went downstairs, Bernard had called in. He winked as he said, 'I was just passing.' Then he took Ellen in his arms and kissed her cheek.

They all laughed at him.

Without taking his arm from around Ellen's waist, he leaned forward and shook Abe's hand then patted Robbie on the back. 'Well, not long now. I hope you've dusted off your suits.'

Abe answered with a grin. 'We're buying new ones;

I've put on weight since I've been stuck in a chair and Robbie's got nothing that resembles a wedding suit. His are all flamboyant.'

This caused them all to giggle. Ruth's heart warmed to see this teasing of him was accompanied by a loving glance at Robbie from Abe.

Bernard had accepted them as a couple as soon as he knew. He'd told Ellen that such relationships weren't strange to him and that many had formed in the boarding school they'd all attended. He was sure that Abe had had one such then.

Once Robbie unpacked the train, Bernard dived in with them. The chat then was about the set that he had stored away at home somewhere. 'It'll be for our first boy, darling.' Ellen blushed again.

'That's if Freddie hasn't either claimed it or chucked it out.'

'You know, Bernard, Frederick hasn't changed, and I don't think he will.'

'Oh, I know that, Abe. He's a good sort really, except for his womanizing and his pig-headedness.'

Abe burst out laughing. It was good to see. It took Ruth back to when she first met him and she blushed too, as she remembered how she'd fallen in love with him — a girlish love, prompted by his kindness.

His grin now was just as it was then, and the fringe of his dark hair fell forward in much the same way, almost covering his deep blue eyes.

As she'd seen him do a thousand times, he brushed his fingers through it in a vain attempt to push it back. It just flopped forward again.

The delight of them all as the train finally got into motion was lovely to see. These, and Amy, were her family. A warm glow filled Ruth at the thought.

After making them all a cup of tea, Ruth and Ellen left them to it. Ellen surprised her by saying, 'I feel like going to see Frederick to give him a few home truths. How dare he treat Bernard how he does! He's ruined all of our plans.'

'Do yer think that's deliberate? I mean, what if he still carries a torch for yer, Ellen? What if this is spite, and a way of delaying you marrying.'

'Well, if it is, it isn't going to work. He always gave me the creeps. He's so different to Bernard.'

'Well, thank Holy Mary for that at least!'

Ellen grinned and tucked her arm into Ruth's as they went along the landing. 'Anyway, I'm hoping Bernard will come with me to Leeds. I haven't asked him yet. I think he will be free as his interview at the hospital isn't until Monday.'

'That'll be lovely for yer both. I only hope Dilly's spirit ain't roaming there — she'll have something to say if she catches yer in bed together.'

Ellen's laughter burst from her. It was infectious and good to hear. When they calmed, she said, 'It would be better if it was Gran. She would clap her hands and say, 'Get on with it you two!''

'Oh, Ellen, would she?'

'Yes. She was a passionate lady.'

'That's where you get it from then, yer hussy, you.'

This made them laugh again, and Ruth thought it a kind of healing laughter as they'd never been able to be this relaxed over anything to do with the intimate relations between a man and a woman. Both had been terrified of it after what they went through.

But something else happened too. A clenching feeling in her groin at the thought of Ellen and Bernard. A feeling that had visited her a few times lately. Always she'd brushed it away, thinking herself unfaithful to her darling Adrian. Thinking that she had no right. But now she suddenly felt emboldened to ask Ellen's opinion on it.

'Ellen . . . I — I . . . can I ask yer something?'

'Of course, anything. You're my sister. Sisters share their most secret secrets.'

'Well, is it wrong of me to want to . . . Oh, this is going to sound so bad . . . but, lately, I've had thoughts. Things like Archie should have a father, not just a father figure — Robbie and Abe are that to him — but a proper daddy he can call his own, and . . . well, I've had other thoughts come to me . . . you know . . .'

'Oh, Ruth, this is all so natural, there's nothing wrong about it. It just shows that you're ready. That you've entered another phase. You've done your grieving. You'll always love Adrian, but you need to move your life on. No one would think that more than Adrian. He'd be so sad to think of you alone . . . Now tell me, who is he?'

'Oh, no. No one. It's just how I have had odd thoughts lately and, like you say, I do feel ready to share me life with someone. Whether I'll ever meet anyone who'd take me on with a kid in tow, I don't know. Anyway, the papers are full of the country being short of men, so I don't stand a chance on all fronts.'

Ellen hugged her waist. 'You never know. Don't give up hope, Ruth, love.'

Ruth gave a wry smile and shrugged as if none of it mattered anyway.

But it did. She knew now after admitting her feelings to Ellen that it did matter a great deal to her. She couldn't bear the thought of the lonely years ahead.

She hoped and prayed she'd meet someone who

could love her enough to take her and Archie as a package and be a good daddy to him.

Archie deserved that.

20

Amy

Amy stood looking down at her mum. Her heart had lifted to find her up and dressed, with her hair done. And even a little rouge on her cheeks and lipstick on her lips.

She loved how her mum had freckles over her nose, just like she herself did.

'It won't be long now, Mum. You'll soon be out of here and we'll be together again.'

''Ave yer got the flat ready, darlin'?'

'No, it needs painting, it's stood empty a long while. I were going to ask if Uncle Cyril was any good at decorating?'

'He's had many jobs, but couldn't keep them — he lacks concentration — but he loved doing that kind of work. I think he'd like to help yer, luv, and would do a good job. But it's up to the powers that be. They might not let him.'

'We can try. After all, it's work as the shop needs doing as well and he'll get paid for that . . . Oh, here he is.' Amy stood and kissed Cyril's cheek. She was beginning to accept him as family and to feel a fondness for him, mostly prompted by how kind and gentle he was with her mum. He seemed a different person to the man who opened the door to them on that first day.

He smiled a huge smile. 'Here I am.'

221

'Yes. Here you are. I'm just fixing yer up for a painting job, luv.'

'Ha, Ethel . . . and a pig might fly.'

'No, it's true, Uncle Cyril.' Amy told him what needed doing.

His face lit up. 'I can do that for yer, girl, and be glad to. When can I start?'

'I'll tell yer tomorrow as I have to arrange it all. Ruth needs to get some paint. And you'll need permission.'

'I ain't a prisoner, yer know. I come and go. It's Ethel as ties us to this place. She's been afraid to go out till now on account of these blokes.'

'Shush, Cyril! Yer bleedin' tongue wags too much at times! It needs cutting off!'

'What blokes, Cyril? Mum, are yer scared of someone? Tell me.'

'It's just these gangster types.'

'Just! Mum, for God's sake! What have gangster types got to do with you?'

'It were from a long time back . . . when I worked the streets . . . You don't need to know, luv. Once I'm away from 'ere they won't know where I am, so we'll be safe.'

Amy felt her blood run cold. But then it came to her that Ruth had spoken of the woman she used to look on as a mum having sons who were gangsters. She'd said that she'd ask Robbie to ask them about hers and Ellen's mum. What if these were the same men? 'Did these gangsters have a mum who worked on the market?'

It was Cyril who answered, 'You mean Bett, Amy. A lovely woman, she'd always give yer a cup of tea, even if yer couldn't pay. Yes, they're the ones. They're

222

a nasty piece of work.'

Both Mum and Cyril looked warily at her. Cyril asked, "'Ow do yer know them, Amy? Yer ain't come from them, have yer? You ain't going to tell of Tild —'

'Cyril! For God's sake!'

'Were you going to say Tilda, Cyril? Mum? Did yer know a prostitute named Tilda?'

Her mum's face registered shock. She stared at Amy. 'What do yer know of Tilda, girl?'

Amy felt hope rise inside her. 'Ruth, who came with me the other day, and Ellen that I told you about, are her daughters. They were at the orphanage with me. We're like sisters, we love each other so much. I live with them. Oh, Mum, they so want to find Tilda. Do yer know where she is?'

Amy saw her mum shoot a warning glance at Cyril. 'No! I — I don't know, luv.'

'But you did know her, didn't yer? How?'

Her mum let out a sigh. 'We were mates. Tilda is — was — the best mate a girl could have. They didn't get her when they got me. She ran away. We lost touch.'

'Ethel!'

'Shut up, Cyril. There's details Amy don't need to know.'

Her mum's body shook as if feeling real fear. Amy sat down on the bed and took her gnarled hand. Squeezing it, she went to say that there was no need to be afraid, but her mum winced. 'Are yer hands painful, luv?'

'Them gangsters did that to her, Amy, and that's why she's scared.'

Amy was aghast as she looked closely at her mum's misshapen hands. 'Oh, Mum, how? Why?'

Her mum gave a withering look to Cyril. 'He can't keep his mouth shut. Look, there's stuff about me yer don't know, luv.'

'Does this have something to do with Tilda?'

'Amy, luv, the least yer know the better, but yes. We worked for Bett's boys, only we double-crossed them. We made money for ourselves by cutting them out — yer see, we should only have gone with men who'd paid the boys for our favours, but they gave us a pittance. They dressed us nice and sent us to nice places to be with the men, but we were poor like yer've never known, girl.'

Amy didn't tell her how much she knew about poverty but let her carry on.

'We used to pray the men who had rented us would feed us first and if they did, we'd put something in our bag for the other one.'

Amy felt her cheeks redden at this detail, but she persevered. 'So, how did yer come to be in here, and how did I fit in to it all?'

'When I had yer, I couldn't keep yer. I left yer with the priest, like Tilda did one of hers — she'd had a kid a couple of years or so before me, yer see.'

'That'd be me mate, Ruth.'

'Yes, she said the priest had named her that . . . Poor girl . . . I mean . . . Anyway, after this happened to me, I could no longer take care of Cyril. Cyril tried to earn money, but nothing he did lasted for long. We were starving and couldn't pay the rent, so we ended up in here. You were with the nuns. But once the nuns knew I was in here, they brought you to me, but I never admitted yer were mine to the governor. He tried to get the nuns to take yer back, but they were closing the facility for homeless kids and said that they knew

I was the mother and should face up to my responsibilities.'

'So, yer didn't want me.'

Cyril butted in. 'No, Amy, luv. It weren't like that. Tell her, Ethel.'

'I knew I couldn't ever give yer a life, me darlin'. I thought yer prospects would be better without me. I thought the nuns would get yer adopted, but that didn't happen, so I took care of yer when yer came here. But then they had yer put into that orphanage. I tried to backtrack and tell them then that I'd lied, and I was yer mum, but they thought I were showing signs of being insane.'

'But you took me to the orphanage yourself! How could yer do that?'

'They made me. They said it were me punishment for lying, then they committed me to this ward . . . It's like a prison. Look at them, they're all like dummies, they never speak, they just stare into space. But it was the first time I felt safe since I came in here, so I've stayed put.'

'And it's better than where —'

'Cyril!'

'Better than where, Cyril?'

'The . . . the loony bin, Amy, where they put them as are screaming mad. I clean the lavs up there, poor bleeders.'

'That's enough, Cyril.'

'Yes, Ethel. Sorry, Ethel.'

'Take no notice of him. He gets mixed up sometimes.'

Amy felt there was more to all this, but her mum looked afraid.

'Why are you still scared, Mum? You've no need to

be. Them rotters have had their revenge on you. And anyway, Ruth were looked after by Bett before the war; they'd have some respect for her, she could talk to them. But if they didn't, there's someone else. Someone who knows them, he'll sort them out. They're his friends, he knows things about them. I'll ask him to threaten them.'

'No! No, please, Amy, just leave it be, luv. I don't want them to ever know that I'm out of here. They'd make me tell them stuff.' She grasped Amy's arm. 'They'd hurt me. And you and Cyril. They mustn't find out. But they won't find me where you're taking me, and they won't know I'm gone. But they will if yer get this 'someone' to talk to them as then none of us'll be safe.'

Amy's stomach clenched as fear rippled through her. There was something these two knew that they weren't telling. She knew it was about Tilda and this posed a dilemma for her. *Should I tell Ruth and Ellen? What if they made Mum tell them? What if Bett's sons find out Mum is out of the workhouse?*

'You know where Tilda is, don't yer, Mum? It's all right, you can tell me. I just want to know that she's safe. I promise I won't tell anyone anything, not even Ruth and Ellen. But that's only because I need to keep you safe too.'

'I — I do . . . She ain't got much of a life, but she's safe, and she must stay there, girl. But she'll get her chance one day. Them . . . boys can't get away with what they do for ever. One day they'll get their comeuppance. Then she'll be free of the fear of them, as we will be. Me and Cyril love Tilda so we'll never, ever tell a soul where she is, not even you, luv, will we, Cyril?'

226

'No, Ethel. I cross me heart and hope to die.'

'Please, just tell me, Mum.'

'No. I can't, me darlin', and neither can Cyril. If we do, we'll put your life in danger too. If they find out yer know, yer won't be safe. That's why you must never let this mate of yours ask them about letting me off. They'll find out where I am then.'

Amy couldn't believe what she was hearing, or the position it was putting her in. She never thought a time would come when she had to keep a secret from Ruth and Ellen, but something told her this was one thing she had to keep from them for her mum's and Cyril's sake. And from what she could glean, Tilda's sake too.

As this thought came to her, she did what she hadn't done for a long time — she looked heavenward and prayed to Ruth's Holy Mary. *Please keep everyone I love safe, Holy Mary, and help me. I'm going to need help to do this as I'm going to have to deceive me lovely Ruth and Ellen.*

As she looked into her mum's eyes, she knew this was the only course open to her. She wouldn't press her mum, or Cyril. Better that she didn't know. Because if she did, she would have to tell Ruth and Ellen then, and that would mean they would move heaven and earth to be with their mum. What would happen then? If these men could do such a thing as to break a woman's fingers, they must be ruthless beyond anything Amy knew and wouldn't have any mercy on anyone.

'Don't worry. We'll never mention it again, I promise.' Amy hugged her mum gently, afraid of hurting her. She'd been hurt enough. Now was the time to try to give her and Cyril some happiness.

'I have to go now, luv. I'll come back in a couple of days. There's a lot to do. By then, I should know when you can come and paint the shop, Cyril.'

'Will it be before Christmas that you take us to live with yer, Amy? We ain't had a proper Christmas for a long time.'

'It will, Mum. I promise you that. Ruth needs the shop to be open before then. But I don't know how we're going to do everything.' She told them about Ellen's wedding and all they had to do for that.

'That'll be lovely, darlin'.'

'And I have a mate I need to help. And that's why I must dash now.' She kissed them both. Cyril came with her to the door. 'I'm sorry, Amy, I have to do as Ethel says. Ethel knows what's best for me.'

'I know. Don't say any more, luv. I'll see you soon, and'll have arrangements made for yer.'

He waved her goodbye. Amy thought he was a strange mixture. Sometimes he seemed like a child, at others determined and scary even. At least, he had scared them when they'd first been to the workhouse. But then, that would be to do with the knowledge he and her mum had of Bett's boys, and of Tilda.

All of this made Amy's heart sink. She hated what she was going to do to Ruth and Ellen, but knew she had no choice.

* * *

When she arrived in Old Nichol Street, Jeff came running towards her. 'Ivan can't wait for yer to come, Amy, nor me.'

'How's Ivan been, luv?'

'He ain't had a drink, Amy. But he's been shaking a

228

lot and emptying his guts into the gutter.'

Amy wanted to tell Jeff not to talk like that, but she was more concerned about Ivan than trying to teach Jeff a bit of decorum. 'Is he ill?'

'No. It does that when they stop drinking, yer know.'

'How do yer know that, then?'

''Cause me mate's mum tried to come off the drink and she was like that. She got so bad that she went back on it! But then, she kicked the bucket . . . Me brovver won't die, will he?'

'No, luv. We're going to take care of him. I have a friend who's a doctor, and one who can sort things out in people's heads. Between them they'll get Ivan right. Have yer packed yer bag then?'

'Are we coming with you now?'

'You are. Me mates are getting yer room ready as we speak.'

'Well, I ain't got no bag to pack, I've got what I stand up in and another pair of pants and that's it.'

Amy looked at Jeff's ragged jumper and filthy short trousers and could have cried. By pants, she didn't know if he meant his undergarment or trousers. But whichever it was, it wouldn't improve things.

He ran off calling Ivan's name. Amy was shocked to see the state of Ivan. He looked clean, but so very ill and as if he hadn't the strength to stand without leaning on the door frame. His grin was the same and this heartened her. She quickened her step to get to him. 'Oh, Ivan, luv, I can see yer feel ill, but we'll get yer through this, I promise.'

Ivan winked at her, and in the gesture, she thought she saw the fighting spirit of the old Ivan and this gave her hope.

'We need to go quickly, Amy, the rent man's due

and I ain't got nothing to give him. He said he'd have me in court for debt. If I've gone and left the keys, he won't bother to find me. He'll just let the place to some other poor family.'

'All right, luv. Have yer got yer things together?'

'I 'ave. They're in me old army bag. Jeff packed it, so I ain't sure what everything looks like.'

Amy didn't worry too much about this. Ruth and Ellen would have ideas about kitting them both out. Ivan looked decently dressed, and this was a relief to her. He laughed at her as she surveyed him.

'Will I pass, luv? I ain't worn these since I came home from the war. They've been hanging up behind me door.'

'You look dandy, Ivan, mate. Have yer got anything for Jeff to change into, or any nightshirts for him?'

'No . . . Oh, Amy, there ain't been any money to get anything.' He looked at the scruffy little Jeff and his face fell in shame. 'I ain't even noticed . . . I'm sorry, Amy . . . Come here, Jeff.'

When Jeff went up to him a tear plopped onto Ivan's cheek. 'I'm sorry, Jeff. I should've took more care of yer. I'll change, I promise. I'll become a brother yer can be proud of.'

'I am proud of yer. You fought in the war! You beat them Germans, Ivan.'

Ivan hugged the boy to him. 'We'll be all right now. Amy'll take care of us.'

'I will. What's yer favourite meal, Jeff?'

Jeff looked up at Amy. 'I think it'll be pie and mash, only I ain't ever tasted it. Me mate said he 'as and he said it were bleedin' smashing!'

'Hey. Yer can cut that swearing out, young man. Me mates won't stand for that, and neither will I!'

'Sorry, Amy, I'll try, but it sort of rolls off me tongue.'

'Well, we'll cut yer tongue out then.'

His eyes opened wide. 'I won't swear, I promise.'

Amy burst out laughing. 'Yer daft thing, I won't hurt yer. But you must try, eh? Try to be a good boy.'

'I will. Ivan said I'll get to sleep in a proper bed and have three meals a day and get to go to school!'

'Have yer never been to school then, Jeff?'

'No. No one ever took me. But I'm clever, I can read and write, I taught meself.'

'Ha, he's fibbing. He has a mate who goes to school and he makes him teach him everything he learns.'

Amy couldn't think why Jeff had not been to school. There were church schools everywhere and it was the law, but she decided not to pursue this. She wanted to get away from the stench of this place and she wanted so much to get them away from it and to take them to a proper home. She made her mind up as she picked up the paper bag that held all of their things and then took hold of Ivan's arm that supper would be pie and mash, even if she had to fetch it from the pie shop herself.

'We need to walk to the end of the road, Ivan. Can yer manage that, luv? Only the cabs go by there and we can get one to take us home.'

'Have you got enough money for that, Amy?'

'I have. Come on, let's get out of here.'

In the cab she sat between them, conscious of the smell of them — a stale, unwashed smell, which clung to them even though they had made an effort to clean themselves. But despite this, her heart warmed when Ivan slipped his hand in hers and squeezed it. 'I won't let yer down, Amy, I promise yer.'

She could feel the shaking of his body that Jeff had

231

told her about. 'I know, mate, yer never have in the past, so I can't see yer starting now.'

Another hand came into hers, a small sweaty one. She looked down at Jeff. He looked afraid. All of this was new to him. He'd only ever known Old Nichol Street. She took her hand from his and put her arm around him. 'Everything's going to be all right, Jeff, luv. I'm going to take care of yer. I promise. What do yer think of being in a cab, eh?'

'I like it.' He looked up at her. His eyes had filled with tears and his bottom lip quivered. She gently pressed his head into her waist, then bent and kissed his tangled greasy hair. She was rewarded by him saying, 'I love yer, Amy,' and this swelled her heart once more. This child, who'd been so uncared for like herself for many years, and had maybe never felt real love, had given his heart the moment someone showed him a little kindness. This touched her so deeply. She smiled down at him. 'And I love you, me darlin'.'

His head drooped and fell onto her lap. She stroked his fringe, the only part of his hair that lay flat. When he closed his eyes, he looked cherubic. She'd care for him, see he went to school, and that Ivan got on his feet. How she was going to do all this and look after her mum and Cyril too, she didn't know. She only knew she had enough love for them all to have a good try and that she would have the help of Ruth and Ellen.

232

21

Ellen

Ellen could see the worried look on Amy's face. Bringing her friend here, who she'd found to be a changed person, must be an ordeal. But she, Ruth and Robbie had chatted while they'd prepared everything. They all agreed that as Ivan had been the saviour of their dear Amy, then they were all going to do the best for him.

They all understood, having been in the thick of war themselves, if not in the trenches like Ivan had been, and they'd agreed the road ahead wouldn't be easy for him, or them.

One main worry was whether Ivan would be considered a deserter. They understood that he'd left the holding camp, where Canadians waited to be shipped home once the war had ended, without leave to, and for this they wondered if he would be punished.

Abe, a high-ranking officer during the war, was looking into this without making anything official. They thought to ease Ivan's mind, though doubted anyone would bother to look for him anyway.

'This is Ivan, everybody!'

Amy had come through the front door and up the stairs. Ivan was behind her, looking unkempt. In his arms he held a sleepy child, but the weight of him was pulling Ivan forward.

Ellen stepped forward. 'Hello, Ivan, we feel like we

233

know you with all Amy has told us. She never stops talking about you and how you saved her in Canada. And you fought to save us all in France. We're grateful for that. Welcome to your new home.'

Ruth made them all laugh. 'Oh dear, mate, don't take notice of Ellen, she's one for the speeches. Come on in and take the weight off yer feet. We've got the kettle on . . . And I take it this is Jeff? Hand him to me, luv.'

Everyone giggled, especially Ellen. 'Sorry, I didn't mean to be formal. I know I don't look as though I do, but I get nervous meeting new people — a legacy of being brought up on my own.'

Ivan smiled at her. 'So, you're Ruth and you're . . . Ellen? I guessed that as you're the one with the fancy speech that Amy told me of. She also said that you're the clever one amongst them.'

'Ha! Not cleverer, mind, I've just been lucky to have had an education. Yes, I'm Ellen. Pleased to meet you, Ivan.'

Ivan put out a grubby hand towards her. She took it, and now that he was relieved of Jeff, she put her arm around him. 'Lovely to have you here.'

'Huh, she's only saying that because she leaves soon!'

This from Amy shocked Ellen for a moment, but then she saw her grin and heard the lovely laugh come from Ivan that Amy had told them about. This lightened the moment again and she laughed with them. 'Don't take any notice of them. They both like to tease me.'

As they sat around the table, Ellen found their chatter was easy, no awkward moments. *This is going better than I ever imagined.* Once more she felt the tension drain from her.

Ruth still held a shy Jeff. The little boy didn't seem at all like Amy had described Ivan's brother, but then, it must all be strange to him.

Once he'd drunk his glass of milk Ruth asked, 'Would you like to go through to meet my little boy?'

'How little is 'e then?'

'Oh, not much shorter than you. Though you're older by three years, which is a lot, so yer need to take care of him.'

'I could teach 'im a thing or two then.'

'No, yer can't, Jeff. He don't need to know the tricks you've had to know, mate. Just play with him and be good to him. Treat him like yer'd treat a brother.'

'Me brothers 'ave all gone.' Jeff addressed this to Amy. 'Me mum hid me under the floorboards when they came for them. She told 'im there weren't any more of us. So then —'

'That's enough, Jeff, yer don't 'ave to give our history.'

'No, let him talk. We want to know. And we'll tell you ours as the time goes on as we have all been in similar boats to you, Jeff. You tell us all you want to, when you want to. It helps to get it off your chest.'

'Yer a posh one, so 'ow come yer've been through stuff like me and Ivan?'

Ellen smiled. 'There's a saying which goes, don't judge a book by its cover, and that means —'

'I know what it means. I read, yer know. It's to say that not everything is as it seems.'

This surprised Ellen but gave her such hope for this little boy. His intelligence was superior to most boys his age and without him having had any advantages. 'That's it exactly. So, you need to apply that to

235

me. Just because I talk posh, you mustn't assume that I don't know what it's like to suffer. Anyway, you go through with Ruth and meet Archie. He's been saying all morning that he has a new friend coming today.'

Jeff looked at her. His gaze said he didn't quite know how to take her. 'I've got a friend at 'ome.'

Ruth put him down. 'Well, now you'll have another. Yer can't have too many friends, mate. Come on.'

As the door closed behind him, Ivan said, 'I'm sorry about that, Ellen. He don't know any better than to speak 'is mind. He'll learn. Like he says, he's educated himself and not many can do that.'

'Don't apologize, Ivan. We want him to feel at home, not inhibited. We don't want him to change. We hope to make things better for him, that's all. He needs to be able to talk freely for that.'

'Be careful not to give him too much rope, luv. He has a few choice words he could come out with.'

Ellen smiled. 'I will.' She knew she'd gone too far. Nerves again coupled with an eagerness to please, but more than that, a desire to help. Ivan and Jeff needed the kind of help she could give them. But she made her mind up to tread carefully.

Amy butted in. Ellen was relieved, till Amy came out with, 'Right, Ivan. A scrub up for you. Yer about the same size as Robbie, who I've told you about. I'll nip down to pinch some clothes from him for yer . . . Ellen, will yer start to run a bath for Ivan, luv?'

Ivan grinned. 'That's me Amy! Now I know I am with yer, luv. Yes, a bath would be lovely. I ain't had one since I left the holding camp . . . I mean . . .'

'Oh, don't worry, luv. They all know what yer did. And none of us blame yer. You know I told yer about Abe? Well, he's sorting it all out, so don't think any more about it . . . and yer needn't look like that, mate. He won't drop yer in it.'

Ellen nodded. 'Honestly, there's nothing to worry about. Now, go and find Jeff and introduce yourself to Archie. Just through there.' She pointed to the door that led off the kitchen into a long, narrow hall from where all the bedrooms, and Archie's box room, led off, as well as the bathroom and their living room, which backed onto the kitchen and overlooked the street. 'He's in the one on the right as you go out of the kitchen.'

As the water splashed and gurgled into the bath, Ellen wished she could start again with Ivan and Jeff. She felt she must have come over so pompous. Taking a deep breath, she determined to be more light-hearted with less of the analysing! She giggled. She'd become a psychiatrist without going through the exams. *Seriously, I must step back a bit and just be friendly. Everything takes time.* She felt relieved to be going away at the weekend. Her heart fluttered at the thought of being at the cottage with Bernard. Since that first time of making love, they hadn't had a chance to come together again. At the thought of it happening again, the muscles in her groin clenched. She couldn't wait.

As she watched the water gradually fill the tub, checking every now and then that it wasn't going cold, she visualized being in Bernard's arms. Soon, it would be every night — well, except for when he'd be on nights in his new job at the hospital. Which would happen as she was sure he would get the position he'd applied for — he couldn't fail. With the bath now full she went in search of Ivan.

As she passed by Amy's old bedroom the door was

ajar. The sound of sobs and Amy's voice drifted to her. 'It'll be all right, mate, I've got yer.'

Peeping in, she saw Amy lying on the bed next to a shaking, crying Ivan.

'Yer can do this, Ivan, I know yer can. Look what we've come through already, luv.'

'Hold me, Amy. Hold me.'

Ellen swallowed. The deep suffering of Ivan was tangible. She wanted to run into the bedroom, to hold him just like Amy was and help Amy to help him, but she crept by. When she got to the kitchen door, she hesitated, then went a little further and opened the door to Archie's tiny room. The joyous noise coming from there was an extreme contrast. 'Yer did it, yer bleedin' did it!'

Ellen held her breath and looked to see what Archie had done. A precarious tower, built with the bricks that Abe had carved out of wood for Archie, stood wobbling between the two boys.

'I breedin' did!'

Ellen pressed her hand over her mouth to stop the laughter she wanted to roar out. The words coming from Archie had almost floored her. Unsure what to do, she closed the door and crept away.

'What're yer laughing at, Ellen?'

'If I told you, you might laugh, but then again, you might blow your top!' This she told Ruth amidst a stutter of laughter as the funny moment still tickled her.

'What? You ain't dropped the towel in the bath, have yer?'

'No.' Ellen shook her head. 'I'm sorry . . . but it's Archie, swearing like a proper cockney!'

Ruth stood still for a moment, her indecision making her expression change from anger to confusion.

238

'Oh, Ellen, what should I do?'

'Nothing yet. It will have to be a gradual process. Anyway, that's not the only problem we have, love.' Ellen told her what she'd seen.

'Oh, poor Amy. She wants to be everything for everyone, and poor darlin' is surrounded by those who are down at the moment. But she can't lift them all up on her own, we've got to help her. I just don't know how.'

'Not like me, like a bull at a gate, that's for sure. Let's just let her get on with it in her own way, but be there for her if she wants us to be, eh?'

'You have changed yer tune! Yes, you did go head-long in, the saviour of all mankind, but I love yer for that, Ellen. It's what yer do, luv, and we wouldn't have you any other way. Come here. I'm sorry for teasing yer how I did.'

As they hugged, Ellen said, 'I deserved it. I've got to stop thinking of myself as the Florence Nightingale of all Florence Nightingales!'

They both laughed.

As they parted Ellen said, 'Speaking of Florence, I came through to make a telephone call to the Red Cross about a job — that's if I can get a line. We never had any trouble in Leeds as we were only on a party line with one other household. Here, it's like the whole of London is rattling on when you pick up the receiver.'

As it happened, Ellen got the operator first time. 'Hello, will you put me through to the Red Cross Headquarters, please.'

'Hold the line, madam.'

A few minutes went by. Ellen was praying that no one sharing the line picked up their receiver. She was

239

lucky this time.

'Hello. Red Cross.'

Explaining that she'd trained as a nurse with them and was looking for a job, Ellen was told they couldn't help with paid employment, only volunteers. 'We still have a few out there looking after returned wounded, but all do it voluntarily.'

'Oh? I'm sorry. I didn't realize.'

'But off the cuff, I can tell you that I do know one hospital that is looking for staff who are experienced at looking after the wounded who returned from war — mostly the limbless, I think. Just a minute. Ah, here is it. It's the Queen Alexandra Rehabilitation Hospital in Roehampton.'

Having no idea where that was in relation to Southampton Way, Ellen thanked the girl and rang off.

'Any luck?'

'I don't know. Where's Roehampton?'

'Haven't a clue, luv, Abe'll know. Pop down and ask him. I'll go and encourage Amy to get Ivan to take advantage of the bath while the water's still hot.'

Running down the stairs, Ellen felt a trickle of excitement at the prospect of going to work. She hadn't thought she would need to until she helped Bernard with his practice, but now they would need all the money they could get together to make that happen.

When she knocked and heard the call to come in, she wasn't surprised to also hear music blasting out. Abe sat in the living room in his small wheelchair, which had been a recent invention of his. He'd had Robbie taking the back and sides off an old one he had. This just left him with a seat and two huge wheels which meant he could propel himself around without

240

bumping into things.

'Hello, Ellen, my dear, how nice. I didn't expect a visit from you. Sorry about the noise, Robbie's running through a few ideas he has for he and Ruth to rehearse. They begin tomorrow.'

'That's okay. Can I get you a cup of tea?'

'No, I haven't long had one, thank you. Funny, but I still stick to old routines. Cup of tea at four on the dot with two biscuits.'

'Old fuddy-duddy!'

'Ha, that's just what I'm becoming. How's it going with the two new lodgers?'

Ellen told him, making him burst out laughing at Archie's swearing. 'Oh dear, I'll have my hands full when I begin to teach him . . . You should be in that music hall show, your cockney is hilarious. So, what about Ivan?'

After he'd listened a few moments, he said, 'Oh dear, that's not good. But I think it's what can be expected. You three have taken on a lot. I hope you haven't bitten off more than you can chew.'

'So do I. Anyway, that's not all I have to bite off.' She told him about hers and Bernard's plans and how she'd found out about the vacancies at Roehampton.

'Roehampton House? I knew it well before it was requisitioned. My father was a friend of Mr Wilson, the owner. But it's a long way from here, dear, too far. I think by car it would take a couple of hours, and by train, a good hour and a half and there'll most likely be several route changes along the way. Do they have live-in nurses?'

'Oh, I hadn't thought of that, but I suppose.' The idea of living away from Bernard for a few days a week didn't appeal and yet, the job did. She'd so like

241

to help those like Abe again — maimed by the war, it seemed their life was over, but surely there was something being done? Maybe at Roehampton she could find out what.

'Not a good alternative for a new bride, eh?'

Ellen blushed.

Abe laughed. 'Sorry, naughty of me. It's living with a theatrical type, and having them visit, they are so free with their speech — but I must admit, it's liberating!'

'Not at all. Ha, I'm one for saying what comes into my mind. I was analysing poor Ivan when he'd only just walked through the door. No wonder he broke down.'

'That wouldn't be your fault, dear. You have a knack of making people see a way around their fears and demons. Never give up. You helped me so much.' Abe sighed. 'I so wish that someone could help me to get out of this blasted chair!'

Misunderstanding him, Ellen jumped up. 'I'll help you, just hold onto me and the arm of your armchair and we'll swing you across.'

Abe once more burst out laughing. 'No . . . I mean, I want to walk again! Give me some legs so I didn't need the wheelchair!'

Ellen joined in with his laughter. When they sobered, she said, 'Do you know, I think, if Bernard agrees, I will go for this job. Maybe I will learn things that will help you, Abe.'

His eyes became wistful. 'Oh, I hope you do, my dear. I hope you do. I feel so useless.'

This saddened Ellen. The war had taken its toll on so many. In this very house they had two lovely men — not that she knew Ivan yet, but Amy had told them so much good about him — whose lives had been changed beyond recognition and there was very little help out there for them. Her heart felt heavy at the thought. 'Abe, if this hadn't happened to you, what would you have done with your life?'

'Oh, probably gone into banking with my father — not at all suitable for me . . . What I really wanted to do was to work in engineering. I know. Not the sort of job a boy born with a silver spoon in his mouth would dream of doing. But I find the idea of inventing and making things for the good of all in the country exciting and challenging.'

'Well, why not? Life changes course at times but that doesn't mean we have to. I don't see why you can't invent things and get them made up by others.'

'I'll see. I'll think about it. But you could be right.'

Suddenly it was as if a light had been turned on in Abe's eyes as he said, 'Actually, we have a small room that's not used regularly — the one that matches your small bedroom. I told Robbie to put the storage in there, but he preferred to leave it with a single bed in just in case a friend wanted to stay over. I could use it as an office.' Abe seemed to come to life. 'I could design a drawing easel for myself and kit myself out with rulers and set squares and all the tools I would need to put my ideas on paper.'

'Exactly!' Ellen could feel the hope rising in him. 'I can shop for you, Abe. Or I can get Bernard to take you shopping for what you need.'

'That would be amazing. I wouldn't have to be pushed everywhere, I can drive my outside chair quite well . . . Oh, but it's too big to go into a car or on the train to even get me near to the shops I would need.'

Abe's outside chair had handles that he used to

propel and steer it. 'Then that's what you have to do, Abe, invent one that can fold and go into a car, or can be strapped on the back, you know, like some people strap a bike to their car. You know what is needed by the limbless, be their champion, Abe.'

'Oh, Ellen, I've never spoken to anyone about any of this. You have made me realize that what I long for, I can invent.'

'That's Adrian's influence. He taught me that in his first words to me. He said, 'I teach by bringing out what you already know.' And he did. I need to learn to be even more like he was as I know I sometimes go too far with my wisdom, but I mean well.'

'And you do a lot of good, don't let the odd slip-up change you. Learn from them, learn when your advice is needed and when not. That's all it takes. I for one have been helped by you, Ellen. I am going to make a list of what I need, and Robbie will get it for me, but one day, he will take me on a train, on a bus, or in the car — me, my chair and all. And that will happen for others too. That's your inspiration, Ellen.'

Ellen crossed the room to stand beside him. She put her arm around his shoulders and kissed the top of his head. Then, as was always the temptation with Abe, she brushed his fringe back from his forehead. His hand took hers. 'That's a losing battle, my dear, it just flops forward again.'

They both giggled.

'Ellen, you're a special person, never forget that.'

For a moment Ellen let in memories of a time when she was unloved, unwanted, abused, hurt and abandoned. Never then had she felt she was special. She didn't now, but she did recognize that she had a gift, and that she should start to use it wisely and not try to fix everyone's world as not all wanted that.

'You've helped me so much, Abe. I'll talk to Bernard this weekend about going to work at Roehampton. If he is all right with it, I'll do it.'

'Good for you. It sounds like the perfect job. You can help those who really need it, physically and mentally. The forgotten war heroes.'

As she left him to go back upstairs, she thought, *Yes, I can do that.* But it was accompanied by a huge sigh, as by doing it, how was she going to help Amy's mum and Ivan?

Somehow, she must find a way to do that too.

* * *

All these worries left her when Bernard called the next day to begin their long journey north. As petrol was still scarce, he told her he'd booked them on a train — a bit of a disappointment to her as she'd thought to bring a few things back from her cottage with her.

'We can still bring them back with us, darling. We'll pack them and have a cab take them to the station. Then we'll pay for them to go into the goods carriage.'

Not sure about this, but accepting it, Ellen was soon smiling again as they sat in a carriage all to themselves and snuggled up close.

Tears prickled her eyes when finally they stood outside the cottage. It looked beautiful. The roses climbing the walls and over the doorway were bare of flowers but had a beauty of their own with their leaves frosted and glinting in the winter sun.

'It's lovely, darling. How can you bear to part with it?'

245

'It's not easy to, but it's so impractical to keep it, and we need the money, darling . . . Come on, let's get in. My solicitor would have had someone in to light the fires, dust it all and air the beds.'

'Beds? Won't we only need one?'

Ellen thrilled at this. She clutched the arm she'd linked into and looked up at him. 'Yes. Just the one.'

The key made the same clunking sound she remembered, and the door creaked in just the same way she was used to. Walking in was like going back in time, with memories sweet and yet the pain of loss raw.

'Darling, you're crying!'

'I — I think part of me expected Dilly to greet me, and Gran to be waiting for me in her sitting room, and Adrian holding out his hands to welcome me home.'

'Oh, my darling. I didn't know your gran, or Dilly, but I can feel the pain of Adrian's loss. He was a good sort.'

'It's lovely that you knew him. It's like our backgrounds have a connection, with you, Abe and Adrian going to the same school.'

'That's how it is in our circles, we made lasting friendships. We just didn't need each other so much, but even if we didn't see each other for years, we only had to meet, shake hands and we were back to the same world again.'

'That's lovely. And it was the same for us. Separation didn't lessen how we felt about each other.'

Bernard smiled and nodded. 'Well, let's get in, darling. I've had a sudden urge to kiss you in front of a roaring fire.'

His kiss burned her; his caresses lit her spirit. Unable to resist the demands she read into them, she yielded to his loving of her as he lowered her onto the rug and felt it accept her and cushion her body as she gave herself fully to Bernard's love for her.

As they lay naked, spent and warmed by the crackling fire, they talked — of their future, and their plans to achieve their dreams. Bernard backed wholeheartedly her plans to apply for the vacancy at Roehampton, though told her it would break his heart to say goodbye to her for a few days each week. Then they made love again, finding new heights each time as they discovered each other's pleasure.

22

Ruth

Two weeks later, Ruth sewed the last stitch into the hem of the last frock. 'There! We've done it!'

She hung it on the last of the picture hooks where three pictures had hung when this was Ellen's room and now all held frocks.

'Oh, Ruth, they look lovely.'

Ruth smiled as she watched Ellen gaze up at the long cream bridal gown and two calf-length deep blue bridesmaids' frocks. 'We've done a pretty good job, I think. Oh, Ellen, you're going to look lovely. But oh, I can't get me head around you going. And not just going to live with Bernard, but to board in the hospital in Roehampton for four nights a week.'

'I know. Come here and let me give you a hug.'

'I need these hugs. And now I won't be able to have them just when I do.'

'I'll save them up for you, eh? Every time I want to hug you, I'll put it in my pocket and bring it home with me.'

'Ha, Ellen, you've a lovely way of saying things. I can imagine you doing that, but . . .'

'Ruth, we got through me being in France, didn't we, love?'

'We did, and I know we'll get through this, but it just won't be the same.'

'You'll have Ivan and little Jeff for company, even

248

after Amy moves into her flat.'

'I know. He's doing so well. He hasn't even had the shakes for these last three days and is a huge help at the shop.'

'Has he got all of your stock there for you yet? He seems to spend endless hours going up to the attic, coming down with boxes, carting them to the shop with him, and then setting to and painting the shop out for you too!'

'I know, he's a godsend. Tomorrow he's going to help sort all the furniture that you have arriving for Amy as Cyril has finished painting her rooms for her.'

'Oh, everything's going to be amazing.'

'It is all going well, I give yer that, but it's all heading towards me being on me own . . . well, not on me own, but not having you and Amy here with me.'

'You'll be so busy, you won't notice. You said yours and Robbie's rehearsals are coming along well. Your music hall engagement will start soon, and your shop will open — you'll not have time to miss us, Ruth. You'll hardly have time to think about us. I just don't know how you're going to do everything.'

'I need to. And having Ivan is turning out to be a bonus as he will be here for Archie. He's really good with him and he's like a father to Jeff.'

'He is. But take care, Ruth. Always look out for signs of him lapsing. It might not happen, as when he was drinking it had only gone on a few months. He told me he was all right till his mum killed herself, then his world fell apart altogether, and everything crowded him. That hasn't gone away, but we can hope that the drink didn't get a real hold on him as it would have if he'd been reliant on it for years.'

'Is there that hope, Ellen? I need there to be. I'll be

afraid if not. I — I mean, not for me, but of leaving the boys with him.'

'There's every hope. I don't think the drinking was something he needed to live, but just needed to block it all out and make life bearable. If his life continues to improve as it has, it can just be a faded drunken memory. It's just that we all have triggers — you do, I do and Amy does. And I'm sure Abe and Robbie do. But we don't turn to something that can destroy us by way of coping. We don't know yet that Ivan will ever again, but just be on your guard. If you see him getting morose, then be ready to help him.'

'I will. Oh, Ellen, it's all such a shame. Such a lovely man.'

Ellen looked at her with that look Ellen could give as if a light was dawning or something. Ruth felt herself colour. She looked away. 'Anyway, I'm glad you're pleased with the frocks, luv. With only a week to go, it would have been a disaster to have you hate them.'

'They are all I dreamed of. And it is in the simplicity that their beauty lies. No frills, no fancy style, just a lovely empire line that's sophisticated and plain and yet elegant. I think you deserve another hug, Ruth.'

They clung to one another, feeling the closeness of their parting and how little they would see each other . . . *But that mustn't be so! I must make it so that it isn't!*

'Ellen, luv, let's make a night when I'm not working and you're home and get Ivan to sit with Archie and Jeff, then me and you and Amy spend time together, eh? It can be once a fortnight even, but let's do it!'

'Yes, that's a good idea. It'll be the Orphanage Girls' night out, eh?'

'Ha, I hadn't thought to call it anything, but that's

250

as good a name as any as that place for all it was brought us together.'

'And that's how I think of it now. The rest . . . well, that happened to a different Ellen, not this one that is me.'

'Oh, Ellen. I've never thought of it like that. Always it haunts me, but yer right, it did happen to three different little girls. We're bigger than that now. We're all our own person, with good lives and we're loved and cherished . . . Oh, luv. In that one little sentence, you've changed something in me. Something hidden, but there. Like a monster hiding in wait for me. Well, yer just killed the monster, luv. Ta, Ellen.'

Their tears mingled as they went back into their hug, but they weren't sad, or frightened tears, they were healing ones.

'Look at us. We're a soppy pair. Come on, let's put the kettle on, girl, we deserve a cuppa.'

Amy came back in at that moment. She'd left them as soon as she'd finished the hem she'd been working on to check on Jeff and Archie. Though both Ruth and Ellen knew it was also to check on Ivan, who was sitting in the living room on his own. She, like them, worried about him. Poor chap couldn't have a quiet moment without one or the other of them checking up on him.

'Ha, yer heard the word 'kettle' then, luv?'

'No, but a good idea . . . Are yer both all right?'

'We are, we were just having a moment — well, me really. I was just getting morose about you all leaving me.'

Amy ran towards her. Ruth went into her arms. 'I'm not, luv. We'll see each other every day.'

'I know we will. I'm being daft. I never liked change.'

'No, we get cosy in what is normal for us, but change is good for us too. Look what it's sparked already!'

Ellen told Amy of their plans.

'Ooh, we ain't never had a night out — not a proper one. We could go for pie and mash, or just go for a walk, or maybe, every now and again, we could go to the theatre!'

Amy's enthusiasm sparked something in Ruth, and she felt better for it. 'You're right. Well, let's get that cup of tea now, we've earned it.'

The door opened. Ivan popped his head around it. He grinned at them. 'I beat yer to it. I put the kettle on the moment Amy left me, as she'd told me yer'd finished yer labours . . . My, they're lovely.'

Ruth shooed him away. 'Ivan, get out! It's bad luck for anyone to see the dresses before the day!'

'Ha, well, that's bad luck yer all going to have then, Ruth, luv. As I've peeped at them before now when they were in the process of being made.'

They all laughed, and Ruth felt more settled inside. Everything was going to be all right. She caught a glance from Ivan that was just for her, and coloured as she had done earlier. Brushing the feeling off, she told them, 'Well, the whistle will be howling the place down if we don't get to the kettle now.'

As she had predicted the whistle on the kettle was shrieking at them. It helped Ruth to go through the process of making the tea. She couldn't understand herself. She seemed to be turning into a dizzy young girl, not a woman in her mid-twenties. Giggling at the thought, she carried the tray through to the living room.

It all looked so cosy to her and more so as Ivan had stoked the fire up. It'd been cold in the bedroom-cum-workroom, even though they'd had a small paraffin heater going.

Once she put the tray down, Ruth crossed to the window. As she thought, there was frost everywhere. 'It all looks so Christmassy out here and with it not being long until the day itself, we should give some thought to what we're going to do. I have a cockerel on order, and I've a pudding just waiting for the final stir from the boys, but we should make an effort this year, as it's the first Christmas with us all together . . . Oh, we will all be able to be together, won't we?'

'Sounds lovely. But where? If you mean all, there's us four and Bernard, Abe and Robbie and Ethel and Cyril and then the two boys . . . Oh, if only we could add our mum to that list, Ruth, love.'

'I know, Ellen, but don't give up hope. I think Robbie was seeing Bett's boys tonight, they might know something.'

'They didn't when she asked them for us when we first discovered we were half-sisters. They said she'd vanished.'

Amy jumped up, startling Ruth. 'I — I just need the loo, excuse me.'

Her demeanour was such that she looked like she would burst into tears. After she'd closed the door behind her, Ellen asked, 'Do you think she's all right? Should I go after her?'

It was Ivan who answered. 'I think she's fine. I know she feels guilty at 'aving found her own mum and you two haven't. I'm sure that's all it is. I'll have a chat with her.'

'Ah, poor Amy. I didn't mean to upset her.'

Ruth went and sat with Ellen on the sofa. 'I don't think it was you, luv. So many things can upset us

— talk of Christmas when we've lost someone, for instance. Don't forget this may have been the first Christmas Amy spent with Teddy if he hadn't been killed.'

'I never thought about that.'

Amy came back in at that moment. Ellen stood and went to her. She held out her arms. When Amy went into them, she sobbed. 'I — I'm sorry, I'm so sorry.'

'Don't be, darling. We shouldn't have talked of Christmas when this would have been your first after the war with Teddy. You're bound to feel it.'

'Ta, Ellen. I'm all right now. I — I just wish everything was different.'

'We won't celebrate Christmas this year, eh?'

'Oh, no, Ruth, luv, I want to. We should, like yer say, it's our first all together again.'

'Are yer sure, luv?'

'I am. We ain't had a proper Christmas ever, have we, Ivan? There were never any kids where we were and farm life just seemed to carry on as normal every day of the year. And we didn't ever have one at the orphanage, did we?' Amy looked from Ellen to Ruth. They both shook their heads.

'Right, let's plan it then, shall we? You and Bernard will be back from your couple of nights away, so it depends on what shift Bernard is working. But as you don't start your job till after Christmas, we know you'll be here, Ellen.'

'I will, and I'm sure Bernard will for part of the day at least.'

'You'll have yer mum and Cyril out by then, Amy, so you three will be here. And we know Robbie and Abe will be, so dinner . . . As I say, I've got the cockerel coming, we just need the veg.'

'I can go and collect that if you put an order in, Ruth.'

'Ta, Ivan. That'd be a help as there'll be a fair bit to carry.'

'I'll do the cooking.'

'We'll all help, Amy, as yer've already taken on a lot by doing the wedding breakfast.'

'Oh, that's not much as it's a help yerself — sandwiches, cakes and jelly and cream. I've got that all planned and me and Ellen just have to do the shopping for that, then I make the cakes, pies and jellies this week and we all pitch in and make the sandwiches before we get dressed on the day.'

'Oh, and look after yer mum and Cyril and settle in to your new home all at the same time, eh?'

Amy giggled, 'Well, I'm going to need some help.'

Suddenly, it all seemed a bit daunting to Ruth, what with her shop opening the day after tomorrow too!

★ ★ ★

The opening day of 'Ruth's Milliner's Shop' fell a little flat, with only one person coming through the door all morning, and then she'd only come in for a nosey.

Ruth would have felt in the doldrums but for the fact that that evening was to be their first night out together and she was so looking forward to it.

'Ha, Ruth, yer've dusted that stand a dozen times already!'

'And you've brushed all the felt hats over a dozen times!'

She and Amy laughed out loud.

'We shouldn't have expected a big rush, yer know. People have got to get to know that we're here and that takes time.'

'I know. We should send Ivan out with a billboard over his neck to walk the streets advertising us.'

This made them laugh all the more.

'Oh, we're going to have such fun tonight, Ruth. Our first night out.'

'Yes, and then yer mum and Cyril will move in tomorrow! Everything seems to be coming together, except . . . well, we ain't found our mum, and I don't hold out a lot of hope.'

Amy didn't answer this. She just turned away and busied herself, vigorously brushing a felt beret.

'Is something wrong, Amy, luv?'

'No! . . . I — I'm sorry, Ruth. I . . . well, I just feel guilty at having found my mum.'

'Oh, you mustn't. We're really happy for yer and want to share your mum with yer, luv. I won't mention it again, I promise.'

Amy still looked as if she was troubled. Ruth couldn't understand this. But then, it must feel uncomfortable knowing that she and Ellen so longed to find their mum and she already had. She didn't want Amy to feel like that and decided to speak to Ellen about the best way to handle it so that Amy could enjoy at last knowing who her mum was and getting to live with her and take care of her.

But this didn't lift the feeling in her of deep sorrow and, yes, Amy was right, the pain was deeper since she'd found Ethel. Anyway, they still had the hope that Robbie would find something out, and he might know now, as he was working at the theatre the previous night.

With this conversation putting a further dampener on them, Ruth was glad when it came to the midday

256

closing hour and she could walk Archie back home to Abe for an afternoon of lessons. She smiled to herself, as she thought of the fun Abe and Archie had together as Abe was teaching him through playing games. It was working too, as Archie always had a new word, or a lovely picture that he'd drawn.

Looking down at him walking beside her, Ruth's inner smile turned to a sigh. She'd brought his carriage with her for quickness more than him needing it, but starved of fresh air, Archie wanted to walk which would take them twice as long, but as it wasn't far, she'd given in.

Archie began to skip along full of joy, and this lifted Ruth's spirit. 'The shop will do well, Archie, won't it?'

Archie looked up at her with a quizzical look. 'I like all the hats, Mummy.'

'Oh, that's good, luv. If you like them, I'm bound to do well!' This made her laugh; Archie could always cheer her up.

By the time Archie and she had eaten with Ellen and Ivan, Robbie still wasn't ready for rehearsal.

Abe teased him about his swollen face. 'You look like a mouse, darling.'

Robbie's sense of humour deserted him, as he'd had toothache all night and had been at the dentist.

Thinking it prudent to make an exit, Ruth told them that as she wasn't needed, she would go back to the shop for an hour. She still didn't feel happy about Amy, and wanted to make sure she was all right. She felt guilty that Amy's mum's homecoming might be spoiled and wanted to clear the air. 'I'll be back at three, Robbie. If yer no better then, we can leave it for today . . . Oi, Archie, give Mummy a kiss then.' Archie was engrossed in a book of pictures that Abe had given him.

The joy she felt at being hugged around the neck and having kisses planted on her cheeks increased as Robbie said, 'I'll come with yer to the door, Ruth, luv, I've some news for you.'

Her expression must have shown the anticipation she felt, but deflation came swiftly as Robbie said, 'It's not good news, luv, I'm sorry.'

Once in the hall, Robbie took her in his arms. 'Keep strong, luv, but it isn't looking good. I'm not a friend of Bett's boys by any means, but they do think I am. They tell me more than they might someone else, or even than they told Bett.'

'What did they say, Robbie? . . . Robbie, tell me!'

'They said they don't know. They asked me who wanted to know, then they said, 'You tell them, Robbie, that if we find that bitch, Tilda, they'll never see her again!"

'Oh, Robbie, no! No! Why? What has Tilda done?'

'They called her a grass. This means that she must have given the police information about them, but that was never going to work as they pay the police — well, a couple or so of them. Those who are in the know about any activity of the law to do with themselves. That's how they get away with everything they do. They are pre-warned of possible raids and information concerning themselves.'

'Oh, Robbie, I — I can't bear it. She's in danger every minute of her life. Where can she hide? What can we do?'

Robbie held her tighter. 'Nothing. Ruth, you must accept that we can do nothing, me darlin'.'

'I can't, Robbie, she's me mum!'

Robbie sighed. 'Look, luv, when you were in the

258

theatre world, you didn't come to know how much it is tied to the gangster world. I want to get out of it all and that is why I'm turning to music hall. I won't be as famous but should still draw crowds. But I'm not an artist who performs alone, I 'ave dancers around me. I 'ave other actors and we bounce off each other, that's why I need you to 'elp me to get out.'

'You mean, you're mixed up with them?'

'I wasn't but I am now that I've shown curiosity in Tilda.'

'Oh, Robbie, I'm sorry, mate. I had no idea. I thought the management only wanted a duo.'

'I know, luv. I didn't want to tell you more. But those boys — well, men — are bastards! And they're very dangerous.'

As Robbie said this, he clutched his mouth. 'Mind, that poxy dentist is worse than them. Bleedin' butcher!'

Despite everything, this made Ruth laugh. Robbie was such a baby when it came to pain, so though feeling sick with fear after what he'd told her, she gave all her attention to him. She gently touched his cheek. 'Go and rest, luv. I'll be back later. I just need a little time to think this all over. There must be a solution, there has to be.'

When she got back to the shop, Ruth had no time to talk to Amy as a group of six ladies arrived. All were about the same age as herself and they had an excited air about them.

One, who seemed to be in charge, announced, 'I'm Dora Thornton. We have been longing for you to open ever since your sign went up. Oh, and your hats are divine!'

'Ta . . . I mean, thank you very much.'

'And the sign in the window says that all the hats

are made by you. That's wonderful, so does that mean that you will make us hats to order, too?'

'It does. If yer give me an idea of what yer want, I can make it.'

Dora looked at her as if she didn't quite know what to make of her. Ruth hoped that her being a cockney didn't put them off — but then, she'd not change that just to get posh customers like these. She was cockney and proud of it.

By the time they left, they'd bought a hat each and told her they would be back in the new year ready to place their orders for the new season of racing.

Ruth should have been elated as they'd turned a disastrous start into an amazing one, but her heart was heavy.

'Ruth, girl, yer like a wet weekend when yer should be over the moon.'

'I can't talk about it, luv . . . I don't want to keep upsetting yer.'

'Oh, Ruth, mate, come here. Don't cry. Whatever it is, tell me.'

When she did, Amy dropped her arms from around Ruth and turned away. She stared out of the window with her arms folded.

Ruth felt exasperated. Her anger rose. 'Amy! For God's sake! Can't I get it through to yer that we're happy yer've found yer mum and it ain't about your good fortune when we talk about our mum, it's about our heartbreak!'

Amy's sob shook Ruth. 'Look, let's close for the rest of the afternoon. We need to talk, luv, this can't go on. You have to understand that we need to talk about our mum . . .'

'It's not that . . . Oh, Ruth, I have information. I

260

feel awful knowing something and keeping it a secret. But, Ruth, if I share it with yer, I'll put my own mum in danger.'

'What? You know something about our mum?'

Amy's sobs increased. Her body bent over. Though shocked to the core, Ruth felt Amy's anguish and wanted to comfort her. Crossing to the door, she turned the lock and changed the swinging card attached to it to 'closed'.

'Tell me, Amy, luv. Don't be scared. I know who we're dealing with. Our mum's in danger too. We need to stand together on this to protect them both.'

'Me mum and Cyril know where she is, but they won't tell me. I — I promised them faithfully that I wouldn't tell you as they're in danger too. Yer see, Bett's boys . . .'

Ruth listened with growing horror and fear to the reason Bett's boys were after Ethel and Tilda.

'So, Ethel knows Tilda — our mum! Oh, Amy, Amy, luv. Come here, I understand, I would have done the same as you to protect me mum.' Though she said this, Ruth wasn't sure that she would. 'Look, if we can find her, we can help her to be in a safe place. Please try to find out, Amy.'

'They won't tell me, I tried.'

'Let's talk to Ellen, Robbie and Abe, eh? Get yer coat, luv. We're going home.'

With the shop locked up, Ruth took Amy's arm, but neither spoke until they got home.

Robbie came out of his flat when they opened the door. 'I saw you coming. What is it? 'Ave yer closed the shop?'

'Amy, go and fetch Ellen down, we need to all be together.'

At that moment, Ivan came back with Jeff from their walk. 'What's going on? Amy, yer've been crying. Are yer all right, luv?'

'Not really. Oh, Ivan, I had a secret, and now I've told it, I'm scared.'

'Ivan, luv, will yer take Amy upstairs, and she can tell yer on the way, and will yer take Archie too, please? We need to talk about things he shouldn't hear, as yer'll understand when Amy explains.'

'Are you all right, Ruth, luv?' There it was again, that look. It held something for her that zinged through her — something she couldn't deal with. At least, not yet, not now. 'I'll see yer in a bit, Ivan, ta, luv.'

Archie, who'd heard her voice had come running to her. His eyes were like saucers, and held fear.

'Ivan's got a good game to play with you, Archie!'

Catching on, Ivan said, 'I'll be down in a minute for you and Jeff, I just need to get it ready.'

He and Amy ran up the stairs, leaving two excited boys behind them. Ruth sighed. How everything would be solved, she didn't know, but there would be a solution, there had to be.

23

Ellen

As she listened to Ruth, fear clenched Ellen's stomach. She felt physically sick. Her mum, her beautiful mum . . . A picture came to her of the distraught lady she'd seen at the cafe when she was just eleven years old.

Her words, 'I luv you, don't ever forget that,' came to her, and she'd known then that she would always love her mum.

'I once vowed to my father that I would find our mum and take care of her. I have to find a way of doing that, Ruth.'

Ruth took her in her arms. Their sobs mingled; their love for one another was the only salve that Ellen had.

'Ruth . . . Ellen, I am so very sorry. This is a dreadful story, and I want to break my heart for you, but we won't solve anything like that.' Abe got their attention with this. 'We need a plan. One that means Ethel and Cyril are safe and feel that they can trust us enough to tell us what they know, then we must make all three of them safe. Really safe.'

Ellen nodded. She knew of only one place that could be a sanctuary. In a flash she made her mind up. 'Rose Cottage — my home in Leeds. I won't sell it. It will become a haven for the three of them.'

'What? You mean me mum too?'

'It's the only way, Amy. No one would find them up

there. They are friends, they could live together, we could visit whenever we wanted to . . . Or, if you like, you could live with them.'

Amy looked from one to the other. 'But the money from the cottage sale is meant to set you and Bernard up!'

'It will put our plans back, but we can still get there . . . Oh, if only Frederick wasn't being such a beast!'

'Bernard said something about Freddie holding up your plans. Is he still doing that, Ellen?'

'Yes, he's a trustee of Bernard's legacy and doesn't agree that Bernard should have a general practice but should continue in surgery and become a top surgeon as he says his father would want. But it isn't what Bernard wants.'

'Right. I'll back you and Bernard . . . No, no, don't object. I want to do this. I should invest some of my money. It will help me to do so. And it may make Freddie see sense. He can be pig-headed at times. You met him, Ruth, you know what he's like.'

'I did. He chased poor Ellen and she didn't want his attentions. He's a womanizer.'

'Oh, Abe, I can't thank you enough, but of course it will be up to Bernard too.' Ellen went over and kissed Abe. 'Now, can you go a bit further and sort out this horrible situation?'

'Well, it has to be that we are told where your mother is before we can do anything . . . Amy, with somewhere safe for you all, would you be willing to persuade your mother and Cyril to tell you everything — and would they?'

'I don't know, Abe . . . Me mum was scared . . . but Cyril. Yes, I think I could if I got him on his own. He

264

lets his tongue say what it wants to. It's me mum who keeps him in check.'

'Good. That's our starting point. We can't do anything till we know where Tilda is.'

'I'll go right now and give it a try. They won't think it strange me turning up as I told them that I might visit to let them know everything is all right for tomorrow.'

'Amy, would you be willing to take them straight to Leeds? I'd go with you.'

'But what about your wedding, Ellen? Amy wouldn't be able to leave them there on their own, luv.'

'Ruth's right, Ellen, dear. I know you want to act swiftly, we all do, but that would complicate things further. Let her find out what she can first, then we can plan, but Saturday is your wedding day, come rain or shine, and whatever happens it's going to be a wonderful day. Robbie and I are all kitted out for our duties, aren't we, Robbie?'

'We are, me darlin' man.'

Abe smiled at Robbie, and Ellen thought the love between these two, who couldn't be more different from one another, was what she wanted for herself and knew she would have with her Bernard.

'All right . . . But can I come to the workhouse with you, Amy?'

'No, Ellen. Yer must stay with Ruth. You need each other. Besides, Cyril won't say a word if you're there, luv. I'll be back as soon as I can.'

As soon as Amy left, Ruth ran upstairs to see if the boys and Ivan were all right. She came back down smiling, saying the boys were having their tea and were full of all the fun they were having.

In the meantime, Ellen contacted Bernard. He

came over immediately, getting there soon after she put the phone down, and listened with concern to all they knew.

'I don't know what to say, darling, I can't take it all in . . . Gangsters!'

Ellen nodded, and as she did her tears spilled over. With this, Bernard was holding her, giving her the strength that she needed not to break down again as, without hesitation, he agreed to their plan.

Her heart swelled as he gently let her go, knowing she was coping, and went to Ruth to hug and reassure her too. 'It will all work out, Ruth. We'll make it our priority to get Tilda to safety.' Ruth came out of his hug and smiled at him. 'Ta, Bernard, yer like having another big brother to care for me. And I love yer like one too.'

As he hugged Ruth close again, he said, 'I'll always be that for you, Ruth, dear. I want you to know you can always turn to me.'

To Ellen, it was a wonderful moment.

Bernard turned to Abe. Robbie was standing by his side. He patted Robbie's shoulder. 'You've got a rival in me now, Robbie.' The two laughed together, but then Bernard became serious as he took Abe's hand. 'I can't thank you enough, Abe. In all this horror, what you have offered is marvellous news. It means that Ellen and I don't have to be separated to earn enough money to save for our dream.' Turning to Ellen, he said, 'Everything will sort itself out, once we know where yours and Ruth's mum is, I promise. We won't rest until it is. And I'll decline the job I've just taken right away. And as soon as we can, we'll begin to look for our practice. You'll see, it really will be fine.'

Ellen smiled. She wanted to tell him how much she

loved him and would support him, though a small part of her was sorry that she wouldn't be going to Roehampton House to nurse those wounded so badly during the war. She didn't say, because Bernard would need her and, more than anything else, she wanted to be by his side.

'Talking of looking for a practice.' Everyone looked at Ruth. 'Do you remember the doctor I told yer about in Bethnal who had a penny insurance going, Ellen?'

'The one who inspired our plans, you mean?'

'Yes. Well, I didn't say, as yer plans seemed to be on hold, but one of the blokes who came to do some brickwork on the shop was from Bethnal and we were talking about how it used to be. I mentioned Doctor Price and he said he still did a marvellous job but can't wait to retire. It's just that he can't find the right calibre of doctor to take over.'

'Oh, Ruth. Where did he have his practice? . . . Bernard, this sounds like the very thing, darling.'

'It does sound perfect for us. I think we should look into it. We might just get lucky and drop on the very thing we are looking for.'

'I could take yer to where he lives, but I can't tell yer as I can't remember the name of the road he lives on.'

The chatter went on along these lines, and then moved on to the wedding and the cottage.

'Talking of the cottage, I'd better ring my solicitor. It will just be my luck at the moment to have a buyer come before I can stop proceedings.'

Bernard caught hold of her hand. 'I'm glad you're not selling, darling.'

His smile sent shivers down Ellen's spine. She knew he meant to convey that he was thinking of the memories they'd made there. Keeping her voice straight, though she couldn't help the little giggle that came from her, she told him, 'I am too.'

There was an embarrassed giggle from Ruth which made Ellen scoot from the room. She wanted to hold on to the joy given to her by the unspoken words passed between herself and Bernard.

With the phone call eventually made after it had taken ages to get a line, they fell into conversation about anything and everything, but with undertones and tension that was almost tangible as they waited to hear from Amy. Ruth broke this occasionally by popping upstairs to see the boys and Ivan and coming down with a tale of the antics they were getting up to, but for Ellen the wait was interminable.

'It won't help, you keep going to the window, darling. You have everyone on edge.'

'I know, Bernard. I'm sorry, darling, but it's been an hour and a half now, my nerves won't stand much more.' The words had only just left Ellen's mouth when she saw a cab pull up outside. 'She's here!'

No one moved. They all stared at the door to Abe and Robbie's flat.

When the front door clicked, Robbie moved to open it.

A trembling, ghastly white Amy came through. Ellen clutched Bernard's arm as she tried to brace herself for this being bad news.

All eyes were on Amy. Waiting for her to speak.

'I — I don't know how to tell yer all where poor Tilda is.'

'Take your time, Amy, dear.'

Amy seemed reassured by Abe's words. She took a deep breath. 'She's in . . . Oh, I'm sorry, me darlin'

268

Ellen and Ruth, but she . . . she's in the loony bin up at the workhouse.'

Ruth's gasp matched her own as Ellen felt her knees give way. Bernard caught her. 'Oh, Ellen, Ellen, my love.'

'It ain't what yer think, Ellen . . . Ruth. She ain't mad. Poor darlin' is pretending to be to get the maximum safety she can. But . . . Well, from what Cyril told me of the conditions she lives in . . . I'm sorry, Ellen, Ruth, but they sound horrific.'

'Please, Amy, we have to know. We have to know what we're dealing with, luv.'

'Oh, Ruth. To convince them she's mad, she acts out hysterical screaming fits. She . . . she picks her skin off . . . and she . . . she pulls her hair out at the roots.'

'Good God! Poor, poor woman.'

As Bernard said this, a tear rolled down his cheeks. Ellen looked around. Everyone was crying silent tears.

Through her own that filled her eyes, her nostrils and her throat, she asked of anyone, 'What can we do?'

Abe answered. His voice croaked as he did. 'We have to get to her. We have to tell her that we are going to make her safe . . . Bernard, you could go. You could say that you've been commissioned by family members to look into her case to see if she can be helped.'

'I will, of course, but I will need to find out who the doctor is that is responsible for the workhouse inmates and speak to him first.'

'Do you think he will agree? Or is that just protocol?'

'Protocol. What you suggest will need a solicitor to back it up, but we can do that. The big question is, what proof do we have that Tilda is your mother, Ellen, or yours, Ruth?'

With these words, Ellen's heart sank. She had no proof, only what her father had told her on the train after the cafe incident when he admitted the truth to her.

'Would the lady who married your father verify this, do you think? Didn't you tell me that they were coming to visit your granny once to bring Christopher to see her? Surely she knew who you were if she was willing to meet you?'

Ellen felt a small glimmer of hope. 'It's something I could try. But what if my father never told her that I was born to a prostitute named Tilda? It's not an easy thing to tell a new wife.'

'No, but he'd have to give her a reason for not having you with him, darling. No one abandons a child born into a happy marriage because the wife has died. Marrying a widower, she would expect him to want his child with him. If he told her the truth, then that would be a reason she didn't want you. He could pass you off as a mistake that he'd rather hide away.'

To Ellen, this was a revelation. 'My God! That's what I was, Bernard. That's how it could have happened, but what about our brother, Christopher?'

'Darling, what you have told me about your father, he seems to have been a cunning and selfish man. As the baby boy was so young, and he had this compulsion, which seems alien to his nature, to look after his children — or keep them from Tilda — maybe to punish her ... he could have passed Christopher off as a son from the marriage just before his wife died ... He did install him in his home before he married his new wife, as I see it. She wasn't there when

270

you arrived from the orphanage, was she?'

'No, she wasn't . . . Oh, Bernard, this theory answers so many questions, my father was exactly like that. He punished those he thought had done wrong by him or got in the way of what he wanted — me, Granny and poor Tilda!'

'Well, then. If you go to the woman who is step-mother to your brother, and who may know who your mother is, you will have to be like your father. You will have to threaten her. Tell her that if she doesn't back you up, you will tell Christopher who his real mother is.'

'Oh, Bernard, that seems cruel.'

'You're trying to save your mother, darling. She wouldn't be where she is if your father had taken care of her.'

'No, and he bleedin' went to Bett's boys and shopped her!'

'What? Amy, tell me this isn't true.'

'It's that true, me darlin', that it made me bleedin' well swear! There! I've done it again. Yer dad caused me mum to have all her fingers broke, and your poor mum to hide in a loony bin!'

Ellen slumped onto Bernard. 'Help me. Help me.'

Ruth dashed forward and was the one to grab hold of her. Lovely Ruth, her adored sister who was suffering just as much.

'Hold on to me, darlin'. Don't let this be one of them triggers yer talk of. Bernard, help her. Don't let her lapse . . . Don't let her be ill again . . . Ellen, we need yer, luv. I need yer.'

Ellen felt the strength of Ruth's voice bringing her back from the brink she'd nearly tipped over.

Bernard lifted her.

Abe's voice came to her. 'Take her into our guest room, Bernard, through that door there on the right.'

As they went through the door, Ellen saw Robbie take Ruth in his arms. Ruth would be all right. As long as she had lovely Robbie, she would be all right.

And she had Bernard. He was her everything. He'd make things right.

As they lay on the bed together, Ellen couldn't sob, or cry out, she just needed to cling to Bernard, to feel his strength. His hand gently stroking her hair, his lovely voice humming gently. Then she knew she wouldn't drown in the misery that was her father's memory. But would she ever be free of him and his wickedness? Would she ever come to terms with him having put her into that horrific orphanage, or abandoning her once more to her gran? She prayed she would. And she prayed she could one day find forgiveness for him, because only in forgiveness could there be any peace.

* * *

It was dark when Ellen and Bernard set out to go to the house that had been her home of misery for the first part of her life. She shuddered when the memory of her cruel stepmother — her father's first wife — came to her.

'Are you sure you're up to this, my darling?'

'Yes, I must do it for my mother. I must.'

The door was answered by a gentleman in his fifties. 'Can I help you?'

Bernard answered. 'Sir, we're sorry to disturb you, but we would like to speak to Mrs Hartington on an urgent matter.'

'Mrs Hartington is now Mrs Farrow and is my wife. What is this urgent matter you could possibly wish to speak to my wife about?'

Ellen wanted to scream that it was to save her mum's life, but she allowed Bernard to do the talking.

'I can understand how you feel, sir, two strangers coming to your doorstep. I'm Doctor Bernard Holbeck and this is Miss Ellen Hartington.'

Mr Farrow raised his eyebrows. 'The war hero? Son of Randolph . . . And brother to Frederick?'

'The latter two, yes, sir, but I wouldn't class myself as a hero.'

'You're one to us, dear boy. Come on in out of the cold . . . In here, this is my office. I'd like to get to the bottom of this before we confront my wife.' He turned and spoke to a gentleman who was obviously in service to him, but not a butler, as he would have opened the door. 'Jelson, tell Mrs Farrow that I have some business callers and I won't be long, and bring us a whisky and a sherry for the lady, please.'

Once inside, he bade them sit down.

'Now, I was sorry to hear of your father's passing . . . Bernard, isn't it?'

'Yes . . . Thank you, sir.'

'And well done on your war effort. Commendable.'

'Thank you again, sir. But I couldn't have done any of it without the Red Cross nurses, of which Ellen was one.'

'Oh? Well, well done, Ellen, too . . . Now, I won't pretend I haven't heard of you, Ellen. My wife thought that you were in a . . .' — he coughed — 'well, a place for those whose minds are unbalanced.'

'I was, Mr Farrow. Put there by horrific things that happened to me. A lot of them at my father's hand,

273

but others by . . . well, I went through some very traumatic times.'

'Oh? I'm sorry to hear that . . . I know a little of what your father did. Excuse me for saying so, but he was a vile man. He broke my wife's heart. She still regrets what she did to your grandmother, but says at the time she didn't see her actions for what they were, but as revenge on your father.'

This gave Ellen a glimmer of hope.

'I understand that completely. And there's no need for your wife to worry. Gran had many valuables that she'd hidden away from my father, some in the attic, and some under his very nose. She managed to make enough money to buy an adorable little cottage and we lived very happily together there.'

'Ah, that's good to hear and it will help Mrs Farrow considerably to have peace of mind.'

'Sir, Mrs Farrow can help us.'

Mr Farrow narrowed his eyes as he turned his attention back to Bernard. 'How?'

'It's a sordid story that goes back to the woman that gave Ellen life . . .'

'You mean, the prostitute, Bernard! . . . Oh, I'm sorry . . . I — I shouldn't have said.'

'No, it's all right. I've known for a long time who my mother is. I met her once and have loved and longed for her ever since. At last I know where she is, but she is in danger . . . not through her own fault . . . I mean, well . . . Have you heard of the gangsters known as Bett's boys?'

Mr Farrow looked alarmed. 'Good God! Yes, of course I've heard of them. Your father was hand in glove with them, young lady. They took everything my dear wife had. Left her penniless except for this

274

house. All in repayment of his debts to them. They left her broken and terrified for her life.'

Ellen was taken aback, but Bernard jumped in, 'Then she may be glad to help us to get one over on them as that is why we are here.'

Mr Farrow looked afraid. In his agitation he jumped up. 'Where's that blasted Jelson?' Opening the door he yelled, 'Jelson!' only to make the poor man jump out of his skin. 'About bloody time. Now pour me a large one, will you?'

As soon as he held the whisky, Mr Farrow drank it straight back. Releasing a huge sigh, he ordered Jelson to pour him another.

The man seemed surprised and shocked as if this was very out of character, but he went about his duties with aplomb. Ellen was grateful for the steadying influence of the sherry and took a good sip, almost choking but managing to swallow hard enough to make her throat accept the liquid.

When they were alone again Mr Farrow apologized. 'You knocked me for six, I'm afraid. Those boys scare the wits out of me. I really don't think I can ask my wife to have anything to do with them. I don't even think I can bring their names up again. It could send her reeling back into her nervous state.'

Ellen felt defeated. She couldn't stop the tears that had been on the brink since the last flood that had almost floored her.

'I'm sorry, my dear . . . Look, tell me what this is all about and then we will see if there is anything that I can do.'

Bernard explained. Ellen felt the atmosphere tensing with every word he uttered, but then was surprised as Mr Farrow said, 'So, all my wife needs to do is sign a declaration that she is witness to the fact that Tilda is your mother, Ellen?'

Ellen nodded.

Mr Farrow's face broke into a relieved smile. 'I can do better than that. I have your birth certificate!'

'What? But my father told me he never got around to registering me! Does it say who my mother is?'

Ellen's heart thudded against the wall of her chest. She could hardly breathe.

'It does. Matilda Dewson. And I have Christopher's, which is registered as him being the son of Hartington's late wife.'

'But he isn't!'

Mr Farrow looked Ellen straight in the eyes, his voice a veiled threat. 'If you want a good outcome from this, then you will promise me that you will never, ever disclose the truth of that and you must assure me that anyone else who knows the truth will never, ever disclose it to Christopher.'

Ellen looked at Bernard.

'It's up to you, my dear. Although I think this is a despicable threat. At this moment, you need to save your mother. You need that birth certificate.'

'And as despicable as it is, and I agree it is, I stand by it for the love of my wife and the young man I look on as my son. But I will put this one stipulation in place. Your promise need only hold until the death of my wife.'

This crumb of hope of ever being able to acknowledge her brother was enough for Ellen, when she weighed it against saving her mum and further hurting Mrs Farrow. 'Thank you. I want you to know that I understand why you are doing this, and that I will abide by it. But one day, I want my brother to know who he is, and who I am. And that I love him and have done since I first saw him as a baby when our mother handed him over to my father.'

'I feel ashamed, truly ashamed, but I have to protect the ones I love, Ellen. Thank you for understanding. I will fetch the certificate for you. It can be authenticated if need be.'

'I still cannot believe it exists, but in one way that's a good thing, as not knowing she had a birth certificate, Ellen was able to lie about her age and become a nurse on the front line at the tender age of fifteen. Which is how we met.'

'Really? Good heavens. You're a very brave young lady and I am honoured to meet you . . . I feel even more of a cad now.'

'Please don't. I promise you that I understand. I would do anything to protect those I love. At the moment, my mum needs me, and Christopher is safe and happy, so my choice is simple.'

'Thank you, my dear. I won't be a moment.'

When he left the room, Ellen looked up at Bernard. He smiled down at her. 'I am so proud of you, my darling.'

'And I of you. I shall be the proudest wife in the world when we marry, darling.'

Bernard moved towards where she was sitting and took her hand. 'We're quite a team, darling, I cannot wait to make it official.' He lowered his voice. 'Do you have to go home tonight?'

'Only to let them all know our success, so they rest easy.'

'I want to kiss you.'

The door opened and Bernard shot back. Mr Farrow smiled. 'I'm glad I've been able to make you both happy. Well, here it is. I'll have to bid you goodnight now, my beautiful wife is becoming agitated at my continued absence.'

Ellen leaned forward and kissed his cheek when he offered her his hand. He looked down into her eyes. 'I haven't known you long, Ellen, but I already know you are a very special young lady. Never change.'

* * *

Once they were outside and in the car, Bernard tucked the blanket around Ellen's knees. He kissed her lightly as he did so. 'Just a promise for later, darling.'

Despite everything, Ellen thrilled at this. She needed so much to curl up in the safety of Bernard's arms and to be loved by him.

She clutched the envelope, wanting to open it, but knowing the words would be lost to her in the dark. But no matter, this was the proof that her mum was her mum and was the first step to getting her released and to safety and she wanted that more than anything — well, probably not at this moment. She smiled to herself. A wry smile, as she thought of what they had planned. How could she dream of such a thing when everything was so horrible? But then she thought of how Bernard loving her would give her some peace and settle the turmoil inside her. Her mum would want that for her.

24

Ruth

Ruth tossed and turned in her bed. Tomorrow was Ellen's big day but it was also a big day for them both as, though it seemed that nothing was going to bar them from their mission to save their mum and all was in order for them to do so, they wouldn't know for sure it would happen until they saw Bernard at the register office.

Bernard had a meeting with the management board of the workhouse in the morning — the very morning of his wedding — and Ruth hoped with all her heart that he would greet them at the register office with good news. For the board had the final say without them going through a legal route of Ellen getting power of attorney for their mum.

Feeling uneasy about this being a possible outcome, she looked over at Ellen. The light from the not yet extinguished gas lamp in the street outside lit up her sleeping face. It was going to be hard to think that this was the last time they would share a bedroom.

A creak of the floorboards alerted her. She sat up. Footsteps walked past her bedroom door towards the kitchen.

Knowing it could only be Ivan, or Jeff, as Archie's room was on the other side of the kitchen door, she listened, waiting for them to come back to bed, thinking they may just have visited the bathroom, or gone to the kitchen for a drink of water. But the footsteps didn't make the return journey, and after a while, Ruth thought she'd make sure whoever it was was all right. Grabbing her housecoat, she donned it as she tiptoed along the corridor keeping to the carpet runner to soften her tread.

What she found shocked her. Ivan sat at the table, his head resting on his arms, his body shaking with silent sobs.

As he hadn't seemed to hear her, she crept back towards the open door, thinking to leave him to his privacy, and yet aching to go to him to offer comfort . . . If only Amy was still here! She would know how to handle this. But yesterday had been her moving out day. She was in the little flat with her mum.

A tinge of envy hit Ruth at this thought. If only it was that simple for her and Ellen.

'Don't go, Ruth.'

'Oh, luv, I didn't think you'd heard me. What is it? Nightmares?'

She went forward and sat down opposite him. Reaching out her hands, she took one of his. 'How can I help yer, mate?'

'Just by being here. I — I need a drink, Ruth, but I don't want one. Does that make sense?'

'A little. Shall I put the kettle on? I know it isn't the kind of drink you want, but it may help.'

Ivan lifted his head. He sniffed loudly and ran his free hand across his eyes.

'Go and swill yer face, luv. I'll have a cup of tea for us by the time yer get back.'

Ivan nodded. Ruth's heart went out to him. He looked like a broken man. And yet a strong one physically, as he only wore his nightshirt and his bare legs

280

showed muscles rippling as he walked. She'd already seen him with his shirt off so knew he was honed and taut.

When he came back, though his eyes showed signs of him weeping, he looked a lot better.

'I'm sorry, Ruth. Sometimes it gets to me, but that is happening less and less. I will beat it, I'm determined to. I want to be worthy of . . . Anyway, I promise you, I'll never touch another drink in me life.'

'I know. I believe in yer, Ivan. Drink your tea . . . Yer can tell me about yer nightmare if it'll help.'

He sipped his tea. His hazel eyes, slightly blood-shot, looked at her with a questioning expression. She held them for a moment, her heart beating faster. Unable to understand how she felt, and yet wanting the feeling that wasn't alien to her.

'Ruth, I — I . . .'

He looked away. Ruth wasn't sure if what she felt was relief or disappointment. Trying to relieve the tension, she said, 'There's no need to apologize, luv. I understand. What you went through in France was an unspeakable horror. And then to come home to your family gone all but for yer mum and Jeff, then . . .'

'Me mum were a good woman, Ruth. She did her best. She loved us all, but she couldn't cope, nor could she stop them taking us . . . She . . . she were like your mum, only she were left with her kids, and she loved us all. But her heart was broken when I returned. That night, she just said, 'You will look after Jeff, won't yer, luv?' I told her I would. Then the next day . . . Oh, Ruth . . .'

'I'm sorry for yer, luv, I am. And for yer poor mum.'

'They came and took her away and that was that. We never saw her again.'

'No funeral?'

'No. Nothing. I just couldn't take it in. I'd dreamed all the time I was in Canada of coming home to her, and then in France, the thought of getting back home got me through the hell, the death and horrendous injuries . . . But yer know all about that, being a nurse over there.'

'I do. Were you afraid?'

'At times I was so scared I wet meself. Many a lad did.'

'I know. And the other too, bless them. It was often my job to clean them up, until I got on to working on the X-ray machine . . . So, when did yer drinking start, Ivan?'

'It was when we landed and were put into a holding camp to await transport. Some of the lads clubbed together and fetched some jugs of ale. I liked the feeling. It made me forget and smile again. Then after me mum . . . Well, it gradually got so I had to 'ave one . . . Oh, Ruth, I've stolen to get a drink. I've let Jeff go without food and spent the parish relief money on drink . . . I'm ashamed.'

He bowed his head. Ruth put her hand over his that lay on the table. 'Don't be. You're making up for it and that's all we can do. Jeff adores you. He trusts yer like he would a dad. None of it means anything to him now.'

'He's the reason I fight like I do.' He looked up. 'Him and other reasons, Ruth.'

Ruth could feel herself being pulled into his lovely eyes.

'But when I have the nightmare, then I — I so want a drink.'

'Is it always the same one, mate?'

282

'Yes.' His head bent again, and his body shuddered. 'He were me friend. A good bloke. We went over the top together . . . There was a blast and . . . and then, I was holding his head . . . I — I caught it like a football, Ruth.' The trembling of his body frightened Ruth. 'It was blown clean off his shoulders.' Tears streamed down his face.

Ruth stood and went around the table to his side and, putting her arm across his shoulders, held him to her. 'Try to think that when that happened, he was gone. He was at peace. He wouldn't have felt anything, just talking to you one minute, then walking the path towards heaven the next, knowing you were cradling him.'

'That's a good way to think about it, Ruth. Next time it visits me, I'll try that.'

'I hope it helps. And about yer mum. Amy needs to have a place to lay her baby to rest . . . well, so to speak, like you do for yer mum. We promised Amy to do something about that but we haven't been able to yet. We could do it for your mum too. Make it the same place so that your mum has Amy's baby to take care of, and then we'll put a rose bush on it and make it look nice. Jeff can help too.'

'I'd like that. Ta, Ruth. Yer've helped me a lot. One day I'll get better and then . . . Well, we'll see, eh?'

Ruth knew what he meant. 'Yes, we'll see, luv . . . Well, I'm off back to bed. I've to be a brides-maid tomorrow.'

★ ★ ★

As she stood brushing Ellen's hair the next morning, she wished with all her heart that they could have their

283

mum with them today, but the timing of everything beat them. Sighing inwardly, she shook herself from her thoughts and spoke cheerily to Ellen. 'Today is about the rest of your life, me darlin'. Try to enjoy it, despite all that is going on. I feel sure that next week, Mum will be safely up in Leeds.'

'I hope so. Everything's in place, the cottage is being made ready. Even groceries being put in the pantry!'

'Will there be enough furniture now that you had some sent down for Amy? Not that she'll need it after all, will she?'

'No. I'm so glad she will be living up there with Mum, her mum and Cyril for a while, but I hope they'll be able to cope on their own without her after a time so that she can come back to live with you. We'll decide what to do with the furniture in her flat then . . . Bernard and I will need some, so we'll probably take it to wherever we settle rather than back to the cottage. There's still plenty up there with Gran having her own sitting room separate to Dilly and Cook's.'

'So, it will all work out. Right, I'd better check on the boys now. I hope Amy's coping with her mum and Cyril while she tries to get ready. It's so tiny in that flat. But she didn't want to leave them any longer than she has to.'

'The boys will be fine with Ivan. What would we have done without him? He's a treasure, always the one to pick up the odds and ends to make things possible for us.'

'I know, he's tasked with getting the boys ready as we speak, and poor thing can't even come to the wedding, with us putting the responsibility of looking after Ethel and Cyril onto him.'

284

To Ruth, Ivan was more than a treasure. She thought about the night before and came to the conclusion that Ivan was one of the bravest men she'd met, and she'd met so many during the war.

But his fight continued, and he was determined to win.

★ ★ ★

The wedding went off as planned, made even nicer by hearing from Bernard that there hadn't been any objections to Tilda's daughter taking her home. He'd smiled at her and Ellen and told them, 'It seems your mother is a handful they are glad to get rid of.'

'Oh, Bernard. I must have got me acting skills from her . . . How has she fooled them all this time? But how will she be with us? I'm afraid she won't accept me as her child even.'

Ellen's hand came into hers. 'I'm nervous too, love, but let's do this together, eh? Like we do everything.'

Ruth smiled, cross with herself for putting a dampener on things.

As they came out of the register office, a voice called, 'Congratulations, Ellen.' Ruth knew who it was without having to look. Ebony, dear Ebony, Rebekah's niece, who ran a restaurant with her husband, Abdi, and who was the main organizer of the soup kitchen that Ellen had set up.

Ebony lifted her hand to wave, but Ruth and Robbie ran towards her.

'You all look beautiful.'

'Ta, darling, I did dress up especially!'

'Oh, Robbie!' Ebony giggled. 'It is good to see you.'

Robbie kissed her cheek. 'And it's good to see you.

It's been a while since me and Abe came for a meal. Is Abdi well?'

'He is. He sends his love to you all.'

Ruth stepped forward. 'Oh, Ebony, it's so good to see you. This is Amy. Do yer remember me and Ellen telling you of Amy?'

'I do, Ruth. And now she is here? How wonderful is that! Am pleased to meet you, Amy. You look lovely, girl.'

'Ta, nice to meet yer. Ruth's arranging for all three of us to come and have a meal at yer restaurant as we're going to have a night out together.'

'I'd love that, Amy. Ruth, girl, when are you going to arrange this?'

'It'll be in the spring, Ebony. I'll contact yer when.'

'Ah, here's the most beautiful bride. Me and Abdi hope you'll be very happy, Ellen, girl.'

Ellen giggled. 'Thanks, Ebony. Give my love to Abdi. Now, let me introduce you to my husband. This is Bernard. Bernard, meet Ebony.'

'Am very pleased to meet you, Bernard. Now you take care of my Ellen. You have a wonderful girl for your bride.'

'I know I do, Ebony. Ellen and Ruth have told me all about you. I thought you wouldn't be able to make it today?'

'I can't stay long. It being Saturday, there's a lot to do at the restaurant. But you all come and see me and Abdi, sometime . . . Oh, and Ruth, Horacio does send his regards to you.'

'Ah, lovely Horacio. Tell him one of these days I will come over to see him when he's home from school.'

'He knows that. He says the first thing he will do is to come to see your shop.'

They hugged and kissed their goodbyes then. Ruth could see the visit had been a good moment for Ellen as she turned a smiling face towards her. 'Oh, Ruth, Amy, it's such a wonderful day.'

'And you look stunning, luv. The most beautiful bride I've ever seen.'

Amy chipped in, 'You are, Ellen. I cried when yer got out of the carriage and came up to the register office.'

'Ah, thanks, both. We've come a long way, girls. And been through a lot together and when we didn't have each other there to support us, we still were close in our hearts. Now, we'll never be parted for long ever again.' Their hug this time sealed this for Ruth, for though in a way they were parting, it wasn't like when they were children.

★ ★ ★

The wedding breakfast was a noisy, delicious affair, with Amy's flapper pie the best dish of the day. Ethel and Cyril seemed relaxed and happy now they had joined them. Ethel cried a lot but assured them they were happy tears.

It was Robbie who dragged them all into what was now called the studio — the room she and he rehearsed in. 'Let's have a sing-song, and then me and Ruth will do a comic number we've been rehearsing.'

Ruth was surprised to see Abe's piano was in the room and even more surprised when Ethel said, 'I can knock a tune out for yer — the good ole London songs.'

Amy looked shocked. 'I didn't know yer played, Mum.'

'I do, luv. I used to make a copper now and again playing in the pub, but Tilda was the best, and her voice! She's got a lovely voice.'

Ruth beamed at Ellen.

Ellen grinned. 'Seems that you've taken all her attributes, Ruth. You look like her and you sing and dance! I don't know how I fit in.'

'You've got her gentle way, luv. She's a gentle person is Tilda.'

This made Ellen smile. Ruth noticed, like herself, Ellen had a tear in her eye. Robbie wouldn't let them become morose. He clapped his hands. 'Take your seats, ladies and gentlemen. I give you Abe.'

Abe wheeled himself across the room and sat at the piano facing them.

'I want to congratulate our lovely Ellen and my long-time friend Bernard on their wedding.'

The noise of the clapping in the empty-of-furniture room gave the impression of a huge crowd. As they cheered, Abe turned to the piano and began to play the most beautiful music. Bernard took Ellen's hand and waltzed her into the centre of the room. To Ruth, as she watched them gracefully glide around, their eyes locked, they made a beautiful sight. She couldn't help thinking about them in Ypres, covered in blood, tending to all the wounded together. They saved so many lives. They deserved this happiness.

Abe gave the piano seat to Ethel next, and though she played honky-tonk music, the next ten minutes were hilarious as they all belted out favourites of London and the war, the one they always sang, 'The Old Bull and Bush', and 'It's a Long Way to Tipperary', which became side-splitting as Robbie sang 'to tickle Mary' instead of 'Tipperary'.

And then it was their turn. 'I have the props here, Ruth.'

Flamboyant as ever, Robbie produced the hat she'd made for the number, a huge affair with a big feather. This played a part as when she strutted by him, it looked like it tickled his nose and he pretended to sneeze. So funny. As were the words and Robbie's actions. For herself, she just had to walk up and down singing as if she was a lady of worth not giving the cockney fellow the time of day, when he was madly in love with her.

The first line, 'She's the apple of me eye,' and Ruth's posh voice commanding, 'Give the poor man a pie!' had everyone falling about with laughter.

That was music hall for you: stupid songs that didn't mean much, but that tickled the audience and had them joining in, as everyone did when these two lines cropped up again. Archie and Jeff loved it and shouted the lines louder than any of them. All ended in giggles.

As they gathered at the front door to see the happy couple off, Archie and Jeff, who'd disappeared with Ivan and Cyril a few minutes before, stood cheering as the old boots they'd tied to the boot of the car rattled and bumped on the ground.

When the car disappeared around the corner, Amy's hand came into Ruth's. 'Well, that's one of us gone, luv.'

Ruth put her arm around Amy's shoulder. 'It's a new beginning for us all, luv.'

'It is. I'm so happy that yer all coming up to the cottage and staying for Christmas . . . and, Ruth, ta for giving Ivan and little Jeff a home. It means the world to know he'll be all right.'

'He's going to be a help, luv. You know, I did think about offering him the flat yer got ready, as you'll move back in with me, won't yer . . . I mean, when yer can leave our mums and Cyril to cope on their own.'

'I will, luv, like a shot! But we'll go up often to the cottage after I come back, won't we?'

'We will. Nothing will keep us away. And nothing will happen till the three of them are able to look after themselves, so that'll be yer challenge, luv. To get them less dependent on yer.'

'I know. It's going to be difficult as I so want to care for them, but I know I have to do what's best for them.'

As they went back inside, Robbie grabbed Ruth's arm. 'I think we're ready, luv. That was amazing. Yer came alive when yer had an audience.' He pulled her to him and hugged her. 'I'm so excited, Ruth.'

'Oh, Robbie. I am, but, well, I will have so many problems with Amy gone. I'll need to work full time in me shop.'

Ivan told her, 'Don't worry, I'll help all I can, Ruth. I know I can't serve in the shop, but I can look after the kids and get yer a meal for when yer come in. You have to do this. Like Robbie said, you were amazing.'

'And it's only three evenings a week, Ruth, please don't pull out.'

'All right, mate, let's see how it goes, shall we. But yer have told them we won't start till after Christmas, haven't yer?'

'I have. We're booked in for the first week in January.'

'Despite all the problems, I can't wait, Robbie. I feel like two people. The one who's a mum and loves making hats, and the other a girl who loves the stage.'

'It's going to be wonderful, luv. Ta. I'll do all I can to lighten yer load as well — I can sell hats in the shop, you know. As I don't look like a navvy like Ivan, I'd fit in very well.'

Ivan punched him playfully. 'Cheeky sod! But yer right, if I wanted to buy a hat, I'd buy one from you.'

They both laughed and to Ruth it was a lovely moment, Ivan and Robbie truly becoming friends. She felt a warm glow blush over her. She didn't know why it mattered so much. It just did.

25

Ellen

Ellen's face glowed. Her happiness was such that she felt it in every fibre of her being.

Everything was coming right. Her wonderful Bernard had given her such joy, such ecstasy and now they were set to begin their new life with a loan and a surety from Abe.

Only one thing topped it all — today, she and Ruth were going to pick their mum up from that awful place. Though mixed feelings assailed her — nerves, and fear, along with anticipation and happiness.

Questions kept coming to her mind. *Will Mum like me? Will she find it difficult to settle? How will all this affect her? Will she be scared?*

But she had to brush them away as she couldn't answer any of them. She had to accept that what would be, would be, and all they could do was their best.

So much planning had gone into it all as it was essential that Tilda was whisked away the moment that they had her through the door. And something none of them wanted to do, but knew they had to — they would give a false forwarding address.

Bernard had said that in normal circumstances, the new address inmates were released to only lay on the file, no one ever needed it, but just in case there was someone who could be got at by Bett's boys, this was

292

the best course of action.

It had been something that Ethel had said which had prompted this. She'd told Amy that gangsters had been to the home in the past and been able to speak to her. They'd threatened her with more pain. They'd found out from someone that Tilda had been seen coming into the workhouse.

Ethel had told them that Tilda had just been to visit but hadn't stayed long. They'd been asked to leave when Cyril went to the matron, but from that day, Ethel's health had deteriorated, and she'd then been put into the more secure ward where she wasn't allowed to leave the building and could only take exercise in the yard.

Tilda had come up with the plan to make it look like she'd gone mad so that she could be safe from everyone — the only problem was, she'd never been able to secure her own release from there, so had carried on the pretence, hoping one day something would change for her.

Well, today, it will, my darling mum. I'm coming to take you out of there and am going to look after you for the rest of your life.

There were just two days left before Christmas Eve was on them. Ruth, Ivan and the two boys had already left by train for Leeds early that morning. They wouldn't get there until four-ish, but it was enough time to get all the fires going before the rest of them arrived. Abe's house wheelchair, and most of their luggage and boxes with their Christmas needs, had gone on the same train in the goods carriage.

Robbie had left early too. He was driving Abe and Amy, and her family.

The activity when they all reached the cottage was

going to be intense as four beds had been ordered. The young man who did the garden, who Ellen had met on her last visit there, had taken delivery and had seen to erecting them in the schoolroom — a barn conversion at the bottom of the garden, with an apartment above it.

It had been Adrian who had overseen the renovations of the barn and had then run his little school in the downstairs rooms until the war had begun and he'd taken up a position in the War Office.

Ellen sighed. She'd thought he'd be safe there and was glad when he'd not been passed fit to go to the front line, only to have his asthma take him from them.

Bringing her mind back to the present, she felt satisfied that everything was in place for them all to spend Christmas together.

They would be a bit short of comfy chairs to sit on as the sofa from the living room had come down to Amy's but they wouldn't miss anything else and chairs from the bedrooms could be brought downstairs. Gran's sitting room was still fully furnished and so was the dining room at the back of the house. It was a big room as it took up three-quarters of the width of the house, so she planned that the long table that Adrian had used for his desk would be brought in and placed on the end of the one in situ and then chairs from the schoolroom brought in to surround it.

They had an abundance of bedding, crockery and a bathroom and toilet inside and a toilet in the yard, besides there being a bathroom in the apartment and a toilet in the small yard behind that too. All in all, what she called a cottage was actually capable of housing them easily for the few days they would stay there and enjoy Christmas together.

294

With all her heart, she hoped Tilda would see what a loving family she was going to be part of, and what a lovely home she, Ethel and Cyril were going to have with Amy staying a few weeks with them and all of them then visiting often. It wasn't London, or anything remotely like it, so it would be strange to them all, but they would be safe. And that's all that mattered.

By the time Bernard and she set out for the workhouse, Ellen felt relaxed about everything, except the coming meeting. She wished now they'd kept Ethel back to travel with Tilda to help her.

★ ★ ★

The hollow sound of hers and Bernard's footsteps as they climbed the carpetless stairs echoed around them, increasing Ellen's nervousness. Her heart raced. She clung on to a small case in which she'd put clean underwear, and warm thick stockings, a woollen skirt and a twin set. Bernard carried a coat and hat over his arm — Ethel had given them the sizes to buy. The hat was a felt bonnet, lovingly made by Ruth.

But when the door was unlocked to the ward for the insane, the noise that met them was much worse than they had heard on the stairs. It tore at Ellen's heart.

All around them, women moaned, or called out for help. Some were on their knees, with blood running from wounds — self-inflicted or not, it was difficult to discern. All looked dirty with hair matted to their heads, and the smell was like nothing Ellen had experienced despite having dealt with horrendous conditions and injuries during the war.

She clung on to Bernard's hand. He shook his head in despair.

'She's in 'ere.' The warden who had shown them up indicated a padded door. 'We tried to wash her, but she wouldn't cooperate. Yer don't know what yer taking on, luv. If I were you, I'd turn and run and don't stop running till yer miles away from 'ere. She ain't the mum yer think yer going to find.'

'I'll manage. I'm a nurse and my husband's a doctor. We'll help her.'

She wanted to say that keeping her here would cause her death, as it would for all those she could see, and that they needed treatment, but her fear of not getting her mum out prevented her. She felt put to shame as Bernard did just that. 'These women need medical attention. How long is it since a doctor saw them?'

'They don't need a doctor; they need a bleedin' noose around their necks.'

Appalled at this, and encouraged by Bernard's outburst, Ellen told her, 'This is cruel. Where are the bathrooms and clean clothes, and where do these women sleep? Who comes in to help them with their mental health issues? Do they see anyone?'

'Look, they brought this on themselves. They're violent, they spit at yer . . . Can't yer see, they're all mad! None of yer fancy doctoring'll help them. You mark my words, you'll be bringing yer mum back to us within weeks!'

'Never!'

'As a doctor I'm ordering you to open some windows, to organize staff to help to bathe these women and wash their hair and then I will examine each one. And let me tell you, madam, this will be reported to the authorities.'

The warden pulled herself to her full height, went to say something, but seeing Bernard's anger, shut up and stormed out.

Turning to the door the warden had indicated, Ellen hesitated. Bernard stepped forward and opened it. It took a moment for Ellen's eyes to adjust to the darkness. 'Mum, are you in here?'

'Tilda? I'm Bernard, your son-in-law. Ellen, your daughter, is here. We've come to take you home. You'll be safe with us, my dear.'

Ellen heard a sob. 'Mum, Mum, it's all right, I promise you. You'll be safe, we'll care for you . . . We are taking you to live with Ethel and Cyril. And, Mum, Ruth is waiting for you . . . Your eldest daughter, Ruth, remember her?'

A gasp came from the figure in the corner. Ellen could now see the form of her mother. She went forward.

'Ellen? Is it really you, luv?'

'It is, Mum. Remember, you saw me at that cafe in Bond Street when I was eleven years old? I was with my father, and you handed Christopher over to him?'

'Oh, Ellen, Ellen, me little darlin', don't come near to me. I stink, luv. I have lice and fleas. Oh, Ellen, Ellen.'

'It's all right, Mum, I've seen and had fleas on me that would make your eyes water. I'm a nurse, and during the war we spent a daily hour de-licing ourselves . . . I — I just want to hold you, Mum.'

'M-my baby.'

Ellen sprang forward as Tilda's legs gave way. Catching her, she held her to her. 'Oh, Mum, I love you, and have done ever since we met . . . well, all my life, really. And so does Ruth. She's always loved you.

She and I met at the orphanage. She looks so like you, Mum.'

'Ruth, my Ruth?'

'Yes. And the first time I met her, she told me she loved her mum. That she knew her mum loved her and one day she would come for her. She always said that you must have been unable to keep her to have left her with the priest, but one day you would be able to care for her and then you would be together.'

'She said that?'

'She did, Mum. She's waiting for you in a safe place.'

A huge sob from Tilda broke Ellen's resolve not to cry. She clung on to her mum's stick-thin body, holding her gently but firmly. Together they sobbed out their pain.

After a moment, Bernard said, 'Let's get you out of here, Tilda. Come into the light gradually, so we can see you and help you.'

Ellen supported her mum, feeling all the love she had for her fill her heart.

When she came into the light, the sight of her broke Ellen once more. Bernard's arm came around her, supported her, gave her strength to deal with the moment.

Tilda's hair was matted and looked as though it hadn't been washed for years. Her face was covered in sores, as were her arms, and Ellen knew from Cyril that most of these were self-inflicted. Some were infected and oozed pus.

Her feet were bony and black with dirt. Her fingernails were long, caked with dirt and curled at the ends. Her eyes were matted with infected gunge. Ellen's tears were of a different kind now as despair filled her.

At that moment the door flew open and the warden marched in. Behind her were an army of women. By the way they were dressed, Ellen knew they were inmates, but these women looked fed and cared for. All of them recoiled in horror at the sight that met them.

Bernard spoke kindly to them. 'Ladies, I need your help. These are women just like you, but they have been treated worse than animals. What you see is cruelty against those who cannot help themselves. They need you to help them. I want you all to fetch a bucket of hot water — the heat of a bath — and to take one patient each and clean them up. Warden, have you arranged for fresh clothes to be brought up here?'

'I'm not made of bleedin' clothes! Where do yer think I'm going to get them from, eh?'

One woman put her hand up. 'I've got a spare frock, doctor.' This set them all off saying they had spare underwear, or a cardigan, nighties, skirts and jumpers.

Ellen knew the spare was probably their only extra clothing, and she loved them for it.

'Thank you, everyone. After Christmas we will visit and replace your items for you.'

One woman piped up, 'St Nicholas the Great 'old good jumbles. They're 'aving one today — the Christmas fayre. I get all me stuff from them. Only cost a penny for a few things, I bring them back for everyone when I can.'

'Are you going today?'

'I am. I've got a penny saved for it.'

'Look, I can't go today, but if I give you a shilling, would you get all you can carry, please?'

'A bob! Blimey, luv, I'd kit them all out for that.

299

Course I will, but I won't be able to carry it all.'

Ellen hadn't thought of this, but an idea came to her. 'Do you know Ebony? She runs the soup kitchen?'

'Yes, I know Ebony, she's a lovely lady. She's what being a Christian is all about.'

'Good. No doubt Ebony will be working at the Christmas fayre. Go up to her with a note that I'll give you and she will see that all you buy is delivered here, and more besides.'

'Right yer are, luv. Now, come on, you lot, let's get busy 'elping these poor sods, eh?'

Bernard took Ellen's hand. 'We should get going, Ellen, but most of these have sores that need treating. I think it best we take Tilda to your house where you can wash and feed her. I'll go to Doctor Price. I've looked up his address on the map as Robbie remembered the name of his street. I did that in readiness of us approaching him. It's within walking distance from here. I'll get iodine and bandages from him and come back to treat these others as the women clean them up. I'll see to it that this place is scrubbed, and clean bedding put on those mattresses on the floor. It's all we can do for now, but we will do more in the new year, especially if we are successful in taking Doctor Price's practice over.'

'Yes, that sounds like a good idea. Only be as quick as you can, Bernard, we have such a long journey ahead of us. For safety, we should go right away . . . Wait a minute. I'll take Tilda downstairs and see if I can arrange to clean her up down there, then I can come up and help. Some of these patients will need bed bathing. I can show the ladies how to do that.'

Tilda whispered to Ellen, 'I can clean meself up, luv, me madness is only pretend. I'm weak, though, so will need a hand to get down the stairs.'

'Oh, Mum, Cyril told me it was a pretence, but will it be safe to expose that here? Cyril says there are those that will inform on you. Will the same ones tell that you're not ill in your mind and make Bett's boys more determined to find you?'

'You know about all of that?'

'I do, love, but don't worry, we understand. And none of it was your fault, it was my father's, and he's dead now.'

'What? No!'

'Oh, Mum I'm sorry . . . I — I know you loved him, but he was no good. He wasn't worthy of your love, or of mine. I'll help you, I promise, as will Ruth. My father wasn't ever worthy of our love, Mum.'

'You're right, luv. I know that but knowing it don't stop yer loving someone.'

Ellen knew this was true. She put her arm around her mum and hugged her to her.

As if this gave her strength, her mum straightened more than she had done till now. 'But, like yer say, I'm not safe, and that was his doing, so I'll put him out of me mind and get on with things.'

'It's the only way. It has been doing so that has helped me too, Mum.'

'He gave yer a posh voice like his, luv, and an education, if as yer say you're a nurse. And me? Well, he gave me you, and Christopher, and you're turning out to be the saviour of me, so I'll not hold any bitterness, but be grateful for that.'

Ellen felt her heart warm a little.

'I think Tilda is right to see to herself, Ellen. You can make a start on helping all the others and I can take the car which will mean I will be back quicker.'

Ellen agreed.

The women were beginning to come back with the water they'd lugged up the stairs. Seeing it and the enormous task ahead, Ellen went into nurse mode, assessing the worst cases for herself to tend to and setting the others to work on the rest of what she now thought of as her patients. 'Don't get rid of any of the water. Swill the floor with it, and don't wash two people in it either, ladies, wash one, then swill the floor of her cell, picking up the mattresses and putting them outside the door until the floor is dry. Can some of you find clean bedding, taking all the dirty down as you go, please?'

The process of seeing to them all and the cleaning took three hours. During this time Ellen was thankful to see Bernard return and have him pitch in. Tilda too, having washed herself the best she could, was doing all she could to help, despite her weak state.

At last, the ward resembled some kind of order. Nothing like it should be, but all the floors had been mopped, and though they wouldn't pass a microscopic scrutiny, they were as clean as they could get them. The women all looked reasonably presentable, and their sores had been cleaned and treated. It was a happier group of women they left than they had found.

When they got to the door, Bernard turned and made a promise to them all. 'Ladies, we will be back on a regular basis and see you're well cared for.'

In the car, Bernard told her that he'd found Doctor Price unwell and not able to tend to his patients. 'We discussed me buying his practice and he was so grateful. Such a lovely man, but everything has overwhelmed him lately. His wife died and she was his right-hand man. I told him that with a rest he could recover. That I was going to prescribe a holiday for him when we get back and then will gladly take him on a part-time basis to help us. He was in tears. Poor man is exhausted and grieving. He's hardly functioning.'

Ellen sat in the back with Tilda. She leaned forward to speak to Bernard, her heart full of pride in him. 'We'll have to come back as soon as we can, darling. We are so needed. Imagine what is happening in people's homes too if they aren't well.'

'Yer not stopping with me then, Ellen, luv?'

'No, Mum. Look, I'll explain everything to you.' She took hold of her mum's hand, still a slender, young-looking hand, though the skin was loose for lack of a fat layer, as was the case for all of Tilda's body.

Tilda listened to all Ellen had to say. She told her all about her cottage, and Christmas, and Ruth. So much to tell about Ruth.

'So, I have a grandson then?'

'Yes, you do! He's adorable . . . And you'll meet Amy. You'll love Amy.' Amy's and Ruth's story tugged at Ellen's heart as she recounted it, and she could see how moved Tilda was as she dabbed at her eyes.

'I never wanted you and Ruth to suffer, luv. I gave Ruth to the priest to care for — he told me he had a family who would take her, and I gave you to yer father, thinking he meant it when he said he would take care of you. But he never did . . . Did he care for Christopher?'

'Yes, he did. He and his new wife took care of him as if they had birthed him together. And she continued to treat him like her own son after he died. He's happy, Mum. He's well cared for and at school in Rugby. A lovely young man who we can be proud of.'

'Yer know him?'

Ellen told her of the contact that she'd had with Christopher and with the man who now acted as his father. 'So, you see, he is loved . . . But one day, when he is a man, I will contact him and tell him the truth. I want him in my life.'

'Me too, Ellen. And you're a special person, luv. Ta for all yer've done for me.'

'I love you, Mum . . . and I didn't do it alone, you know. Ruth played a huge part, as did Amy. Once we found her mum, we found you.'

'I can't take it in that Ethel has found her daughter. I was broken-hearted when Cyril stopped coming up and giving me news of Ethel. I didn't know what had happened. Then the warden told me they'd left and it made me flip. I felt my whole world had ended as they were the only two people I had in me life. It was then they put me in that padded cell yer found me in.'

'So, you were never mentally ill? You kept strong all this time?'

'I did, Ellen. I had to hide where them boys couldn't find me as I knew if they did me life would be over. All I could do was keep telling meself that where there's life there's hope.' She suddenly lifted her arm and pulled Ellen into her. 'And I was right, me lovely Ellen. I was right.'

'You were, Mum. And we're going to have the best Christmas ever. Ruth has taken all we need up to the cottage, with some clothes for you too. We'll soon feed you up and get your hair right. It looks better already, but a few shampoos and it will be the shining crown I remember.'

304

'I expect there'll be a few greys in it now, luv.'

They both giggled together, and Ellen felt they were bonding as mum and daughter, and soon that would happen for Ruth too. Her happiness at the thought of them all being together at last broadened her smile.

'You're beautiful, Ellen, just beautiful and I love you.'

Ellen's world felt complete.

26

Ellen and Amy

It was as they were about to leave London on the A5 that shock zinged through Ellen. Suddenly she was flung forward. Her head hit the back of the front seat. A crashing noise and the sound of breaking glass took the space around her.

Feeling dazed, she clung on to her mum as best she could, but then caught sight of Bernard. 'Bernard! Bernard! Are you all right?'

There was no answer. Bernard was slumped over the steering wheel.

'Mum, are you hurt? Oh, Mum, you're bleeding!'

As she said this, there was a screeching noise. The car was moving. They were being pushed off the road! Fear made it difficult for Ellen to swallow. She looked around, trying to see out of the smashed windows. Turning, she saw the back window had completely gone. Through it she could see the bonnet of a van locked onto their car. 'What's happening? Bernard! Bernard, please wake up!'

The movement and the noise stopped. A figure appeared at the front side window. He had a thick wooden club in his hand which he smashed down, shattering the glass. His hand came inside and found the handle, opening the door. He put his head inside.

'It's been a long wait, Tilda, but I've got yer now. There's no more escaping yer punishment, girl.'

'No! No, leave me alone, Roly, I've a chance of a new life now.'

'Oh no yer 'aven't, yer slag. The only life yer going to see is the life after death!'

Ellen's heart thudded as Roly tried to pull the front seat forward. It didn't give. Someone tried Bernard's door, but it wouldn't open. Ellen thanked God there were no back doors. Maybe they would give up?

The sound of her mum's terrified whimpers helped Ellen to be strong for her. 'It's all right, Mum, don't be afraid, they can't get to us, the seat is stuck.'

'It . . . it won't stop them . . . Oh, Ellen, what have I done to yer, luv?'

'You haven't done this, Mum, you're a victim, not the . . .' Something splashing on the front windscreen stopped Ellen's words. The distinct smell of petrol filled the car, burning Ellen's throat and stinging her nostrils. She looked at Tilda. Her eyes were wide with terror.

'They wouldn't! God, no! Bernard! Bernard, get out . . . Oh, Bernard, my love, my darling. I love you with all my heart. I'm sorry. So very sorry.'

A face appeared through the front window. Ellen's temper, fuelled by her horror and fear rose. 'And what do you think Bett would say to this, eh? She'd break her heart, after she'd rung both your necks!'

The man looked stunned.

''Ow do yer know me mum?'

'Bett took care of me and Ruth, you remember, the girl who became famous on the stage.'

'I do. And what's she to you then?'

'Me sister. Bett loved us both and looked after us like a mum, and she wasn't proud of you, but she did get you to help us by hurting Belton so he couldn't get up to his tricks again. She was lovely, and she didn't deserve to have sons like you two!'

'What gives yer the right to talk about me mum? Shuddup.'

'She was a lovely lady and you two broke her heart.'

'We looked after me mum. We gave her the best of everything.'

'She didn't want it . . . Oh, she didn't show you two, because she loved you. She was thankful for the titbits you gave her. But she wanted you to be decent boys, not to terrorize, murder or extort money from hard-working people.'

'I said shuddup!'

'Well, I won't. Bett deserves for you to be told the truth. She cried buckets of tears over the pair of you.'

Roly stared at her. His face went white, he gasped for breath, then slowly slumped down out of sight.

His brother's distraught voice screamed, 'Roly! Roly! 'Elp, someone, 'elp!'

'Get me out of here, I'm a nurse. I can help him!'

'No, don't, don't, Ellen.'

'I have to, Mum.'

The blows to the seat thudded as, like a maniac, Roly's brother smashed the back off the front seat.

Ellen climbed over, leaving her mum cowering in the back seat.

One glance told her Roly was dead — probably a heart attack, but she must look as though she was trying to help him to delay whatever the consequences of this would be.

As she tended to him, the sound of bells in the distance coming ever louder gave her hope.

She looked up into Roly's brother's face. Fear held him in its grip. He looked from his brother to his van. To the back of their car. Tilda sat there shivering. Deciding to run, the brother jumped into the ditch then scrambled up the other side and climbed the fence. He was out of sight by the time the police arrived. Ellen didn't know how it happened that they were here, but she sobbed with happiness.

Out of the back of the van they spewed one after the other, all carrying truncheons. The one they all called Sarge shouted orders, sending four of them running after the escaped brother. Then he kneeled down beside her. 'So, Roly's in hell at last. Good riddance! Now, what did you do to him to have this happen to you, young lady?'

'Nothing. I'm sorry, my mum will tell you everything. I must tend to my husband, the driver, he's hurt.'

'There's an ambulance on its way, love. We called them, but they're a bit further away than we are. He'll be all right, you leave him to the professionals.'

'I am a professional. I'm a nurse and he's a doctor.'

The sergeant touched his cap. 'Very well, madam. I'll talk to this lady in the back.' Putting his head inside the open door, his voice held disbelief as he said, 'Tilda? Is that you? What the blazes?'

'Yes, it's me, Steve. This is me daughter, they were taking me home. She only found out where I were a little while ago.'

'And where were you? Why didn't you ever come to me for help?'

'Huh! Fat lot of good that'd do, yer all on their payroll.'

'I'm not and never have been, and nor is our new inspector. Inspector Garland was, but he's long had the boot. It's been the mission of me and me inspector to nail this lot. We don't normally react to a shunt on the roads, but a passing motorist called in and he was in a state. He described what he'd seen. I can smell the petrol still. It looks like they were going to burn you alive, Tilda. We knew such actions could only be the work of one gang. Bett's boys! Well, Roly's dead, and Ricky will swing at the end of a rope, as will all his gang, because Ricky will squeal like a stuck pig if we let him think he'll get a pardon for it.'

He looked up at Ellen then. 'How is he?'

'He's coming round now. He has a few cuts and a huge bruise. My main worry is if he has suffered concussion.'

Bernard made a moaning sound, then opened his eyes.

'Darling, it's all right, we're all fine. It was a car accident. The ambulance is coming.'

'Ellen . . . Oh, Ellen, how did it happen?'

'I'll tell you all about it when you're better, darling.'

His eyes opened wide. 'Your mum . . . is she . . . ?'

'She's all right. And she's going to be more all right than she's ever been as she's going to be truly free, Bernard.'

'What? What are you talking about? Bett's Boys, they'll always be a danger to her.'

'They won't. Look, I don't want you to worry as it's all over now but . . .'

Thinking it now best to tell him to alleviate his worries over her mother, Ellen described what had happened. She'd hardly finished doing so than another set of bells rang out in the distance. But the sound of shouting from over the road drowned them out as the policemen who'd chased Ricky could be seen dragging him back across the field.

The sergeant helped Tilda out of the car, his voice

310

gentle as he said, 'Tilda, you should have contacted me, you know. I would have protected you . . . Anyway, I need you all to promise to contact me when Christmas is over. You are my witnesses, but I won't hold you up now.'

★ ★ ★

Five hours later, all with bandages somewhere on their body and with Ellen and Bernard both sporting blackening, bloodshot eyes, they managed to stiffly get off the train. Ruth ran towards them. 'Oh, Ellen, Ellen, I've been worried sick since your phone call . . . Look at yer both . . . and, Mum? Oh, Mum, Mum, yer here, yer all right . . . Yer truly here, luv.'

With this Ruth burst into tears.

'Ruth? Here, mate, that's a nice greeting, ain't it?'

Although Ellen saw tears glistening on her mum's cheeks too, she felt this was a bit of a harsh hello after Ruth's longing for this moment since being a baby. But then they were in each other's arms, clinging on as if they would never let go, and Ellen's mind rested easier.

Bernard's arm came around her and pulled her close. She knew he'd detected her feelings. 'It's all going to be fine, darling. And it's over. Truly over. We're all free to do what we want, no more clandestine operations. You and Ruth can enjoy your mum and Amy can enjoy hers, and none of them have to live up here if they don't want to. Now, don't worry. Some things take time.'

'I know. I just hope Ruth isn't disappointed. I know Mum loves her. But isn't it just so wonderful? All of it? I cannot believe it's happening.'

311

'I know. And I've been thinking as we travelled here that even though everyone will probably come back to London now it's safe, maybe we still needn't sell your cottage, darling.'

'Our cottage, Bernard. There's no you and me, only us.'

Bernard smiled down at her. 'Yes, us. Oh, darling, I love you.'

'Even with a black eye and a bump on my nose?'

'Yes, even with that.'

They giggled, then Bernard said, 'I mean it, though, we could keep the cottage. With Abe being a partner in our practice, we can manage now. We can come up to the cottage for breaks, as everyone can, and then one day, who knows, we may come to live in it.'

'I'm so glad that you have fallen in love with it, too, darling, but we'll see. It is a big expense.'

They didn't have time to say more as Robbie came over to them.

'Well, quite an adventure yer both had. Can't wait to hear all about it.' He shook Bernard's hand, then grinned when he winced. 'Now yer know what yer patients feel like, eh?'

'I certainly do, Robbie. I'll be more sympathetic in the future.'

They laughed together and Ellen thought how comfortable they all were with each other. The thought gave her a warm feeling. She put her arm around her mum, now that Ruth had busied herself collecting the luggage together.

'This is Mum, Robbie.'

'I would know yer anywhere, luv. Ruth's the image of you and so is Ellen, but not as much as Ruth is. And I can't tell yer 'ow pleased I am to meet yer,

Tilda. You're going to mend some hearts that have been missing a piece of them for a long time.'

'I'm pleased to meet yer, Robbie. I'm a bit over-whelmed with it all to tell the truth. This morning I were still in that hellhole thinking this was me life for ever, and how much worse it was now Ethel and Cyril had gone, and then, like a bolt of lightning, I'm here, battered and bruised and I have me daughters back. Yer couldn't make it up.'

'Ha, yer right there, luv. But for the girls it's been years of longing and trying to find yer. And now you're safe, as one of Bett's boys is dead, they tell me, and it won't be long before the other is. Good riddance to them, they've made a lot of people's lives a misery.'

Tilda's bottom lip quivered. Robbie took her hand. 'Yer safe, luv. I promise yer.'

'Ta, Robbie.'

Ellen took her into her arms again. Her thin body was trembling. 'It's all been too much for you, love. Let's get you to the car, eh?'

Ruth came back to them then. She took her mum's arm. Tilda looked at her and told her, 'I have always loved yer, Ruth. All me life. I'm sorry I did what I did.'

Ellen understood now why she had been a bit stilted with Ruth. With herself, she'd been taken away by her father, leaving Tilda no option, but Tilda had given Ruth away.

'You don't have to be sorry, Mum, not ever. I've always understood why. And I've always known that you loved me.'

'Ta, luv. Yes, Ellen told me how you used to say it. And that warmed me heart as I've always felt guilty. But I had no choice, luv.'

'I know. It's behind us now. We're together, and the

313

love I imagined yer had for me is something I can really feel at last. Please don't feel guilty about me. I love you, Mum, with all me heart.'

This time as Tilda went into Ruth's arms, it was as a loving mum.

27

Amy

The kitchen was a hive of activity mixed with excitement.

'That's the spuds peeled, luv. I tell yer, I never thought I'd enjoy peeling spuds, but I ain't done no ordinary stuff for such a long time.'

'Oh, Mum. You make chores a pleasure. I can't imagine what life has been like for yer.'

'It weren't bad in the beginning. I had you, luv, and we worked in the laundry. The other women were good company, and you were adored, me little darlin'.'

Amy saw Ethel glance at the clock. She couldn't wait for Tilda to arrive. It had been a long day for them all, but the news of the demise of Bett's boys had cheered them all up and given them a second wind.

Cyril, Robbie and Ivan had done wonders shifting furniture in the three hours they'd been here, and Amy, Ruth and Ethel had made up beds, set fires and sorted the dining room ready for dinner.

Amy loved the cottage on arrival and found its layout quirky but workable, with a central hall leading to a living room on the left and another on the right; the room on the right led to the dining room and the one on the left to the kitchen, which also led to the dining room. This made part of the dining room have a slanted roof as it fell beneath the stairs.

The living room on the right was now a bedroom, its beautiful furniture brought into the second living room as that had been emptied to furnish Amy's flat.

Bedrooms had been allocated. Robbie and Abe in the downstairs room. Ellen and Bernard in Ellen's gran's old bedroom. Herself and Ruth in Ellen's old bedroom. Ethel and Tilda in the one next to theirs that Ruth said used to be Cook's and Dilly's room, and finally, Cyril, Ivan and the two boys in Adrian's flat, though Archie had the option of sleeping in with her and Ruth if he wanted to when it came to bedtime.

Just thinking about it all made Amy feel exhausted. 'I bet everyone would like a hot drink when they come in, Mum, I know I do. Will yer fill the kettle while I get this pie in the oven, eh?'

The sound of the water hitting the bottom of the kettle did nothing to soothe Amy's nerves. She'd gone from being elated that Bett's boys could no longer harm her mum and Tilda, to feeling the shock of her beloved Ellen hurt and in the situation she had been, to being anxious about the meal and there not being much time to cook everything. But then after rooting around in the kitchen she had found a meat grinder! This had made a huge difference as minced meat took a lot less time to cook. So, meat and onion pie with mashed potatoes and swede it was. With apple dumplings for pudding. She still had the custard to whip up, but that didn't take long.

The garden, she'd found, was laden with Brussels sprouts and swede, as well as fruit trees, potato farrows and parsnips that should have been lifted a month ago but were still pulling from the frozen soil

316

in good condition — these she wanted to roast on Christmas Day.

Sighing contentedly now she'd sorted everything, Amy looked around the beamed kitchen with its long scrubbed table in the centre, its black-leaded stove, the clothes airer hanging high above it and the dresser displaying lovely china pieces. And then the deep pot sink under the window with matching yellow, patterned-with-roses curtains hanging from the window and around the sink and knew that this cottage was her dream home.

It was so similar to what she'd been used to in Canada and from day one she'd found London stifling and living in a flat unfamiliar to her. You couldn't just go out in the garden, you had to go downstairs and through Robbie and Abe's kitchen and then you were only in a yard — a pretty one, she imagined, in the spring and summer as Abe had planted pots all around it, but still just a concrete yard.

Sighing, she went to the back door to cool off a little. When she opened it, she was surprised to see a young man digging a root of potatoes. 'Hello, you must be Jack . . . the gardener?'

'By, yer made me jump. Yes, that's me. I were told yer were all coming. I keep the kitchen garden stocked even if Miss Ellen ain't here, and I'm allowed to have veg for me ma.'

He sounded just how Ellen did when she mimicked Dilly, the one-time housekeeper at the cottage.

'I'm Amy.'

'Pleased to meet you, lass. Thou's up from London, ain't you?'

'Yes, there's a load of us coming.'

'I know. I covered the root veg so they'd still be

317

fresh for you. But by, it's been a cold spat, so that's helped an' all.'

'Ta, mate. I appreciate it. We brought most of the food we need and had some fresh delivered today, but we didn't bring vegetables.'

'What about a Christmas tree? You've young 'uns with you, I hear.'

'We hadn't thought about it, but it would be nice.'

'I'll get you one. I allus cut them on this same night every year, and some holly. I'd say we're in for a harsh beginning to 1920 as the berries are plentiful this year.'

'That'd be lovely, ta. We've enough hands to get the place decorated. I know Ellen said we have a box of stuff in the attic — garlands and that kind of thing — but she didn't think we'd get a tree!'

'Aw, Christmas is grand with a tree decorated. I'll be back in the morning with it.'

'I'll have the kettle on, Jack.'

'Eeh, ta. Though I hope you Londoners know how to brew proper northern tea. We have it that strong you could stand the teaspoon up in it.'

He laughed then, a lovely deep laugh. His deep blue eyes lit up with the merriment. Taking his flat cap off, he ran his fingers through a shock of thick black hair. Then he looked at Amy as if seeing her for the first time. She held his gaze for a moment. His half-smile told her he was feeling the same shyness that now crept over her.

He doffed his cap. 'I'll see you on the morrow then.'

She loved the way he spoke and as she watched him pick up his bucket and walk away from her towards the end of the long garden, she noted his strong body and that he wasn't over tall, just the right height for her. She blushed at this silly thought and went inside.

Cracking egg yolks into a bowl for the custard, she whipped them with a frenzy, trying to quieten the butterflies fluttering around her heart.

The sound of a car horn brought her back to normality. 'They're here, Mum!'

Ethel came running out of the pantry with the tea caddy in her hand. Her expression showed her excitement. Calling out, 'Cyril, Cyril! Tilda's 'ere, mate, come on!'

Amy laughed. It pleased her to see the friendship and love the three had for one another and that was compounded when they opened the door and Ethel ran forward and hugged Tilda.

When Amy caught sight of Ellen's face, the tears sprang to her eyes. She rushed forward. 'Ellen, oh, Ellen, luv.'

'I'm all right, I promise, Amy, love. I just need a hug and a nice cup of tea — Oh, and to take my boots off, my feet are steaming!'

'Ha, I know that feeling. Everything's ready for you, love . . . And, oh, Ellen, I love this cottage, it's so homely . . . I love it!'

As they went inside, Ellen told her, 'Well, stay as long as you need, love. Everything is in place back in London, as we thought that you'd be up here for a while.'

'Oh, ta, luv, I would love that, but I think Mum will want to get back.'

'Well, we'll see. Now, I want you to meet our mum, Amy.' Ellen hugged herself. 'Ooh, it feels so good saying that.'

Amy grinned as Tilda came towards her with Ethel linking in one arm and Ruth the other. She looked

319

overwhelmed. Amy put out her arms to her. 'It's so lovely to meet yer, Tilda.'

Tilda seemed more nervous than Amy, so Amy told her, 'It's a lot for yer, luv. Why don't yer take yer mum upstairs, Ellen? My mum'll go up with her. I can take their cup of tea up to them and they can have a chat while we get the rest of the things sorted. I noticed there are two chairs next to the window in the bedroom that they are to share, and we lit the fire for them.'

'Yes. Dilly and Cook used to often sit up there in the afternoons watching the children coming and going from Adrian's school, and looking over the fields. You'll love it, Mum, and it will give you a chance to catch your breath before you meet everyone.'

Tilda looked gratefully at Amy and smiled. 'Ta, luv, I do need a moment.'

Ruth stood next to Amy as they watched the two new women in their lives climb the stairs behind Ellen. When they were at the top, Ruth turned to Amy. 'It feels like we're whole for the first time, Amy.'

'I know, luv. I know exactly what yer mean. It's as if someone said, yer do have a right to be here, you've got a mum.'

The girls hugged.

'Hey, yer blocking the way, you two. This is no time to turn the taps on, I've a boot box full of stuff and another load to fetch from the station's left luggage. Poor Abe's stuck in a chair in the front room till I bring his house wheelchair here.'

'Sorry, Robbie. Just leave those cases there and I'll move them.'

'And I'll go and see to that tea . . . Oh, Ruth, I love it here!'

Amy skipped off towards what she already considered her kitchen. She could honestly say this was the happiest she'd felt since leaving Canada, but she couldn't have said why.

28

Ruth

Christmas Eve was hectic. Jack had brought an enormous Christmas tree, and there'd been fun and games getting it inside the house, with Amy going mad at everyone as pine needles fell about what she called 'her kitchen' much to the amusement of Ruth and Ellen.

'I don't think Amy ever wants to leave here, yer know, Ellen.'

'I know, she said as much last night when we arrived. She's certainly bedded in. How on earth she managed to cook such an amazingly tasty meal for us all when we arrived, when she'd only been here a few hours, I don't know.'

'The pie was lovely, wasn't it? She said she found everything she needed in the garden, even herbs in the greenhouse. It does seem to suit her here.'

'I suppose Canada's like this, rural and with lovely fresh air, and she wasn't unhappy for the last few years of being there.'

The smells wafting from the kitchen seemed to confirm what they'd been saying. They'd all offered to help her to prepare the Christmas Day vegetables, but she'd only wanted her mum and Tilda. All three were happily chatting away, though Ruth did notice that once the tree was inside, Amy dashed out to chat with Jack, who she'd learned was Ellen's gardener.

Ellen voiced these thoughts. 'Amy seems taken with the gardener too.'

Ruth giggled. 'Two great minds think alike!'

'Ha! We're matchmaking! Talking of which, you seem to be getting on well with Ivan, love.'

Ruth felt the colour rush to her face. She hadn't thought it obvious. She'd only recently recognized her own feelings as being more than just liking him. 'It shows then?'

'A little.'

They both giggled.

Ruth picked a red and white garland out of the box that had been brought down from the attic. 'Where does it come from, this feeling of attraction to a man? I'm always doing it.'

'Always?'

'Yes, I fell in love with Robbie, then he became like a brother, and I met Abe and promptly fell in love with him. Then along came Adrian, and I was taken right off me feet, and now Ivan's having an effect on me . . .'

The door from the kitchen opened and Ivan stood there staring at her. Ellen coughed. 'I — I think I'll go and see what Bernard's up to. They're all in Robbie and Abe's room.'

Ruth hadn't moved and neither had Ivan. Their eyes were locked on each other.

'Did yer mean that, Ruth?'

'You heard?'

'Yes. Me 'eart's still racing from what you said.'

'Well, I do fall in love a lot.'

'And you've fallen in love with me?'

Ruth stood stock still. It was as if she was being asked to confess. And yet it was something she wanted

323

to tell but couldn't. She nodded her head.

Ivan came into the room and closed the door behind him. 'Oh, Ruth. I think whatever it is that hit you has hit me too. I love you, Ruth . . . but, I'm not worthy of yer.'

Ruth rushed to his side. 'You are, Ivan. More worthy than anyone I know, and yes, I do love you. I love you so much that I ache.'

She wasn't sure how it happened, but she was in his arms and his lips were on hers. To Ruth, it was like the last pain locked in her heart released and all she could feel was Ivan's love and his caring for her. She was no longer trapped in a cold shell, she was feeling, loving, and loved.

'Ooh, Mummy's kissing your brother!'

They jumped apart and were confronted with two giggling boys.

'Archie . . . it wasn't . . . Mummy . . . Mummy hurt herself and Ivan was kissing it better.'

'It didn't look like that to us, did it, Archie? We caught yer at it, Ivan.'

'No. It didn't, Jeff. We caught them at it.'

Ruth was bursting to laugh. Ivan did just that. He put his head back and let out a loud laugh that held happiness and relief.

'We're sussed, Ruth. Well, boys, yer right, I confess. I love Ruth . . . your mum, Archie. And she loves me. But not more than you, just in a different way.'

'Like a man loves a woman, Archie. They'll be between the sheets next.'

Ruth, used to Jeff's coarse ways, and trying to gently change them, coloured once more — this she wasn't used to. But then to have Archie mimic him again was too much.

'Will you be in the sheets with Ivan, Mummy?'

She looked at Ivan. Saw he desired that more than anything. Swallowed hard as the feeling took her too, but with it had come shame to hear her little Archie speaking like this and about her. Ivan handled it.

'Jeff, you should be more careful and respectful, lad. This ain't Old Nichol Street. Yer don't talk to ladies, or in front of them, like that, and yer need to be careful what Archie picks up from yer. Can yer do that for me, mate?'

'Yeah, I didn't think. Sorry, Aunty Ruth.'

Ruth went to hug him, but stopped. Jeff might think it cissy. But then he surprised her. He ran at her and hugged her waist. 'Does this mean yer'll be me big sister?'

'Are yer proposing for me, mate? Ha, I reckon I can do that for meself when I'm ready.'

'Oh, you're not ready to take me on then?'

'Oh, Ruth. Yer me girl now. And'll always be. I'd take yer on tomorrow if you like. In fact, today, this minute.'

'I do like, Ivan. I like very much, ta.'

'He has to go down on one knee, Aunty Ruth.'

'Yes. On one knee!'

To try to stop laughing at such two serious little boys was the most difficult thing she had to do, and she could see it was for Ivan too. But he gallantly went down. 'Will yer do me the 'onour of marrying me, Ruth? I've no job and no prospects, but I love yer and pledge meself to take care of yer and be a dad to Archie.'

Ruth's heart swelled. It was the most beautiful proposal. 'I do, Ivan. I do.'

No sooner were the words out than she jumped out

of her skin as simultaneously the kitchen and the hall door opened, and a loud cheering and clapping went up.

Ruth looked from one to the other, shocked rigid.

'Sorry, luv.'

Amy didn't look at all sorry as she explained, 'I was just coming in to ask yer something when I realized what was going on and beckoned Mum and Tilda to listen in . . . Oh, Ruth, Ivan, I'm so very happy for yer.'

Before Ruth could react, Ellen piped up, 'And I was just coming back in as the men were talking boring talk when I heard too and fetched the menfolk. Oh, this is a happy moment.'

She was encased in the arms of her beloved sister and her very best friend as the two of them had rushed at her.

Archie was clapping and saying, 'Mummy's getting married,' and Jeff was being hugged by Ivan. The moment for Ruth dispelled any doubts she'd had about betraying Adrian, as now, with it happening here — the place where he had first told her he loved her — it was as if he, too, was in the room nodding his head with approval. Yes, there was a long road to travel, as Ivan still had a journey back to full health, but she would be by his side, and she knew that would be with the blessing of her beloved Adrian.

'Well, this makes Christmas even more special. Congratulations, Ruth. And, Ivan, you're a lucky fellow.'

'Ta, Abe, I can't believe it. I've loved Ruth from the moment I set eyes on her, but never felt worthy enough to have her love me back.'

'You're the worthiest person of all, Ivan. You have a lot of courage, you've shown us all that. And with

326

Ruth supporting you, you'll win through.'

Robbie tapped Ellen and Amy on the shoulder. 'I take precedence in the hugging stakes, ladies. Me and Ruth go back a long way.' He leaned back a little. 'Ruth. The love of me life, you're deserting me again, darling.'

Ruth giggled. 'Never, Robbie, luv. You'll always be at the top of me tree. Well, below Ivan, that is.'

Ivan caught hold of her hand. He looked around him at all gathered there. 'Yer know, when I met Amy, I had a love for her, which I still have, so I understand how yer feel for Ruth, Robbie. But me and Amy are like sister and brother, like you two are. For me now, I feel as though I have been healed. That nothing that has happened to hurt me matters now. It's all led me to Ruth, and that's what matters. And now, as I look around at yer all, though I will never forget me family, I feel as though I have a replacement, all just as nice and one that I can love and find love with too.'

They all cheered, and Ruth could see there wasn't a dry eye amongst them. Ivan had been torn in pieces by the things that had happened to him, but all of them were playing their part in putting him back together again. She looked from one to the other. She loved them all, and she could think of no one she'd rather be sharing her happiness with than them.

Amy, as practical as ever, brought them back to normal. 'Well, I was coming to shout to you all for your lunch, as the posh ones amongst us call the meal in the daytime.' Clapping her hands together, she said, 'Everyone to the table. Jack's mum has sent pork pie and mince pies, and I've put them out with a cheese board, so it's help yourself. The teapot is on the table as well.'

As they filed in, Ruth holding Ivan's hand as if she'd done so all her life, she thought how kind they all were. This would be the time when they would have their first glass of sherry of the festive season, but no one questioned that it wasn't available. All cared for Ivan, and all wanted to help him by not putting temptation in his way.

The talk around the table was all teasing of them, asking when the wedding would be. Amy joined in even though she must have been feeling a bit left out with Ellen married and now Ruth finding love, but she didn't show it and joined in with the rest of them.

'Yer not giving me time to breathe! Shut up, all of you! You'll be told in good time. I ain't had five minutes to talk to Ivan since I knew he loved me.'

This made them all giggle, but they changed the subject. The men talked about the Boxing Day sport that was to come, and the women chatted about all the arrangements for Christmas dinner — a very important event for them all, their first ever since their reunion.

Cyril, after eating his pie, took himself off for a walk. He was a bit of a loner and more used to women's company, and Ruth worried about whether he was enjoying himself, but Ethel didn't seem concerned. She was the first to volunteer her services towards the dinner. 'I'll do the spuds.'

'Mum, you've only been here a day and yet we all know yer love peeling spuds!'

Ethel beamed. 'Well, that's because I can't do much else. No one taught me. If we had nothing else for tea, we always had spuds! I grew up peeling them.'

This made them all laugh.

'Well, I'll dress the cockerel. I'll start tonight and

you and Archie can help me, Jeff. We have to pull out every feather then scorch off any small ones that we can't get out.'

'I don't like hurting the cockerel.'

'It won't 'urt it, Archie, yer daft thing. It's 'ad its neck wrung. It's dead as a dormouse.'

'Jeff!'

'Well, he's a softy sometimes, Aunty Ruth, he needs toughening up.'

Ruth didn't deny this as she agreed with it. Maybe Jeff was the one to do it too. She had babied Archie too much. Starved of love while Ellen was nursing in France and grieving for Adrian and lonely beyond words, she'd smothered Archie.

'Well, just go a bit easy on how yer do it, mate. Not too much all at once.'

'All right. But he has to be a man!'

Ruth wanted to laugh at this. Jeff was so funny and made more so as he acted like a man in a boy's body. Not his fault, he'd had to bring himself up for the most part and that had meant being tough and taking a lot of knocks with no one to turn to.

'So, that's settled then,' Ivan announced. 'Me, Archie and Jeff to dress the chicken. There's stuffing to make as well, yer know, boys.'

'Well, I don't know how to do that, but I can learn.'

'That's right, Jeff, yer can always learn.'

'But ain't cooking women's work?'

'Not all. Men can do some of it. See what yer think when we get round to it. If yer think it's not what yer want to do, yer needn't, mate.'

Jeff seemed happy with this. Suddenly, he jumped up. 'Come on, Archie, Jack's 'ere again. He said he'd show us how to cut the fruit trees back.'

Ruth wanted to say that Archie couldn't get involved with that, it was too dangerous, but she stopped herself. She had to let him try things for himself, so instead she distracted herself. 'I'll do anything yer want me to, Amy, you just direct and I'll do it.'

'Well, there's the Christmas pud yer made, Ruth. That needs to have its final stir and the lads to make a wish and then put it on to steam overnight. There's the Brussels sprouts to prepare and the parsnips to peel, and gravy to make. Oh, and the cream to whip, and the trifle must be done this afternoon or it won't set.'

Ruth saw a bewildered look on her mum's face as she listened but didn't volunteer to take on any of those tasks. Had she never prepared any of this in the past? But then, Ruth doubted she had as she'd never had a proper home.

'I'll work alongside me mum. We'll get through a few jobs that way.'

Ellen piped up, 'Can I do that too, Ruth? I'm hopeless in the kitchen, as you know. It comes from always having been looked after. Or I'll just help where anyone needs me.'

'Can't yer cook either, luv?'

'No, Mum, no one ever taught me . . . I mean, well, Dad always had a cook and so did Gran. I just didn't get the chance.'

There was a look that crossed Mum's face that Ruth understood. It was shame mixed with the pain of all she'd missed out on. 'Mum, I know things didn't go right for yer, and when yer want to yer can talk to me and Ellen. We'll understand, won't we, Ellen?'

'We will, Mum, but in the meantime . . .' — Ellen took Mum's hand — 'no guilty feelings. None of what

330

happened is your fault. I saw the love you had for me and for Christopher that afternoon, and now Ruth is seeing the love you have for her. Don't spoil our happiness at having found you and being with you by self-recriminations.'

Tilda smiled through her tears. She was delicate and all of this was a lot for her to take. Suddenly Ruth had an idea. 'Shall me, you and Ellen leave the others to wash up and go for a walk, eh, Mum? We can do our part when we get back?'

'I'd like that. But yer won't be cold, will yer, me darlin's?'

'Oh, Mum. In that one question you have sealed for us both how you feel about us, hasn't she, Ruth?'

'You have, Mum. Yer sounded like I do when I'm dealing with Archie — a mum. A proper mum, and yer ours and we love yer.'

Tilda smiled a wider smile than either of them had seen till now. She looked beautiful.

★   ★   ★

They walked hand in hand, talking as they went. All had told of their journey to this point by the time they got home.

To Ruth, no matter what she and Ellen had been through, which was horrendous, what Tilda had been through was much worse. She felt angry when she thought of how men had used her. The gangsters had made her into a prostitute for their own profit, taking no heed of how some of the punters treated her. And Ellen's dad's treatment of her, saying he loved her, giving her hope, then dashing it. And his ultimate betrayal of her, taking her children and then grassing to the cops about her and Ethel.

Even though she adored Ellen and would never do anything to hurt her, Ruth knew that she hated Ellen's father with a vengeance and was glad he was dead. If he wasn't, it was as sure as anything, she would be hanged for his murder.

On the way back with all demons laid to rest, they linked arms and to Ruth, it was the happiest she'd ever felt. This was her family — at last she had one.

29

Ellen & Ruth

Christmas seemed a distant memory by the time Ellen and Bernard began their search for their new home in mid-January.

With Amy choosing to stay up at the cottage for a while, Ethel, Cyril and Tilda had stayed too, and this had given both Ruth and Ellen some breathing space. Both had a lot to contend with and felt they couldn't give the time to their mum that they wanted to until they'd sorted themselves into a routine.

For Ruth, there was the new show starting and her hat business to launch properly. Robbie was proving a godsend to her.

Ivan was too, with taking the boys under his wing and seeing to their needs, though Ellen wondered how it was working out for Ruth and Ivan being under the same roof now that they had declared their love. She smiled to herself with the thoughts that came to her of clandestine creeping along the landing. Then chastised herself for even thinking such a thing. But she giggled anyway.

'What's amusing you, darling?'

'Oh, just happy.'

Bernard took his hand off the steering wheel and sought hers. Ellen knew the happiness in her to increase with his touch.

'Doctor Price has been amazing, hasn't he? To

think, it's only a few weeks since we bought his practice, and he has found us a house to rent.'

They were on the way now to view the house. Ellen's stomach was jittery with excited tingles. 'Yes, I can't wait to see it. And he's been so generous with his time, going with you on your rounds to introduce you to his . . . our patients, and teaching me how the penny insurance works — though there must be those who can't afford that. Those large families and all the poor folk who live in Ivan's old quarter.'

'We went to see one of those yesterday and she tried to give Doctor Price a slice of bread pudding she'd made, but he wouldn't take it.'

'Ah, that was lovely of him. I wonder if they will get used to us, though. I mean, technically she should have offered it to you as you were the one treating her.'

'I know what you mean, darling, but don't worry, they will when he isn't around as much. It's a transition for them, too.'

'Oh, I didn't mean . . . I just, well, want them to like us and, more than that, to trust us . . . Actually, Bernard, I have an idea. It won't make us rich, but I worry about those who are slipping through the net. Look at the poor condition Jeff was in when he came to us. He had sores all over him, he was underweight and his eyes were infected.'

'Hmm, it was so sad to see, but where is this leading?'

'Well, you know about the soup kitchen, don't you?'

'Yes, I feel so proud that you were instrumental in setting that up, darling. But how does that connect to your idea?'

'Why don't we do a free clinic there once a month

334

on the same day? There is a room we could use. I could tend to all the small things, and the obvious bigger ailments come to you, or I may spot something I need you to look at.'

Bernard was quiet for a moment. When he spoke, he said, 'I think it a marvellous idea, but a little flawed. Ethically, we could only accept those registered to us, so I would have to make sure they were. I would have to run the idea by the Medical Council and any local doctors would have to be informed. We don't know the scale of the problem yet, so we need to bed in first, but I do think it is huge, especially in the slum areas. The Nichol estate, for instance. I've seen things there that made me want to vomit, and I thought I'd seen it all. It's not all of the people. I came across a lady the other day with five children, and her cottage, though in dire need of repair, was clean, as was her frontage, but she was worn out with the effort of trying to keep respectable amongst such filth and dilapidation.'

'Well, no battle can be won unless it is fought — even a hopeless one. And I don't believe in them — everything is possible. The women need help and encouragement — to know that someone cares, to help them beat the everyday curses of lice, and infections. To educate them into knowing that dirt begets disease. We can do that.'

Bernard laughed out loud. 'Oh, my darling, you're priceless, but do you know, I do believe that if anyone can, you can. And if we aren't granted permission for our free surgery, I don't see that stopping you.'

'It won't, I'll go amongst them and help them in their own street. I can help with all the things I've mentioned. I know I can.'

'You're a special person, Ellen . . . Oh, here we

are, Bethnal Green Gardens and the next turn is ours — Cromwell Road.'

The three-storey house with a plain frontage was made eye-catching by the lovely Georgian leaded windows. 'Ooh, I love it!'

'Hmm, it does look nice, and it has a nice outlook too. It's huge, though.'

'We need it to be, remember? The downstairs will be taken up with your surgery and treatment rooms. Only the kitchen will be used as part of our home.'

'Let's get inside and get a better picture of it, shall we?'

When he'd unlocked the front door, Bernard turned and lifted her in the air. Ellen gave a little squeal of delight mixed with shock as she hadn't expected this. 'What are you doing, darling?'

'I'm carrying my bride over the threshold.'

'But what if this isn't the house for us?'

'Then I'll do it at every house we view.'

They both laughed. Ellen snuggled into his neck. 'Thank you, my darling. I do love you.'

'I love you, Ellen, more than I'm able to express. I feel now that I wasted so many years when we were working in France, though I'm glad I didn't act as I didn't know then that you were so young. I still marvel at you passing yourself off as over twenty-one when you were only fifteen!'

'Ruth's stage make-up helped with that.'

'I never noticed you wore any.'

'It was very subtle, but once you all accepted me, I hardly ever did. I think we all got that tired that it aged us anyway. And being brought up with older people gave me a different outlook on life than most fifteen-year-olds would have.'

Bernard nodded. 'So, now you're like a sixty-year-old!'

He put her down as he said this, and she slapped his shoulder. 'You cheeky devil!'

They were laughing again, but then became serious as they turned and looked at the hall with its mock-arched ceiling, beautifully carved with fleurs-de-lys that looked elegant painted gold against the whiteness of the arch. 'So lovely. I wonder who this house was built for?'

'It *is* lovely, Ellen. A very nice first impression, as is the carved stair rail. Let's look around the rest of it.'

By the time they'd seen the two reception rooms, the kitchen, the pantry and the dining room, they just knew it was for them.

Upstairs sealed the deal, as the huge main bedroom at the front of the house with views over the park would easily lend itself to being a living room. Besides this there was a bathroom and three more bedrooms on this landing and two further bedrooms on the second floor. All of the rooms had odd bits of furniture in, and of good quality, so it didn't seem a problem to complete the job of furnishing it. Bernard had quite a bit of furniture and she had the pieces she'd brought down for Amy, so they would have very little to buy. One thing she would insist on would be a new bed. Bernard's was so small that whilst it was lovely to cuddle up together, sleeping with Bernard, who sometime flailed about, wasn't so good.

'You could make your mum a flat up here — a bedroom and a sitting room, at least.'

Ellen looked around the bedroom on the third floor that they were in. It was big enough to hold a sofa and a chair. It had a fireplace, and not so much of the sloping roof that the one next door to it had, which in itself was plenty big enough to make a bedroom.

'Yes, it would be lovely. Though I'm not sure where she will make her home yet. She may want to live with Amy, Ethel and Cyril up in Leeds, or if they come down here, in a little place of their own for the four of them. It would need to be bigger than the little flat at the back of the shop, though. Or Mum may choose to live with Ruth. I'm just glad that she stayed up in Leeds for now. It will give her a chance to find her feet after being imprisoned for so long. Poor Mum.'

'You're right, though, it must be her decision. Wherever she feels comfortable, that's where she must live.'

Ellen smiled. To her, the thing that mattered was that she had found her mum and that she was safe. Nothing else, as the feeling of being an orphan went along with the feeling of being unloved and unwanted, and that wasn't pleasant. Now, they were all loved and cared about. Her thoughts went to those orphans they left behind — what kind of lives had they now? And what of those who still lived there?

'You know, Bernard, one day I might pluck up the courage to go back to see how things are now.'

'Back to where, darling? You went into your head again then, something you often do. And I haven't a clue what you're talking about, but you think I do.'

'Sorry, love. Back to the orphanage.'

Bernard grabbed her and pulled her into his arms. 'My sweet Ellen. You want to fight everyone's corner. It's what I fell in love with you for. You cared about every soldier we tended. You never saw them as casualties of war, but as people, as I did. And you're still doing it. I promise, I will make a visit there to check up on the children. I don't think it is part of my

338

practice. I think you would have known if Doctor Price had visited there.'

'No doctor ever did to my knowledge, darling.'

'Well, they may now, but I will check, I promise.'

'Let's go and look outside, shall we?'

There was a surprisingly long garden to the back of the house. 'Oh, look, a rose garden.'

'Oh, Bernard, that will look lovely when they are in bloom, and the scent will be perfect for us when we sit out here . . . You know, I must get a rose — or maybe take a cutting from one of those. That was a lovely service we held in the garden of Rose Cottage on Boxing Day, for Amy's lost baby and Ivan's mum. It would be lovely to plant a special rose in the spot we designated as theirs.'

'Oh, it would. Though it looked nice how Jack arranged those white stones in a cross.'

'Yes. I get the feeling he would do anything for Amy, and that he's the reason she didn't want to come home yet.'

'Really?'

'Yes. That and the fact that being on the edge of Leeds, Rose Cottage is rural, and we think she is more used to that setting than a city atmosphere. She did live on farms and Canada is a vast country.'

'Yes, all mountainous air and flowing rivers. It must be wonderful.'

'Well, we have our little oasis opposite. The gardens are lovely, I cannot wait to see them in bloom.'

Bernard squeezed her tighter. 'You see good in all. I love you, my darling.'

As she was held close to the smooth cloth of his suit, Ellen thought of how lucky she was. The little girl, lost and lonely, abused and cruelly treated, seemed like another person to her. She just couldn't think now of that once being her life.

'You shuddered, darling. Don't worry. Nothing bad is ever going to happen to you again, I promise.'

Ellen prayed that it wouldn't.

* * *

Ruth wondered how she deserved so much happiness as she turned another hat on her milliner's hat block. Stitching as she went, she thought about the decoration she would put on it. These warm felt bonnets were selling so fast, she could hardly keep up.

'Cup of tea, darling?'

'Oh, Robbie, that would be lovely. My back aches leaning over this block.'

'You're doing a great job, darling, I just sold another two! I stood outside having a fag and these two girls came looking into the window. I told them, 'All handmade, girls. And in any colour you like!' They came straight in, tried one on each and bought them!'

'Ta, Robbie, mate. I love that yer helping me.'

'That's the way it always was, Ruth. Me and you. And it will always be. And I love my life now. I can run along the road to see that Abe's all right — he always is. He's in his element teaching the kids and making an easel so he can get on with his designing. He has so many ideas of things that can help those afflicted by the war, like himself.'

'That's good to hear. And the music hall's going well.'

'It's getting better. Last week's audiences were bigger, and the interaction was so spontaneous.'

'I know. On that first evening we struggled, didn't

340

we, mate? They sat there like wooden pegs!'

'Ha, they did. But I loved it last night when they were shouting answers to us and singing along with the chorus.'

'Even your smutty jokes went well!'

'Ha, they ain't as smutty as I could get . . . Did I tell yer the one about —'

'Go and get that tea, yer daft thing!'

Robbie did a little dance and gave a kick of his leg as he left her. Ruth giggled. He was a tonic. It seemed that life was getting better every day.

As she worked, Ruth hummed 'A Pretty Girl is Like a Melody', the song Robbie had sung to her on stage the night before. Only Robbie, being Robbie, had the audience howling — the men shouting 'hear, hear' and the women play hitting them as they laughed, when he sang his own version of the second verse:

> 'A pretty girl is like a melody
> She's on at you all night and all day,
> Just like the strain of a haunting refrain,
> She'll start up and nag you again and again
> You can't escape, she has her eye on you
> She'll smile as she commands what you have to do
> She will leave you to kiss another under the moon
> Oh, yes, a pretty girl is just like a pretty tune.'

All the while, Ruth had to act out his words with gestures. It was so funny, the audience stood and clapped afterwards, and that was as the curtain came down.

They had to do two curtain calls, finishing off with 'Daisy, Daisy', a huge favourite singalong. The evening was a resounding success.

How life had changed for them. Ellen, Amy and Robbie were all happy, as she was. It seemed to her that all their troubles were over. Especially if the shop continued to make money as then she would be able to pay Amy a really good wage, and she could find a house or flat for her and her family. *Family! I didn't think that word would ever be part of our world, but now it is. I have my family and Ivan and Jeff are part of that. Ellen has hers, and I'm part of that, as our mum is part of us both. And Amy has hers, too.* Life was good at last for them all.

On arriving home that evening, Ruth called in with Robbie to say hello to Abe. He was full of what he'd done with his day, which was so lovely to see. Often, she'd thought of him as unfulfilled, but now, as Robbie had said, he was excited about the ideas he had and showed her his template for his easel. She kissed his forehead. 'Clever you! So, how did the boys do today?'

'Archie's a bright spark, Ruth, you need to use the money left for him wisely. He can go a long way with the right education. Jeff? Well, he has a lot of catching up to do, but he will get there, because he wants to. And that's half of what it takes. He does have one talent, though. I gave them a piano lesson each, and Jeff took to it very quickly. He learned the keys in no time, so I'm going to nurture that.'

'Ta, luv. I'm so grateful to yer. Well, it looks like I might need to buy a piano then. Poor Jeff deserves all the help he can get.'

'He's a fine boy, a bit rough around the edges, but he has a good heart. He loves Archie and is sometimes like a cross father and sometimes like a loving one with him.'

'I know. I have to be careful over some of the things he thinks Archie should know, though!' Ruth laughed as she went towards the door. 'Well, see yer later. Ivan's having a go at cooking a stew today, so I'll bring yer some down.'

'Ha, taste it first, Ruth. We can manage to whip something up if it's rubbish.'

'Robbie! Yer'll eat it now, mate, even if it tastes awful!'

'I'm only kidding, it'll be lovely, I'm sure . . . But, Ruth, luv, be careful. Don't make Ivan's life about looking after the kids, cooking and cleaning. He should be thinking about a job, or he'll lose his own self-respect.'

Ruth stood still for a moment. These were thoughts she'd had, but Robbie seemed to use them as an accusation.

'Don't be upset with me, mate. We've always spoken our minds to each other, ain't we? I'm just 'elping yer to see the truth, me darlin'.'

Ruth looked from Robbie to Abe. 'I agree with Robbie, Ruth. You need to think of ways to manage the children being looked after to free Ivan up.'

'I — I haven't forced this on him . . . He didn't feel well enough to go out into the world.'

'That's the point, Ruth. He never will if you give him excuses not to, but at the same time, he will feel less of a man. He must have skills that he learned on the farm that would stand him in good stead in a job?'

'I've been an idiot. I thought I had my life sorted, but that was at the expense of Ivan's. Ta, both of you.' Ruth went back towards them. 'Oh, I do love yer both. Yer like big brothers to me, keeping me on track and looking out for me. What would I ever do without yer?'

'And we love you, Ruth. We both have for a long time, and we've both been *in love* with you, and still are. You can always rely on us.'

'Ta, Abe.' Ruth hugged him and received a hug back, then turned to Robbie. 'Oh, Robbie, never stop telling me how it is, will yer?'

'I won't if yer promise never to fall out with me. You're our special person, Ruth, me darlin'. You've given us a safe place to be together and, like Abe says, we both love you for it.'

Ruth had tears in her eyes as she ran upstairs. Ivan opened the door on hearing her footsteps. ''Ello, me darlin'. You're home at last!'

'Has it been a long day, luv?'

'A bit. But all's well now yer here.'

She went into his arms. He held her to him. She could feel his desire for her, so gently pulled away. 'Soon, me luv, soon.'

'How soon, Ruth, luv? It's driving me mad living with you, being in the next bedroom. But I am willing to wait. I just wish we had a date to aim for.'

'I know. I want you so very much, but I'm scared after what happened with Adrian. I want to be married. Let's set a date, eh?'

'Three weeks from now! I can post the banns tomorrow!'

'Yes, yes, let's do it. Ellen's wedding gown will fit me, and my bridesmaid's dress will fit her — we can alter them a little to make them a bit different . . . Oh, Ivan, I love yer.'

His kiss took away any tension and lit her heart with flames she dared not fan just yet. The memory of making love to Adrian, just the once before they were to be wed, and then losing him almost straight after, held her back. But three weeks did seem to be a long time away.

★　★　★

Lying awake in bed much later, Ruth had the curtains open and gazed at the clear sky. A blanket of stars twinkled at her, a beautiful sight, but one that would mean there would be a frost. Not that the thought helped to cool her longing. Giving in, she swung her legs over the side of the bed, then giggled at herself as she crept stealthily across to her bedroom door, as every floorboard creaked under foot. She felt hot with embarrassment at the thought that Abe and Robbie lying below her would guess what she was up to.

She just got to the door when an almighty banging of the downstairs front door stopped her in her tracks and had her standing stiff with fear, her heart pounding as the words, 'Open up, police!' came through the letter box. Running to the stairs and down them, she met Robbie in his nightshirt coming out of his and Abe's flat. Neither of them spoke as Robbie opened the door.

The two policemen brandishing truncheons barged in.

'What . . . ?'

'Robbie Grant, we have reason to believe you and another man are engaging in homosexual behaviour. We're here to arrest you both!'

Ruth felt her legs go to jelly. *This can't be happening, it can't be! Dear Holy Mary, help us. Help us, please!*

30

Amy

Amy had run down the stairs knowing that the phone ringing this early in the morning wouldn't be good news. But she hadn't expected anything like she'd heard. She stared at the handset she'd just replaced on its hook on the wall. Disbelief held her in a kind of stupor as she tried to take in what Ruth had told her — Robbie in custody! And Abe would be too, if it wasn't for his condition and his standing in society. But he had been read his rights and told that he was to attend the station later in the day.

Cyril came through to the hall at that moment. 'Everything all right, Amy, luv?'

Something clicked in Amy's head. Her mum saying Cyril's tongue wagged without him thinking about the consequences of what he was saying. 'Uncle Cyril, Robbie has been arrested and Abe too, though he has been allowed to stay at home. Have you told anyone about them? I mean, what they are . . . how they live their lives?'

Cyril's face showed that he had.

'Oh, Uncle, who?'

'Just me mate. 'Onest, no one else.' Unaware Cyril had a mate, she asked, 'Where was that and when?'

'It was just after we moved out of the workhouse . . . Charlie, 'im on the gate. He was always good to me, so I went to visit him to tell him about me new

346

life. I — I told him about everyone.'

Wanting to fly at him but keeping calm, Amy asked, 'How did he react to yer telling him about Robbie and Abe?'

Cyril dropped his head.

'Uncle Cyril?'

'He didn't like it. He said they were the scum of the earth. Then he surprised me as he spouted the Bible and said 'ow they were sinning against the flesh and would burn in hell. He scared me, Amy. I — I never went to see him again.'

'Oh, Uncle, you were told yer weren't to tell anyone.'

'What will happen, Amy, luv? They'll let them go free, won't they?'

Amy felt a pain in her heart as she told him, 'Not for a long time if they can prove their guilt. You may have to call this Charlie a liar if it turns out that he informed the police. They did tell Robbie in front of Ruth that someone had informed on him and Abe and that they had been watched ever since. It seems Robbie was seen tucking a blanket around Abe when out for a walk recently. Whilst doing it, Robbie planted a kiss on Abe's head, and that was that. The police came last night. Ruth thinks they were hoping to catch them in bed together, but Abe was having a rough time and Robbie had taken him to his chair where he is most comfortable. He was just making him a hot drink when the coppers knocked on the door.'

'So, they didn't catch them then?'

'No, but that didn't stop them reading their rights to them and taking Robbie to a cell . . . Oh, Uncle Cyril, I asked yer not to tell a soul.'

A tear plopped onto Cyril's cheek. Amy went over to him. He was a funny one to understand. He would never intentionally hurt anyone, but didn't seem able to grasp how his actions could do just that. 'Look, don't worry, luv. Yer didn't know this Charlie was a religious man, did yer?'

'No, it shocked me. I wouldn't 'ave told him, 'onest, luv. I know them sort don't like stuff like that. Though he never spoke well of me sister Ethel. So, I should 'ave known. He always said that it wasn't right how they'd made their living, that it was sinful.'

'Who didn't speak well of me, Cyril, luv?' Ethel asked this as she came through to the kitchen with Tilda. Both had housecoats on and their hair in hairnets. Amy ran to her mum.

'Amy, luv, what is it, me little darlin'?'

Shocked when she heard the tale, Ethel turned to Tilda. 'That bleedin' Charlie! He shagged me and paid me by giving me a fag, then spouted the Bible about me being a temptress. I'll bleedin' kill him, the hypocritical bleeder!'

'Me too, Ethel . . . H-he forced himself on me. He said he knew who I was and the trouble I was in . . . He even had me once in the ward. He came up at night. He must 'ave paid the janitor.'

Amy felt sick. It was to her as if she was hearing Belton had come alive again.

'Amy, luv . . . Amy! I'm sorry, me darlin', it just made me that mad, I didn't realize what I were saying.'

Her mum's arms took hold of her and held her close. 'Yer shaking, me little darlin'. Let's sit yer down.'

Once she, her mum and Cyril were sat around the kitchen table, Tilda put the kettle on. While they

348

drank their tea, Amy felt the pity of what they had all been through. She dabbed at her eyes.

'Now, darlin', stop yer worrying, it don't 'elp nothing. But I've an idea. I think me and you, Tilda, should go to London and see Charlie boy. I think if we threatened to tell of his behaviour, he might change his story — tell them that he'd been thinking about it and had overreacted. That Cyril hadn't told him that the men were a couple but just that they lived together, and he'd added one and two together and made four!'

'But what about Robbie being seen to kiss Abe?'

It was Tilda who answered. 'Robbie's theatrical, it's how they behave. Everyone accepts that they're the only men who kiss other men — well, in public. It's what they do. No judge will convict on that, or on what evidence they do 'ave, come to think of it. I've been up in court and been guilty but got off because of not enough evidence.'

'Me too. We can change this around, luv. We can.'

'Oh, Mum, I hope so. It's unbearable.'

'You ring Ruth back, at least she can comfort Abe . . . And as for you, Cyril, I'll tape yer bleedin' mouth up one of these days . . . Cyril, Cyril, luv, don't cry . . . It's all right. Yer didn't mean it, and neither did I, luv.'

Mum got up and put her arm around Cyril. 'Shush now, me lovely brother. No one will blame yer.'

Amy went to him, too. Not for the first time she wondered how his mind worked. She patted his back. 'We all love, yer, Uncle, we don't blame yer, you weren't to know.'

Cyril looked up. 'Do yer love me, Amy?'

''Course I do. You're me uncle and the only one I've got and a lovely one yer are too.'

Cyril grinned. Amy bent and kissed the top of his head. 'It'll all be all right, you'll see. Mum and Tilda will sort it. I'll go and telephone Ruth . . . Now, don't worry, she'll understand, she won't blame yer. No one will, or they'll have me to contend with, luv.'

Almost running out to the hall, such was her hope that all could yet be saved, Amy dialled the number. 'Ruth? Oh, Ruth. We might be able to save Robbie and Abe.'

'How? Oh, Amy, do yer really think yer can?'

Amy told her what had happened. 'So, me mum and yours are coming home. They're sure that they can get this Charlie boy, as they call him, to change his story.' She told Ruth what she'd heard. 'And as for the kiss on the top of Abe's head, your mum said that can be passed off as a theatrical gesture of the type them actors are always at with each other. Robbie's Abe's carer, he cares for him lovingly, the kiss was just an extension of that.'

'Oh, Amy. I feel there is a glimmer of hope. Abe's solicitor has engaged a lawyer for him. He's coming later. I'll put all this to Abe now, so he has something to tell the lawyer.'

'He won't say it's true, will he, Ruth? Robbie could be imprisoned for years.'

'No, Abe will deny it. He has already spoken to his solicitor over the phone. His solicitor said that no judge will take anyone's hearsay or a silly action over the word of a war hero anyway, so I was going to ring you back with a little bit of hope.'

'Oh, Ruth. Pray to yer Holy Mary and I will too. She'll get us all out of this.'

'She will, and don't worry, luv, I've had a long conversation with her already . . . I don't know how she stands on such as this, though.'

'She's a mother . . . and anyway, Jesus himself was theatrical and had a lot of men friends, and some of them left their wives and families to follow him, so she probably understands better than we do.'

Ruth's lovely laughter came down the phone, making Amy long to be with her. But the tug here was too great for her to leave right now.

'Oh, Amy. Yer shouldn't say that about Jesus! . . . Though, thinking about it . . . Oh, stop it! We'll be cast down to hell!'

Amy giggled now. She felt happy that Ruth had cheered up, and glad to have made her laugh even if it was with a bit of blasphemy!

'Amy, changing the subject. Me and Ivan are going to wed soon . . . well, we are if this all turns out all right.'

'Oh, Ruth, that's wonderful news, luv. Ooh, I love you both so much. It's like me brother and me sister marrying!'

'What? Amy, yer at it again!'

'Ha, yer know what I mean. That's how I love yer both . . . I still can't believe you and Ivan have fallen in love. It's like a bright star in a murky sky.'

'That's a bit poetical, ain't it?'

They laughed again and Amy began to feel that everything really was going to be all right . . . She might even have news herself soon.

Saying her goodbyes, she went back to the kitchen to find no one there but she could hear movement upstairs above her. She sighed. *Can me mum and Tilda really save Abe and Robbie?* She hoped so with all her heart.

The back door opened then. 'Have you got the

kettle on, lass?'

'Jack! Yer startled me.' The startling of her had taken the form of her heart skipping a beat, but she had to cover up this feeling and give a reason for her blushing with the sheer pleasure of seeing him.

He grinned. She loved his grin. She loved everything about him.

'Well, it's nine o'clock, me usual time to start work, lass.'

'I know, but . . .' Suddenly, Amy felt her tears coming again. She quickly turned away.

'Amy . . . Amy! Aw, lass, has sommat happened?'

Plonking herself on one of the chairs that surrounded the table, she nodded. Jack came into the kitchen and over to her, and put his hand on her shoulder. To Amy, the feeling that zinged through her was like a sudden earth tremor. She knew Jack had felt it too. 'Eeh, Amy, lass, I can't bear for you to be hurt. Can you tell me about it? I'll allus be here for you, no matter what it is, lass.'

She didn't think she could ever tell Jack things about herself; they all seemed a million miles away from his tranquil life. She felt he'd be shocked — no, more than that, disgusted.

'Amy, whatever it is, I can take it . . . I think the world of you, lass . . . I — I've given me heart to you.'

If she thought she could shock Jack, at this moment, he'd shocked her more than she could take. She looked up at him.

'I mean it, Amy. I'd like you to be me lass.'

'Oh, Jack. Yer know so little about me.'

'I know about your babby . . . I don't know how that happened, but it don't matter. I know in me heart it wasn't through sommat you wanted to happen, but

352

you loved your child and that's what mattered to me.'

It came to Amy then that if she was going to give her love to anyone ever again, she had to be truthful with them. Teddy had known all about her and loved her despite of it all, hadn't he? And this was the only way to have a true love, wasn't it? She had to know that who she gave her heart to could accept her for all that she was and all that had shaped her, and she so wanted to give that love to Jack.

'There's a lot more, Jack. Yer may not like me after yer know it.'

'Put yer coat on and come out to me shed . . . Aw, lass, please. Give me a chance to know all about you . . . only to help you, mind. I knaw I'm not going to change me mind on loving you.'

Amy's heart flipped over. *He said the words — he actually said he loves me!*

As she went for her coat, she called up, 'How are yer getting on, Mum? Are yer packing?'

Her mum came to the top of the stairs. 'We are, luv . . . Where're you going then?'

'Oh, just to the shed, Jack has something he needs me to see.'

'Oh?'

'Mum!'

'Ha, I'm only kidding, luv. I'll get some breakfast for everyone once we're ready. Go on with yer . . . and good luck, me darlin'.'

Amy blushed, but she giggled too. She loved having a mum who she could talk to and loved how strong her mum had become. In her, Amy could now see the brassy young woman she must have been and knew she would have loved her then too. The salt of the earth, a typical cockney and lovely with it. Tilda was of the same mould. She wondered if Ruth and Ellen would be happy with the woman that had emerged as the real Tilda, for she had become strong too. They were both unrecognizable from the two women they had first met. Instead of needing looking after, these two were going to be a force to be reckoned with.

Amy felt like a naughty little girl as she stepped inside the shed. Well, it was a bit brazen of her, but she had to do this, and this was somewhere private for her.

Her love for Jack had deepened over the weeks as they'd worked together in the garden and then, when there wasn't enough work in the garden, had sat long hours on his bench behind the shed together, both wrapped up warm and drinking hot cocoa, his favourite drink. He'd told her that gardening was his first love and that he had worked alongside his father when he'd been the gardener for a big house out in the country and that that was his ambition, but that he hadn't been successful when he'd applied for a few jobs. That he'd been turned down to serve in France, because of his flat feet, which gave him a lot of gyp still as the arches often felt very painful. And how much he had suffered being at home when other lads around had all gone to war and many had been killed. She knew him inside out but had never given more than a hint about herself.

As she entered, the shed door creaked. Jack stood up from the stool he'd been sitting on. He didn't speak, but to Amy, his eyes spoke volumes.

'I — I . . . this ain't going to be easy, Jack.'

'Then don't put yourself through it, love. I don't need to knaw. Or you can tell me bit by bit, when you feel ready, if it's important to you to do so.'

'No, I want to tell you.'

She sat on the stool he'd vacated, and he sat on a log that was fashioned like a stool. He took her hands. Again, the feeling she'd had earlier shot through her. She drew in a deep breath. 'I were an orphan . . . well, I thought I was. I only found me mum recently . . .'

Jack never once interrupted, though when she told of Belton raping her, his grip on her hands tightened and she could see the pain in his face. She didn't stop. She knew now that she must get it all out; that if she didn't, the horror and deprivation of it all would stifle any love she hoped would be hers.

Exhausted as she came to the last chapter of her falling in love with Teddy and then later her coming home, she saw tears running down his face.

After a moment, he whispered, 'Can I hold you, Amy, me little lass?'

They stood as if compelled to. And then it happened, Amy felt her world had truly come right, even more so than it had done when she came home to Ruth and Ellen. More so than when she'd discovered that her beloved Ethel was her mum, for now, inside, she felt whole, truly whole.

'I love you, Amy, and if you'll let me, I want to take all of that hurt out of your life.'

'I'll let you, Jack. And I love you, too. I have since the moment I set eyes on yer.'

'Aw, Amy, me Amy.'

His lips seared hers and sealed their love. She clung to him as if he was a lifeline, and she had to admit, he was just that to her. The saving of her, like nothing before had been. Even Ruth, her beloved Ruth, couldn't do this for her, nor Ellen, who she loved just as much. Nor could finding her adored mum have

355

done this — not completed her . . . For it was as if she was being cleansed, accepted as a woman, a worthy woman, worthy of a man's love.

'By, Amy, lass, you've took me heart from me and wrung it through the wringer with knowing all that happened to you. But I'm here for you. I want you to knaw that none of what you've told me has affected me in any way, other than to make me love you more than I did already. And hearing it has made me want to protect you and take care of you, so that nothing like it ever happens again.' He went down on one knee. 'Will you marry me, me little lass?'

'I will, Jack, luv, I will.'

They hugged as if they had never been hugged before. When they came out of it, Jack told her, 'About what you told me about your friends, Abe and Robbie. I had guessed, and I never thought to meet any blokes who were like that. The thought of it had repulsed me. But when I met them, I guessed what was between them and came to like and respect them. And it made me think that the world was made up of all kinds of love, so as long as they don't . . . well, behave like those men you told me about did to Robbie and other boys, then what they do together is their own business.'

'Ta, Jack. I understand what you're saying. It is a difficult thing to accept, I know that.'

'Maybe one day everyone will be free to live how they were born to be. And I really hope your ma and Tilda can save them.'

'Talking of them, I'd better go. They are going to try to catch a train today. They're all packed and need to have a good breakfast as it's a long journey.'

'Aw, I don't want you to leave me, lass, but I know

you must.'

'I'll never leave yer, Jack, never, luv.'

He held her to him once more, and Amy thought this was the place she always wanted to be, in Jack's arms.

As she left him, she looked around the garden he'd fashioned, his beloved kitchen garden, with potential to have far more produce than could ever be used by whoever occupied the house, and his landscaped haven that looked a bit dull now, but had promises of spring as shoots of daffodils had pushed through, and she thought to herself that she never wanted to leave here again. The thought of living in London repulsed her. She'd hated every minute without being conscious of doing so. She hoped with all her heart that Ellen would let her and Jack have this cottage for their home when they married.

Then she giggled. *Yer getting ahead of yerself, girl. There's a lot of water to go under the bridge before we can wed.*

As she reached the kitchen door, she sent a prayer up to Ruth's Holy Mary. *Please let it all run smoothly. Let it be that Abe and Robbie are freed, that Ruth's wedding can go ahead, and please let all me dreams come true.* Somehow, she knew they would.

31

Ruth

The anxious wait for their mum and Ethel had Ruth trembling. Ellen took hold of her hand. She could feel that she, too, was feeling the strain.

'Please let them succeed, Ellen.'

'We'll know in a moment, love.'

They were sitting in Bernard's car just around the corner from the workhouse. Ethel and Tilda had left them five minutes ago, hoping to catch the hateful Charlie before he left for home.

The darkness and smog of this early February winter morning made it impossible to see what was happening a few hundred yards away and this in itself was making Ruth nervous. She'd wanted to be in sight of their mum.

'What did Abe's lawyer say, Ruth? I didn't like to ask him.'

'He said they had a very good case, that he was appalled by this accusation, that he knew Abe's family well and as long as Charlie would admit that he'd twisted what Cyril had told him, then he thinks the explanation of Robbie being an affectionate theatrical type and his carer only would be accepted by the prosecution service as the police having no grounds to continue with the case.'

'So, Cyril can be relied on to say that he didn't say what he did?'

'Yes, he's mortified, but he may not be questioned. It all depends on Charlie's story. Mum's going to put it to him that he's to go to the police and tell them he is a Christian man and that what he said wasn't right, but an assumption. He's to say that he's now had an attack of conscience and would like to retract his story.'

'Do you think Mum and Ethel can make him do that?'

'I do. They both know of a birthmark he has on the top of his leg. They will tell him they will use that as proof they are telling the truth when they go to his wife and to the papers.'

'They're willing to go to the papers! Oh, Ruth, it's so sad to think of what they've both been through. It — it brings back what happened to us.'

'It does. Yer know, there's something in this women's rights movement, and I hope it includes the treatment of women and girls, not just getting us the vote.'

'We should join, they're always calling for women to take up the cause.'

'Ha, I can see me with a banner.'

'I can too, love. You could sing your protest; they'd all listen then.'

'Oh, Ellen, will Robbie and me ever be on the stage together again? I'm so frightened for him.'

Ellen squeezed her hand. 'I don't know. If we can get them free of this charge, wouldn't it be better if they moved away? The police can be like a dog with a bone.'

'Abe has said as much.'

'Oh, where? Has he said?' Bernard had sat in the front of the car drumming his fingers on the wheel listening, but until now not joining in the conversation.

'He spoke about his sister, Lucinda, being in Paris. He said they are more liberal there.'

'Oh, we would miss them so much.'

'We would, Ellen, darling, but I think that is an excellent idea and I will encourage Abe in it. I will never feel they are safe here again. And Paris is a good place for Robbie, too. They love artistic people, and he knows a lot of the French language. He told me he picked it up easily during the war. Yes, I think that's an excellent idea for them both.'

'It does sound it now with how you explain it, darling.' Ellen turned to Ruth. 'And we can go to see them, it's not the other end of the world, as we know. I would love to see it in peacetime.'

Ruth, who'd been worrying Abe's plan might happen and not wanting Robbie to go, now felt differently about it. Yes, she could see it really was the best way — the safest way. And thinking about it, not even the stage was important to her against the safety of her lovely Abe and Robbie.

'Oh, someone's coming. I'll get back into the front with Bernard, love.'

Ethel appeared. She was shivering. Ruth opened the door. 'Get in, luv. Where's me mum? Is she all right?'

'She's staying there. He's agreed to go to the police station, but won't go till he's been home as he says his wife frets if he's late. We don't trust him, so we've told him we're going to follow him and wait outside his house. If he don't come out and go to the police station, then his wife will know what he did . . . He were like putty in our hands, luv. It seems he truly loves his missus and she's not well. He said if she knew what he'd done to us, it would kill her.'

'Really! He said he'd go to the police station? That's wonderful news . . . Oh, ta, Ethel, luv, ta ever so much. I didn't want to put you both through this, but we had no choice.'

'I know how you feel, Ruth, but will Mum and Ethel be safe?'

'Oh, what am I thinking! I'll go with them.'

'No. Your mum said to tell you both you're to leave this to us. We can handle him, I promise yer. He won't be dealing with two scared, beaten women now. Me and Tilda are strong and can stand up to the likes of him. You go 'ome and let Abe know that all's going to be all right. We'll catch the bus home.'

It was Ellen who made the decision. 'Ruth, we have to let Mum and Ethel do this their way, love. It doesn't sound like this Charlie wants anything to come out. If he hurts them, then it will.'

Ruth relaxed a little. 'Ethel, tell Mum we love her. And Ethel, we love you too, so take care of each other, eh?'

'Don't you worry, luv. We'll be home with good news in a couple of hours. I promise.'

★ ★ ★

The wait seemed interminable. Ellen and Bernard couldn't stay as they had papers to sign and other business to attend to. Ivan went to the shop for Ruth and put a sign up saying *Closed* for a couple of days, while Ruth sat with Abe.

He shocked her by asking, 'Do you think it's wrong the way Robbie and I love each other, Ruth?'

361

'No I don't. Why should love be owned by just men and women couples? Anyone can feel love and want to express it.'

'They call us queer. Maybe we are.'

'Abe, love, don't doubt yerself now. This will pass.' She told him what Bernard had said. 'And though I don't want you to go away, I agree now. Just think what it will be like to live freely together, no pretence.'

'It would be wonderful. I hate having to present Robbie to the world as my carer. I want to be able to say this is the man I love, and who loves me and makes me happy.'

'Then go to Paris ... How will Lucinda be with you? And Andrew ... I remember, yer had a brother Andrew, does he know?'

'Lucinda was happy with it all from the beginning, but then she is another who's artistic. She and her husband live a bohemian lifestyle. They seem away with the fairies half the time. She'll love presenting me and Robbie to her friends ... Andrew, I'm not sure. He's a lecturer at Oxford now. I wrote and told him, but he just said that he didn't mind, but didn't want to hear about it. So, when we write, I never mention anything about Robbie. Andrew is married and has a child now — a girl. I would so love to meet the little one but have to accept that Andrew isn't sure. I know he loves me, he tells me in every letter, so I have made myself content with that.'

Ruth wanted to hug him; she hadn't missed the glistening of a tear in the corner of his eye as he spoke about Andrew.

When that tear plopped onto his cheek, she did rise and put her arms around him. He leaned his head on her shoulder. 'Ruth, darling, I have always loved you, you know. But I couldn't have made you happy. I know Adrian did, and I know that even though Ivan is so totally different to me and to Adrian, he will make you happy too.'

'Poor Ivan hasn't had many chances in life. I've been lucky considering the background that we both had, but he hasn't. I want to change that.'

'I know, my dear. And I know that Robbie chatted to you about that. Heed his words. Don't mother Ivan, but help him to be his own man again, as that is where your happiness will lie, Ruth.'

'I will. I'm going to get the boys into school as soon as everything settles down. That will free Ivan up to pursue what he wants to do. He loves working on the land but there isn't much chance of that around here. But he'll come up with something.'

'Why not sell this house and move to where he would have a chance?'

'Oh, I don't know. That's too drastic, I have me shop and Ellen . . .'

'But you needn't move too far away. Ellen is going to Bethnal Green, where we both lived. There's loads of opportunities there — the docks, the markets, industry. Though to me, with his background, Ivan needs to be on a farm, or running his own business. I can't see him in a factory.'

Ruth knew this conversation was helping Abe. He needed to focus on something and sorting her future out was distracting him, whereas she wanted to talk about him and Robbie as she worried so much for their future.

The telephone ringing gave her a chance to escape for a moment.

It was Abe's lawyer. 'Ah, Miss Faith. Can you please

get Abraham to come to the telephone? I have good news.'

Ruth looked at the clock. *How can he have good news? Mum and Ethel aren't back yet!*

Abe had hardly put the phone down when the front door opened. Ellen, Bernard, Ethel and her mother walked in. Just behind them was Ivan with the boys. She hadn't noticed how long they had been, but now suspected Ivan had taken the boys to the park for a while.

When all were in Abe's sitting room having hugged their greetings to one another, Abe looked around at them all. Ruth followed his gaze. Everyone looked anxious as they waited for his news.

'Robbie's coming home!'

'Oh, Abe.' Ruth leaped at him, tripping on the wheel of his chair and landing in his lap! The room erupted with laughter, a sound she never thought to hear again.

'Well, you took the wind out of my sails, Ruth. Are you hurt?'

Ruth stood up. 'No, just feel silly. Tell us what yer know, luv.' Ivan came to stand near to her, and she was glad of his arm coming around her.

'Well, it seems that my lawyer had gone to the crown prosecution even before the workhouse man changed his story. He was giving the angle of it all being hearsay and how Robbie was a theatrical type. It seemed the man he talked to is a fan of Robbie's and completely understood the gesture of him kissing my head. He had already said he had his doubts, as he also knows my family and my war record and he agreed that the police evidence was all hearsay other than the witnessed kiss. He'd only just finished giving his agreement not to prosecute when he received a call from the arresting officer withdrawing his application for prosecution, as the man who had tipped them off had just been in and confessed to having made up the story based on what Cyril told him.'

All cheered. And Ruth thought, yes, this wasn't all the truth, but the truth was that the lies they told and what had happened had been caused by bigotry, not by any wrongdoing on Abe's and Robbie's part. Not in her eyes anyway!

Talk turned to Abe and Robbie moving abroad and Bernard said he would give all the help they needed.

'Well, if Robbie agrees, then I'll speak to my sister. She will find us a place to go to, but in the meantime, I'm not leaving this house and will get my fresh air in the backyard!'

Although Ruth thought this sad, she felt relieved. He was safe here, and if they weren't seen out together, then they shouldn't be in any danger.

★ ★ ★

Three weeks later, they were all at the chapel where Ebony and Rebekah first took Ruth when she was a young girl of fourteen, the preacher smiling down on Ruth and Ivan from the altar. Ivan's eyes told her how much he loved her. And as she'd arrived by his side, he'd whispered, 'Yer look beautiful, me darlin'.'

Her heart sang with joy as she looked up into his handsome face.

The chapel was packed with all those she had known in the days of coming here and had worked alongside on the odd occasions she'd helped with the soup kitchen too.

And standing proudly holding her hand to give her away was Robbie and, next to Ivan, Horacio, son of Ebony and Abdi. Tall and handsome, so very different to the little boy in the park that she'd met when he was just four years old and she was thirteen and had run away from the orphanage.

Though she'd seen little of him since he went away to school three years ago, he had written to her and she to him. When she knew he would be home, she wanted him involved in her wedding day. She loved Ivan all the more for choosing him to be his best man after only meeting him the once when they'd gone to Ebony and Abdi's restaurant to celebrate and to invite them to the wedding.

Happiness filled Ruth as she looked around her. In the front pew was her mum, all dressed in pink and looking so lovely. Sitting with her was Ethel, just as lovely in navy matched with lemon, and between them sat Archie, looking so much like Adrian, it was like having him there. And in Archie's smile, she read Adrian's approval of her choice.

Next to Ethel was a proud-looking Cyril, who'd been very quiet since the incident, but they had all let him be, knowing he had lost his confidence a little. Robbie and Abe had been kindness itself to him, so they knew he would be all right eventually.

And behind them, Bernard, Jack and, at the end of their pew, Abe in his wheelchair, looking happy and relaxed. Tomorrow, he and Robbie would set off in Robbie's car for Paris. Both were very happy about this and, she could tell, couldn't wait. They'd had a massive scare and she knew they wouldn't feel safe until they had left here.

Then there was Ebony, bringing so many memories

of Rebekah in her high hat and frock of many colours.

Looking upwards, Ruth sent a 'hello' to Rebekah, the woman who'd given her and Robbie so much love when they were homeless. For a moment, she thought she heard Rebekah's tinkling laughter, and to her it was saying, 'Rebekah is happy for you, Ruth, girl.'

And Ruth knew that she was set on a path of happiness now, as were the two women who meant so much in her life — Amy and Ellen.

Amy would soon marry her Jack and they were to rent the cottage, and would also start a market garden from there. Ellen had said that if it went well, they could have the chance of buying the cottage from her, which had completed their happiness.

Ellen and Bernard were about to move into their new house. Ellen was bursting with plans, which Bernard said he would have to gently curb a little. 'Otherwise we would end up working for nothing for twenty-four hours a day as my lovely, caring wife wants to heal the world for free. And whereas my heart wants to do the same, my head says that won't feed us, or the many children I intend to have!'

Ellen had laughed along with them and had wholeheartedly agreed about the large family Bernard wanted.

For Ruth and Ivan, there was all the future in the world to sort out what to do. Now having the chance to put the house back as one, it would be worth a lot more and give them the capital to have choices. What they would be, she didn't know yet. She did know that whatever plans they made, children were included in them. Both, like Amy and Ellen, wanted to make children happy. Give them a good life. And never let them experience anything like they all had as kids.

As she said her vows, she thought, *This is what life is about, happiness, family and friendships, and love. More than anything, it is about love.* And that's what would take her, Ellen and Amy forward. They would always be the Orphanage Girls, but the misery of those days was gone for ever, and their paths were strewn with happiness.

Acknowledgements

Many people are involved in getting my book to the shelves and presenting it in the very best way to my readers. My commissioning editor, Wayne Brookes, who I love dearly. He works tirelessly, overseeing umpteen processes my book goes through, and keeps me going with his cheerful encouragement — always optimistic, a joy to work with.

My desk-editorial team headed by Samantha Fletcher, whose work brings out the very best of my story to make it shine. And Victoria Hughes-Williams, who is responsible for the structural edit and makes sure the story flows. Thank you — an author is nothing without her editors.

Thank you too to my publicists, Chloe Davies and Philippa McEwan, who seek out many opportunities for me to showcase my work. My thanks to those who complete the team, the sales team, who find outlets across the country for my books.

A special thank you to my son, James Wood, who reads so many versions of my work, to help and advise me, and works alongside me on the edits that come in.

And last but not least, special thanks to my readers, who encourage me on as they await another book, supporting me every step of the way and who warm my heart with praise in their reviews. My heartfelt thanks to you all.

No one person stands alone. My family are amazing. They give me an abundance of love and support and when one of them says they are proud of me, then my world is complete. And so, I acknowledge the part played by you all. You are all my rock and help me to climb my mountain. Thank you. I love you with all my heart.

Letter to Readers

Dear reader,

Hi. I hope you enjoyed reading *The Orphanage Girls Come Home* — the third and final instalment in the Orphanage Girls trilogy.

Thank you from the bottom of my heart for choosing my work to curl up with.

I would so appreciate it if you would kindly leave me a review on Amazon, Goodreads or any online bookstore or book group. Reviews are like being hugged by the reader and they help to encourage me to write the next book — they further my career as they advise other readers about the book, and hopefully whet their appetite to also buy it.

And so, Amy's story completes a journey that took Ruth, Ellen and Amy from the depths of depravity in the orphanage to the theatres of war, to London, to Leeds and to Canada. Theirs was a personal journey too, as they coped with all life could throw at them and came out triumphant.

Always a mixed feeling for me when my characters' journeys end, and I leave them to live their lives in a much better environment than when we met them. I have feelings of sadness at saying goodbye and of hoping I did them proud. But then comes the excitement as I venture on a new journey with new characters.

This time it is a trilogy entitled The Guernsey Girls. Here is a taster:

For Annie, a maid to a household living in a Cornish manor, life is a struggle. Working a gruelling twelve hours a day, her only respite is her once-a-year trip to visit her beloved East End family — her ailing mum and her younger sister, Janey. This is when she gives them her entire salary which, along with the little that Janey can earn between caring for their mum, has to sustain them.

For Olivia, born on the island of Guernsey to a rich banking family and engaged to be married to Hendrick, her only concern is her quest to gain language skills to further the plans Hendrick has for their future. For this she will spend a year in London living in her father's West End apartment while she studies.

But when Annie is assigned by Olivia's Cornish aunt to accompany her to London, it is a trip that will turn both of their lives upside down and their worlds will collide in a way they could never have dreamed of.

In Germany, Hendrick's homeland, the Nazi Party are growing in power. He fears for his father's safety. There is only one option — Hendrick must work for the Nazi Party. He comes up with a plan to teach Olivia to codebreak — it is then that Olivia and Annie must step up as they take on the codename 'The Guernsey Girls'.

And finally, I am always available to contact personally, if you have any queries or just want to say hello, or maybe book me for a talk for a group you belong to. I love to interact with readers and would welcome your comments, your emails and messages through:

My Facebook page: facebook.com/MaryWood Author

My Twitter: @Authormary

My Website: authormarywood.com

I will always reply. And if you subscribe to my newsletter on my website, you will be entered into a draw to win my latest book personally signed to you and will receive a three-monthly newsletter giving all the updates on my books and author life, and many chances of winning lovely prizes.

Love to hear from you. Take care of yourself and others.

Much love,

Mary xxx

We do hope that you have enjoyed
reading this large print book.

Did you know that all of our titles
are available for purchase?

We publish a wide range of high
quality large print books including:
Romances, Mysteries, Classics
General Fiction
Non Fiction and Westerns

Special interest titles available in
large print are:
The Little Oxford Dictionary
Music Book, Song Book
Hymn Book, Service Book

Also available from us courtesy of
Oxford University Press:
Young Readers' Dictionary
(large print edition)
Young Readers' Thesaurus
(large print edition)

For further information or a free
brochure, please contact us at:
Ulverscroft Large Print Books Ltd.,
The Green, Bradgate Road, Anstey,
Leicester, LE7 7FU, England.
Tel: (00 44) **0116 236 4325**
Fax: (00 44) **0116 234 0205**

THE ORPHANAGE GIRLS REUNITED

Mary Wood

Abandoned by her father for the second time, left scarred from the orphanage, Ellen finally finds happiness and hope — reunited with her long-lost gran. But it cannot compensate for being torn apart from her beloved friends Ruth and Amy. When a devastating encounter leaves Ellen broken and desperate, she is forced to fight her past demons.

Ruth has found peace, building a new life as an actress and surrounded by friends. But still she longs to be with Ellen and Amy, after everything they endured together in the orphanage.

Amy was shipped to Canada with hundreds of other orphans — what hope can anyone have of finding her?

One wish comes true when Ruth's acting career leads her to Ellen. But no sooner has the dust settled than war is on the horizon . . .